LOW
M

A novel by William Gasston

The British Channel Islands lie in the Bay of St Malo, just south of the Cherbourg peninsula closer to France than England. In 1940 the Germans invaded the islands and thus began five years of purgatory for the local population.

First published in February 2018 by William Gasston
Cover, page design and overall production by William Gasston

Disclaimer

Low Water Men is a work of fiction which has been based on historical fact. Except for some historical wartime leaders, the characters are all figments of the author's imagination . Any similarity with any living person is coincidental.

Acknowledgements

Many thanks must go to the Jersey Evening Post for their permission in being able to reproduce the text of the orders of the German High Command during the Occupation.

I am deeply indebted to Peter and Verity Cruickshank of Jersey who have been a major source of information, their family and friends being low water fisherfolk since long before the war. Thanks also to my good friend Phil Greaves of Lambley, Nottingham, England who undertook the edit and encouraged me to push on.

Website

Whatever you think about the pros and cons of the internet, it is probably(up to now!) the major game changer of the twenty first century. It disseminates information and opinions faster than a speeding bullet. I have set up **www.lowwatermen.com** so that any reader, who has been kind enough to peruse and enjoy my story, could access information regarding the Channel Islands and the German Occupation.

ISBN 978-0-6482693-1-1

LOW WATER MEN

FOREWORD

I was one of the lucky generation. Born in 1947 in England , I was never called upon to fight in any wars, to be in any army, navy or air force. My parents and grandparents were the innocent victims of two world wars which punctuated their lives and left a trail of death that spanned the globe. I spent my youth on the island of Jersey in fresh free air, not dodging bullets and bombs. I had freedom of choice and I lived in a democratic society where the majority held sway. All I endured was the austerity that followed in Hitler's wake , a bit of food rationing and a shortage of oranges. Small fry indeed. My childhood in Jersey was spent playing on the beach or in the park and around the concrete bunkers which remained after the German Occupation of the Channel Islands. I pretended I was Battler Briton, the famous British air ace, fighting off the Panzer Divisions of the Third Reich. My friends and I had little knowledge of the horrors of the conflict that had gone before and this small part of Hitler's Atlantic Wall was our playground. All of our parents had war stories of bombing raids, death and deprivation. I was fascinated by the tales that Jersey people told of life during the German Occupation between 1940 and 1945. Everywhere you look in the Channel Islands the evidence of those strange and awful times remains, hopefully as a reminder to the world not to let it happen again. Perhaps also to a new generation who has only known entitlement, it will remind them that it was not always so. They say history never repeats but recent world events would seem to lend the lie to this saying.

My interest in the incredible low water landscapes of Jersey's coastline was fired by my maths teacher, Mr M.C.Green, affectionately known as 'Gloop', who used to organise field trips on Tuesday afternoons under the guise of 'Local History'. His amazing enthusiasm was unfortunately not matched by the behaviour of his twelve year old charges and we looked upon the afternoon as a total skite. We went everywhere round the island on those outings, invariably catching a bus to get there and back. La Fontaine des Mittes was a stand-out memory. It was an ancient natural spring on the north coast, nestling down a slope surrounded by gorse and heather. The path to it was sparse and little used but we caterpillared our way through the dense vegetation to get there. For the courting couple who thought the gorse provided sanctuary for their romantic inclinations, it would have come as an unpleasant surprise when thirty of us trampled through their secret hideaway. This, of course, was just an amusing (to us!) adjunct to the interest in history that Mr Green sparked in a few of us. He is long since gone but I thank him profusely for putting up with us rotten adolescents. History is difficult to teach to young people as they themselves have no history. So it was for me when as a twelve year old I went on a school ski-ing trip to Koenigsee in the Bavarian Alps in the late fifties. As a side trip we visited nearby Berchtesgaden. I have the photographs still but at the time it meant very little to me that less than fifteen years previous to our trip, Hitler would have been taking tea on the terrace up there. The war was something our parents spoke of but for us it could have been a hundred years ago. Not so now, as memories like this are like gold to me. We grew up amongst all the concrete that the Germans had left behind, a spooky reminder of difficult times. The bunkers were eerie places with dark corners that smelled of stale urine. There were so many of them that, after the liberation, government simply did not have the resources to make them safe or remove them altogether. A friend of mine was tasked in the fifties with demolishing one of the concrete bunkers on Gorey Pier. An expert in explosives, he made many attempts at completing the task but had to eventually admit defeat having made little impression on the German architecture. After that experience, they were practically all left in situ and sealed off. When the scars of the Occupation became less vivid, a lot of brilliant work has been carried out by the Channel Islands Occupation Society and the Societé Jersiaise in rehabilitating these structures so they can be viewed in the context of history.

To my friends in Guernsey, I am sorry not to have included you more in the narrative of the story. There are some who say Guernsey and Sark had it far worse than Jersey in respect of food supplies and with a population of just a few thousand less than Jersey, they did it tough as well.
Alderney, too, twenty odd miles to the north east and close to the Cherbourg peninsula was almost totally evacuated .While maybe not an extermination camp, it served as a last stop work prison for many unfortunates. There is no doubt there are awful tales here that will never be told. Alderney is a mystery because there was no body of locals to witness what went on. The SS were involved here but not on the other islands. It was also fortified on a similar scale by slave workers and the infamous Todt Organisation. But why? There was nobody left there.

The more stories I hear and the more history I read then the more I realise that wartime has a ludicrous randomness. Events and situations happen fast . Did Hitler visit Jersey that warm and sunny summer's day in 1941? Did Glenn Miller, the famous American band leader, crash land on the rocky shores of Jersey that stormy December night in 1944?
It just might have happened.

LOW WATER MEN
CHAPTER 1

15 DECEMBER 1944   13.30hrs

It was bitterly cold and fog swirled around the small airstrip of R.A.F. Twinwood Farm, just four miles north of Bedford, a market town near London, England. A black car was parked by the front door of the air traffic control tower .The two Americans inside the car, Lieutenant Colonel Norman Baessell and Major Glenn Miller, peered through the gloom in expectation of a light aircraft landing. The weather had been so bad the last couple of days that the majority of non essential flights had been postponed. The war was stuttering to an end in Europe. France had fallen to the Allied forces which were now pushing eastwards towards their ultimate target of Berlin where Adolf Hitler was mustering his final defences. Five years of warfare had taken its toll on the local population but they nonetheless welcomed the Americans.

"Even the birds are grounded today", said Miller, despondently. He was anxious to join his band of wartime musicians who had already flown to the recently liberated Paris to start a new tour.

" Nah, don't fret ", said Baessell. They had met each other the night before at the nearby Milton Ernest Hall , a large country house used as a covert base by the Allies . It was close to the airfield at Twinwood just a mile down the road. Baessell had offered the musician a lift to Paris. He wound down the window and leaned his head out into the icy air.
"I think I hear it."
He did indeed hear an incoming aircraft droning overhead but the noise receded.
"Perhaps he's going round again", said Baessell.
"Perhaps he'll have more sense and head for the Bahamas",

replied Miller.
The fog swirled around them again.

The drone returned and got louder. There was a squeal of tyres on runway and a few seconds later the aeroplane appeared through the mist and taxied to a halt about fifty yards from the control tower. An airman came out of the tower, banged on the car roof and yelled,
"There's your lift, gentlemen !"
The two men got out of the car, sniffed the air and walked slowly towards the runway. They circumnavigated the large propeller and clambered up through the open door which had been opened by the pilot. Flight Officer John Morgan pulled them in and said, "Sorry I'm late, sir. Bit difficult to see up there. "
Baessell thanked him for his efforts but the conversation did little to ameliorate the feelings of foreboding that Miller had been experiencing the last few months. The flight across the English Channel was still fraught with danger and in these weather conditions it was certainly not going to be an easy trip. He was well aware of all this but , surprisingly, still insisted on going.

The small plane was a Canadian made Noorduyn Norseman C-64 powered by an extremely noisy Pratt and Whitney single engine. The Norseman was made of metal, wood and fabric and had a reputation of being able to fly cargo or passengers into difficult terrain. It nosed the few yards to the middle of the runway, paused as if to draw breath and accelerated in a crescendo of noise into the fog. It seemed to take ages to trundle down the almost invisible tarmac and eventually the tyres parted company with the ground and they were airborne. Miller looked at his watch. It was nearly two o'clock and he hoped he would be at band rehearsal in Paris by six.
It took a few minutes for the aircraft to rise above the clouds which seemed to stretch out for ever like a depressing grey

blanket. Morgan found himself with a navigational compass which had seen better days and visibility was so poor, he could barely see the tips of the Norseman's wings. Unbeknown to them all, the original flight path was no longer a viable proposition. If only he could see where he were going . He guided the Norseman south and within a few minutes passed over Maidenhead en route to Beachy Head on the south coast of England. Here he intended to change course and fly south east across the English Channel to Dieppe. He kept below the cloud and mist until he saw the white horses on the surface of the Channel. The swirling fog then closed in around them. An hour or so after take-off, the Norseman slipped from view and disappeared, as if sucked in by the dense impenetrable mists of wartorn Europe.

CHAPTER 2

March 2008 Jersey, Channel Islands

The church of St Pierre de La Rocque was just over half full as Peter Marinelle's coffin was carried down the aisle. It was a cold and crisp Spring day and most of the congregation wore overcoats of some description. The inside of the church was colder than the air outside. The early daffodils had just started to bloom and were in abundance on the altar, at the end of the pews and on top of the coffin, their yellow flowers in contrast to the darkness of the occasion.

A battered old wicker fishing basket nestled amongst the flowers on the oak casque. The older members of the congregation murmured in approval and recognition, feeling not so much grief as a sadness of another friend gone. The irrefutable certainty of death had been confronted by most of them already. The older they grew the less it worried them. The deceased was a couple of months short of his eighty second birthday and had seen off a good proportion of his contemporaries. Peter Marinelle had been a fisherman all of his life. The circumstances of his death could not have been more simple or apt. He had been found, stone dead from a heart attack, stretched out in the bottom of his clinker-built wooden bass boat which had drifted back to shore on the incoming tide. A hand held fishing line was hanging from the back of the transom on which no fewer than eight mackerel had snared themselves on the staggered hooks. The local doctor had declared him dead and his body was transported to the mortuary in St Helier.

"Waste not, want not." said one of the onlooking fishermen as he tidied the boat .He grabbed the trailing line which had snared the now dead fish and proceeded to gut them.

"How did he manage to catch mackerel in March?" said another.

"Yeah, guess he was a bit lucky like that," came the reply.

None of Peter's friends seemed to mind. It seemed such a fitting end to a long and active life. The vicar shuffled into the pulpit. The congregation stood up.

"Please, sit down", said the vicar as small clouds of condensation burst upon the solemn cold air. He was in his thirties and still full of hope and enthusiasm, but old enough to gauge exactly the mood of the congregation.

"Gosh, it is cold, isn't it ? " he went on."Perhaps some of you would like to contribute to our central heating fund on your way out"

This remark elicited a good natured chuckle from the front row and just did enough to prick the bubble of tension.

Many of Peter's friends said a lot of good things about him, the organist played "Abide with me" and the audience stumbled through the words as they made a feeble attempt at singing. The dead man's son Cameron and daughter Crystal , now in their sixties, shed tears and hugged each other. The pall bearers then returned to carry the coffin out to the hearse and off the four miles to the town crematorium for the final farewell. The courtege followed the hearse along the coast road and, as requested by the family, they stopped opposite La Rocque Harbour where Peter had for so long set off across the sand banks with his wicker basket slung over his shoulder.

It was low tide and a light mist clung to the shore. The sea would retreat almost a mile over sand and craggy rock, turn and then with long black fingers would inch its way back in. It was indeed a mysterious and wondrous place. Crystal and Cameron stared through the open window.

"What a wonderful way to go", said Crystal.

There was a pause. A few more seconds passed.

"He was one of the last ones, you know." she said finally.

"The last ones ? What do you mean?" said Cameron.

"The last parishioners who reckon they saw a Glenn Miller concert in the parish hall towards the end of the German Occupation. Dad reckoned he rescued a couple of Americans

from a plane crash out by Seymour Tower the night before. ”
Crystal's words trailed away.
Cameron raised his eyebrows.
“Yeah, yeah, I think that was one of his taller stories......but I do remember Aunt Sophie saying something about it. Bit of a mystery really. Shall we drive on?”

CHAPTER 3
JERSEY, CHANNEL ISLANDS, JUNE 1940

It was June 1940 and Peter Marinelle was fishing at the low water mark off the east coast of Jersey, the largest of the British Channel Islands which lie below the Cherbourg peninsular off the west coast of France. It was a glorious day and as the tide receded he marvelled at the expanse of rock and sand that the sea had unveiled. Jersey, measuring nine miles by five, was the southernmost of the islands and had a tidal movement of some forty feet which meant that ,when the tide went out, mile upon mile of seaweed and craggy granite outcrops appeared, concealing a multitude of marine life. No trace of wind stirred the mirror like surface of the sea which seemed to mark time at its lowest point before charging back up to the sea wall. Today the sun had cast a calming mellowness upon the scene.
Peter squinted and through his eyelashes, the water threw up diamonds of sparkling light and , through the layers of hot air, a mirage shimmered in the distance.

At fourteen years old he was still at school but had been itching to leave so that he could help his father on his fishing boat. This ambition had been thwarted by the outbreak of war with Germany nine months previously and he had tearfully said goodbye to his father who had joined the Merchant Navy at the earliest opportunity . As a Jerseyman and a Channel Islander, constitutionally he could not be conscripted into the British Forces but most of the local menfolk of sound mind and body felt it their duty to sign up at the first sign of hostilities.
His father had taken him aside and entrusted him with the safety of the family- a huge responsibility for one so young and he undertook it reluctantly.

He remembered going down to the harbour in St Helier just a

few months ago with his mother and baby sister Sophie to see him off. It seemed like years now. They had trudged along the quay toward the mail boat Isle of Sark, his mum and dad hand in hand and Peter pushing the pram. Cliff, his father, had not been feeling too well after last night's farewell party when it seemed every friend or relative had called in for a drink. His dad loved company but today they were together alone, just the four of them .They waited for what seemed like ages by the side of the mailboat until a man with a megaphone warned of its imminent departure and the crowd that they were part of started to disperse.
His father kissed the baby and carefully lowered her back into the pram. He turned towards Peter and it suddenly struck him how tall his son had grown. He put his arm round his shoulder and looked him fiercely in the eye.
"You're in charge now, son. Don't let me down. Just do your best. Keep the boat in good nick and with any luck I'll be back for Christmas". With that said they both started shadow boxing as if embarrassed by the mood. His dad clipped him round the ear and they clinched for a brief moment.
"Don't forget to keep your guard up,son," he said quietly but firmly. With that they both hugged and laughed and the dreadful tension lifted. Peter stepped back to allow his parents some space. The boat's siren hooted and dockers started unravelling mooring ropes. With that, his father turned and disappeared up the gangplank and was gone.
Peter had been so upset that, unlike his mother, he could not bear to stand at the end of the pier and wave the ship out. He had walked back with the pram towards the town and sat on a bench overlooking the smaller boat harbour to wait for his mother. He sat there for a while and rocked his baby sister off to sleep. After a few moments he began to feel such a deep despair that his throat hurt from trying to suppress it all. He began to sob quietly. His best friend, who had taught him how to make a spike to catch plaice, who had taught him how to whack a cricket ball to the boundary, had gone away. He felt a

hand on his shoulder and a voice said,"Come on,Peter. You've got to look after Mum and your sister, now." He kept his head down, embarrassed that anyone should see him like this. He felt annoyed that someone should invade his moment of sadness. Who were they to tell him what to do? He waited a few minutes, regained his composure and turned to face this intruder but the man, sensing his presence had not been welcome, had already gone.

Peter quickly snapped out of his daydream and returned to the task in hand.
This vast expanse of shoreline was his playground, shared only with a few old timers and weekenders whose knowledge of the tides overcame the potential dangers of marching a mile seemingly straight out from the safety and comfort of the high tide mark at the sea wall. His father had the knowledge and had passed all of it on to his much loved son.

The low water fishing was a hobby he enjoyed and it provided a varied diet for the supper table whilst allowing him to enjoy his own company. The tide was a long way out and he checked his watch to make sure how long he could remain before it turned and rushed back over the mile of gullies. Many unwary people had drowned in these waters, cut off by a sea that gave no warning as its liquid fingers crept silently along.
Peter was confident he had time enough to investigate the splash in the large pool in front of him. He skirted the gully and inched nearer with his home made harpoon. As the tide turned, the larger fish set about grabbing their own supper as small crustaceans presented themselves, inviting their predators to break cover. A large plaice had done just that and, given away by the flick of its tail, was immediately pierced by the ugly three pronged weapon and dumped, still wriggling, into Peter's wicker fishing basket.
"Must be all of a pound", said Peter under his breath. "Better go." and he set off back towards the beach and dry land. He

paused and took one last look out to sea and thought how clear it all was. The coast of France to the east , less than twenty miles away, glinted in the sun. On other days, with the aid of his father's telescope, he had been able to see lorries turning at the bottom of the hill on French soil directly east and it had been so close he felt as if he could row there and back in an afternoon. He could just hear his Dad saying, as he always did, 'just a few miles away they speak another language and drive on the other side of the road'. His eyes suddenly filled up as he wondered where his father was and whether he was safe. The war was nine months old and he had had no news for the last six. Able Seaman Marinelle was providing convoy cover somewhere in the Atlantic.

Determined not to dwell on it, he sniffed and set off on a predetermined route through the labyrinth of rocks. It was now late in the afternoon .The drone of a distant engine broke the serenity just enough to stir him but he thought nothing of it - probably a fishing boat, it was very still. The noise got louder and, as he looked instinctively behind him out to sea and about a mile away, he could pick out the shapes of three aircraft coming towards him at a level of about two hundred feet. "Bloody hell. Better take cover", he said. "They could be enemy".

The island had attracted the attention of many aircraft over the last couple of weeks. The one which had scared the life out of him the last time had turned out to be British but he was loath to take any chances so he scrambled behind the nearest granite outcrop and wedged himself into a position where he could not be seen. He peered over the top of the rock and at that moment he could pick out the swastikas on the wings of the approaching Heinkel He-111 bombers. His heart raced and he ducked down, wedging himself still further into the crevice of the rock.

The aircraft screamed overhead flying towards the shoreline. He watched them intently and before he had a chance to think of what they could be there for, they unleashed a hail of explosive shells onto the slipway at La Rocque which was where he was heading. The noise was deafening and shattering as the bombers dumped their lethal cargo on an unsuspecting Jersey parish.

One minute all had been peace and quiet down at the low water mark.......

and then the world caved in.

His house was a hundred yards directly up the road and, at the thought of his baby sister in the pram in the garden and his mum in the kitchen, a wave of panic hit him. He jumped down onto the sand but his legs buckled under him. His wicker basket rolled away, spilling his catch amongst the seaweed. The injured plaice, in a last act of survival, manically flapped its way into a pool of water and disappeared. Peter grabbed the handle of the basket and yanked it to his side. Using his harpoon, he levered himself up and sprinted towards the beach. He cursed his wellington boots which slowed him down as he galloped through the gullies. At last he left the rocks behind and hit solid sand. It took him the best part of five minutes to reach the carnage that confronted him at the coast road that ran at right angles to the top of the slipway.

There was wreckage and soil everywhere, at least two motionless bodies in the road and smoke coming from the houses opposite, the roofs of which had been blown apart. It seemed like slow motion to Peter as he raced up the road scanning the horror as he went.

One, two, three, four houses and he was home. Up the garden path.....what garden path ? Where was the boat? It had gone, along with the front of the house. He scrambled over the rubble into what had been the hall. Through the smoke he screamed, "Mum,mum,MUM". Nothing. His ears were ringing and his senses seemed numbed by the enormity of the events of the previous few minutes. He lurched against the splintered bannisters and fought with himself to regain a hold on reality. He breathed deeply, like his father had told him to do when he

had been sent by the midwife to tell him of the news of the birth of his little sister. He calmed down and searched the house for signs of life. He pulled manically at shattered floorboards, a broken wooden chair fell through a hole in the ceiling grazing his arm and he kicked it out of the way. There was no sign of life.
"Peter! Peter! are you there?"
A lady appeared by the road.
It was the reassuring figure of Mrs le Plongeon who ran the post office.
"Are you safe?" she said and then she said it again."Peter. Are you okay?"
"YES!"he yelled in irritation. Surely she can see, he thought.
"Your mum and Sophie are up at Mrs Le Brocq's house. They'd gone there for tea - they're quite safe", she said in a quiet matter-of-fact voice. He suddenly felt quite calm and, instead of that dreadful void in his soul as he thought that not only his father but his mother and sister too had now deserted him, the relief caused by Mrs Le Plongeon's matter-of-fact statement swept over him.
He sat down on the bottom step of what remained of the staircase. His ears were ringing and his eyes could barely take in the mayhem that surrounded him. His heart was pounding from the five minute sprint up the beach and he struggled to breathe. The eerie silence that was the aftermath of the exploding bombs was gradually replaced by the noise of people shouting.
"Get yourself up to Mrs Le Brocq's place as quick as you can", said Mrs Le Plongeon. She grabbed his hand and pulled him to his feet. She pushed him gently in the right direction. He only had two hundred yards to get there but it seemed to take an age as he picked his way through the debris on the road. He eventually got there and fell into his mother's arms at the gate.

The Channel Islands had joined the war.

CHAPTER 4

Germany reaches the Atlantic coast

The days which led up to the air raid at La Rocque had been full of anxiety and uncertainty for the whole population of the Channel Islands. Situated as they were just off France in the bay of St Malo, they were still distinctly British despite the efforts of their Gallic neighbours over the previous centuries. The German Army was marching west and Paris had fallen just two weeks ago. This had precipitated a wave of panic as rumours were spread and discredited in rapid order. The islands were, not altogether unexpectedly, totally unprepared for war. They were hardly blocking the advance of the Third Reich across the English Channel and it was a good bet that they could keep a low profile.

Within days the Wehrmacht had driven the Allied armies on to the beaches of western Europe. Hitler had hesitated to drive home his advantage and at Dunkirk thousands of troops had managed to climb on to an armada of boats and escape to England. The net was also closing further south at St Malo on the French coast where French and British civilians were being evacuated .

An untidy fleet of fishing boats and pleasure yachts had set off from Jersey, many of which were skippered by close friends of the Marinelles, and, as the beautiful walled town of St Malo was being bombarded by the advancing enemy, several evacuees were rescued and brought back to the island, a distance of some twenty miles.

At midday on June 21, 1940 a motorcade of large shiny Mercedes staff cars pulled up in a clearing of a forest outside Compiegne some fifty miles to the north east of Paris. The railway carriage ,where the World War 1 armistice had been signed, stood a few yards away . A large block of granite by its side was inscribed with the following words........'Here on the eleventh of November 1918 succumbed the criminal pride of the German Empire - vanquished by the free peoples they tried to enslave.'

The Fuhrer alighted from one of the leading cars and shuffled over to the plinth. On reading the inscription, his facial expression told of his anger and torment at the demise of his people some twenty years before but this was mingled with the triumph he felt at overrunning Holland, Belgium and France and pushing the British back in just a few weeks since May 10. The powerful German Army stood thumping their chest all the way up the Channel coast. Times were good and he was happy to humiliate the French as much as he could with the signing of its surrender.
After a few minutes exploring, he entered the railway carriage which stood as a commemoration of the Versailles Treaty of 1918. He was followed by Wilhelm Keitel, the Obercommandant of the Wehrmacht and Reichmarschall Herman Goring, head of the Luftwaffe . They were followed by all the other members of the hierarchy numbering a group of eight souls. Chairs were drawn up around the large table and a map was produced and laid out in front of the Supreme Commander.
A general discussion ensued with much triumphal banter which seemed to ameliorate Hitler's mood. There was much movement of hands across the map and military movements were assessed. The Fuhrer's finger moved along the lines of the coast of France in a southerly direction before coming to rest on the bay of St Malo.

"...and these Channel Islands are British, are they not ? Is there any reason why we should not occupy them seeing as we are so close?"

A murmur of approval rippled round the carriage.

"Perhaps the Kriegsmarine could come up with a plan. Are they defended and if so, how heavily? Are the Royal Navy defending the area? Does the RAF use it as a base? Give it top priority."

The message was noted and passed down to headquarters which had been set up in Cherbourg. Here the plan was taken up by Major Albrecht Lanz , a battalion commander of 216.ID and his naval friend Kapitanleutnant Koch both of whom had a romantic notion of the Channel Islands which lay tantalisingly close to where they were having lunch while looking to the south. After the meal and together with others, they hatched Operation Grune Pfeil which translated as Operation Green Arrow. Things were moving fast with the Germans.
On the other side of the channel, battered and bruised by the defeat of his European allies and heavy losses of the British Expeditionary Force , Prime Minister Winston Churchill, moving at a much slower pace, was persuaded that there was no viable reason for defending the Channel Islands and declared them a "demilitarised zone" on June 19, 1940.The previous two weeks had been pock marked with indecision by the War Office in their deliberations with the Channel Island governments. Much of the discussions were conducted on the telephone. Military, naval and air support was initially promised then just as quickly withdrawn as the German Army closed on the French coast.
This meant that the islands were undefended and was literally an invitation for the Germans to move in. The big question was *how long would they take.*

Such troops home on leave that were on the islands had to be evacuated along with those locals who chose to leave and seek

the safety of mainland UK and beyond.
Several families had taken the opportunity to leave on the British Rail ferries which steamed to Weymouth on England's south coast - many with stronger ties to England than Jersey had found the decision easy. Other nationalities also chose not to be stranded and left. The call to escape was sudden and dramatic - many houses were left unlocked and pets were left to roam or worse still, taken to the Animal Shelter to meet a sad but convenient fate. Open doors in empty houses swung to and fro and half finished meals lay on unattended kitchen tables.
Jersey's sister islands of Guernsey and Sark lay a few miles north and were suffering the same painful decisions of whether to stay or go. Much further north, the third largest island of Alderney bucked the trend and, almost to a man, left everything behind in their haste to reach the closest Channel Island of Guernsey or mainland England.

Peter's mother Christine had decided her family was staying. Her roots were very firmly in Jersey and she was confident that the war would pass them by. Her father had been killed in France in the first World War when she was barely nine years old and she , understandably, could not forgive the Germans. However, she could see no immediate threat from them as they would surely have their sights set firmly on England.
She had been to the main town of St Helier to pick up some shoes and on the return journey the bus had passed the docks. Through its grimy windows she had witnessed the chaos ensuing. Mothers with babes in their arms were queuing to get on a boat, any boat. Suitcases were piled randomly against the barrels of potatoes which were also vying for space on board. Worry and desperation were etched in the faces of the waiting. She sighed with the reassurance that her decision had been right. There was no way she was going to put Sophie and Peter through that. As the bus followed the winding road over Mount Bingham which skirted high above the harbour, the whole sorry scene of confusion unfolded like a bag of dirty washing.

It was a warm day and the bus was belching out thick black diesel fumes as it struggled up the hill. Visibility was exceptionally good and as they reached the top of the rise she could see the group of rocks called the Minquiers some miles to the south across the sea. It was low tide and the huge reef sprawled across the horizon like a string of black beads. Before Sophie was born, they had taken Peter on a fishing trip there one day two years ago. The sea had been flat calm that weekend and they motored off in the bass boat Fair Winds to arrive at the reef at high tide. They had anchored up near the main island of the reef and Peter had been goggle-eyed as acre upon acre of sand and craggy outcrop were uncovered as the tide receded. They explored and swum in the pools as the sun got higher. Christine suggested lunch and they had returned to the boat to eat their sandwiches. Her husband Cliff and young Peter were fishing for prawns with home made nets. How fine they both looked and she felt a warm glow of pride as she watched them. Cliff broke off to open a bottle of wine which Christine had unpacked from the basket. He half filled a glass, took a swig and said,

" That'll do nicely, waiter"

"I'm a waitress, actually...just in case you hadn't noticed.."and she unbuttoned her blouse to reveal the swimsuit underneath. They had been married for fourteen years and she still knew how to put a twinkle in his eye.

"I think I see what you mean," he beamed."Is that a new swimsuit?"

"Might be", she said as she peeled off the skirt as well,

"Got it at Noel and Porters' yesterday. Only half a crown"

"Let's have a good look then"

Christine paraded up and down the sandbank imitating the models who would walk up and down just like on the newsreels at the cinema.

"We'll have to christen it, won't we..."

Cliff moved towards her and picked her up in his arms.

She screamed and was promptly dunked in the nearest pool,

kicking her legs up and down as they went.
Peter turned and clucked disdainfully. He was used to their antics and just carried on fishing.
Cliff grabbed her outstretched hand and pulled her gently to her feet.
"Anyway,it's very nice. But then again.."
He was about to say"..you look better with *no* clothes on" but the words seem to get stuck in his throat. He had things on his mind. One or two of his younger friends had recently joined the Merchant Navy. He had married young and had the responsibility of Peter thrust upon him at an age when he felt he should have been off seeing the world. He had never regretted it but he still felt there was a piece missing. Christine had felt it too, a certain dissatisfaction with his lot. She loved him deeply and was determined not to lose him. She sensed his eye was firmly in the distance somewhere.
She remembered opening a cooked mussel one day and finding a small pearl in the flesh. Cliff had explained that the mussel had originally been troubled by a piece of grit which it could not flush out of its shell and , as he said it, she thought that was exactly the problem with him and somehow she knew that she could not help him with this one. He knew it too but could not find the words to explain it to her. They both drew a veil over it and set out to enjoy what was a glorious day.
They finished lunch and sunbathed while Peter continued to explore the rock pools. They both dozed off and were awakened by a trickle of cold water being poured over them by their offspring who had finally had enough of prawning. The wriggly crustaceans were in such abundance that they were hardly a challenge to catch - unlike those on his own patch of La Rocque which always seemed to be one size smaller than the mesh on his net.
The day wore on and they were joined by other keen fishermen and their entourages. Peter came across one of his school mates, John Le Ross, whose father was the Assistant Harbour Master in St Helier. His dad was combining business with

pleasure on a boat trip to check all was well on the reef and that the French had not raised the Tricolor in his absence. Raising the flag was usually an act of defiance brought on by half a dozen drinks and the cider apple brandy Calvados had a lot to answer for on those occasions. Events like these were not taken that seriously by the Jersey authorities but nonetheless had to be checked out.

By four o'clock the tide was on its remorseless way back and the vast sandy landscape was quickly eaten away by the sea. They collected their things and climbed back aboard the boat. It was decided that John Le Ross would come back with them as his dad had some business to attend to and as they lived just up the road, it was more convenient for them all. Peter and John sat on the bows of Fair Winds as Cliff started the engine. They eased gently out of the inlet and waved goodbye to all the others.

Getting away from the reef took a skilled seaman as many a rock was just beneath the surface. Cliff knew the marks he had to steer for but Peter had to look out for these hazards in case the currents made them drift off course.

"Big rock on the starboard side-about fifty yards", said Peter.

"Got it", said Cliff as he strained his neck to see. He pushed the tiller away from him and they eased past the obstruction towards the open sea and Jersey. Once into deeper water, Peter and his friend climbed back into the cockpit and Peter produced a couple of fishing lines. After a few minutes the boys had managed to attach some feathers to various hooks on the hand lines and, once the weights had been put at the tackle end, they unravelled the lines over the stern of the boat.

"Can you slow down a bit, Dad", said Peter,"the weights aren't sinking".

"Right you are, sir. Full speed astern", said Cliff. Christine smiled and so did the boys as they all entered into the spirit of the day.

The lines began to sink. Within seconds, John yelled,"Got one".

"Me too", replied Peter as they both began to haul in. John's

was first out and his eight hooks produced two beautiful mackerel, their shimmering colours sparkling in the sun. Peter had a real handful and only just managed to yank his line over the side to discover all five of his hooks were occupied. They had hit a shoal at feeding time.
There were fish struggling in all directions as Cliff cut the engine right back so that he could help, and succeeded only in falling on his backside, much to everyone's amusement. Once the confusion had subsided, the fish were dispatched into a hessian sack and the boys refeathered their hooks. The shoal was still close by as the surface of the water was disturbed by their threshing and shortly the gulls joined in for a meal. Peter and John caught forty four mackerel in the same time as it took to tie the hooks and cast the lines overboard.
What a feed they had that night. Most of the mackerel were delivered to friends who lived close by and the rest they gutted and grilled along with the prawns. John Le Ross' family came to share the meal and left after midnight when the bottle of Calvados had been drunk. Peter had long since gone to bed, sated with the happenings of the day.
The air was still warm and all the windows remained open. Cliff and Christine left the dirty dishes and staggered upstairs to bed. They fell into each other's arms and made love but Cliff's head was somewhere else. He quickly fell asleep and Christine was left staring at the ceiling once again. Over the next few months the situation continued and when she fell pregnant with Sophie she thought that things might change.However, world events decreed otherwise and Britain joined the war against Germany on 3 September 1939. Christine gave birth to Sophie on the very same day. Such a lot was happening that it was hard to keep a grip on reality.

It was no surprise to Christine when Cliff enlisted with the Merchant Navy a few weeks later.

"Tickets,PLEASE,madam", said the bus conductor. Christine was jerked back to reality and quickly fumbled in her bag. "Sorry....miles away", she said as she recovered her poise. She quickly checked her surroundings and realised that the bus had travelled about three miles along the coast road and none of the journey had registered in her mind. She had enjoyed the daydream but it didn't help the ache in her heart.She got off at the top of La Rocque slipway and scuttled the few yards up the road to the house where Peter had been happily looking after his little sister Sophie for the last four hours.

CHAPTER 5

Occupation!

The decision to demilitarise the Channel Islands had been a difficult one. To deploy so much manpower defending a group of rocks which may or may not assume some importance to the enemy would have been foolhardy.
The difficulty lay in whether to tell the enemy or not. The longer the knowledge was kept from them, then the longer the population had to sort themselves out -whether they left or stayed was their choice.

As the long, long days of June began to wane, Hitler's army drew ever closer to the coast of France. Tension rose as more and more German aircraft flew low over Jersey. Unbeknown to the people down below, the activity on the docks had taken on a more sinister light to the enemy above. The potato lorries, innocently offloading the precious crop of Jersey Royal potatoes, were deemed to look like troop carriers. Eventually the tension was broken when Peter Marinelle's low water fishing expedition had been so rudely interrupted by the Luftwaffe's bombing raid.

The next day, as the island tried to recover from the shock, Germany was informed of the previously secret demilitarisation decision. After two days of low level aerial reconnaissance, leaflets were dropped from these aircraft to tell the population to surrender and in so doing, white flags were to be flown from all buildings.

Later that day, July 1st 1940, and two thousand feet above, one of the German Luftwaffe's finest, Hauptmann Ziggy Heinzel became part of that story. He led a flight of four Dornier Do17Ps and was briefed to fly in low to test the reactions of the locals.

Days like this were few and far between - he had taken off from Cherbourg , on the French coast, in perfect conditions for a picnic but not so perfect for wartime aircraft, with no cloud cover whatsoever. Still, he had had a good lunch and he was a member of the all-conquering German Air Force which had swept everything before it. He was 22 years old, the girls in Paris had been very friendly and he was going to live forever. No one would dare fire on him when he wasn't looking.
From the cockpit of his Dornier , through his field glasses he had been observing the islands below for anything resembling anti-aircraft activity but all he could see were white flags. He wasn't to know, but a lot of those flags hanging from the windows of houses were a strange and malodorous collection of dirty linen put out by an island race who were none too pleased at being abandoned by their mother country.
Ziggy spotted the airport on the west coast of Jersey and, cannons at the ready, made a low pass over the large green fields in order to precipitate some sort of hostile reaction. The other three aircraft followed. Again.......nothing. He gained height and banked the aircraft round over the sea. The airport was not huge and was built on high ground which sloped gently down over sand dunes to the Atlantic Ocean. He peered down and noted the white lines of surf creaming over the beach. The water was very clear and the dark brown reefs could be discerned just below the surface. It was far too quiet for him. He was eager to be attacking lands further north but, for the meantime, this would do.
"*Ah! To hell with it*", he said and pushed the joystick forward to propel his aircraft towards the beckoning runway.
The radio crackled. " *Cover me, lads. I'm going in* !! "
With the other three planes covering any counter attack, he did exactly that.

The lush green grass caressed the tyres as he made a perfect

landing and taxied towards the main building. He stopped twenty yards short and cut the engine. He pulled back the cockpit , climbed onto the wing and jumped effortlessly down to the soft turf below. Several skylarks wheeled into the air in the distant long grass.
A shimmering heat haze added to the overall drama. He felt the warmth of the sun and suddenly the whole situation had an air of peace and calm. He hesitated as if enjoying the moment but soon he realised there might be fifty rifles pointing at him from who knows where.

A man was standing by a fuel lorry, leaning on a broom. He pointed toward the main doorway. Ziggy paused and lit a cigarette. No bullets so far. He was loving it. Still nothing stirred.
Discarding the half finished butt, he decided to make a move. He marched smartly to the doors and disappeared inside the building. Fifteen minutes later he returned to his airplane and took off once more. He had received information that the islands were ready to comply with the German demands. Hauptmann Heinzel was unaware of the significance of his landing. To him it was just another piece of Europe crumbling before the might of the Third Reich. To Hitler it was the first piece of the British Isles to fall and that fact would also not be lost on the British Government. To the Jersey population who had remained to face the uncertain days, it was the beginning of five dark years of occupation.

Later that afternoon,several German aircraft returned with about a hundred troops and officials led by Hauptmann Gussek who was met by the heads of the Jersey government led by Bailiff Basil Dechevaux. An ultimatum was issued, distributed and conformed to. Captain Gussek was escorted to the main town of St Helier where he set up headquarters at the Town Hall. All communication with mainland Britain had already been severed and a bucket brigade of regulations was issued.

The main signal station for approaching shipping stood on Fort Regent, an old granite fortification which commands a sweeping view of the capital of St Helier. The flagstaffs there could be seen for miles.

By July 2, 1940, the German Imperial War flag was fluttering in the breeze.

A small part of Britain had been occupied by the Wehrmacht who had clearly come prepared. Europe was in turmoil and the sound of the jackboot now echoed around the streets of Jersey. The Germans were here to stay.

CHAPTER 6

The Germans move in

During the first month of the German Occupation the life of the island had been turned on its head. Families had been split, some had left, some remained and those that stayed held their breath while the Germans took over. The local newspaper ,the Jersey Evening Post, was used to inform the population of the new regime . Subjugation was the name of the game and if you didn't like it then there were consequences which had been well documented during the Nazi advance through Europe.
The main town of St Helier saw the most change as buildings were requisitioned for administration. Hundreds of German troops poured in through the docks and the airport. Hotels and guest houses were now requisitioned for the newcomers.
In the Mayfair Hotel two German Luftwaffe staff were sharing a room.

"*Well, Gunter, we have certainly fallen on our feet here.*
Sunshine and sand.
Better than Berlin !"

Corporal Fritz Doenig leaned out of the window and breathed in the fresh air.

"Certainly smells better, my friend", he replied.

Outside the room more soldiers had arrived and were clattering along the corridor. In the general hubbub of conversation one voice overpowered the others.

"So this is the Island of Wight. According to the map we are only about three hundred kilometres from London. We won't be

here for long".

On hearing this, Gunter looked at Fritz and laughed out loud.*"What an idiot!"*

"Must be from the map reading section", added Fritz drily and he closed the window.

The Isle of Wight lay just off Southampton on the south coast of England. The Channel Islands lay 100 miles further south, less than 20 miles west of the French coast. The soldier's misdirection was a serious error !

It was now August and after the initial horrendous bombing raid which had nigh on obliterated their house, the St Clement parish authorities had rehoused the Marinelles in an abandoned seaside house called St Kitts, a few hundred yards from where they lived before. It was a cottage built of local granite with a garden which stretched down to the beach. It had a porch on the road side of the kitchen and a door led to the living room which overlooked a scrubby garden. Thirty yards of scratchy grass and sand led down to the beach, the only differentiating line being a few rocks which were the remains of a low wall long since beaten down by a previous storm. There were three rooms upstairs.

The Marinelles lived about three miles from the town of St Helier and were currently far enough away to be almost unaffected by the arrival of the German forces. Peter still went to school in St Helier on the bus, as normal, albeit with depleted numbers and Christine got on with the business of the new house and looking after Sophie while her son was studying.

The summer was at its height and the seasons paid no attention to the new regime. The beach could be seen from most of the windows and more than once a couple of German officers had

pulled up in a requisitioned car on Le Hurel slipway to the west to enjoy the pleasures of an afternoon swim at high tide. Peter watched and walked slowly down the garden and over the low wall that led directly onto the sand. He was barefoot and the clean dry sand above the high tide mark squeaked beneath his toes. He thrust his hands deep into the pockets of his old grey shorts and watched from a safe distance. The two officers had stripped off on the beach and left their clothes in two neat piles on the sand. They were a good hundred yards out and swimming strongly. Peter was impressed and was even more impressed when he saw a small figure sprint down the slipway and gather up the clothing before making off equally fast back up the slipway. He was certain it was his friend John Le Ross. He had timed his run to perfection as the two swimmers were too intent on their exercise to notice the action on the beach. The figure scuttled back up the slipway and disappeared.
Peter walked slowly back to the garden of his house, slowly because he did not wish to attract attention to himself. Once out of sight himself he made his way through the house and out of the front door onto the main road where he spotted John Le Ross coming towards him with the bundle of clothes under his arm.
"In here", said Peter. "Come and watch the fun. I saw you nicking that stuff. It'll be ages before they even notice".

John's heart was beating fast. He couldn't believe how easily he had got away with it. They hurried inside and laid the kit out on the kitchen table. Concealed down the leg of a pair of trousers was a leather holster with a sinister looking Luger pistol. John removed it and pretended to aim it at a picture on the wall. Peter was first to realise that they must not be caught in possession and said,"Don't be daft John, we've got to hide this lot and I've got just the spot". He went up the stairs and pulled down the ladder to the loft. They both scampered up with the uniforms under their arms. Peter peeled back the material from the roof beams and shoved the stolen goods behind before

resealing the beams. They scampered back down the ladder before closing the loft and going back into the garden. They peeked out from behind the little shed which butted onto the beach.
The swimmers had returned and after a brief search of the slipway and surrounding area they retreated to their car, still in wet bathing trunks, and drove off.

There was a period of about an hour before the tranquillity was abruptly pierced by the arrival of three German trucks which spilled out at least fifty troops all armed with rifles. An officer barked out instructions and the men quickly formed a unit of three ranks before coming smartly to attention. A large open topped Mercedes field car then pulled up and the more than ample figure of Oberst Von Schmidt, the newly appointed military commander of the Channel Islands, stepped out from the back. Accompanied by two more officers he strode briskly towards the assembled troops. The officers conferred and dispersed the awaiting men to form three groups. What happened next can only be described as a vigorous and indiscriminate search of all the houses in the immediate vicinity. Doors and protesting householders were all pushed aside as each home was turned upside down in the search for the stolen uniforms and of course the Luger sidearm.

In short time a posse of fresh faced grey uniformed Wehrmacht squaddies had noisily entered the Marinelles' house and swept through like locusts. Unfortunately for the boys, they broke into the loft where, without too much effort , they discovered the missing items which were brought down and thrust onto the kitchen table. The Luger slid across the shiny surface of the wood and toppled onto the floor with an almighty noise. For a second the boys and the soldiers watched each other in silence .Suddenly everybody was shouting in German and an officer entered.

"Do you boys know anything about this?" he said in perfect English.

Peter and John both shook their heads but looked as guilty as hell.

A high ranking officious German officer arrived and immediately barked out an order. In that moment the reality of the situation was driven home to all those locals who thought they were in for an easy ride. At gunpoint the boys were frogmarched out to the waiting staff car and driven off at high speed with an armed escort.

The crowd which had gathered to watch this unfolding scene stood in amazement while the remaining troops boarded their lorries leaving the carnage of a neighbourhood search behind them. The onlookers were clearly in shock and it was a good minute before any of them voiced an opinion.
"Bastards!!! "

It didn't take too long before the Constable of the parish had been informed of the boys' arrests and by a combination of telephone calls and messengers the Bailiff of Jersey, the island's political and judicial head, was informed of the situation.
The boys themselves were taken to the Newgate Street prison in the main town of St Helier, offloaded from a truck and unceremoniously bundled into a cell where they were left for the best part of three hours. A soldier brought them some bread and cheese and told them they would be tried in front of the Oberst in the morning on a charge of an act of treason perpetrated against the Fuhrer himself. A few minutes later the lights were turned off and the seriousness of the situation started to dawn on the pair who had, to them, just been having a lark. But this was no longer the peace time that they had

known, the island was occupied by a foreign army and things could never be the same again. The Newgate Street prison itself was a cold and forbidding place, originally built as part of the hospital in 1765. Comfort was not one of its strong points.

John Le Ross started to cry.

"Come on, you wimp," said Peter, "we'll probably just get a bollocking. It's not that serious."

John carried on sniffling and Peter had a feeling deep down that a bollocking was not all that was in the offing. A small piece of plaster fell from the ceiling and a small furry creature scuttled over his foot. All was not well.

CHAPTER 7

Trial and sentence

The hours of darkness in the prison cell did nothing for the boys' confidence and after a sleepless night, dawn broke all too soon for them. Peter felt as if time was going too fast and feeling of foreboding had gripped him. His eyes were drawn to the graffiti which previous prisoners had felt the need to leave behind. A sketch of a hangman's noose etched into the flakey plaster of the wall did nothing to elevate the mood. His friend John was still tearful and despite his hunger, could not bear to eat any of the bread which constituted breakfast under the new German rule. Peter used the bread to stimulate the saliva in his dry mouth but the effect did not last long.

At 7.30 a.m. the door clunked open and a small posse of soldiers escorted them out to a waiting lorry. It was a short journey onto the seafront and into the driveway of the nearby Grand Hotel which had been requisitioned by the invading troops. They were led under gunpoint into a large room which had previously been a dining area for guests of the previously upmarket seaside hotel whose impressive facade had stood sentinel over the Bay of St Aubin since 1890.

After a few minutes a few smartly dressed officers filed in and arranged themselves at two separate tables. Peter and John recognised two of them as the officers who had been involved in the incident on the beach. Someone said something in German and everyone in the room stood as Oberst Von Schmidt, the newly appointed military commander of the island, marched smartly in and took a seat in a large captain's chair behind a large desk.

Another order was barked out and everyone sat down. There followed what seemed to be a preamble followed by a translation of it in English. The charge which followed was based on the theft of a weapon from the occupying army. This was a serious offence and the officer defending the boys implored them to make a full and frank confession as it appeared that no facts were in dispute. The offence had been committed, and the boys had, by their own statement, stolen the weapon and had hidden it in the loft. Under further questioning John had confessed to the actual theft and Peter to acting as a partner in crime.

To the bewilderment of the boys, much of the rest of the proceedings was discussed in German and the rather large officer in charge of the prosecution launched into a tirade as to how an example must be set to the rest of the population if this sort of insubordination was not to be repeated. A long heated argument developed and at the end of a further half hour a break was taken and after Oberst Von Schmidt had filed out, most of the officers took the opportunity of lighting cigarettes. Consequently the room had filled with smoke catching the rays of sunshine which streamed through the large restaurant windows. The presiding officer returned and delivered what appeared to be a verdict of some sort. He read deliberately and at length from a sheet of paper which he held in his hand . He banged his other fist on the table from time to time to emphasise the seriousness of his impassioned speech. He came to the end of the diatribe with a final flourish.

All eyes seemed to be on the boys as the defending counsel approached them with what they knew to be the verdict and sentence.

“John , Peter. You have both been found guilty as charged. Unfortunately you have been sentenced to two years in prison. I have managed to persuade them to let you serve your sentence here in Jersey.”

There was silence all round and Peter felt a strange ringing in his ears. John was terrified and thought he was having a bad dream. Reality finally took over and while John wept uncontrollably, Peter's jaw set tight and his face went very white. They were led away and back to the prison.
The young boys were in deep shock. It was barely midday on Monday. Some cheese , sausages and apples were brought in but neither of them had the stomach for food. They could hear voices outside in the street. The voices got louder . A crowd seemed to be gathering.

By three o'clock the small crowd had become a thousand strong as news of the verdict and sentence was carried throughout the island. As more people gathered, German troops arrived in force to keep the peace. The protests became louder until suddenly the general hubbub was silenced as warning shots rang out in the street and arrests were made. Peter watched the scene unfolding from their cell window on the first floor of the prison. He felt totally bewildered.

The atmosphere on the island had changed dramatically. Jersey had previously been a sleepy holiday island perched enigmatically between English and French cultures. It now held its breath as two young lads were perched along with the rest of the population on the edge of a precipice. If any of the local population had any doubts as to whether the invasion and subsequent occupation by the Germans was all that serious, then those doubts had been thoroughly laid to rest. The streets were cleared but the fallout was immense and had only just begun.

CHAPTER 8

The Bailiff protests

Local government was already in disarray since the arrival of the Wehrmacht and the trial had certainly not resolved any issues. The parliament consisted of upwards of fifty representatives from the twelve parishes of the island . The head of the judiciary and also the local parliament was the Bailiff , Basil Dechevaux, and on hearing the news, he sent a message to German HQ asking for an immediate audience. The upshot of his request was a meeting with Oberst Gruber, the German administrative commander , at 7p.m. that same evening at the German Headquarters at Victoria College House.

The Germans had requisitioned a number of properties for administration purposes. Victoria College itself was a magnificent granite building with a commanding position on a hill overlooking the main town of St Helier . It had massive strategic views to the south west and the east and had been a seat of learning for the sons of Jersey since 1852 when Queen Victoria had visited. There was an equally impressive granite building a couple of hundred yards further up the hill where school boarders from all corners of the world were housed. The school had decamped almost en masse to mainland England before the advance of the German Army or were transferred to other schools where classes could continue. This building bore the name of Victoria College House and the administration of the island for the foreseeable future was from these comfortable quarters .A soldier could walk from here and then down through the extensive grounds of Victoria College to where he was billeted in one of the hotels at the foot of the hill in town in about fifteen minutes. It was downhill all the way and the return journey by foot was for the fittest only.

Being a former pupil of Victoria College, Bailiff Dechevaux was familiar with the layout of Victoria College House. During his formative years there, he was a day boy who used to trudge up from the main school at 1p.m. every school day for lunch. College House lunches were not always to his liking but he got used to it. He studied hard and after a couple of years in London, he returned to the island to work for his father's law firm. Eventually he got the call to cross over to the public sector and, not long after his 56th birthday in 1938, by reason of the illness of the previous incumbent, he rose to the position of His Majesty's Bailiff of Jersey. The job was an onerous one. He was elected to be head of the judiciary by his fellow legal officers but his duties included being the head of the Jersey States government. The island had been part of the British Isles since the days of William the Conqueror and the position of Bailiff was an ancient, time honoured title. However, he figured no former Bailiff had ever had to handle the circumstances that he now found himself having to handle.

His official car, an old black Peugeot, turned right off the main road and edged between the two granite pillars which formed the gate. He made his way to the impressive entrance hall and made his presence known to the guard at the door. While waiting for the door to be opened, he turned and took in the view of the cricket field which stretched down to the school itself. Over the last few weeks of indecision and uncertainty, the grass had already grown long and neglected but was still green and lush. You could still make out the square in the middle where the cricket pitches were. They would lie fenced and fallow during the football season only to spring back into life in the summer months as the sound of leather on willow echoed around the oval.
He sighed. The Bailiff was one angry man. This was his old school, dammit, and these people had marched in and just taken over .

He was ushered in through the main door, across granite flagstones polished by decades of schoolboy feet and into a large room which was lined with portraits of previous headmasters whose common steely gaze bore witness to former times. He was met by the not insignificant figure of Oberst Gruber. Born in 1891, he had served with distinction in the Cavalry in World War One and was the holder of the German Cross in gold. A trifle overweight , he cut an impressive figure in his officers uniform .The two leaders had already met on a number of occasions. They exchanged formalities and cut directly to the topic of the day.
Neither man would be trifled with but obviously Gruber held all the cards and would be dealing them for the foreseeable future.

“Herr Bailiff, what can I do for you?”

"Herr Gruber, you know exactly what you can do. You can release our....our children from prison!"

A look of feigned surprise came across Gruber's face.

"Herr Bailiff, these boys deserved their punishment and should consider themselves lucky not to have been *shot* for stealing a weapon” said Gruber in perfect English. He emphasised the word 'shot'.

"But these are just children! You commit an illegal act by taking the island by force of arms and you say to me that these boys are lucky not to have been *shot* ! That is outrageous. What you are doing is against all decency and fairness and very likely a breach of the Geneva Convention. I cannot believe what you are doing!"

"Believe it, Herr Bailiff," replied Gruber. "Our two nations are at war and there is very little that's fair in war, so much of what we do as the occupying force you will just have to endure. If you bear with us, we can all get through these times unharmed !"

Gruber reached for the cocktail cabinet and turned condescendingly towards his accuser, "Do sit down, Herr Bailiff. Brandy?"

"I demand you release these two boys immediately !" he surprised himself with the vigour of his outburst.

" Herr Bailiff, you are in no position to make *any* demands ! Now, please sit down and also perhaps, calm down"

He poured a brandy from a bottle left by the last College housemaster and offered the glass to his guest who immediately ignored the gesture but still sat down. He repeated his demand but in a more ordered fashion this time.

"I implore you to release them. There is nothing at all to be gained by imprisoning them"

Gruber paused, took a sip of brandy and replied." I repeat, Herr Bailiff, that they are lucky not to be facing a firing squad. They will serve the full sentence and you must get accustomed to the new regime."
The two men were now locked in an eyeball to eyeball stand-off. The Bailiff broke the tension and, leaning forward, he plucked the brandy glass from the table, raised it to his lips and downed the not inconsiderable contents in one emphatic move. He turned and marched out of the still open door, down the hallway, out the door and into the back seat of the official Peugeot.
The brandy had not assuaged his anger and , in truth, it was

burning his throat. His first attempt at speaking failed miserably but he eventually cleared his throat and tried again "Just drive, Arthur, please. Just get us home." he said to the driver in a husky voice.

The interview was definitely over .

CHAPTER 9

New Regime

With the two lads locked up in Newgate Street prison and not likely to be released any time soon, the islanders and the occupying force reached a kind of uneasy stand-off. The prisoners were not short of food as they were allowed victuals delivered by friends and relatives so , in this respect, their conditions were not as harsh as those being experienced on mainland France which sat less than 20 miles due east. The Wehrmacht were not unaware of what was going on there as the Free French resistance, the Maquis, gathered force but the country was huge and a man on the run would be hard to track down. Jersey and the rest of the occupied Channel Islands were tiny in comparison and any major acts of resistance would be easy to quash.

Back at St Kitts, Christine had overcome the initial shock of the few minutes of madness that had resulted in the boys' incarceration. She gazed wistfully towards the French coast across the water on a beautiful summer's day. Crystal clear seas like glass peppered with granite outcrops took her eye but the view could not assuage her anxiety. An absent husband and an imprisoned son did not paint a happy picture and her mood was one of resigned sadness. Her youngest child cooed from the pram and the intrusive noise pricked the bubble of depression. She had had no news of her husband Cliff since January and she could only fill in the gaps with information that could be gleaned from the BBC news on the radio. She could only guess that he was manning ships on convoy duty somewhere.

How her life had been turned upside down in the last year ! She got up from the kitchen table and put the kettle on the stove to make a cup of tea. In general she kept busy because busy stopped her mind from fragmenting into pieces which she felt could not be put back together. The community had rallied round since Peter had been imprisoned and she was not short of moral support, witness the number of callers she was getting. One or two of the local farmers had kept her going with supplies of vegetables, and babysitters were not in short supply – not that she was out much, but she did bus into town once or twice a week to see the boys, albeit just delivering food and trying to hold a conversation from the street below their cell on the first floor of the prison in Newgate Street. She was thankful that they had not been shipped off the island.

What she did miss in these daydreaming minutes was her husband – she loved him dearly and yearned for the warmth of his body. At this thought, her eyes welled with tears which she held back as she filled the tea pot with hot water. Baby Sophie needed feeding and the cooing transformed into a whinge as her belly complained. Christine picked her up and fed her from a bottle. She missed also the plentiful supply of fresh fish that her husband and more latterly her son would bring home. Pretty soon the local fishermen would be dropping the odd basket of prawns at her door.

Although the German civil authorities had ordered everyone to carry on as normal, nothing was normal anymore .The local uniformed police were now subservient to the Wehrmacht and you could see the town policemen opening the doors of German staff cars as they arrived at the town hall. The menfolk who remained had to work to feed their families and what little work that was available was provided by the invaders. It was clear that most locals were treading a stressful line between surviving or collaborating with the enemy.

By September , the Battle of Britain was mushrooming over the skies of England where the Royal Air Force fought with the Luftwaffe . Hordes of cocky Luftwaffe officers were seen swaggering along the pavements of St Helier in search of rest and recreation. They did not create a very good impression but, like swallows in Autumn, they disappeared as suddenly as they had arrived . Not all were ecstatic at their departure – one or two local ladies had succumbed to their Prussian charm, and

now had to suffer the consequences of being shunned by their friends. This turned out to be an ongoing scenario as the Occupation continued.
The airmen's arrogance manifested itself on the pavements of the town. The locals had no option on many occasions but to step out onto the road to avoid phalanxes of invaders milling round the shops. One local lady, just short of her fiftieth birthday and obviously tiring of all the heel clicking and Heil Hitlering that was going on, could take it no more. As she stepped out onto the road yet again, she yelled out at the top of her voice,
"Heil Churchill !!! Get out of the bloody way you bloody Krauts. Get out of the way. Eff off all of you. Eff off back to Germany. Fuck Hitler. Fuck you. Heil Churchill!"
The vigour of Maisie Le Cac's verbal volley took even the locals by surprise. A stunned silence ensued for a few seconds before she was arrested . Despite seemingly being a tad deranged (or "cuckoo" as the locals would have it) she was ignominiously shipped off to a French prison for six months. She returned unchastened and remained a vituperative critic of the intruders for the remainder of the war albeit in a less confrontational way.
The German response to her somewhat legitimate outpourings had shocked Jersey people as much as the boys' punishment. As the months pushed by, however, six months in prison became the norm for minor misdemeanours.
Life went on all over the island as people adjusted to the presence of the invaders. It was clearly a case of how long they would have to put up with it. The Channel Islands had been cast adrift to the vagaries of war and they were clearly, at least at this stage, not high on the priority list of the Allied Forces who were in disarray all over Europe. The Battle of Britain was being fought in the skies over England and Churchill was desperate to get the Americans involved in the fight against Hitler.
Occupied France was suffering all kinds of deprivations and

hostility towards the enemy was being met with cruel brute force. Horror stories emerged of mass killings in retribution to resistance to the Germans and these filtered through via the various supply links that were maintained between the French mainland and the islands.

The Jersey population were in no doubt whatsoever that to resist indiscriminately and belligerently would be to induce barbaric retribution.

And yet... and yet, at present there seemed to be a delicate stand-off between the occupied and the occupiers. Who would blink first ?

CHAPTER 10

Prison life

Whilst the new German Occupation was developing with its new rules and regulations issued on an almost daily basis, our two young prisoners had overcome the initial shock of the events which followed their prank on the beach. Thrown into a state of depression after their trial and sentencing, they took solace in each other's company. They shared a cell of reasonable dimensions and made the most of their two hours in the exercise yard every day. Their cell was on the first floor of A block at the Newgate Street prison and their little window with its iron grid commanded a good view of the street below. No visitors were allowed but this was no burden as it was possible to hold conversations with people in the street and they had an endless stream of morning and afternoon visitors who were all familiar with the timetable of the prison day. Food was brought in and after a few days the lads were in a much happier state of mind.

As Autumn moved on and the nights became longer and the days shorter, they listened for planes flying overhead and guessed whether they were friend or foe.
The aerial activity was intense in September as the Battle of Britain was won and lost and all sides involved drew breath . From the snippets of information shouted to them from the street below on a daily basis, they put together the scenario in their imagination. John would be Battler Britain, the youngest pilot in the R.A.F. and he would shoot down bomb carrying Heinkels and feisty Messerschmitts. Peter was Powerful Pierre who flew the R.A.F.'s secret weapon, a Spitfire which could render itself invisible. They passed hours of fun with the soundtrack going on overhead.

The prison quickly filled up with locals all accused of minor misdemeanours and news was disseminated by word of mouth through the bars of the windows. The boys had assumed hero status amongst their friends and came to enjoy the limelight. They even managed to get a small supply of ping pong balls sent in and together with wooden rulers which were delivered as part of a maths homework assignment, they quickly improvised their own particular form of 'prison cricket' in the confines of their cell. The prison guards were almost all German and they quickly realised that if everybody behaved themselves, this particular tour of duty wasn't so bad. Of the three long term prisoners they had inherited after the invasion, only one was considered dangerous .He was serving the second year of a five year sentence for manslaughter and was prone to verbal outbursts, usually in the middle of the night.
As December approached and the temperature dropped, blankets and bedding were
sent in. The initial shock of the military trial had now well and truly passed and the boys had just begun to fret with the boredom of it all. Peter longed to be out and about on the beach and John just wanted to be out on his dad's boat with a fishing rod in his hand. They had had an argument or two but it was clear that the confines of the cell were beginning to hurt them and the prospect of another eighteen months or so was depressing them both. They talked endlessly in the dark hours about how they missed their families and what they were going to do when this chapter had run its course when, hopefully, they would be released.
Surprisingly, they did not have to wait long.

CHAPTER 11

Surprise

The island's civil government had not been idle. Despite being burdened by the relentless issue of new military orders which had to be communicated to the public, the Bailiff had been badgering Oberst Gruber on a regular basis. At least once a week, his chauffeured Peugeot had arrived unannounced at College House where he shirtfronted his German counterpart. Gruber was particularly patient with him as his lack of courtesy in not making an appointment often meant rearranging his duties.

The two became not quite friends and not quite enemies. There was always a distance between them which could not be breached. However much Bailiff Dechevaux reproached him, Gruber knew who was in charge.

"...and what about this young lad who you have imprisoned for a month for reading a pamphlet dropped by the R.A.F.? Is that the mark of a civilised nation,Herr Gruber ? "

" Oh, please call me Werner, Herr Bailiff. I shall be here for a while so surely you and I can dispense with formalities. Unfortunately that boy is a troublemaker and is very disrespectful by all accounts. He was lucky he did not get six months. Now next, how is the registration of milk retailers going and also the licensing of food merchants ?"

Dechevaux shuffled his papers, searching for the relevant notes. A shaft of sunlight broke through the net curtains of the large office.

“..and perhaps I should call you Basil, Herr Bailiff “

Dechevaux stiffened visibly. Gruber was definitely toying with him and carried
on the dialogue before his guest could turn on him.

“I think I have some good news for you. I have decided to release the La Rocque boys, Marinelle and Le Ross, as a gesture of goodwill . I think everybody has learned a lesson by now. I have signed their release papers right here. Perhaps you will arrange for their removal from Newgate Street as soon as possible. We can deal with the rest of our agenda tomorrow.”

Dechevaux spluttered and found himself unable to utter anything meaningful in that instant. Eventually he took and examined the release papers, pretending to read the finer details despite feeling overjoyed. There was no way he was going to show Gruber that he was the slightest bit pleased. He collected his briefcase from the floor and shoved the documents inside. Not wanting to appear too enthusiastic, he rose slowly to his feet and drew breath.
“ Well, it's not before time. It was totally unnecessary.... what you did....and are doing.”
He paused, rose and moved toward the door. He hesitated and, before leaving, spoke again.
“Thank you......er........Werner”

Gruber offered his hand but Dechevaux was already on his way and marching through the massive front door of College House, his briefcase in his hand. He climbed into the back of his large black Peugeot, catching his chauffeur unawares.

“They've released the boys, Arthur. We had best go back to Green Street and I'll make a couple of phone calls to their parents and also I had better notify a few people. After that I suggest we go and pick them up at Newgate Street."

Arthur had previously been catching his employer's eye in the rear view mirror but, on hearing the news, he swivelled round and blurted out,

"Oh, well done, sir. Well done!"

"Thank you, Arthur but all I did was to keep badgering Feldkommandant Gruber and all he did was feed me brandy. Never mind. Let's go."

The Peugeot nosed its shiny black bonnet back between the granite pillars on to the main road and headed back to town. Dechevaux sat grinning in the back seat.

CHAPTER 12

Christmas comes early

Our two young prisoners were surprised when a German guard came to their cell door and spoke through the grill.
"Christmas , she is coming early for you boys. *Raus, raus, raus* !! "
They looked at each other blankly but then the door was unlocked and through it they recognised the figure of Dechevaux who had visited them in an official capacity in the early days of their sentence. They remembered him as a sympathetic man and realised quickly that something was happening.

"Come on, lads. I have good news for you....... the best news! You're being released. Put all your stuff in your blankets and follow me to fresh air , friends and family. I am taking you home."

There was a strange silence. "Well, come on then! Hang around much longer and they'll lock the door again."

The boys were dumbstruck but there was no third bidding. It took five minutes to shove all their belongings into their blankets and, gathering the four corners into their hands, they followed Dechevaux outside, down the steps, stopped briefly at an office to pick up some paperwork and then out into Newgate Street. With the help of the chauffeur they piled their stuff into the boot of the waiting Peugeot and climbed into the back seat.

"We are taking these boys home, Arthur. Coast road to La Rocque, please. "

The chauffeur looked over his shoulder from the drivers seat and smiled at the boys. Simultaneously they gave him a thumbs-up sign. The Peugeot moved off from the prison , down to the Esplanade and headed east.

Meanwhile at La Rocque, Mrs Le Plongeon from the local store and post office was already scuttling along the road with a message from the Bailiff's secretary for Christine .
Dechevaux was aware that the sudden release of the boys would come as a major shock to their families and was anxious for them to know as soon as possible.
Mrs Le Plongeon reached St Kitts where she found the front door ajar. She pushed it open and shouted, " Christine, are you there, dear? ". Christine shuffled out from the back with little Sophie in her arms. " Sorry to barge in but this message came through from the Bailiff."
The note was delivered and the note was read. Both deliverer and recipient were ecstatic!
"Peter Marinelle and John Le Ross to be released immediately . I will deliver both personally before noon." It was signed Basil Dechevaux, Her Majesty's Bailiff.

Edith Le Plongeon hugged Christine and the baby. "Must dash,dear. Have to let the
Le Ross' know the good news as well ! Happy days , my love."

With that, she scuttled off to deliver the other message.

The boys could barely speak and kept smiling at each other as the car passed various landmarks along the way. Autumn had passed them by and Peter noticed how bare all the trees were. A blustery wind blew sand across the road. They took the coastal route via the harbour and Mount Bingham, Havre des Pas with all its little guesthouses, and then along the coast until Dechevaux turned round from the front passenger seat and

enquired “Which house are we passing first?”
Peter gave instructions and eventually St Kitts came into view. The front door was open and a good looking woman was cleaning the windows outside. It was his mother Christine. As the car approached and stopped, she stepped down from the chair she was using and turned to face them. The Peugeot stopped by the house , the doors were flung open and out piled Peter, his face creased between a smile and a frown. He ran straight into his mother's arms and, to his embarrassment, she smothered him with hugs and kisses. He drew back and said, “Any news of Dad yet, Mum?”
Christine shook her head. “Nothing yet. Best you say goodbye to John and be sure to thank Mr Dechevaux. Without him, you'd still be inside the prison.”

Dechevaux climbed out of the front passenger seat and introduced himself to Christine, explaining the situation and how the boys' sentences had been commuted. Peter strolled back to the car to chat with John and they could not have been happier, all smiles and lively chatter. He collected his blanket and belongings from the chauffeur who had unloaded them from the boot.
“I'll see you tomorrow,Johnnie boy. Come down anytime.” He punched him playfully on the shoulder. “We're bloody well free!”

They did a little jig until Dechevaux interrupted them.
“Best we get you home now, John. But before you two go, I have one or two things to say. Under our present circumstances, we must all take care. You've both caused a lot of heartache to your families with a careless prank. In future, you'll be more aware of what can happen. God willing, one day this nightmare will end. Now, go away and behave yourselves .”
The boys nodded in agreement, totally in awe of Dechevaux who then shook their hands solemnly. He then gave them a conspiratorial thumbs up as if to say 'well done'.

“Peter, look after your mother. Let's go, John. Goodbye Mrs Marinelle.”

The car started up and slowly they disappeared along the road and out of sight before turning left to John Le Ross' house.

Peter and his mum felt the cold wind. “Come on, son. Let's have some tea.
Your sister has grown quite a bit.”
She put her arm round him and shepherded him through the front door. Tears were streaming down her face. Peter rushed to the small bedroom where his little sister lay asleep.
Christine stared blankly out of the front room window which looked straight out to sea.
She spoke under her breath to no-one in particular.
“ One out of two isn't too bad but two out of two would be better.”

The kettle whistled and the cold wind blew spits of rain against the glass. She drew her
cardigan tightly round her and cried some more. Her son's absence in prison had put severely into focus how much she was missing her husband.

CHAPTER 13

Low water meeting

The days following his release from prison were happy days for Peter, although he had to admit that imprisonment had been a bit of a lark. After the sheer terror of the trial and sentencing, the first couple of weeks of being locked up had been an ordeal but after that it had been a little boring but not unbearable. He and John had got to know each other pretty well and when one was down, the other would cheer him up.

They had been well fed and what with extra blankets being brought in , it felt like three and a half months of camping . They had just started their school summer holidays when the Germans arrived and would have been setting off on their fourth year at secondary school at the end of September so it really felt like extended summer holidays. To their mates they were heroes and both houses were inundated with friends and relatives who had dropped by to shake them by the hand.

Before they knew it, November was over and Christmas was nearly upon them. Up to this point , the regular links and supplies with the British mainland had been cut off but the slack had been taken up by a local government supply committee, the Department for Essential Commodities, which was allowed access to mainland France and goods were reasonably obtainable. However, Peter had decided that a couple of lobsters might make the festive season go better and one grey overcast and misty day when the tide was half way out, he slipped unnoticed onto the sand in front of St Kitts, wicker basket and spike in hand and slowly walked the hundred or so yards to where the rocks started. He could taste and smell the saltiness of the sea on the mist which hung peacefully on the landscape. He loved the mist. It drained away the subtle colours that the sun was so good at encouraging and all the surrounding features were contrasting black and white. An eerie scene but a calm and peaceful one, he felt totally at ease in his surroundings slipping from rocky outcrop to rocky outcrop. Quickly he was out of sight of the foreshore and heading towards Seymour Tower behind which he knew there were lobsters lurking in secret lairs. Seymour had been built near the low water mark about half a mile from the beach as a defence against the marauding French in the previous century. It had been built on a large granite rock base and stood guard sixty feet up and its one main room big enough to hold a dozen people with ease.

It was a mild day for Christmas and he quickly worked up a sweat underneath his thick jersey as he trod the fisherman's well worn path out to the tower, carefully noting features on the way, features that seem to whisper a welcome as he passed by on a rocky road untrodden by him for a half a year.

His last trip down there was the day the Germans came, when the planes flew over his head and dealt death and destruction at the top of the slipway. It seemed like longer, so much had happened. He didn't think he could ever forgive them for that . He felt so much older in himself now.There had been an order that week to keep all locals off the beaches while they were mined by the Wehrmacht sappers. So far the beaches in front of St Kitts had not been visited so he considered it safe to slip down to the low water mark . It would be nearly dark by the time he got back so he knew he probably wouldn't be seen and how could they possibly mine the vast areas of rock and sand anyway? It wasn't a really big tide so this was more of an exploratory trip for him. Next time he could bring John and plan it a bit better. The slippery tide had not gone beyond the tower today and was on the turn. He could sense the stillness as the sea paused and sighed before easing back up to the land again. He foraged along the edge where the bigger fish lurked and chased small crustaceans. Winter was not a great time for fishing but today was an exception. A couple of good sized bass

were darting around by the water's edge. He stood as still as a heron until he was sure the bass was oblivious to him and then plunged the spike downwards swiftly parting the fishy flesh as it impaled the creature to the sand.
“Wayhay! Gotcha.”
He picked up a stone and clouted the spiked and wriggling fish about the head until it wriggled no more. It was despatched into the wicker basket and he was aware of its eye gazing up at him as if to condemn him for his foul deed. He quickly closed the lid and began his search again only to be interrupted by a scuttling sound behind the nearest outcrop of granite, a scraping of shoes on gravel.
A voice cut the calm. “Nice one , young fella! That's a bonny wee fish.”.
The voice was unmistakably Scottish and Peter recognised it before he saw the face.
It was Angus Cameron Mackintosh, Angus to his family, Mac to his friends and Mr Mac to anyone under twenty.
“Hello Mr Mac. Had any luck today,” said Peter.
“Aye, I have. I managed to get a decent wee lobster .More by luck than judgement though. I reckon he was just moving into a new hole when I got him. Have a wee look.”
Peter peered into the Scotsman's basket and gasped when he saw the size of it.
“Wow, a two pounder at least! Where did you get it?”
“I'll let you know next week, laddie. Did ye think I was born yesterday?”
Peter smiled. The two of them were on the same wavelength. Low water fishermen kept their secrets and whilst sharing notes about the weather, their inside leg measurements and the tides, they steadfastly refused to divulge knowledge such as where lobsters were hiding.

Angus was a single man in his early fifties, young enough to have seen the horrors of the first world war but too old to get a call up to fight the Hun again. He was physically and mentally scarred like millions of others across Europe who had had the misfortune to be involved in the bellicose abyss of 1914 -18. The shrapnel wounds in his mind steadfastly refused to leave and sleeping was a luxury to him these days. He would read all night or simply walk on the beach until the sun came up . In the summer he would often be found snoozing down by the low water mark , usually tucked up at the top of a rocky outcrop where nobody could sneak up behind him, but usually given away by his quiet snoring. His house was about half a mile from St Kitts and he was the first to knock on the Marinelle's door with an offer of help when Peter and John had been thrown into prison. He was an independent soul and kept himself to himself. An engineer by trade, he had worked on the railways on the mainland after the Great War.

Eventually his war wounds got the better of him and he retired to Jersey when a distant relative died and left him a house right on the beach. His affair with the sand and the sea started right there, the day he arrived on June 29, 1925. He travelled on the overnight boat from Weymouth and arrived at the house at 8 a.m. on a windless morning with the sun rising overhead from the east and the tide lapping at the bottom of the garden. He recalled later thinking that someone had removed the plug from this beautiful bath as, when he looked again after five hours of unpacking, the sea was a distant glint on the horizon. His ragged mind was soothed and he loved the place from the first day. He had been engaged to be married to Miranda, beautiful Miranda, just before he went off to war. When he returned, the beautiful Miranda had left him a note to say she had left him and had married another. Now heartbroken and broken of mind and body, he constructed a new life because the alternative was too hard to imagine. The best part of seven years of sheer grind had elapsed since war's end when Aunt Agatha , his mother's sister, died and left him this small and intimate house at La Rocque. He left the mainland in a heartbeat and arrived, breathless that very morning. After five days of summer at La Rocque, he proposed to the view from the front room.

“Marry me ,darrlin.” he said. He didn't need a reply. She was his until the day he died. After all, she was much more trustworthy than bloody Miranda.

He had known the Marinelles because Cliff was a fisherman whose boat was moored in La Rocque harbour and in such a tight-knit community , everybody knew everybody. He had watched Peter grow up and was appalled when the boys crossed swords with the invading army and got dealt such a heavy blow. He liked Peter because he figured the boy got it, the 'it' being their current ever changing surroundings and his unconscious desire to be part of it.

“How was your wee holiday?” he said , a smile flickering at the corner of his mouth.

“Ah,that.” replied Peter. “It was okay. Rather have been here though.”

“Aye. You won't get caught next time, that's for sure! Did ye know they will be mining the beaches around here very shortly ? We shall have to be a wee bit careful in the future. We won't be allowed on the beach and if we sneak down we stand the risk of being blown up.” He paused and took Peter totally by surprise when he suddenly swore. Mac spat it out.
“Fucking Krauts, fucking Krauts!”
After his experiences of the Great War, the Germans were not his favourite people.

He recovered his composure. “ Look, laddie. There is a way. You can see this section of the beach from your house, can't you ?When you see them laying mines , you must draw their positions as accurately as possible on a map. I'll do the same from my front window and with a little bit of luck we should be able to carry on our business down here. Knock on my door when they have finished and moved up towards me. Ok? “

“Good idea, Mr Mac. I can do that.”

“Best we get back now laddie. The light's fading and the tide's comin' in.”

With that the unlikely pair beetled off back towards the beach, the low sun set weakly way to their left and the mist settled in again. They diverged where the sandy beach began near the southern slipway. Mac went right towards home and the pub, Peter went left towards St Kitts.

“Fucking Krauts. Fucking Krauts,” said Peter, mimicking the Scottish accent of the older man. The words trailed into the misty air but Mac had overheard. He stopped , turned just twenty yards away and thundered into the misty air, his exhaled breath blasting the moisture in all directions.

“Oi, laddie! Would you be taking the piss?”
“Aye, Mister Mackintosh. Aye”, said Peter. He couldn't help himself.
Mack exploded with laughter. “Gud on ye, laddie. Gud on ye. A piss taker, another bloody sassenach piss taker! A wee bairn! A bloody wee bairn! Don't ye love it!”

He disappeared along the beach into the fog, his last laugh fading into the dying light.
Peter had quickened his pace just in case Mr Mac really *had* taken offence and was home in three minutes to face his mother's ire.

“Where have you been, Peter? You said you would be an hour.

That was at two o'clock. It's now a quarter to five !"
Christine was not happy with the boy. He was fourteen years old and was as gangly as a newborn foal . He had gone into prison a boy and come out the other side as a stroppy youth. She used to tell him what to do and he would do it. Now there were perpetual negotiations and arguments when his behaviour was pulled into line. Now she needed Cliff more than ever and so did Peter. The kid was adrift at sea and needed pointing in the right direction. Not that Peter wasn't dealing with it all. The hormones that were racing round his body were changing him from a timid slender boy into an altogether more attractive being. He was now shaving on a regular basis and his growing frame was now hung with a similarly growing musculature. He didn't love his mother or little sister any less but just felt there were things that he didn't need to do or be told to do. Even his pubescent spotty face was on the mend. His mother was acutely aware that he needed more guidance than she was able to give.

"I've been fishing,Ma. We have fish for supper... a nice bass. I met Mr Mac and he snagged an enormous lobster. At Christmas....that's unheard of !"
"Well , next time, young man, be a bit more accurate with your plans. If you are down at low water and get into trouble there's no way we're going to be able to help you. AND the krauts are going to mine all the beaches soon so you just won't be able to get down there .... Besides which , I could do with a bit of help with Sophie"

"Yeah I know, ma. I can do that."
"Can you......can you,though? You're going to have to try harder."
Peter knew he could try harder but nobody, nobody was going to stop him from fishing at low water.

CHAPTER 14

First Christmas of the Occupation

Christmas 1940 was the first under the Nazi regime and it was a disjointed occasion with most families divided. Husbands and sons were away at war and those that remained found it difficult to position themselves in what was, after all, a totally new life. There was an ongoing curfew from 11 p.m. to 6 a.m. This caused little problem except for those who were challenged after hours, usually on the way back from friends' houses. These unfortunates could expect to spend a month in a cell . One of these was one Angus Mackintosh , who was caught after curfew walking home from an illegal lock-in at the Grenadier Inn. As it was between Christmas and the New Year, the publican one Brian Le Rouge , had decided on a secret session in the back room of the pub with some Calvados that he had put aside at the outbreak of hostilities. Now Mac, being a Scotsman, was a whisky aficionado and looked upon this French drink as somewhat inferior but, nonetheless, his viewpoint did not distract him from taking pleasure in drinking it.

On this occasion, he took a little too much pleasure. Time was forgotten and at midnight he bade his host adieu. The publican , himself three sheets to the wind, advised him of the late hour and further advised Mac to walk home along the beach and if a patrol approached then he was to dive immediately into the stinking morass of rotting seaweed which always clung two or three feet deep to the high tide mark close to the wall.

Mac , however , was so drunk that the plan of walking along the beach went immediately out the window when, as he exited the pub, he turned right instead of going straight on to the beach slipway and found himself on the main road. He followed his ever shifting centre of gravity this way and that, like a seal chasing a balloon. The footsteps of the approaching German patrol were loud and regular but they could have been

riding on a tank with all guns blazing for all Mac was aware. With the time honoured desperate Scottish cry of "Aww for fuck's sake!", he lurched one more time and passed out in the middle of the road, offering no resistance as they immediately gobbled him up and had him shipped off into St Helier for a month's detention at Hitler's pleasure. He regained consciousness an hour later, confused as to his new surroundings. To say he was annoyed would be an understatement. He was apoplectic with a rage induced by the French brandy. His language was indecipherable and, if it had been understood, he would probably have done six months instead of 30 days. He was impossible to question as the interpreter could not discern anything from his Scottish invective. In this respect, he couldn't implicate the publican at the Grenadier. He realised pretty quickly that if he continued with his broad Glaswegian accent, his interrogators would soon get bored and leave him alone which is exactly what happened. He was out after curfew, he did the crime and then he did the time.
He was released at the end of January , he was jailed in 1940 and was released in 1941, a fact he was quite proud of. A badge of honour, he thought. A wee holiday, he said.

The Germans had been busy laying land mines on open land next to the coast and on exposed beaches. On his return, Mac's neighbours soon filled him in on the activity. He remembered he had left instructions with his young friend Peter Marinelle to observe and map any German activity on his stretch of the coast. He didn't know the family well enough for them to quickly overlook his drunken escapade so he didn't feel confident enough to knock on the door of St Kitts .He would take a walk up to La Rocque Harbour and chat with the locals who were tinkering with their small boats.

January had been a cold month with frosty mornings and occasional outbreaks of snow. Today was no different. It was

grey and overcast with a light easterly breeze blowing off the sea, which sat sullenly two or three hundred yards from the slipway seemingly catching the mood that this was a quiet day and it wasn't going to move anywhere fast. It shone silvery grey even though the sun was hidden behind the seamless cloud cover which cast a gloom over the landscape. This was what the locals referred to as a 'nip' tide , when the moon's gravitational influence was at its lowest during the lunar month. The opposite of the nip or neap tide (as mainlanders would more correctly call it) was the 'spring' tide which occurs when the moon is full. A nip tide was the tortoise sometimes barely moving and the spring tide was the hare, racing breathlessly the mile down to the lowest low water mark before sprinting back up to the beckoning sea wall. From high to low and back again, it took just over twelve hours. This was Mother Nature's call, a never ending cycle of movement, of unseen forces working together since the universe was born.
Not that Mac was waxing lyrical about the meaning of life today. He was on a mission. He took the road to the southerly La Rocque slipway and stopped at the top to see if anybody was about. An outcrop of rocks ran straight out from the slip for two hundred yards before joining the man made pier running north east providing an excellent shelter and dry berth for the day boats. Someone was pulling and checking on a mooring rope but Mac could not discern who it was from so far away. He strode down the beach towards the pier when a voice from behind him bellowed,
" Did you enjoy your holiday, you old bugger ?"

He turned to see none other than his erstwhile drinking companion Brian Le Rouge who was grinning from ear to ear. Mac's face lit up.
"Aye........aye. I did. Wall to wall sunshine and a lassie on each arm! I had a bonny time, you stupid sassenach"

Clearly good friends, they knew each other well enough to cast

abuse without fear of retribution.
"I didnee dob ye in! They didna understand my incrrredible Scottish accent !"

"Yes, I figured that out, but only after a few days. There was no knock on the door from the Jerries in the middle of the night! I didn't sleep for a week."

"It wasnee too bad. A tad cold at times .Now you'll be able to tell me. What's the story with the landmines around here? Are we all to get oor legs blown off ?"

"Well," said Brian, "this area around the pier is okay and fishing from boats is still alright so long as you register your trip beforehand. Otherwise you might be the target of a potshot from the shore. The foreshore north to the golf course is now officially out of bounds and landmines have been placed there but that's not to say they aren't anywhere else. A mine exploded last week at La Collette near St Helier and yesterday a mother and two young children were injured when a mine exploded at Fliquet on the north coast. Generally speaking, if you're low water fishing you'd be pretty safe walking straight out past the pier as I don't reckon they have put any beyond a couple of hundred yards out. Young Peter Marinelle would know. He's a mate of yours, isn't he? Apparently he has plotted a few places on a makeshift map just from observing them over the last few weeks.
Hang on........." he looked over Mac's shoulder, "here he comes now!"
"I hope you haven't been wagging school, young man," said Brian as Peter came close.
"Er, no Mr Le Rouge. We finished early today. Something to do with blocked toilets. School hasn't really recovered from the freeze of last month. Hello Mr Mac. How was your holiday?"

"Och, it wasnee too bad. It would have been a damn sight colder in the Newgate Street Guest House than when you were in there. You had it easy. Anyway, ladee, Brian here says you know where the krauts have put their landmines. Did you map them ?"

"Yes I did . I don't think I missed any. There were only three .None of them were more than a couple of hundred yards down the beach. The map's in my satchel......right here."

Mac laid the scruffy piece of paper on the sea wall and they both studied it, giving and taking bits of advice here and there. "Now listen, ladee, and listen well. You are not to go near the foreshore until I have figured out some safe areas and even then, I reckon it's all going to be out of bounds until the Krauts have left. Apparently, we can still use a boat to go fishing so the safest way out is going to be straight out from the pier, but I will check it all out thoroughly because I am expendable as I am Scottish !! Ha, ya didnee see that one comin', ladee. " Peter laughed and thought how much fun the wily old Scotsman was. He would leave all the ground inspections to him as he certainly knew what he was doing. There was no point in taking a risk when someone else was volunteering to do it!

"Don't worry, Mister Mac . I won't be going out there for a while. You'd need a fur coat at present."

"Aye. You're right on that one. I'm off. Take care, ladee."

With that, they all went off in the same direction, Peter on his bike and Mac and Brian striding to keep up , all talking about Mac's enforced "wee holiday".

CHAPTER 15

School holidays

The early months of 1941 were a period of consolidation for both the invading army and the local population. The war raged on in Europe while prime minister Churchill tried in vain to turn back the tide of Nazi aggression. There was heavy bombing by the Luftwaffe over London, Liverpool and Glasgow. Buckingham Palace was hit. Rommel and his Panzer divisions were ruling North Africa. There was no good news and all the bad news was disseminated over the radio. Foodstuffs were not in regular supply with the consequence that there were shortages, and rationing came into effect. At a local country sale, eggs were sold at the hideous price of eight shillings a dozen. Town shops were exhausted of stock . German orders were promulgated via the Evening Post which was now overseen by a special Wehrmacht propaganda squad keen on censorship. Orders were altered or withdrawn as soon as they were put out. Eventually the confusion settled into some sort of order.

Any notion that the Germans had gone soft was dispelled when a party of sixteen young Frenchmen , intent on escaping from France in an open boat to the British mainland, were captured in the northern island of Guernsey and brought back to Jersey for trial. They had mistaken Guernsey for the Isle of Wight, some ninety miles further north and just off the coast of England. They sailed into harbour there, singing the Marseillaise only to be captured and sent to Jersey for trial. Four were sentenced to death by firing squad but only one, Francois Scornet, was eventually executed on March 17, 1941.

His final journey was a cruel long drawn out affair. His parents were ordered over from North Brittany to witness his final

demise. He was taken by lorry from the Grand Hotel in St Helier with his own coffin in the back, six or seven miles out west to St Ouens Manor where he was tied to a tree and executed by firing squad. A vast contrast to the six months imprisonment that the Jersey boys Peter and John had been given. Here lay the difference in the treatment by the Germans of the French and the English. The 22 year old's body was then placed in the coffin on the back of the lorry and driven back to town where he was buried in a St Helier cemetery. A harsh and brutal event, it shocked the locals and cast a long , dark shadow.
February and March passed relatively quietly, new laws came and went to the amusement of the locals but generally the mood was one of wait and see. Peter and his erstwhile fellow prisoner John Le Ross resumed their friendship. They had spent that six months together and neither of them felt the need to be in the other's pocket , a fact that was unspoken but with which they were both happy. During the Easter school holidays it was John who knocked on the door of St Kitts and it was Peter's mother Christine who greeted him.

"Hello stranger. We haven't seen you for ages. Come on in."

She waved him towards a chair by the kitchen table.

"Peter ! Peter! Your jailbird mate has come to see you!"

John smiled." Steady on, Mrs M."

Peter came thumping down the wooden stairs from his upstairs bedroom, through the hallway and into the kitchen.

"How you doing,mate. Stolen any guns lately?"

John clutched his stomach in mock agony. " Oh, haw haw haw....so funny, my stomach hurts from laughing so much."

It was clear that John had recovered his confidence which had previously been shattered after the trial. Christine couldn't help noticing the difference in size between the two boys. Peter had grown a lot in the last year, his voice had broken and he was a willowy youth whereas John was still the same polite lad with a lad's voice and clearly he was the shorter of the two by a few inches. He blushed profusely when Christine insensitively pointed out the height difference. John was acutely aware that when it came to the joys of puberty, he was clearly at the back of the field. Communal shower time after school football was a cringe making ordeal for him being surrounded by hairy spotty youths while his own hormones steadfastly refused to kick in. He would scuttle through the showers as quickly as he could hoping that nobody would notice his total lack of pubic hair. Peter was aware of his embarrassment and, true friend that he was, quickly changed the subject.

"Good news, Johnnie boy. We had a Red Cross letter from the old man a couple of days ago. First news for well over a year. We don't know what ship he's on or where he is because of all the censorship....but it looks as though he is well but he's a bit upset that he can't come home on leave, on account of Jerry being here. Mum knows all the details, well at least the ones the censors let through."

Before John could speak, Christine was delivering all the details.......... Cliff had rejoined the Merchant Navy in London and had been sent down to Warsash to retrain . After a period of a few weeks he had been sent overseas and that's all we know except he is safe and well........... Overseas could mean one of many outcomes because that's what sailors do..............they go over seas but there was a good chance he had been sent to the

Mediterranean. Possibly Egypt.

There was a good deal of chit chat that went on between the three of them as they were all clearly excited to hear such good news after such a long interlude.
The sound of Sophie whimpering came through from the back room and the conversation ground to a halt.

John suggested that he and Peter should wander down to the harbour and check out his dad's boat and after telling Christine they wouldn't be long, they left through the front door, pleased to be once again in each other's company. Christine was pleased too as she heard the sound of their laughter receding into the distance. The boys went ambling along the road the three or four hundred yards north to the slipway and down onto the sand, generally poking fun at each other the way they had always done. The weather in April was showing signs of warming up and, in reality, things were not too bad.
As it was low tide, the vast majority of the boats tied up in the now dry harbour had nestled into the mud. They checked the mooring ropes of the Le Ross' boat and then made their way out past the rest of the boats to the bottom of the ladder at the end of the granite pier and climbed carefully up the slippery rungs until they were on the pier itself. The rungs were covered in green slime from being submerged by the sea on its daily journey so it was usually a perilous climb up the thirty feet of near vertical wall. After gazing eastwards towards the coast of France, they both wondered what was going on over there. What a strange situation had befallen our two young heroes. They had both reached an age when they could be relied upon to start making a few of their own decisions when suddenly a foreign army had invaded their space. Fortunately they were both young enough to think it was all part of normal life, a bit of an adventure to be turned to your own advantage.

John spoke first, breaking the spell of their peaceful stare.

“Dad is organising the Easter nets this weekend. He's cleared it with the Jerries and we are all set to go this Friday. Coming? ”

“Sure thing!”, came the reply. “Hope it ain't too cold,though.”

They sidled off back along the pier and along the path around the outcrop of granite that the pier had been built on. The path eventually joined the top of the slipway which was where the boys parted company, Peter to the left and John to the right.

CHAPTER 16

Easter fishing

Good Friday 1941 was on April 11 and whilst not being too cold, it was dull and did nothing to lift the spirits. Traditionally the local fishing and farming community would come together and lay nets in the low water gullies of the east coast of the island, using tractors to transport the heavy nets down the beach and, more optimistically, to transport them back again filled with fish. The Assistant Harbour Master Roger Le Ross, John's father , had arranged safe passage for the weekend with the German authorities who were generally intrigued by this local event but also disclosed that the only active mines were well to the north of La Rocque. This was good news for the low water fishing fraternity as now their activities did not include the risk of being blown up.

Families coerced friends and relatives to join the party but at Easter it was a mostly joyless experience punctuated by freezing cold water and muscular discomfort. The nets were heavy to set and the sea temperature was still as low as six or seven degrees centigrade. Sometimes the nets were set or harvested in the dark which made the task even trickier but it was all treated as a bit of a lark and was invariably fuelled by seemingly infinite supplies of French brandy. The weather was cool and quiet for the Easter weekend which ensured a good turnout. Each family team of at least ten members were out early jockeying for the best low water gullies. In summer, the more adventurous would happily wade into waist deep water to lay nets in fast running water as the tide either breathed in or out, anchoring the mesh with the multitude of rocks which lay around. The basic idea was to set them then retire back to shore and wait for the tide to shepherd the sea and the fish down the gullies into the waiting trap. You could

set them in the daylight and collect in the dark or vice versa, either method meant a hiatus of three or four hours which had to be filled with a party back at the family homes.
The Marinelles and Le Ross' were always together for these expeditions but this year was totally different. Peter's father was away at war and the occasion served somehow only to underline his absence . This year however, at Peter's invitation, they had a willing guest in the form of Mr Mackintosh. In previous years Mac tended to flit between families and had become quite an expert at netting and was a popular choice of those lucky enough to be in his thrall and also lucky enough to understand what he was saying. He had a wealth of local knowledge and knew exactly where to set the nets.
Knowing that Mac was on board, our Assistant Harbour Master Roger Le Ross deferred to his experience and let him lay the plans. As the tide times varied so much , it was important to set the net at the right time and return at the right time to harvest the catch. Mac worked it all out and on the day before Easter Friday, ten friends and relatives were marched out to the low water mark , carrying a weighty length of mesh like a rolled up carpet. This old net had been sitting in an old farm shed for the last six months and those six who drew the short straws and bore the weight on their shoulders, also had their noses fairly close to the action and had to endure last year's fishy smell on the journey. Mac's secret gully was located and the team members were sworn to secrecy, punishment was having to do it all again on another day. The expedition set out two hours before dark.
Mac referred to John Le Ross as 'wee man' and Peter was 'big man' and the rest of the crew, mostly cousins, were allowed to use their real names. The trip down was like a caterpillar weaving in and out of rocky outcrops. The gully Mac picked was still under about two feet of water but he insisted the net was set straight away so it was a manic thirty minutes of freezing cold activity as he kept them hard at it.
“Get those stones fixed at two foot intervals and look lively,

wee man, afore you get washed away! ”
“If I drown, Mister Mac, you can have my winter coat.” replied John.

“Och, yerrr winter coat wouldna fit my budgie, wee man. Now look lively!”

John missed his footing and fell sideways, wetting half his heavy jumper. He recovered quickly and, quick as a flash, came straight back at him.

“Will we catch a whale, Mister Mac ?” said John, clearly intent on humouring the Scotsman.

“If we do, wee man, it'll be you hauling it back up the beach! ”

….and so it went on. Nobody was left out of the gentle ribbing and the job was quickly done to Mac's satisfaction before they collected what kit was left and turned en masse back to the beach . A hundred yards away a tractor's engine was idling away while the Le Gresley family went about the business of setting their net. Cheery waves were exchanged as the blue smoke from the old engine drifted across the shore and dissipated into the cold air.

Mac's crew reached the slipway just before darkness descended fully, to be met by Eileen, Roger's wife and John's mother, and Christine who was standing by a large upright pram with Sophie inside surrounded by what groceries could be sacrificed to the party about to begin at Eileen and Roger's house. This turned out to be quite a low key event, being a mix of young and old and, as there had to be a before dawn meeting at the slipway in the morning, the crew broke up just before ten o'clock. This was long enough for Mac to have a long chat with Christine who knew little of the Scotsman's history. He was

aware of Christine's concern at his friendship with the boy and did his best to chit chat about this and that and generally put her mind at rest.
“He was a bonny wee lad, Christine, when he went into prison and he's turned into a bonny big lad now. He is so much taller than wee Johnnie. Your boy has a cheeky way with him but he makes me laugh. So does wee Johnnie. Must be tough for you all, not having Cliff around.”

Christine's eyes filled with tears and Mac quickly apologised for upsetting her. “It's not your fault,Mac. I live with it every day. Sophie is no problem but Peter is at an age when he needs an example to follow and I'm just afraid that he is forgetting his father, and what with the Germans and everything, it's like a juggler has thrown all the balls in the air and we don't know where they are going to land. Peter has gone from a controllable lad to a lanky youth in a few months. He's a good boy but doesn't always do as he's bid.”

“Aye,aye. I can see that. Is he getting to school alright?”

“I think so .....but I 've had to give him a bit of leeway what with the prison business. It's only been four months after all. I think they have both got over the shock and disruption of it all but I certainly haven't ! He and John have had a bit of a break and it's good to see them back with each other again. They both caught the same bus to school last week just before they broke up for the Easter holidays. That was good to see.”

And so it went on and with every word that fell from Christine's gorgeous mouth, Mac fell more in love with her. She smelled divine and looked stunning. If she had asked him to move the house an inch to the right, he'd have done it. She had a friend for life.

Just before ten o'clock, Mac decided he had had enough and bid everybody farewell.

“Dinna fergett!!!! Six o'clock on the slipway and wrap up well. It'll be cold before the Easter sun warms us up. Chances are, howeverrrr, that it will be just as bloody cold all day. Thank you and goodnight!” Mac disappeared down the road in a relatively sober state. Christine had that effect on him.

CHAPTER 17

Tea and hot cross buns

Easter Saturday hadn't yet surprised anybody as it was still dark at six in the morning but it was a tad chilly on the slipway as the fishing crew met to harvest what they hoped would be a full net. The tide was two thirds out although you wouldn't have known it. It was a little misty so Mac decided to delay the outward journey by a few minutes so that they could at least see something as the sun came up. Everyone was well and truly rugged up in whatever passed for winterwear. Mac had turned out in a pair of yellow oilskin trousers that were so big that the waist was at chest level and over the top was a yellow oilskin jacket. He was very visible but also very warm. Mac's crew was now a motley crew of coloured jumpers and jackets. They were all equipped for the job in hand.
Hot tea and coffee was being distributed by Eileen Le Ross who had brought a Thermos flask down with her. The condensing steam rose gently from the flask as she gave out the mugs. Eventually the sun rose enough to poke its head above the layer of fog which clung to the shore and off they set, Mac clearly in charge.

"Keep together. I don't imagine the mist will stay for long but stick together anyway."

The sound of ten pairs of wellington boots trudging down the slipway was overwhelming. A group of German soldiers looked on in amusement. Mac saw them and started singing a chorus of Happy Wanderer which everybody joined in with. He was surprised at the vocal support he got as they marched seaward. The singing amused Mac as invariably it would be the Germans who would be singing the Happy Wanderer, albeit in German, as they marched smartly along, their jackboots rapping the tarmac in time with the singing. The German patrol thought it amusing too, as the fishing crew left the slipway and swished their way through the shingle and sand beyond. Most of them knew the way through the rocks. If you went in a straight line to any visible point off the eastern coast, you would take twice as long as the terrain was such that you would be wading waist deep one minute and climbing over a twenty foot rocky outcrop the next. The safe ways were well trodden and one or two rocks had been painted with arrows to help the unwary. Thirty minutes later they were at Mac's secret gully which was still underwater but it didn't take long for the sea to fall back with a rush. As the level dropped, it became apparent that there was not an abundance of fish in the net. Whilst there was no surprise there, it was still fun to watch the net being revealed little by little. A few minutes later and the catch was revealed as being two good size bass, a few undersized chancre crabs and one very ugly and extremely large octopus. Peter and John prised the bass from the net and then discovered two more bass and a three foot conger eel wriggling underneath.

“I'm not going near the octopus, thank you”, said Peter as he extracted one of the bass and put it into a hessian sack along with one that John was juggling with. Of the four bass that were netted, only three were big enough for a feed of any sorts. The conger eel , always a tricky customer with its sharp teeth and restless ways ,was despatched to fishy heaven with a few blows from a large stone. The conger's unique nervous system meant that, post mortem, it would still be writhing in the sack for a couple of hours.

Mac was more interested in the octopus and was poking it with a long fisherman's knife.

“That's a bonny size. What say we have a good feed of calamari tonight! ”

Roger Le Ross looked at him quizzically and questioned him as to how he was going to manhandle the octopus into a sack, especially as it had a wingspan of about five feet.

“Och, leave it to me. It's a man's job ! You just gotta grab it by the head....like so....and
prise the tentacles off whatever it's hangin' on to.......four..five...six...seven and then the last one and hey presto! You cut the head off.”

Unfortunately before he could wield the knife and decapitate the unfortunate creature, the octopus latched on to Mac's oilskin trousers, the large ones that came up to his chest. In a whirling mass of wriggling tentacles, the suckers stuck to Mac's crotch like a magnet to iron.
A wrestling match developed with Mac prising one tentacle off only for it to stick down somewhere else.
The watching crowd respectfully contained their mirth for a few seconds only before dissolving into riotous laughter.

Mac was wrestling too hard to notice at first he had become the cause of their hilarity.

“Get off me, ya slippery bassa! ”

Man and octopus created quite a picture as they struggled at low water. Eventually Mac grabbed its head and with a quick motion, lopped its head off and despatched it into the sack leaving the still squirming tentacles in motion.

Still laughing ,the rest of the party stepped forward to help remove the suckers. Each fishy arm was quite thick so they were in for a good supper. At this point Mac started giggling which set everybody off again.

“Come, you sassenachs, it's time for us to collect all this kit and get back for breakfast! Let's get as much of the rubbish as we can out first and then we'll clear the stones. ”

It took a good half hour of sweating and bending to get the mesh clear and able to be rolled into portable form. Mac gave John the sack containing the fish .

“Here,wee man. Grab the sack and don't let it go. You'll be safe from the octopus but the conger may get ya!!!

The sack was tied at the neck with string and John held on to it. The dead conger suddenly thrashed around inside the hessian and took the young fellow by surprise.

“ Mind the conger doesn't rip your throat out, Johnnie boy,” said Peter.
“ Ooooooo, I'm so scared!!” said John in mock terror.

At that moment, out of a still grey sky, the rain started to fall and in a steady downfall managed to dampen all in its path.

“Come on, team. Lets get this lot back and get the fire lit!”

The team needed no more encouragement and, with one accord, lifted the magic mesh carpet and caterpillared back to the slipway. Mac led the way , taking the front end and whilst they trudged along, he reflected on the sombre grey look of the surrounding rocks. He felt cocooned against the elements in his oilskins as the rain dripped across his vision from the hood that he had pulled over his head. The oilskins squeaked as he moved, their yellowness giving a pleasant contrast to the

surrounding gloom . Mac felt strangely comfortable and at ease.
He loved this place and felt blessed that his aunt had left it to him at such an opportune time in his life.
The rest of the party were not so comfortable and after a few choruses of the Happy Wanderer , an inch or so of torrential rain and a half hour route march, the slipway was reached and not a moment too soon. After a bit of moaning all round, the team pushed on the extra five hundred yards to the Le Ross' house where the net was unravelled and laid out on a low granite wall so the rain could wash it clean of all the small bits of debris that were too tedious to remove by hand.
John lifted the hessian sack onto the draining board of an outside porcelain sink and emptied the catch. He turned the old brass tap anticlockwise and washed the fish under the stream of ice cold well water. A sharp fishing knife hung on a string over the sink . John reached for it and after a few minutes huffing and puffing, he had expertly gutted the catch and carried it into the kitchen of the house.

"Hi Mum, bit wet and cold out there today," he said as he laid the catch on some newspaper on the kitchen table.
His mother Eileen looked it over and enquired as to where the rest of the catch was.
"Very funny, mother. Very funny."

The party of fishermen trooped in and headed for the fireplace where they warmed their freezing hands. A mock fight broke out as they jostled for a better place to stand.

"Get out the way"
"No, *you* get out the way!"
"Now, now, children. If you don't behave, you won't get any *hot cross buns,*" said Eileen.

The mock fight stopped instantly and all those engaged in the jostling contest turned in surprise. A lot of foodstuffs were in short supply but Eileen had managed to barter some garden vegetables for enough flour to make a batch of Easter hot cross buns which were cooking up nicely in the woodfired stove.

"Come on, somebody put the kettle on. We have just enough tea for everybody. You had better enjoy all this because it's not going to last much longer," said Eileen.

Her husband Roger concurred. " You're dead right, love. Supplies are getting harder to get. What we used to get from the mainland is now a damn sight harder to get from France. Everything we import comes by boat and that short stretch of water gets more dangerous by the month."

In his capacity as Assistant Harbour Master, Roger was privy to a lot of information which wasn't widely known. The island government had permission from the Germans to send emissaries to nearby France to buy stocks of food. All boat movements in and out were known to the Harbour Office and he knew that there was no certainty as to future supplies.

Our team of damp fishermen totally ignored his words and drew up the available chairs to the kitchen table to await the small Easter feast which did not disappoint them. Mac made the tea, using a hotchpotch of mugs and cups while Eileen opened the oven door and removed the now perfectly cooked buns. A smell of cinnamon filled the air. The audience sniffed in approval.
" Ahhhhh, just smell that... beautiful, " said Peter.
" Why's that," said John. "Have you farted?"
Both the boys exploded into uncontrollable laughter and the rest of the kitchen winced at their adolescent mirth.

“That's enough you boys! Grow up.” said Roger, sternly.

Mac smiled inwardly. They were just kids but he thought they were good kids. To them, all this upheaval was an adventure but Mac knew that the lives of all the Jersey people had changed and would continue to change until the Germans left.

Tea and buns took precedence over his dark thoughts and he tucked in at the trough with the rest of his buddies.

CHAPTER 18

Tragedy strikes

Easter came and went and life, generally, seemed to limp along without too much further upheaval . There were food shortages and rationing had begun. Fishing was banned off Elizabeth Castle breakwater to the south of St Helier. The Harbour Office implored fishermen and boat owners to share out their fish. Boat fishing from the main eastern harbour of Gorey was banned but La Rocque, two miles south, could be used which made it a lot busier. As petrol became scarcer, transporting boats became problematic so many owners decided to leave their boats at La Rocque or closeby in farm sheds and driveways.

The Whit Sunday public holiday fell on the first day of June and the day broke with sunshine and a chilly easterly breeze. John had collected Peter from St Kitts and they set off together to work on the Le Ross family boat. John's dad, Roger Le Ross, was already sanding and priming when they arrived. He set them both to work with the sandpaper, a hard and unfulfilling task guaranteed to weaken the shoulder and arm muscles in double quick time.

Lunchtime approached and, despite the cold breeze, the warmth of the sun was causing a lot of sweat. A lunch break was announced and the sandwiches were spread upon a makeshift table on board the boat. It was a welcome rest and the three of them were happy to sit down and relax. There were two slipways down to the sand at La Rocque ,the southernmost one tucked into the corner nearest the pier and the other, a couple of hundred yards to the north west, marked the corner before the Royal Bay of Grouville came into view. A mile or so of golden gravelly sand stretched north, the view dominated at the top end by the magnificent Mont Orgueil castle. Its history stretched back to the eleventh century and it was built to ward off intruders, mostly French but ,as time went by, included incarcerating political prisoners in the time of Charles 2nd. The Island's people were staunch Royalists. The castle commanded high views to the east, north and south over Gorey harbour and in medieval times would have been painted white to be visible from miles out to sea , serving as a warning to those who thought the island was easy prey. Clearly the Germans had been unimpressed as their bombers flew in, with invasion on their minds, last summer. Despite all this, the Castle was still immense, both in aspect and architecture. The latter of which had already been added to with the building of various gun emplacements and machine gun nests.

A gang of primary school age kids were throwing stones into the sea at the north end of the beach half hidden by outcrops of rock. The neap tide was an hour short of full, not destined even to reach the sandy beach today. One or two families spread picnic rugs on the sand, meagre rations stretched to make it an uplifting day out. Things didn't seem to be so bad when the sun was shining. More boat owners arrived and one or two boats which had migrated from Gorey Harbour on trailers were shuffling down the slipway. Gradually the dry harbour became a hive of activity, sanding and painting, the furling and unfurling of sails , in general a happy mood descended over La Rocque, warmed by the first real sunshine of the year. A small fishing boat, previously moored further out, gently throbbed its way out to sea leaving a trail of blue smoke in its wake. The wind suddenly dropped and every sound, no matter how small, seemed amplified but instead of destroying the peace, it appeared to add to the general quietude.
Squeals of delight came from the rock throwers at the far end. They had identified a floating black object about four foot across which was working its way shoreward buoyed up by the incoming tide. A good target by all accounts and many rocks

landed close. It was only a matter of time before somebody hit it.
The picnic lunch remained open and breadcrumbs left while our workers returned to the task.
Working on the hull of the boat on a stepladder, Peter succumbed to the call of nature and shinned down and round to the seaside of the boat, away from public view, to have a pee.
At that moment John shinned *up* the ladder to carry on the work.

At the far north end of the bay , little Jimmy Le Cocq had been throwing stones into the sea for a good five minutes. He had a good arm for throwing and it made a nice change to have a floating target. Usually he and his mates had to build a small pile of rocks and then retreat ten yards before attempting to knock it down again with a well directed lob or a coconut shy throw .The menacing black buoy was just out of range so he selected some flatter disc like stones in order to skip them over the surface of the sea , thereby achieving more distance. His last throw was perfect, six seven eight skips he counted, each skip registered by the splash marks momentarily left on the glassy surface of the sea. Each contact with the sea made the stone lose energy but as it died on the last skip, it made one more desperate slow leap as if inspired by the devil himself. It made a melodic ping as it struck the Polish made floating mine which was once tethered to the seabed by the Royal Navy to protect an English harbour against the Kriegsmarine.
A couple of seconds later an enormous ear splitting explosion ripped through the bay followed by the sound of breaking glass as all the windows of the houses in the vicinity were blown in by the compression wave. A disjointed plume of water rose hundreds of feet into the air and shrapnel and rocks as big as footballs rained down in a terrifying shower with a noise like hail on a tin roof. Pitter patter, pitter patter, evil shards of shrapnel sought out their own random targets.
John Le Ross, up the ladder with paintbrush in hand, heard the

explosion and just had enough time to turn his head in the direction of the noise before his young life was snuffed out by one of those evil shards of black metal which had come so violently and intrusively spiralling towards him with barely a seconds warning. He heard a clunk and then all went black as it struck him beneath his right eye. He fell from the ladder straight down in a crumpled, appalling heap on the foul smelling mud below. His father, working inside the hull resealing some of the woodwork, heard the noise of the explosion but neither heard nor saw him fall. It was only when Peter came back from his toilet call on the other side of the boat that anybody realised anything was wrong. John's body lay in a heap with blood coming from his head. Peter immediately screamed for Roger to come and help.

Panic had set in all round with people crying and yelling. A German patrol had been close by and they summoned reinforcements and medics. In a few minutes a couple of ambulances arrived and one by one the injured were carried up to the slipway. The stone throwing kids miraculously had escaped injury apart from burst eardrums. Most of the impact had gone over their heads. A couple of householders had been cut by flying glass as their windows caved in. That was it...... apart from the forlorn figure of Roger Le Ross carrying the lifeless body of his son John up the beach from the muddy harbour . Roger did not realise the extent of his son's wound and hoped beyond hope that he would just be concussed and would regain consciousness shortly. He laid the boy out on a low wall until help arrived , then put him on to a stretcher which was loaded into the ambulance. Doctor Legarde came from across the road to offer help. He climbed into the back of the vehicle and he set about examining the head wound as quickly as he could. He felt for a pulse or a heartbeat but it was clear from the size of the wound that nothing could be done. He searched desperately for any sign of life until reluctantly he declared the boy dead. It was 2.25p.m. Roger and Peter looked on in shock. The doctor beckoned Roger inside the ambulance.

“ I'm so sorry, Roger. I'm sorry to have to tell you that John is dead. He has a massive head wound. He had no chance. Now listen carefully....you understand that he is dead. Roger?”

Roger stood there, taking it all in but not quite understanding the horrendous moment he was living in. He climbed into the ambulance and stood by his son, held his hand, stroked his hair , hoping he would come round and say something like “Hi,Dad”. Time was standing still and he didn't really know quite what to do .Then he put his arms around the boy's shoulders and pulled him into a sitting position, rocked backwards and forwards and hugged him and hugged him and hugged him. Silently the tears poured down as he smelt his son's pale and cold skin. He kissed the boy and laid him back down. John's mother Eileen arrived within five minutes from up the road and Roger broke the news.
“He's dead , my love. There was an explosion on the other side of the beach and they think a bit of shrapnel got him in the head.”
Eileen nodded and held his hand. She lay across her son kissing his face. His skin became colder to the touch as the minutes ticked by. Roger gazed on, frozen with the shock of it all. Eventually the doctor suggested he be moved to the mortuary by ambulance. Roger had to pull his now wailing wife away from their boy. He clutched her to him and they both sobbed uncontrollably.

Peter sat on the seawall , staring into the distance , not really taking it in. He had been waiting by the back door of the ambulance while John was being examined. He had heard the doctor delivering the bad news to John's father. It felt like a scene from a film and he was just watching whilst not taking part. Eventually the ambulances left and a German officer, a

Major Schumacher arrived with more troops. He gathered the support of the honorary parish police and took details of the incident. Despite the initial anger of the locals that the Germans had laid a mine in a safe area, it soon transpired from eye witness accounts that the explosion had been caused by a floating mine, probably cut adrift from its defensive position in the English Channel by a spell of rough weather. The explosion had been triggered more probably by touching a rock rather than Jimmy Le Cocq's excellent throw.

At that moment Mac swung off the main road onto the slipway and spotted Peter , still sat on the sea wall but now sobbing quietly. Mac immediately went and sat next to him.

"What's happened, laddie . I was home when I heard the explosion. Is anybody hurt?"

"It's John....he's been blown up by a mine. He's dead. It should have been me. It should have been me. I came down the ladder and went for a pee round the back of the boat. He climbed up the ladder and now he's dead. It should have been me!"

Out of nowhere, Mac produced a blanket and draped it round the boy's shoulders.
" It's not your fault, laddie. It's not your fault !"

Mac paused and took in the tragedy of the situation. He got up and broke into the discussion going on between the parish police and Major Schumacher who was investigating the accident. He was told what had happened and after a minute or two's discussion, he returned to the boy.
"Come on, laddie. Let's get you home."

Mac put both hands on one of Peter's arms and guided him back towards St Kitts. The boy's sobs became more audible

and urgent. Mac found himself crying too and in that moment the two of them stopped by the side of the road and Mac hugged him close, trying to comfort him. Peter's sobs turned into an awful wailing sound and in that moment, Mac pulled himself together. He wrapped the blanket tightly round his charge and, using a fireman's lift, carried him the last hundred yards to St Kitts. He freed one of his hands and banged manically on the door before it opened under the force of his attack. He set the sobbing body down on a kitchen chair and yelled for Christine to come and help.
Christine had just settled little Sophie and appeared from the back. Mac delivered the awful news. Christine comforted her son and managed to get him into his bed where he sobbed until he fell asleep. She returned to the kitchen and immediately produced a bottle of brandy from a high cupboard and put it on the table. She opened another cupboard , produced two glasses , filled both and pushed one towards Mac.
They sipped in silence, barely able to take in the tragic events of the day. Neither felt they could articulate clearly just what they were feeling and consequently it was a few minutes before either spoke.

Mac was first in.

“ You know Peter had just come down from that ladder before John shinned up just as the mine exploded. He thinks it's his fault. It's going to be hard to explain to him that it was just a fluke accident. What a terrible, terrible thing to happen. I canna believe it.......”

Another couple of minutes went by before Christine spoke and the conversation continued in this staccato style for the best part of an hour.

"Poor John. That poor boy. How were Roger and Eileen?"

"They had already left with the wee man's poor wee body in the ambulance off to the
mortuary at the General. Brian was down by the slipway and he said they were absolutely devastated," replied Mac.

"Chrissie, are you going to be okay? Not only are we all in shock, but you are going to have to deal with Peter and his reaction to all of this. Is there anything I can do to help ? It must be tough with Cliff away. Anything at all. Just let me know."

The mention of Cliff tipped Christine into a flood of tears. "Oh bugger", Mac thought and he realised the moment may have been a bit raw to be confronting her with a new challenge and , while still seated , he screeched his chair next to Christine and put his arm round her shoulder. After a few minutes sobbing, she suddenly stiffened and rose from the chair before heading for the bathroom which was upstairs. Mac remained seated and stared into the fire. The embers of the coal which glowed brightly and comfortingly, mesmerised him and he forced himself back to reality.
He thought what a mess the whole situation had become. A young lad's life snuffed out and for what? He was in the wrong place at the wrong time, killed by shrapnel from a mine laid allegedly somewhere up the English Channel by the Royal Navy and forced loose by a recent storm. How unlucky was poor wee John. That piece of shrapnel had the boy's name written on it for sure. He got up to check on Peter who was snoring quietly and fitfully in the back bedroom, shrouded under a pile of blankets and, thankfully , fast asleep.
He rearranged the blankets and closed the bedroom door quietly on the way back to the kitchen. He waited for Christine to reappear before he began to say his goodbyes.

It was nearly six o'clock in the evening and there was still plenty of light left in the day.
“I had better be off, Christine. I just hope he sleeps for a long time. I'll nip back to the harbour and see if there is anything I can do down there. Take care, wee girl.”

He turned towards the door and Christine followed him and gave him an unexpected hug before he left.
“As I said before, take care. I'll maybe drop by tomorrow to see the boy?”

“Yes,that would be a great help. Thanks Mac.” Her eyes were still full of tears and one burst the dam over her cheek and rolled down over her chin and dripped on the floor. Mac was off down the road and, when he was out of sight, he stopped, threw back his head and roared at the sky, a guttural bellow that summed up the desperation he was feeling. The noise brought one or two householders to their doors to see what was going on. Most of them came to the conclusion that it was just the barmy Jock on a drink fuelled bender. How wrong they were.

It was just another summer's day until those ten seconds of explosive madness changed the lives of many people. Ten seconds that took a young lad's life, ten seconds that robbed a family of their beautiful son, ten seconds that drove a dagger into many peoples hearts and ten seconds that managed to tip the young lad's best friend into a dark chasm. Mac clearly had a job on his hands.

CHAPTER 19

Sad day

Peter slept for twelve hours, woke up and remembered what had just happened and went back to sleep eventually rising at midday on the Sunday. Mac had dropped by in the morning, as he had promised, and Christine had made him a cup of tea. The pair were a bit more talkative than yesterday and had no difficulty in discussing the terrible accident. Mac had been down to the harbour the previous evening and found out at first hand what had happened. He questioned anybody who happened to be around and the consensus of opinion confirmed that the mine, whilst being made in Poland, was decidedly British and probably laid by the Royal Navy around one of the English Channel ports, from where it probably broke free from its mooring in a storm . It then drifted south with the prevailing winds and currents and fetched up at La Rocque. The post mortem had revealed that a piece of shrapnel had entered John's skull just below the eye and passed clean through , leaving no chance of survival. It exited at the back of the head taking with it a large portion of bone. The verdict was accidental death.

On the days that followed, sadness fell like a cloak on the tightknit community that surrounded La Rocque and there was no other talking point in those over the garden wall conversations. At local government level, Bailiff Basil Dechevaux became involved from the outset and was at the scene of the tragedy the next day accompanied by Oberst Gruber. The investigating officer Major Schumacher, filled them in on the facts. Dechevaux impressed upon them both that this was an event that could have been avoided if Germany had not invaded Europe. It was a manifestly simple statement that could not be refuted by either German officer. Neither Gruber nor Schumacher felt like arguing the point anyway.

The funeral took place the next Wednesday at noon at the tiny church of St Peter La Rocque which was about three hundred yards inland from the northern slipway and a stones throw from the Le Ross' house. The tiny church could hold about a hundred souls and was packed to overflowing. Shafts of summer sunshine beamed through the stained glass of the windows picking out particles of dust in their light. The vicar coughed , dispersing the dust towards the congregation. The large wooden doors were kept open and a light breeze riffled the hair of the vicar as he waited in front of the altar.

John's coffin was carried from the house by four of his father's friends . The crowd outside respectfully stood aside in the graveyard as the pallbearers made their way through the iron gates and through the doors into the church. The service was brief and the singing was muted. John's parents, Roger and Eileen, struggled with it all. Everybody struggled with it all. It was not in the order of things for a lad to die so randomly and so young.

Mac had accompanied Christine and Peter to the church. Sophie was being looked after at the village hall .

The vicar gave the address and struggled to make any sense of the tragedy. His advice of "the Lord giveth and taketh away" fell on particularly stony ground. Most of the congregation were deep inside their own wells so the glib bible quotes probably didn't even register. Roger Le Ross' friend Terry delivered a eulogy outlining the highlights of young John's short life. His task was a difficult one and he lurched through it, the words sticking in his throat at regular intervals. Roger consoled his wife Eileen as she wept uncontrollably. It was a sad , sad day and then as if almost on cue, a butterfly skipped its way into the church through the open wooden doors. It was a Red Admiral and its bright colours distracted the mourners as it danced through the sunbeams before settling momentarily on a fat lady's hat. As the final hymn was sung, it landed on

Peter's shoulder before departing the same way as it had flown in.

In the crowd outside , Major Schumacher stood at the corner of the graveyard in full uniform keeping as low a profile as possible. He also had young children back in Munich and whilst he knew that his presence could have caused some resentment, he felt qualified to offer some sort of moral support for a bereaved family. Although some may have blamed him, his presence did not go unappreciated. Nevertheless he shuffled out of the back gate when the coffin moved out to the graveside. This war was not his war and he had no say in his call up for duty. He walked briskly and smartly back down the road where his chauffeured car was waiting.

Peter had not been to a funeral before in his fifteen years. Weatherwise it was a lovely sunny day which didn't match his mood. He wished it could be raining. That would be more in keeping with the ridiculous loss of his good mate. Their time in prison had brought them close together and he felt like he had lost a brother. He had come to realise that it had been a totally random accident and, even if he *had* been standing up the ladder instead of John, there was every chance the shrapnel would have missed him. John's head had been in that particular space at that particular point in time and there was no sense in denying it. He had been desperately unlucky and that was it. He was determined never to forget his buddy.

The service over, the crowd moved out and close friends and relatives shuffled the few yards from the church to the freshly dug grave where the vicar continued his spiel. Ashes to ashes, dust to dust went the same way as 'the Lord giveth and taketh away.' Peter stood at the back of the small gathering when the butterfly returned, fluttering round the heads of those assembled before moving off towards the back gate of the churchyard. As if mesmerised, Peter slipped away unnoticed from the throng and followed it slowly out of the gate. It skipped skittishly down the road towards the sea, pushed along

by a north westerly breeze. It seemed to pause briefly outside John's house before moving on down the three hundred yards to the coast road and then across onto the northern slipway. Peter was now sprinting to keep up and accelerated hard as he barrelled down the slipway before he fell upon the sand. The Red Admiral fluttered on towards the sea and the rocks, the tide was way out. He got up but finally ran out of sand and tripped, sprawling on to the gravel. The butterfly was gone, being blown towards the coast of France stopping only when the breeze dropped. Peter stood up and waved.
"Bye Johnnie, bye. Never never never never........ forget you"
The words drifted off over the rocks.

He sat down on the nearest boulder expecting to cry some more but he felt somehow calmer. He looked back towards the slipway and saw Mac making his way towards him, calling him.
Peter stood up . Mac looked really strange wearing a suit.

"You okay, young fella?" said Mac as he approached

Peter nodded and stood up.
"Yes, I'm fine"

Another Red Admiral butterfly glided skittishly past soon to be followed by another and another. Soon the sea air was filled with butterflies all caught on the offshore breeze, seemingly hell bent on a watery grave, their fragile wings unable to fly against the wind. Then, over a period of two or three minutes, the wind fell out and the temperature rose a degree or two. The sea started to shimmer in the distance. Little by little, the wind started to fill in but this time it blew from the east and back to shore. The hundreds of butterflies borne previously on the westerly breeze now returned to shore and safety.

“Would you believe it! A bloody flypast. A bloody flypast!” Mac yelled and Peter cheered. They both felt that John had not gone at all.

The butterflies, of course, had not appeared as if by divine intervention. The warmer weather had produced conditions such that hundreds of cocoons in gardens and hedgerows prematurely disgorged their colourful living metamorphosed contents into the scented air at about the time of John's funeral. Even Mac , the craggy Scotsman, could not help but marvel at the timing and he shook his head, half in disbelief but half in the hope that it really *was* something rather special. He struggled to find words to explain what they had just witnessed.

"What are the chances of that happening ? Nature is such a wonderful thing. All the Red Admirals in the district shedding their chrysalis' at the same time. Eh, big man? What d'ye reckon? What are the chances?"
"About the same as being struck dead by a piece of shrapnel from three hundred yards."

Peter's instant reply killed the conversation stone dead and left Mac thoroughly deflated. He wished he could take back what he had just said.

"Me and my big fucking mouth, what a fucking idiot" said the Scotsman under his breath. He gestured towards the slipway and said,
"I'm sorry laddie. Come on, let's go back and have a wee dram to kill the pain."

The butterfly moment was well and truly over . They traipsed back up to the sand about ten yards apart, then up the slipway and back up to the Le Ross' house where a very subdued wake was in progress. Sherry was being sipped and a respectful hush dampened any meaningful conversation. As to be expected at a young person's funeral, there was little celebration of a life well lived but more statements of the injustice and randomness of it all. There was much quiet weeping and eventually Eileen Le Ross could stand it no more and shuffled quietly off to her bedroom. Mac was looking after Christine and, unbeknown to them both, young Peter downed a couple of glasses of sherry which had been abandoned by departing guests. Before long he had added to the total and became decidedly maudlin. Mac suddenly realised what had been going on and said to Christine, "I reckon he's had a few by the smell of his breath. I'll get him back to yours before he gets any worse."

Peter could hardly stand and Mac managed to sober him up by marching him down the lane towards the beach while Christine made her way to the parish hall to collect little Sophie. They all made it back to St Kitts within minutes where Mac said his goodbyes and carried on down the road to his piece of paradise. As the community fell asleep that evening, they all came to but one conclusion. It had been a long, sad day and they were glad it was over.

CHAPTER 20

The islands become part of the Atlantic Wall

The Battle of Britain had been won by the Royal Air Force late in 1940 . The islands were spectators to it all as German and British planes alike flew high above leaving the odd trail of smoke as young pilots fought for their cause. Hitler decided that the Russians could not be trusted to keep the peace and as a result of the the build-up of troops on the Soviet border, Operation Barbarossa was conceived. It was put into action finally on 22 June 1941 when Germany attacked Russia. This relieved the pressure felt by the British on the European west as Hitler's gaze was averted.

At a meeting in the Reich Chancellery in Berlin the Fuhrer was discussing his strategies with Goring, Goebbels, Bormann and Frank. A huge map of Europe and beyond lay on the table.

"*I don't think we have another option. I don't trust Stalin. My dear Field Marshal Rommel, with his magnificent Panzer tanks, is going well in the push towards the oil fields of Libya. If we overstretch on the Western Front across the Channel then we shall be vulnerable to invasion by the Russians .*"

He drew his finger along the French coastline and hovered over the Channel Islands. He paused for a minute, deep in thought. "*....and these British Channel Islands must surely be subject to attack sometime. Churchill is probably plotting their recapture as we speak. I would like to keep them occupied . Can we fortify them further?* "

There was a lot of nodding of heads and murmurs of affirmation.

" *I will speak with Fritz Todt and get him to do an appraisal"* spoke a voice from the back.

On the 16 June 1941 a letter from German Army Command West was received in the islands to the effect that the Islands were to be fortified. In November a visit by Fritz Todt took place . Todt built a lot of the road infrastructure pre-war in Germany and was responsible for the Organisation Todt which brought together private and public German companies to build a massive defensive wall from Holland to the north and Switzerland to the south. This was the so called the Siegfried Line. Now, it appeared, he had another project on his hands. In the months that followed a workforce of 16,000 workers arrived, mostly French, Russian and Spanish prisoners who were treated abominably by the Organisation Todt, operating along military lines. Later Moroccans, Algerians and Greeks caught out by the advance of the German Army through France joined the force , effectively slave labour. Hotels and houses were requisitioned for the OT personnel whilst the workers were housed in primitive conditions and fed very little. Whatever the deprivations they suffered, they were put to work on the massive job of fortifying the islands.

In the Annexe at Storey's Gate just across from the Houses of Parliament in London, Prime Minister Churchill was in conversation with members of the War Cabinet. They stood around a large map table pointing to this and to that whilst a pall of blue smoke arose from Churchill's cigar. He puffed on it and and turned to Brendan Bracken, his Minister of Information.
"Brendan, what news do we have of the Channel Islands? "

He then swivelled his head to immediately pose a further more general question to all his advisers.

"Is there any chance of recapturing them now that Jerry is stretched on the Soviet front?"

At this point there was a lot of negative intakes of breath. Bracken told him that the islands were well and truly occupied and, because of the German naval presence in the Bay of St Malo and the seas around it, the chances of a successful attack were minimal at this stage of the war.
"That's a great shame. We could do with a victory and some good news right now.
Those poor Channel Islanders will just have to keep buggering on!"
This was Churchill's favourite expression, sometimes abbreviated to KBO. He had been using it for rather longer than he had wanted to.

Churchill spent the rest of the year wooing President Roosevelt and the United States of America into joining the war. Despite supplying munitions and armaments on a lend lease scheme at very advantageous terms , America declined to come fully to the party until the Japanese attacked Pearl Harbour, the HQ of the American Pacific Fleet in the Hawaiian Islands, on December 7 1941 and, at last, Britain could feel less isolated. Clearly though, the Channel Islands could rightly feel that, as a consequence of all that was going on in the world, they were small fry indeed and had to all intents and purposes been abandoned.

The local civil governments of Jersey and Guernsey were cognisant of all these events and decided to simply get on with the job of survival. They were given permission to bolster diminishing food supplies by doing deals on mainland France which of course was under German control .A lot of foodstuffs were rationed and it was clear that sooner or later petrol would run out. It was not unusual to see huge queues at the town depot when the milk , bread , flour or butter ration was being distributed. These shortages were destined to worsen over the course of the Occupation.

The mood at La Rocque , after the funeral, was lifted by a spell of good weather and light winds. Peter was back at school and found it a worthy distraction. Every week day he would catch the bus which took him along the south coast to the bottom of Mont Millais on the outskirts of St Helier and from there he would walk the half mile up the hill to Victoria College. He was up early two weeks after the funeral in preparation for school when he realised that he need not have bothered. Saturday had previously been a half day filled with a double English and a double French period but because of general shortages of fuel, the headmaster had decided on a shorter week.
Peter was up at first light which was exceptionally early as the island was a week short of mid summer's day . He suddenly realised that today was the first Saturday of his long weekends and he no longer had to write descriptive essays or 'parlez francais' at the weekend.
"Oh, happy days, no school today. Thank you Adolf."

It was still only 5.30a.m. when he took his mug of steaming hot tea and sat down on the wooden bench at the end of the garden just a couple of yards short of the beach.
The low wall which marked the boundary of the property had long since crumbled to be replaced with random lumps of smooth granite garnered from the seashore. The sun was rising directly out to the east, the wind strength was zero and the air was crystal clear. Already it was quite warm and Peter felt it was warm enough to take off his pyjama top. He squinted and focussed his eyes on the incoming tide. It was two hours short of high and already past the bottom of the fifty yards of shelving soft sand which stretched down from where he sat. To

the south east and over a mile away out to sea stood Seymour Tower, its square shape in contrast to the craggy shapes of other rocks which were still above water. He sipped his tea and caught sight of a number of splashes a couple of hundred yards out . He held his breath as a pod of dolphins surfaced, arching out and back underwater as they cruised across his field of vision before disappearing to the left behind the pier.
Just a week past his fifteenth birthday, he still felt confused about John's death. He had spent those months in close company with him in prison and they were as close as siblings. He just could not figure out any reason for it and struggled to get a handle on the awful randomness of it all. There was no answer and in his quieter moments there was no light that would guide him. He was stuck with it forever.
The back door opened behind him and Christine called to him. She held Sophie in her arms. The two year old wriggled in her grasp and held her arms out for her older brother.
"Peeeet.Peeet! Me want Peeeet", she reached for him and climbed over into his arms.

"Come on, little sis. Come and see the dolphins. They might come back in a minute."

As if on command, the dolphins arched back into view from behind the pier, disturbing the still, quiet water as they chased a school of bait fish.

The three of them walked the few yards to the bottom of the garden and stood gazing seaward. Peter had grown taller than his mum and Christine had to reach up to put her arm around his shoulder. With his free arm he reached around her shoulder and they stood there intertwined.

"We'll be okay, Mum. We'll be okay."

Christine sighed and said,
"I hope so, son. I hope so".

There was a short silence broken only by the lapping of the tide as it crept up towards them.

".......shouldn't you be getting ready for school ? "

"No, Mum. I told you last week there was to be no more Saturday school and if things get any worse there will be no Monday either. God bless our wonderful Headmaster."

"Probably means you will get more homework!"

Peter groaned but had to agree with her. His mum dropped her hand from his shoulder and rubbed it up and down his bare back.

"Yes, we'll be fine, son. We'll be fine. "

CHAPTER 21

Boat trip

Half an hour later, Mac came knocking at the door saying that he had the use of Brian Le Rouge's boat and with it, a signed permit from the Germans to go out fishing for the day. The permit now included a demand that twenty per cent of the catch had to be handed over to them as a levy and also to ease the food shortages of the occupying force. This did not seem unreasonable but it didn't stop the majority of fishermen stashing whatever they caught in the hidey holes of their boats. Usually a token pollack, a particularly bland fish, was enough to keep the Krauts happy.
Christine opened the door.
"Hi Mac. Cup of tea?"

"Thanks but no thanks, hen. I'm on a mission. I've got a fishing permit and the loan of Brian's boat for the weekend. What d'ye reckon, Christine. Would you all like to come? It's a cracker of a day."

"Thanks Mac but I can't today. I'm taking Sophie round to Iris Legarde's for lunch and won't get away till mid afternoon. But take Peter, he'll be thrilled."

Peter's face lit up . It was a big spring tide due in about an hour. They could fish the dropping tide and potter round the gullies before dropping anchor out by Seymour Tower. The low tide would be way, way out so conditions were perfect for their expedition. Brian was in town that day so couldn't make it but was anxious for Mac to use the permit so that it wasn't wasted. It had taken him a lot of trouble and he made sure that Mac was aware that he was expecting a percentage of the catch.

"You're worse than bloody Jerry ! There'll be nothing left for us at this rate" said Mac as he grabbed the precious piece of paper before arriving at the Marinelles' house towing a collection of fishing rods, tackle box and lunch in a botched together trolley which was more used to carting a bag of golf clubs around.

Christine quickly cobbled together some lunch for Peter and kissed him goodbye. She was expecting him back on the uptide at about 7 pm. The days were long and it was light until way past the curfew time of ten o'clock. She trusted Mac implicitly and was confident that he would keep her boy safe.

"Don't forget your cork life jacket." she said.
"No, mum." he said and exhaled a huge sigh as he did. He could swim really well and saw no need for this bulky garment.

Off went the odd couple down the road, the cranky Scotsman and the lanky Jersey boy. They turned down the southern slipway and, as the tide was nearly high, waded out to the Crazy Doris. Mac had been down at sunrise to prepare for the expedition and had already put the outboard motor in the bottom of Brian's eighteen foot fishing boat. Mac went through a check list and, when he was happy, he mounted the engine on the back, gave it five pulls before it fired and off they went past the pier. They gently carved their way through what seemed like liquid glass. The almost total lack of wind meant no sign of a ripple save the wash that the boat left behind. The wash slapped against the pier as they pushed on out towards the tower.

Peter peered overboard marvelling at the clarity of the water. It was about twenty feet deep and he could see the rocks on the sand without any problem. He wanted to jump in and feel the cool water caress his warm skin.
'What a day!' he thought to himself as he squinted at the sun

rising to the south east. He leaned out and dragged his hand in the sea, turning it this way and that to feel the pressure of the water. He let his arm bounce along as he gave in to the sea.

"Let's nip out to Pebbly Gully and drop anchor there for an hour or two with the rods. I dug some really feisty redcat worms behind the pier yesterday . Let's see if they're any good," said Mac.

Fifteen minutes later, Mac idled into a spot at the end of Pebbly Gully navigating by lining up the end of the pier with the house with the pink roof and holding that line until the Elephant rock was ten yards away. Such was the way of the experienced boatmen. They needed no charts, just familiar rocks and landmarks on the shore.
Peter stood at the front, balanced with the hook anchor in his right hand. It weighed about twenty pounds and he had no problem manhandling it overboard when Mac gave him the nod and cut the engine. The dinghy drifted with the current until the anchor rope went taut and the anchor held fast.
"Let's get to it, young fella. The worms are in the tin can mixed with seaweed."

There was a whirlwind of activity as rods and reels were set up, lines were fed through rings, hooks attached , wriggly worms threaded painfully on and various bits of lead added to make all the tackle drop to the bottom which was about twenty feet down. The water was as clear as gin. Rocks, seaweed , sand and gravel all blended in a kaleidoscope of colour. Our two fishermen made themselves comfortable, two rods each hanging overboard. The rod tips swayed this way and that with the movement of the dinghy. The sun rose in the sky and Mac dozed off at the stern, the brim of his large straw hat tilted over his face . He kept one finger on the line of the rod by his side. For an hour nothing stirred, not a bite or a nibble. The lines were wound in and rebaited two or three times.

"Water's too clear. Never catch anything when the water's too clear," said Peter.

Mac sat upright, looked around and interjected, "Too little wind. Too bright and not enough time! Anything else we can think of?"

"The sky is too blue. The worms have gone off. Never catch anything when the worms have gone off," said Peter and, almost as a afterthought, he added ...."and Johnnie's not here any more."

Mac arose from his reverie with a surprised look on his face. He leaned forward.

"What !!!! Are you blaming Johnnie for the lack of fish? Och yerr bum's oot the windee, young fella."

He paused for a second as he knew Peter was having a moment of soul searching and he would have to tread carefully.

"What about all those butterflies at John's funeral? Do you really think he's not here?" said Mac tapping his head.

"Well, if that's all true, why can't he send us some BLOODY FISH? "

There was a few seconds while both of the odd fellows struggled to size up the situation. Mac broke the ice and shouted back,
"Because the water's TOO BLOODY CLEAR,that's why!"

Peter smiled and they both broke into laughter until they were interrupted by the sound of Peter's reel spinning as the line paid out and his rod bent under the weight of the fish snared in the depths of the gully. He started winding in , struggling to bring it to the surface. Mac stood by with a landing net and peered into the water. "Looks like a bass!"
"Feels like a bass!" said Peter, now breathing hard. Mac pushed a landing net under the fish and swung it onboard.
"It IS a bass! and probably aroond a poond. Nice fish,ladee! That'll be Johnnie's bass, I guess. What do you reckon? "
"I reckon you're right, Mister Mackintosh. I reckon you're right."

That was the extent of their angling success that morning and around midday they laid down their rods and took lunch. The tide was falling rapidly and as it did so the landscape became filled with previously submerged rocks and sandbanks now standing proud under the sun. The water below was now only about six feet deep. As Peter hauled the anchor up , he caught sight of movement on the seabed, as clear as day. He released the anchor back into the sea.

"Hang on Mac. Take a look at this! Wow.!!! "

Mac leaned over on the other side so as not to capsize the boat and saw what Peter was on about."Oh, happy happy day, ladee. Happy happy day !"

Crawling on the sand just ten feet below were hundreds of spider crabs, each one four to eight inches across the carapace and with long spidery legs giving them a span of two or three feet.
Pink in colour, the Maja Squinado, was an edible crab with ten legs and in early summer migrated in large numbers to moult

and to mate. This is exactly what must have happened. Spider crabs were an annual visitor but not even Mac had seen them in numbers like this. It looked like a giant mesh of interlocking limbs spreading out across the gully.

"The question is how are we going to handle this? " said Mac.

"How do you mean?" came the reply.

"Well, I guess we can grab the biggest and best ones."

".......and fill up the boat !!" added Peter.

Mac quickly assessed the situation.

"I reckon at dead low water this gully will be about three feet deep maximum so the boat will still float. We can hang around here for an hour or so, fill up and then wait for the incoming tide to carry us back over the sand bank .We'll be stranded for an hour but it will take that long to fish them out of the water and sort them out. It means our rod fishing is finished and we won't be able to explore around the tower and beyond as we'll be stuck here. Sound good to you? "

"Certainly does," replied Peter. "And there's nothing to stop us having a wander round here while we anchor up. We can easily wade on to the sand banks .On the other hand I think I would rather swim than wade over that horrible lot of nibbling crabs. Eeeeeurgh!"

"Aye ladee. Aye,"

They anchored up and made the boat secure. On the dropping tide, the gully was effectively now a lagoon about twenty yards

across and would reduce to about four feet deep as the sea leaked out and before the tide returned in an hour or so. This was a different world out here. The sea was draining out like water down the plughole of a bath leaving great swathes of sand and rock exposed . Little fish took refuge under rocks, crustaceans scuttled under cover and ever adaptable species of seaweed clung to the granite outcrops seemingly knowing they would soon be submerged again and safe once more. The whole place was drying in the hot sun and creaked in protest. Our two low water men surveyed the view and decided to go in different directions and return in half an hour which would give them both an opportunity to check out at least a couple of their favourite hidey holes and pull out a lobster or two. There would usually be quite a few other hopeful low water people on days like this but fishing permits were becoming harder to obtain so competition was light on the ground.
One such character, Gaston Guilleaume, could be seen just beyond the tower. Age had wearied him and his back was permanently bent . His silhouette could not be mistaken and neither could the smell of his Gauloise cigarette which drifted across the sand.

Mac shouted to him, "Bonjour Gaston ! Ca va?" .

The figure straightened slightly. With a typical Gallic shrug of the shoulders, he burbled something in French and waved back. Mac spent a few minutes wandering here and there across the sand flats before returning empty handed to the boat. He sat down on the nearest rock and stared into the heat haze that made the houses on the shore shimmer . He saw Peter coming towards him, a few yards away, waving a wriggling lobster in each hand.

"Look at these two beauties!"

He held them out for Mac to inspect. "You lucky little bugger. Make sure you tie up their claws before you put them in the sack or they'll tear each other to shreds. Nice ones. Where did you find them?"

Peter shot a sideways glance and said without any interval or hesitation,
"Just over there, a bit to the left, a few paces to the right under the big rock."

Then, in a broad Scottish accent, he followed it up with

"Did ye think I was born yesterday, Mister Mac ? "

Mac grinned.

"Ya bloody wee piss taker!" came the reply. "Ok, point taken. Let's catch some crabs!"

The tide had nearly reached its lowest point and, as they had predicted, the Crazy Doris was in about three to four feet of crystal clear water. They waded across and prepared for battle by first clearing the deck of all the debris and clutter . Fortunately the floor was covered with loose hessian sacks which they peeled back to use as bags for their catch. After that it was a simple task of selecting the largest crabs at their feet and then dipping underwater to retrieve them. Some of them were quite feisty but mostly their carapaces were an easy handspan and easy to grab from above thereby avoiding being nipped by the claws at the front. Nevertheless it needed quite an effort to manoeuvre them into the sacks and there was an outbreak of bad language every few minutes. Eventually the craft began to sink lower in the water with the weight of the catch and, with the depth of the gully increasing with the uptide, there came the time when Mac made the call to climb

aboard .This was not an easy task in itself but they managed by Peter straddling in first and pulling Mac up. Mac was surprised by the 'wee ladee's' strength and the ease with which he pulled him over the side. The boat tipped and swayed as they climbed in but they managed not to ship any water over the side.
It was noticeable that there was now only about two feet of clearance out of the water and Mac had to organise a spreading of all their cargo to maintain an even keel. Both of them were perched precariously , Mac on the seat at the stern and Peter at the bows facing him, with their feet being nibbled through the walls of the sacks. The gully was now overflowing and reconnecting with the sea in a flurry of foam like a fast flowing river but, as the levels equalised, the crescendo of movement was dulled until eventually all was calm again. With an act of acrobatic dexterity, Peter pulled the anchor aboard and they drifted gently away from the place they had now rechristened Crab Alley.
With a full load there was nothing more to do than potter in with the tide which was going to take three or four hours. Still about a mile out from the shore and with time to kill, Mac idled the engine northwards towards the mighty Mont Orgueil castle which dominated the headland a mile or two up the coast. Now over sand and with the sea like a mirror, they decided to drop anchor in order to eat cake and drink lemonade.
Within minutes they were shipshape once more and Mac's old tin lunchbox was on his knee. He distributed slices of fruit cake and uncorked the lemonade bottle, decanting the fizzing liquid into eager enamel mugs.

"Well, this ain't so bad, young fella. Get that lot down you. You wouldnee want to die for a quid on a day like today! "
Peter devoured the cake, making sure he caught the crumbs in his tee shirt so as not to waste anything.
"Ladee, I'm going to propose a toast now so listen up. Ladies and gentlemen, be upstanding.........well, it's best if we don't upstand as we don't want to rock the boat..........and raise

yourrrr sassenach glasses to this wonderful day!"
They raised their lemonade mugs in unison.

"...........and to Johnnie," said Peter quietly ....."My good mate Johnnie."
He suddenly caught his breath. His eyes filled and a tear rolled down his cheek.

"Aye, well said, ladee. Well said.".......and the words stuck in his throat as he choked back his own emotion. To his surprise , it was Peter who picked up the ball and ran with it.

"Cheer up, Mac. He's here. He spoke to me when I got those lobsters."

Mac was blowing his nose and Peter's words stopped him in his tracks.

"Well, what did he say? " Mac enquired softly.

"He just told me where the lobsters were."

A silence descended on them. Mac wasn't sure how seriously he had to take this disclosure but his train of thought was interrupted by the movement of a shoal of fish and the noise of a following flock of seagulls.
"Quick ladee, break out the feathers. I don't know where we're gonna put them but we've got fish to catch!"
The mood was, happily for them both, well and truly broken. While Mac steered towards the shoal, Peter delved into the tackle bags for sets of mackerel feathers and hooks which he attached to handlines and lead weights before dropping them overboard while he wound out the line. Five minutes passed while they trolled the sand banks and suddenly the mackerel

struck. An hour later the hessian bags, filled with spider crabs, were now covered by a layer of fifty or so sparkling, writhing,blue and grey flashing , tasty mackerel. They could not go wrong as the shoal hung around but eventually they ran out of energy and space.

Sunburnt and exhausted, they chugged the few hundred yards south west back to La Rocque with Mac on the tiller and Peter with his head on the gunwhales looking out for submerged rocks but generally marvelling at the world below. Seaweed, previously drying out prostrate on the rocks, now stood up proudly and waved as the shadow of the boat passed overhead. Soon they were closing in on the pier with a couple of hours until the big spring tide hit the seawall and closed out the bay. Mac, in his wisdom, had decided to borrow a trailer and cart the boat back to the Grenadier Inn where the owner, Brian Le Rouge, would be waiting. His plan was to evade having to declare his catch to as few people as possible. To the casual observer , they had a good haul of mackerel and at the most they would have to give away ten or so fish to the German authorities to keep them sweet. Hopefully, thought Mac, the hessian sacks would be taken for what they were, hessian sacks in the bottom of the boat. He headed for the north slipway and floated up fifty yards short. Peter jumped out and held the boat on a rope as it floated with the tide. Mac disappeared up the slip and acknowledged the German patrol at the top.

"Just fetching the tractor and trailer," he said as he handed the German soldier his permit.

"Be back in a jiffy, Jerry."

"My name is Gunter, Jock."

"Don't call me Jock, Jerry."

"Don't call me Jerry, Jock."

It was clear there was previous history here and the conversation had been played out a few times before. There was laughter on both sides.
Mac returned with tractor and trailer, drove down the slipway and reversed the trailer towards the boat. With difficulty they winched the heavily laden Crazy Doris on to the trailer and took off back up the slipway to confront Gunter who was delighted with the four fat mackerel that were presented to him as the regulation twenty per cent of catch levy. He had a quick look into the dinghy and saw nothing but hessian sacks and fishing rods. He waved them through and our crew turned right towards the Grenadier Inn where they offloaded the catch into an outhouse. Mac then returned the tractor and trailer which he had borrowed from the farm up the road and walked back the few hundred yards to the Grenadier Inn .

Peter and Brian were waiting with the catch laid out on a sheet on the floor.

"Fifty three mackerel and ninety three spider crabs! " said Brian, smiling......
"What a day. What a day! "

It was now six o'clock and Mac had promised Christine that Peter would be back by seven.
"Peter, how much do you think you'll want to take back for family and friends tonight? My idea is to get Brian to trade whatever is left when we've taken our immediate needs. He's in the best position to do it as he knows everybody and their business round here and he can do it quietly. How about six of one and half dozen of the other for both of us and trust Brian to get us some other goodies. After all, it *is* his boat.......oh and

you should keep yer lobbies."

Peter was in total agreement and got his kit together before selecting six of each which he put in separate sacks.
"I'll walk you back, big fella. I promised your mother I'd see you back. I'll see you in an hour or so, Brian. "
Brian nodded in agreement. "See you, Peter.......and well done. There will be some bounty in this for you, don't worry. And Mac, I've found another bottle of Calvados, if you've a mind to a glass or two when you get back."
"Och no, see the trouble it got me into last time. Six months holiday in Newgate Street prison!"
"There is such a thing as moderation, Mac. You should try it!" replied Brian.

"Come on, Peter. Let's get you back. See you, Brian."

All the goodbyes were said and they set off back down the road, past both slipways of La Rocque where Mac was a little worried that Gunter may have lost his sense of humour . The tide was now at its highest right up against the sea wall and the bay looked stunning. Gunter and his patrol thought so too for they were gazing thoughtfully out towards France and beyond , thinking what a wonderful posting this was. They weren't to know that within two weeks Germany would declare war on Russia and a posting to the Eastern Front would not be such a good proposition.

St Kitts was still another three hundred yards past the big house, Platte Rocque, that overlooked the southern slipway but they marched on singing The Happy Wanderer just to annoy Gunter who was staring after them.

"Bloody stupid Jock!" he yelled in German.

" German bastard!" he yelled back, smiling broadly as he did and waved a greeting.

Mac didn't want to prolong the discussion and the two of them moved swiftly on.
He and Peter were absolutely exhausted from their day out and he didn't have the energy anyway. They were soon at St Kitts and Christine invited him in for a cup of tea which he gratefully accepted as it would give him an opportunity to gaze upon her loveliness. He tried ,without much success, to hide his feelings.
"Did you catch anything, you two?" she said.
"Just a couple of mackerel and a few spiders," came the reply from both of our conspirators at the same time. Christine couldn't let this one go and said,

"Been down the fishmongers then, have you?"

'Oh, ha ha Mum. My stomach hurts from laughing."

"Och, no Christine. We've had a bonny day. Sunshine, fish, crabs, lobsters and good company."

"Peter didn't go then?" She was relentless but it brought a chuckle from Mac.

'Och no. He's a bonny lad."

"Did you want to stay for supper, Mac. I can boil the lobster with some garlic and stuff. We have bread as well"

"Much as I would love to," replied Mac, "I have to get back to Brian's place. But thank you anyway."
After tea, Mac made his way home and took the opportunity to abuse Gunter as he passed the slipway. He quickly visited

Brian, refused the Calvados and at last got home and collapsed into the old but very comfortable armchair. He poured himself a small whisky.

"What a day......... What a day!"

Within a minute he was, unusually, fast asleep.

CHAPTER 22

Bartering time

While Mac slept that evening, Brian Le Rouge went to work. With a wheelbarrow full of spider crabs and mackerel , he was already doing the rounds of the farms close by bartering the catch for eggs, potatoes, tomatoes and anything else that was edible. They were fortunate indeed to live where they did as crops were still being harvested, cows were still being milked, butter was still being churned, bread was still being baked, chickens were still laying eggs , pigs were still getting fatter and fish were still being caught. In short, the country folk had it a lot easier than the town folk of St Helier where the queues for rationed goods were always long. He had been lucky to have enough fuel for the boat but it was clear this would be rationed soon. Everything seemed to be in short supply and the reason was that they were in a war zone and any goods that were shipped from France (they clearly weren't coming from anywhere else) were in danger of being intercepted by the Allies. It was a weird situation.
Brian's first port of call was the house of Roger and Eileen Le Ross. He knocked on the door of Sunny View and it was Roger he heard shuffling on the other side.

"Who is it?"
"Why don't you open the door and find out?"
Roger recognised the voice and opened the door. He looked terrible and his sad demeanour took Brian by surprise.
"How's it going, good friend?"
Roger paused for a moment and replied, "It's tough, Brian. It's tough. I try to sleep but when I wake up, I remember it all again. It's there, always there......."
His voice trailed off as his concentration wavered.
Brian felt awkward but still managed to say,

"I can't find any words that will help you, mate. None of us can. But there's a lot of people out there who are feeling your pain. "

"I know, Brian, I know......but they get on with their lives and forget about it. I can't.
It sits there like a big black cloud. Eileen is worse. She just cries all day and I don't think she can ever get over it. Come to think of it, I don't think I have much chance either."

Brian had preselected the biggest mackerel and the biggest spider crab from the wheelbarrow.
"Where shall I put these?"
"Blimey, where did you get those?"
"I sent Mac and young Peter out on the boat today as I had some legal stuff to do in town. They brought back........quite a few."
He had paused because he suddenly remembered that Roger was still the Assistant Harbour Master and it was probably better that he didn't know the extent of the catch in too much detail. The less he knew, the less he could pass on.
"Good catch,eh? Don't worry, I know where you are coming from. I don't give the Krauts anything to feed on. How much did it cost to get past the slipway with all this?"

"I believe it was four fat mackerel. Mac's a canny bugger. He seems to get on quite well with that guard in charge. They just swear at each other in their respective languages and smile. I think it must be love. Anyway, I must get on. Got things to swap."
"What do I owe you for these? It'll have to be cash as there ain't much in the pantry."

"No,no, I didn't mean *you*. Those are a gift. Just hope you bloody well eat them."

"Well......thanks, thanks Brian. It's appreciated. I'll...er.... get Eileen to cook the crab straight away and I can salt the mackerel for later. It'll divert her mind for a while."

"Okay, Roger. Gotta go. Take care," said Brian, lifting the handles of the wheelbarrow in readiness for his next delivery. It was still light and he had nearly two hours of trading left before curfew.

"G'night, Brian and thanks again!"

He watched Brian as he pushed his way up the lane, hamming it up as he weaved from left to right. A smile crossed his lips. He felt a bit better. "You bloody fool!" he shouted after him. Brian carried on further up the road and called on the three farmers that he counted amongst his friends. Without lingering too long with any of them, he returned back down the lane with fresh eggs by the dozen, bags of potatoes and tomatoes, two pounds of butter together with an odd leek, a large swede and a pumpkin. He figured he had done well and was home in good time before any wandering German patrol could investigate what he was carrying. The smell of fish on his hands was overpowering and he scrubbed them until it was all but gone. All the goods were then stacked in the cold room in readiness for sharing with Mac and Peter in the morning.

Darkness was descending and he reached for one of his many hidden bottles of Calvados. He poured himself a drink in his rooms above the pub and headed for his favourite chair which gave him a view across the coast road and down the slipway. He took a swig from the glass and he felt it burn his throat before it pumped some joy into his brain. He watched the colours of the sunset fading. His wife was safe in England , stranded by the Occupation while visiting relatives in Portsmouth. This was his favourite time of day. He would have long conversations with Beryl even though she was a hundred or so miles away. He missed her badly.

He had had a successful evening but he felt, as many of his friends did also, that things were definitely getting worse.
He nodded off and was surprised when he woke at first light. He was surprised because he was still in the armchair and surprised because he had slept there for about seven hours straight. He got up stiffly and stretched, the muscles of his 55 year old body groaning in protest. He walked into the kitchen and lit the gas for the kettle. Today he had the prospect of a decent breakfast. He had eggs, fresh bread, butter and bramble leaf tea. He normally drank Darjeeling tea but that went out the window last Christmas when supplies ran out . He was now accustomed to this new hedgerow vintage which was passably palatable and readily available. He filled the teapot with boiling water from the kettle and immediately put the frying pan where the kettle had sat. There was congealed fat in the pan from the last fry up and as soon as it melted he put in a piece of bread. The smell was overwhelming and he sniffed the air long and hard. He cracked the egg and in it went, bubbling and sizzling. He wondered if Beryl was awake yet, she was an early riser. He stared wistfully out of the window and decided to dedicate this breakfast to his absent wife. He raised his mug toward the rising sun .
"Here's to you, Beryl. I make that 30 years of married life today .Happy anniversary, my love. Happy anniversary."
He had always had trouble remembering the date but now she wasn't here, he found himself remembering all sorts of dates when they'd done things together. The day they met, the day he proposed, the day they took on the Grenadier Inn and of course, the day they married, all sprang easily to mind. He knew she was probably thinking the same thoughts at exactly the same time at her sister's place in Portsmouth.

"Oh well, let's go. Another day in paradise. Let's see if Mac wants some eggs for his breakfast!"

He loaded up a large sailor's duffle bag with two shares of last night's bartering and set off the few hundred yards to Mac's house. Mac had been up and about since first light and he was delighted to see Brian.

"Come in, come in. I'll put the kettle on. What did ye get on yerr wee expedition to the farming community?"

"Plenty, my son. Loads of eggs, butter, vegetables, leaf tea.....even a couple of rashers of bacon! ......

"Whoa, bacon. I can smell it already. Where's my bit ?"

"......yeah, I ate that already. Sorry about that."

Mac rounded on him.

"You sassenach bastard. Och, yerr winding me up. There wasnee any bacon!. Was there?"

" Do pigs fly? " said Brian.

"Och, you're a bugger. I'll put my *real* coffee back in the jar then."

And so it went on, a continuous stream of jovial mickey taking which only good friends can attempt. Brian got his coffee and Mac cooked his rasher of bacon before Brian departed, leaving Mac the task of delivering Peter's share of the contraband.

CHAPTER 23

Hitler visit

The days leading up to the middle of July 1941 were fairly quiet for Jersey except for the surrender of wireless sets from various districts. No sooner had the selected district surrendered their sets than they were given back a week later. This was one frustrating characteristic of the German command. Notices were issued and withdrawn shortly afterwards. However , the wireless set order gave notice of what was to come and many plans were made by the locals to hide their sets in readiness for the next notice to surrender. The wireless had assumed massive importance in knowing what was going on in Europe. The local newspaper was important for local news but could not be relied on for truthful international news as the Germans were censoring it. Before anything was printed, it had to pass muster with the weasly Colonel Getz and his cohorts, who took up residence in the offices of the Evening Post in St Helier . It was difficult to get anything past them. Propaganda was the new weapon of the times and the Nazi regime was extremely good at producing it. There was much activity around the harbours that week as they were cleared in readiness for a visit from Field Marshal Von Witzelben, commander of the German First Army stationed in Cherbourg and responsible for the Western Front. He duly arrived in style early on the morning of July 11 but at the airport at St Peter and not at the docks. The plane that flew in that morning was a Focke-Wulf FW 200 Condor, a four engined machine that could carry over 20 passengers. This one was rather special as firstly, it had been customised for a few less people to travel in comfort and secondly, it was piloted by Hans Bauer, Adolf Hitler's personal pilot. Bauer was a WW1 flying ace and was the only person Hitler would fly with. Alongside Von Witzelben sat the Fuhrer himself, anxious to see these jewels in the British Crown. They were met by Oberst

Gruber ,the local administrative commander, and Oberst Von Schmidt, the overall Channel Island Supreme Military Commander. They set off in a large black highly polished Mercedes and three other staff cars which contained an armed escort. The trip had been planned from Cherbourg at very short notice the night before and had produced quite a lot of panic in the military command in Jersey.
It was clear the Fuhrer was following through on his personal directive for the fortification of the Channel Islands. He and Von Witzelben were whisked off sharply
on a whistle stop tour of the existing coastal defences.
The motorcade drove from the airport straight down past the end of the runway they had arrived on and down to the seas on the west coast of St Ouen's Bay. Sand dunes led down to the beach which stretched for three or more miles north to south. A sparkling blue sea was spitting large waves onto acres of clean hard sand, in total contrast to the shores of La Rocque on the opposite side of the island.
The motorcade reached the coast road and edged on to the hard standing overlooking the massive beach.
The Fuhrer looked impressed with the view and poked at the map of Jersey which nestled on his lap,
"This coastline would have to be defended against an attack from the sea, regardless of the huge waves generated down here."

He had already spotted three or four peculiar round towers dotted up the coast on the shore line. One of them had been built on a group of rocks just four hundred yards west of where they were beyond the sand line and surrounded by sea.

"Did the locals build these?"

"Yes, I believe so, Fuhrer. In about 1800 to keep out the French."

"They knew what they were doing. They are well positioned. That's a big beach and we would need decent artillery to cover it from the high point,"...............he stopped and pointed...... *"here,here,here and here. Can we go this way now?".*
He nodded towards the north and they drove the three miles which took them around the far north west tip of the island before winding up the very steep hill at L'Etacq and onto the open land at Les Landes which gave panoramic views back south from where they had driven and also to the north west where Sark and Guernsey lay. It was a day, also, when the most northerly of the Channel Islands, Alderney, could just be picked out on the north eastern horizon some twenty five miles away. Hitler and Von Witzelben got out and stood mesmerised by the magnificent vista which stretched all around as they stood on a carpet of verdant purple heather. Rugged granite cliffs dipped down to a sea that had been stilled by weeks of glorious sunny weather. Skylarks , disturbed by the intrusion, soared suddenly upwards, singing in annoyance. There was a buzzing of happy bees and the sweet sound of chirruping crickets enjoying another warm summer's day. Most of the rest of the world was in conflict with the man standing just a few yards away.

"Quite magnificent, Witzey. Quite magnificent. Those other islands are really quite close. My decision to invade was a good one. With so much high ground , this will not be too difficult to defend. This area particularly would also make an excellent command post. "

The posse walked casually along the cliff paths and stopped briefly to observe a kestrel which hovered above its prey just a few yards away, perfectly stable in the light breeze. They then turned back to where the cars were parked. Just then a canteen truck, driven by Captain Hans Bauer, arrived. Tables and chairs were unloaded and placed on a patch of flat gravel .

The Fuhrer turned to see this flurry of action. Von Witzelben spoke first.

"*Your pilot is back again and it looks like he has brought some lunch as well. Is that part of his duties?*"

Hitler drew his finger back and forth across his upper lip.

"*Yes. When I am away from Berlin, he looks after my dietary requirements. I trust him implicitly and he gets to taste it all before I eat it. Let's hope he's in form today! I did ask him to seek out some fresh local produce.*"

Bauer had indeed done the day proud as he had commandeered the canteen truck at the airport and ,with the help of one of the catering corps, had visited one of their supplying farmers close to the airport. A fine selection of tomatoes, lettuce, runner beans and various herbs were laid out on the table. His assistant had been busy in the back of the truck boiling up some of the local new potatoes . Holding the large saucepan steady on top of the coal fired stove while the vehicle swayed at top speed around the many corners en route to Les Landes, was a job normally outside the remit of the young soldier. With Bauer's encouragement, he managed to retain most of the contents inside the saucepan and not set fire to the truck. With some sprigs of mint and copious amounts of melting butter, he delivered the potatoes on an enormous hot plate but nearly dropped the lot when he looked up and realised just who he was serving. His expression of total bewilderment amused the Fuhrer no end.
"Have no fear, young man. I am who you think I am. Where are you from?"

"I am from Stuttgart, mein ....er ...Fuhrer."

" I hope you are happy to be serving the Fatherland. Your work is important. Well done."

"Thank you, mein Fuhrer."

Flustered, he backed away without dropping or spilling anything, leaving his superiors to have their lunch. The potatoes and salad were well received and Bauer even produced some chocolate which pleased Hitler immensely. A German motorcyclist with side car swung into view about five hundred yards away and was intercepted by the armed guard. He handed a written message over and returned back down the road. The message was delivered to Hitler as he devoured the last piece of chocolate. He swallowed hard and read the note.

"Alas, Witzy, we have to return to Cherbourg as soon as possible. The Luftwaffe have had heavy losses over Moscow and I must get back to Berlin. Never mind, a complete day off was not to be."

"Jawohl Fuhrer, " came Von Witzelben's reply and he relayed the information to the local commanders. It took barely a minute to arrange an extra seat for Bauer in the Mercedes and to set off back to the airport, the same way as they had come. As they rounded the top of the hill at L'Etacq, the view to the south and west was even more stunning than on the way up because they were now facing in the right direction. Hitler asked Bauer to stop while he got out to take it all in.
"Wait there Witzey, I'll only be a minute."
He walked across the road and onto the thick grass. He breathed deeply and took in the fresh sea air. The breeze riffled his tunic as he stood gazing this way and that. He took a penknife from his breast pocket and crouched down to dig out

some earth. Holding the dirt in his hand, he remarked, *"Britischem Boden. Britischem Boden. British soil. Wunderbar, wunderbar!"*

He tucked the knife and the soil back into his breast pocket. Taking one long last look , he climbed back in alongside Von Witzelben and ordered Bauer to drive on.

Twenty minutes later, the party stood by the steps of the Fokker-Wulf and said their farewells. Hitler buttonholed the two local commanders and issued his orders.

"You will of course understand these are my specific instructions. I don't want the British to just sail up and think they can recapture these islands. Strategically and psychologically, they are of the utmost importance and they will be defended heavily. It is only a matter of time before the Fatherland conquers England and here, you will be leading the way!"

Von Schmidt and Gruber saluted as their Supreme Commander and Field Marshall Von Witzelben climbed the steps into the aircraft.

He had been on British soil for barely four hours but Hitler was absolutely delighted to have been on it and to have subjugated it to German rule. Leaving Sark and Guernsey to the left, they flew over Alderney back to Cherbourg. As they climbed down the steps from the plane back on to French soil, Hitler made another observation.

"I have already spoken to Fritz Todt . He can see to all this. We shall issue a Fortification Directive by November. What a beautiful place. I think it would be nice to return there some day. Thank you Witzey! We should do this again. Maybe stay

longer next time."

The three of them had left Cherbourg just after breakfast and were back on French soil in time for afternoon tea. Hitler had much on his mind as, just three weeks before, the Germans had invaded Russia and were now stretched closer to home than the west coast of France. The Fuhrer had clearly been enchanted by the islands and they stuck very firmly in his mind.
By the end of August there was a development in the Middle East when Churchill decided, with the help of the Russians, to invade the essentially neutral country of Persia who he feared were Nazi sympathisers. The move essentially safeguarded the oil supply and also made sure that the Germans could not access it either. Their Panzer tank divisions in North Africa would be thus be starved of fuel. The upshot was that 690 German nationals, mostly working on oil installations, were to be deported and imprisoned. In truth most of these 690 souls managed to escape across the border but nothing could ameliorate the mood Hitler had taken on. This invasion of a neutral country was, he thought, outrageous so he took it upon himself to enforce some retribution by ordering the evacuation to Germany of 2000 Channel Islanders to be selected by virtue of being not born there or not normally living there. The order was given but was mysteriously buried for a year.
Its ramifications were dreadful but the islands continued their stand-off with the Germans unaware of the heartache to come. Hitler had made the order and it stood there like a ticking time bomb.

CHAPTER 24

The band receives a gift

As Autumn 1941 arrived , the build up of troops became more apparent and most of the hotels in the main town of St Helier had been requisitioned to accommodate these newcomers. There was a continuous turnover, some units moving to the Russian front and others returning from service in Poland. Members of the Hitler Youth, all well indoctrinated in the ways of Nazism , were also arriving. The pupils at Victoria College were ousted in favour of these master race trainees and moved into other premises down in town. The College's commanding south west facing granite façade provided an impressive backdrop for the propaganda photographs and movies which the Third Reich was so fond of. Further up the hill at the College's boarding house, the Feldkommandantur was now firmly established and was effectively running the island.
A well trodden footpath ran behind the school and through the grounds before descending quickly down several flights of granite steps into St Helier. A large wrought iron gate marked the exit on to St Saviour's road along which lay a ribbon of guesthouses and large hotels. This was where most of the new intake of troops was being accommodated.
The impressive Mayfair Hotel had seen a massive change of clientele. Early last summer it was welcoming tourists from England and France, momentarily escaping the worsening effects of war in Europe. Happy holidays were still on the agenda. A year later it was host to an invading army in grey uniforms. Where a bowtied hotel manager once stood behind the ornate reception desk, now stood an armed guard. An army catering corps had now replaced the busy , neat waitresses in the dining room. The parquet floored ballroom, where many a romantic couple had previously waltzed the night away, was now the scene for band practice of a more military style.
Fritz Doenig and his room mate and fellow musician Gunter

Muller, had already completed a year's service as part of the original intake in July of 1940. The debris of the bombs dropped in the first attack had barely been swept away before the members of a Luftwaffe band had been ferried in. With a few additions over the last few months, they now totalled more than twenty members who could play instruments varying from trombones, tubas and trumpets to clarinets, saxophones, flutes, flugelhorns and drums. Some were more accomplished musicians than others but their job was to provide stirring German marching songs to raise the morale of the troops and provide a backdrop for more ceremonial occasions. Every morning there was band practice and at half past noon they would stop for lunch. After moaning about the culinary skills of the catering unit, they would usually relax in the ballroom. Today was no exception but the peace was disturbed by the noise of a large piece of furniture being scraped along the parquet floor.
"Hey, hey,hey! Take it easy. You are ruining the floor! What the hell is that?" said Fritz.

One of the military removal men explained the situation.

"Which one of you is Doenig? Ah..you..okay. This is a mahogany radiogram which my commanding officer Major Brandt of Government House said you might be interested in. It is extremely heavy and as big as a cow and the four of us have already carried it about two kilometres down the road. We would appreciate a more hospitable welcome."

"I am sorry,my friend," said Doenig. *" How kind of Major Brandt. How about sticking it by the stage near the electric socket. We'll give you a hand and then maybe you can get some lunch in the canteen."*

There were smiles all round and the radiogram was lifted over

the precious floor into the space by the stage and immediately plugged in to the power source. The removal men departed to claim their free lunch and Fritz and Gunter set about firing it up. With a lot of knob twiddling, it burst into life with a deep bass sound which pleasantly surprised the assembled bandsmen. They further discovered that the wireless dials boasted three frequencies, short, medium and long wave. Within a few seconds they were tuned into Radio Hamburg on short wave. The reception was not great and the volume swirled like a fairground organ. Radio Hamburg was the only station now broadcasting out of Germany and, with the guidance of German Propaganda Minister Josef Goebbels, was now disseminating news, information and music with an understandably Nazi bias. Goebbels was a clever man and realised the importance of the radio in spreading the Nazi message. Radio Hamburg was not only adept at raising the morale of the troops of the Fatherland but also could be used to dispirit the enemy. A dark and distinctly English character nicknamed Lord Haw Haw was employed to broadcast tales of further British setbacks and German victories.
Gunter turned away from the sideboard sized radiogram and faced the audience.

"That's brilliant. Radio Hamburg ! Wow! We can listen to some other military bands for a change! That's got to be better than listening to Werner playing out of tune!"

They all laughed and there was no animosity from Werner Turner because he knew he was the best horn player there and the last time he played a wrong note was five years ago. His unfortunate rhyming name was the result of his German mother's marriage in 1919 to a British engineer who was working in Berlin after the end of World War One. Although Alfred Turner pointed out that Werner would not be the best name for their newborn son, the new Mrs Eva Turner prevailed and Werner Turner was stuck with a name that nobody could forget. He played in school bands as a teenager and conscription saw him join the Luftwaffe as a musician. He saw himself flying Messerschmitts between concerts but that particular dream was shattered when they discovered his eyesight was not up to standard. He figured he would survive longer playing the trumpet on terra firma so he was not too disappointed .

The band still had their military duties to perform and they were trained to fill in at various defence posts around the island. They hated this side of their duties as it was inevitably boring but it did provide them with a bit of variety and also made them aware that they had it pretty easy. They played a variety of marching tunes which became familiar and amusing to the locals. If a squad of soldiers was marching somewhere then you could be assured that they would be singing Der Frohliche Wanderer in time with the rhythmic noise of their jackboots scraping on tarmac. On ceremonial parades the Luftwaffe Band did it all for them , their instruments setting the pace for the marching soldiers.

On the other side of the cabinet, the top lifted to expose a turntable for playing records. Packed inside this section were dozens of small boxes containing needles for the pickup arm. The radiogram finally surrendered more of its treasures when the cabinet under the turntable was opened to reveal fifty or more shiny black records all in their cardboard covers. They had clearly been well looked after by a rich music lover. Fritz Doenig made a mental note to ask Major Brandt the story behind this fine piece of furniture. They had a few minutes left before mustering for a short sit down concert at a tea party up at Government House . The time was well spent inspecting the record collection. There was Mario Lanza, Maria Callas, the Band of the Coldstream Guards, the London Symphony Orchestra, the Vienna Boys Choir..... a cornucopia of music of the pre-war decade. Gunter found a brand new record still inside a mailing packet with a U.S.A. postmark on it. He pulled out the contents which bore the His Masters Voice legend in

the middle. He screwed his eyes up to read the label. The name of the song sounded strange but the name of the orchestra was familiar to him. He had often listened surreptitiously to the Voice Of America radio programme which was President Roosevelt's answer to Radio Hamburg as far as news and propaganda went. Every weekend there was a request show which was broadcast for the army stations all over the USA. The band that played on the radio was the same as the one on the record......the Glenn Miller Orchestra. The tune was Chattanooga Choo Choo.
Gunter held the disc tightly in his hands and whispered,

"Das ist Gold. Das ist Gold!"

CHAPTER 25

Bad news

After his day trip to Jersey, the Fuhrer directed operations from the Cherbourg military command post before returning home to the Berghof, his private fortified headquarters near Berchtesgaden. From here, just two months later on 22 October 1941, he issued his fortification order for the Channel Islands. He still suspected that there may be an attempt to recapture them , consequently jeopardising sea communications.

"..we need to convert them, with the utmost speed, into an impregnable fortress.
For the army, we need a network of concealed emplacements which give flanking fields of fire and big enough to house guns of sufficient size to penetrate heavy armour plate.
For the Navy, one heavy battery on each island and two on the French coast to defend the sea approaches.
For the Air Force, strongpoints to be created to accommodate anti aircraft units.

The High Command of the Army will be responsible for completion.
Foreign labour to be used especially Russians, Spaniards and French.
Progress reports to be sent first day of each month to C-in-C Army "

These orders were quickly initiated but one unrelated order should have rung alarm bells.

"Another order will follow for the deportation to the Continent of all Englishmen who are not natives of the Island i.e not born there."

The order was signed by the Fuhrer himself. The defence constructions had been in the planning stage for at least three months so Hitler had simply confirmed the general plan. Teams of expert engineers had visited the islands during the summer months, completing geological and strategic surveys .These were the same engineers responsible for the the soon to be built Atlantic Wall which would stretch from Spain to Scandinavia. These were massive projects which needed huge quantities of concrete, steel and manpower.
As we have seen, the regrettable order for the deportation of non-native Channel Islanders was Hitler's retribution for the Anglo Russian takeover of the neutral territory of Persia with all its oilfields. The order was not best received by the German Military Command in the islands and was ignored for the best part of a year.
The construction of Festung or Fort Jersey, however, was far from overlooked and began in earnest with the arrival of hundreds of troops bringing the total up to ten thousand with many more to follow. On one day in early November the docks in St Helier saw the arrival and departure of no less than forty steamers and barges, all laden with cement bags, steel and barbed wire.
After a year of relative calm, things were changing at a pace that the local population were not accustomed to.

Coastal areas were particularly vulnerable to this new era. Information was dispensed through the local newspaper and for a while it was hard to keep up with all the notices being issued. There was heavy mining going on , not only on the foreshore and beyond but also in meadows and dunes thought to be of strategic importance. If you ventured out for a walk on the coast without consulting the notices in the Evening Post, you stood a high risk of being blown to pieces by stepping on an explosive device. It behove the Germans to be precise about their warnings because their own troops were at serious risk as well and an officer was killed when the dog he was exercising triggered a bomb at Fort Regent.

Fortifications at La Rocque were on the agenda but the area was no stranger to invasion. The very last battle on English soil had taken place at that very spot in January 1781 when the French landed 1000 men . In the eighteenth century, much of the area would have been rock and sand dune .The small plateau called Platte Rocque, next to the present south slipway , gave a commanding view of the east and south approaches, unencumbered by houses in those days. The French were a constant threat to the island and not even the mighty castle at Gorey, just three miles north, could deter them from the odd attempt at a landing. The island was defended by its own Militia and the British Army, a force of some two thousand souls. Platte Rocque was defended by a guard post but, on the night in question , they were either asleep or absent and consequently the French met with no resistance. They marched west into St Helier and, in the early hours of January 6, 1781 managed to talk the Governor of Jersey into capitulating. Major Pierson and his 95th regiment, however, had intelligence of the attack and were having none of it. He marched into St Helier from a westerly direction with a force which outnumbered the French by two to one and , after a fifteen minute skirmish in the Royal Square, quelled the invasion with the loss of eleven men. Major Pierson was one of them, being mortally wounded with a musket shot to the chest. The French fleet lay off La Rocque with over a hundred men ashore. The Eastern Regiment, possibly billeted at Gorey Castle, repelled their retreat at Platte Rocque with just 45 soldiers until reinforcements arrived.
The repulsed attack sped up the construction of a number of armed Round Towers which were built in strategic places all round the coast. These were in addition to the existing medieval forts and castles which already dotted the coastline. The Round Towers were built of granite to a height of fifty or sixty feet with two floors and a roof top all accessible by ladders. There

were observation and firing apertures at each level and provided a level of early warning still effective one hundred and sixty years later. One was built on Platte Rocque where the Eastern Regiment performed so well and another was built on the rock known as L'Avarison down at the low water mark. This was now known as Seymour Tower , the central point of most low water fishing expeditions. Seymour was officially a Round Tower design but, because of constructional restraints, had been built square. It was sufficiently far out to command views north to Gorey Castle and west to Green Island, a massive field of fire. From Platte Rocque Tower to Gorey Castle, there were another half dozen towers, one of them a few yards from Mac's house.

Bringing us up to date, a notice was issued to the effect that all the towers, many of which were privately owned, had been commandeered by the Germans. This displeased Mac no end as it meant he would have six or so trigger happy Jerries overlooking his garden on a permanent basis.

Further to this, the golf course which lay on public land amongst the dunes leading up the east coast to Gorey was declared a military zone and mined accordingly. Its foreshore was also out of bounds with anti tank obstacles to be built there. The foreshore to the west of La Rocque was also deemed a military zone . It seemed their low water playground was in jeapardy. Seymour Tower was also to be armed and manned on a more permanent basis. Previously it had just been part of a tour of inspection which a squad would visit occasionally at low tide. Now it was to be a first line of defence with guns pointing in all directions.

As 1941 drew to a close, the local population was becoming thinner as the rationed food stocks dwindled. The Germans themselves were so far unaffected which caused a lot of unrest and indignation in those over the wall neighbourly conversations.

At St Kitts, Christine Marinelle was not looking forward to Christmas which was only a week away. The gas supply was

becoming unreliable but Peter had managed to gather a large stack of fire wood for the kitchen stove. Coal was still available but in small quantities. The winter had not been bad until today when the temperatures had plunged. She was surprised when Mac turned up one evening just before curfew at nine o'clock.
"Hi Chrissy, sorry to turn up so late."
"No problem, Mac. It's always nice to see you, good friend. Come in."

He stepped inside and edged towards the stove.
"Warm yourself up. You look frozen. I thought you Scots were used to the cold!"

"Aye, we are. I reckon the climate down here has made me soft. Never mind, your stove is mighty welcome. How's the bairn and the big fella?"

"They are both good, thank you. Peter will be down in a tick. He'll have heard your voice."

"Lassie, would a leg of pork go down well for Christmas?"

Christine felt a bit stuck for words, she opened her mouth but nothing came out.
Mac could see she felt confused so he went on and explained the situation.

"I've been saving all my cigarette ration coupons and I'm about to redeem them all in exchange for a leg of about to be freshly killed pork and some other stuff......... it would be a Christmas present and to thank you for your kindness over the last few months."

"Oh Mac. That is so sweet of you....but I'll only accept on one condition and that is that you join us on Christmas Day to eat it ."

Peter's footsteps came thumping down the stairs announcing his arrival at the kitchen door. He had overheard the conversation.

"Oh no! Not Mister Mac for Christmas. You mark my words, he'll be asleep before the pudding arrives!"

It was a second or two before Mac realised that Peter was pulling his leg again.

"Very gud, young fella, very gud. No, it's a gift. You don't have to invite me and Peter's probably right, I'd be asleep pretty quick."

He turned to Peter and said, under his breath, "You'll keep , you little bugger."

"I won't accept it if you don't come. It's as simple as that!" said Christine, herself warming to the banter.
"Deal?" she asked.
"Deal." said Mac.
"Bugger." said Peter and Mac chased him round the kitchen table.

CHAPTER 26

Christmas 1941

The weather improved as Christmas 1941 approached. The cold snap abated and the temperature became quite bearable. The Mayfair Hotel , host to the musicians of the Luftwaffe Band, managed a few decorations in the German style. They were mostly wreaths made from fir branches with four candles attached to mark the four weeks of advent, leading up to a day which was celebrated by both sides of the conflict sharing the same Christian beliefs. On the afternoon of Christmas Eve, the band had been playing carols up at Government House and this usually involved a bit of marching practice thrown in to keep the bandsmen fit enough to have enough puff to blow their instruments and to march in time. Unfortunately a visit to Government House, where the Military Kommandant, Oberst Von Schmidt, was in residence, involved a half mile walk on a level road to the bottom of St Saviours Hill which was accomplished quite easily in ranks of three with the bass drum banging out left, left, left , right, left in time honoured fashion. They then had to ascend another half mile up the steep hill to the bottom gates of the Kommandant's mansion. This caused much amusement to the guards on the gate when everybody arrived red faced, sweaty, and out of breath. Today it was different. Major Brandt, the Kommandant's personal assistant, had sent a troop lorry down to the Mayfair to ferry the boys all the way. They were delighted and responded to the Major's kindness with a brilliant exhibition of Christmas music to the assembled top brass.

During the intermission, Unteroffizier Fritz Doenig made a bee line for Major Brandt with the intention of thanking him for the gift of the magnificent radiogram.

"Major Brandt, can I thank you for the fine gift you sent down

to us."

Major Brandt gently grabbed his arm and led him away into the corner.
"Keep it down, Fritz. Nobody knows it's missing yet. It used to be in that corner over there ."
He nodded in the direction of a mahogany sideboard which now stood in the space previously occupied by the now departed radiogram.
Major Brandt added with a wink and a smile,
"It's mahogany, isn't it? Looks the same, doesn't it?"

Klaus Brandt and Fritz Doenig were friends from kindergarten right through to when they left school. They had ambitions which were stripped away when war loomed in the mid thirties. Doenig smiled.

"You crafty old bugger, Klaus. Thanks anyway. There were some fantastic records in the cabinet and Radio Hamburg came through loud and clear! Any idea who it belonged to?"

"Apparently, my dear Fritz, the previous Lieutenant Governor of Jersey, whose official residence this was before we arrived, had two sons, one of whom worked in Washington for the British Embassy. The other had a furniture business in London. The staff here reckon it arrived a couple of years ago, as a seventieth birthday present for the old man. I thought you lot would appreciate it more than the Oberst who incidentally is unaware of its existence. We have not had this conversation. Understand?"

"What conversation was that, Major?"

They smiled and downed another glass of schnapps before the second half of the performance. The assembled guests had all

tucked into the schnapps and by the time the session closed with the band's version of O Tannerbaum, they were all singing along loudly and merrily. Their duties over for the day and a spare bottle of schnapps hidden in the bowels of the tuba, the band returned to the Mayfair. A huge fir tree had been erected in the ballroom and was being decorated by the kitchen staff. Fritz made sure all the instruments were cleaned before being put in the band store room. He watched quietly from the doorway as bits of crepe paper and string were threaded round the branches of the Tannerbaum. Everybody seemed to be having a good time. His thoughts went to his home town and family and he wondered how they were faring.
"What on earth are we doing here? These people don't want us." he mused.
He knew there was nothing he could do. The great German machine was rolling and the whole world was finding it hard to stop it in its tracks.

Five miles away at La Rocque, Mac had just dropped off the leg of pork at St Kitts before heading back to the Grenadier Inn to have a festive drink with Brian. Christine was preparing it with herbs and spices that she found in the larder. She sliced the skin and rubbed quantities of salt into the cuts .
"That should give us some good crackling."
Peter was helping Sophie decorate the little tree that the Le Ross' had cut from their field. They were having a lot of fun. Her tall, gangly, handsome son had knuckled down after the tragedy of losing his best friend. Despite the horror, he was turning into a humorous, sensitive young man. She could not stop staring at him, the way that mothers do with their sons.
"Your dad would be so proud of you," she said quietly.

"What's that, Mum? I didn't catch that."

"Oh, nothing."

"Why is that, Mum?"

"Why is what, son?"

"Why would he be proud?"

"You *did* hear me then."
There was a pause.

"What?" He looked at her quizzically, grinning.

"Come here, Peter. I need a hug."

He smiled, got up,walked across the room and gave her a hug. Sophie laughed out loud and slowly stood up and took her very first steps towards them. Christine and Peter yelled encouragement. Things weren't so bad after all.

At the Grenadier Inn there was a gathering of the locals. Brian had begged and borrowed whisky, calvados and, together with his own illegal hooch, was definitely in business. The dartboard was in use, barely visible through a thick fug of cigarette smoke. The smell of cigarettes was no longer the romantic aroma of French Gauloises or Gitanes but a fuzzy melange of burning hedgerow leaves as the locals try to outdo each other in their quest for a tobacco substitute.

A dart rebounded from the wire on the bristle board and a collective groan went up. The next dart missed the outer wire and failed to score. The third dart nestled neatly in the double nineteen and three people cheered.

On a table far enough away to eliminate the risk of being impaled by a stray dart, the shove h'apenny board was being primped and polished. At least three hundred years old, according to Brian, the wood had been hewn from an ancient oak tree which had been felled in the Great Storm of 1620. It was actually mahogany and he had bought it just five years ago at George D. Laurens, the sports supplier, in St Helier. Although still young , it had been battered way beyond its years, suffering the indignity of the spillage of the odd pint but the myth had been happily perpetuated. The ha'pennies were old coins of the realm which had been rigorously cleaned and meticulously polished so they shone like new brass, so much so that the dates and king's head on them had been ground down to near invisibility. The aim of the game was to shove the coins up the board to land between and not touching a series of parallel lines etched into the wood. The contestants spent most of the playing time complaining that the opponents coins were touching the bed lines.

In the corner, a couple of old fellows were playing dominoes. Neither contestant was particularly eagle eyed and to an onlooker it appeared as if they were having trouble counting the spots.

A game of crib was erupting by the bar. The two card players sat on high bar stools with the crib board on the bar. The crib board had seen better days. Most of the holes where the pegs were inserted to mark the score, were bunged up with bits of tobacco and ash which had dropped from the lips of the players.

"It's fifteen two, fifteen four, fifteen six, fifteen eight, two for a pair and ONE FOR HIS KNOB! I make that eleven. Savvy?" The wrinkled Frenchman Gaston Guillaume just shrugged his shoulders in typical Gallic fashion, an evil smelling home made cigarette stuck to his bottom lip. He still managed to move the crib peg on fifteen holes without his opponent noticing.

Brian looked on benevolently from behind the bar, amused by

the behaviour of his regulars. He had now been at the Grenadier for twenty years and had not missed a Christmas behind the pumps in all that time. The pumps and barrels had not been used for the last six months since the brewery suspended production and what business he did do depended on what spirits he could buy on the black market. He was also experimenting with his own brand of hooch which he distilled off the premises using potatoes.

Things weren't so bad. The curfew had been extended and everybody was having a good time. Christmas dinner was a few hours away and Mac was on his third large whisky. He made up his mind that this was his last drink as he wouldn't want to upset Christine by turning up in the morning smelling of booze. No, things weren't at all bad He left the party at midnight, his limit of three whiskies had been exceeded by another three. He felt pretty good as he walked home, sniffing at the mild salty air as he went. He fell into bed, hoping that he might nod off and dream about Christine . He dozed off but woke up with a start when his recurring nightmares cranked up yet again. There were bullets whistling overhead and a shell exploded in his trench. The mud was welling up around him, sucking him down.

He rubbed his eyes and stared at the ceiling.

"Fuck it fuck it fuck it fuck it FUCK IT! Just leave me alone."

He adjusted his pillow and lay his head down again.

"Now come on, I want naked ladies, not bloody muck and bullets."

Once again he dozed off only to be wakened by another nightmare. An image of his former fiancee floated into his whisky addled reverie and she was nagging him about his drinking. He could see her angry mouth moving in time with the invective she was delivering. He forced himself awake. This was a trick he had learned a year or two after the nightmares started. They had become so intense that he figured there must be a way of unlocking the horrors that haunted him. One night while his mind was going down the plughole of another muddy trench and with the Hun about to stick a bayonet in his guts before wiggling it around, he realised he was dreaming. Whilst balanced between unconscious and conscious thought , he tried to force himself awake by squeezing his eyelid muscles as if he were squinting with his eyes closed. After what seemed like a huge effort, he managed it. At first he thought it was a fluke but he managed it again and again until eventually when a dream interrupted his sleep, he was ready for it. His brain kicked into consciousness and he woke up. There were a couple of side effects that he didn't like. The first was that when he forced himself awake, he couldn't get back to sleep which was why he tended to read a book or go for a stroll on the beach in the middle of the night. The second side effect he *really* didn't like. The erotic dreams which used to delight him, no longer visited him and when they did, his newly trained brain interpreted them as just another nightmare and he couldn't help but wake up.

He guessed it was a fair trade.

CHAPTER 27

A time for reflection

Back at St Kitts , the day before Christmas had been a quieter affair. Christine woke up thinking of her husband Cliff once again. She never seemed able to dismiss him from her mind. Looking after a two year old was becoming harder the more mobile Sophie became, but Peter had stepped into the breech. She found this a godsend as she enjoyed the moments when she could take her thoughts to another place and 'talk' with Cliff. The last news they had was a Red Cross letter a month ago. As usual, not much information could be gleaned of his whereabouts except that it was hot. Their last theory of the Mediterranean and the Middle East was entirely correct but there was no way that Purser Marinelle could communicate his whereabouts without the letter being heavily censored or even destroyed. Christine wrote back in similar terms with vague references which she hoped he could decipher.

There was a special Christmas Eve service at St Peter La Rocque which the vicar had put on for families with young children. Christine put Sophie in the pram and accompanied by Peter, the three of them walked the few hundred yards up to the church. The atmosphere was very festive inside and was almost full. Carols were sung and the vicar delivered an optimistic lesson extolling the virtues of patience. Sophie was mesmerised by the twinkling lights on the tree as she sat on Peter's lap. The two kids were at opposite ends of the spectrum. Sophie was too young to understand Father Christmas and Peter was way past getting too excited. Nonetheless the evening was enjoyed by all.

By nine on Christmas morning, it was only just light but she was already stoking up the stove and preparing the pork and

vegetables for roasting. Sophie had been up and about for ages and Christine had washed and dressed her before she made a beeline for Peter's room. He was still asleep but not for long with a two year old jumping up and down on his stomach. Mac arrived at midday with presents for everybody , much to Christine's embarassment as she had specifically told him "no presents". She gently chided him.
"Mac.....I told you not to do this."

"Och, nae worries ,pet. They're just things I had lying around."

The things he had lying around were a fishing tackle box for Peter, a wooden pull along toy for Sophie and for Christine, a large seagull sculpture that he had whittled from a piece of wood over the last few months.

"You can always put it on the fire if you run out of fuel."

"I don't think so, Mac," she said as she stroked the smooth wood. "I don't think so.........aw thanks Mac."

She gave him a big hug and a kiss and he blushed.

"Och, away with ye lassie."

At one o'clock the Christmas dinner was on the table. The roast pork sizzled on the plate and they fought for the crackling while wearing silly paper hats. The
radio was tuned in and they listened to the King's Message , hoping for a reference to the Channel Islands. There was none and there were no mentions in any of the request programmes which followed. The mood turned sombre as the disappointment set in.

"Forgotten us again!" said Mac. "Let's get the cards out!" They had a couple of hours of rummy and crib before Mac stood up and said his goodbyes.
"You don't have to go,Mac. You could sleep on the sofa, you know." said Christine.
However Mac had made up his mind , hugged her and Peter in one movement and then kissed Sophie before he was out the door and heading home.

Mac was not a fan of Christmas. To him it was just a watershed at the end of each year when he would make an appraisal of what he had achieved in the last twelve months and he always felt as if he had pulled up short. His mental demons remained with him but he felt that he was coping.
Christine used to like Christmas but this last year was just twelve pages in her calendar that she was happy to screw up and throw on the fire. The festive season just marked another year away from Cliff.
Peter always liked the festive season. Last Christmas had been a good one because he and John Le Ross had just got out of prison and it was one big celebration. This year end he was a quieter person, the death of his best friend weighed heavily on him and he missed his father's guiding hand.
At the Grenadier Inn, Brian was nursing a thick head. The general feeling that week in the pub was that the Germans were not nearly as cocky as they had been last year and that it wouldn't be long before Churchill would come charging over the hill to rescue them all.
Meanwhile at the Mayfair Hotel, the band were contributing to a fine celebration . After church in the morning, a fine meal was cooked up and served by the catering corps. The band then got stuck into their full repertoire of festive music in the ballroom. An extra ration of schnapps had been given out and the occupying forces were having a good time.
Unteroffizier Fritz Doenig, as musical director for the day, then introduced himself publicly to people who already knew him

and said,

"Merry Christmas, everybody. I'm glad you enjoyed that. And now for something completely different. Today we have Werner Turner on the trumpet......"
but he was shouted down.

"....ah, please yourselves, you Philistines. This is Chattanooga Choo Choo!"

With lips and fingers oiled with a little alcohol, the Luftwaffe Band breezed through the tune they had been tinkering with all week. It didn't sound too bad but was lost on the partying soldiers who were enjoying a day off. As the song finished, two people clapped.

"I was right. Bloody Philistines!" said Fritz.

The cheerfulness and optimism of the previous Christmas was beginning to wear off. Soldiers were coming and going, some to the Russian Front and other more lucky ones were returning from it. For the band, it was a cushy number but, realistically, they all wanted to be home with their families and not in this faraway island.

Both sides of the conflict were understandably confused by the situation. However, things were beginning to change. As the year ended, it was clear that the honeymoon period of the German advance across Europe had ground to a halt. Their gains now had to be defended. Occupied mainland Europe was suffering atrocities to the civilian population as the activities of the Resistance were cruelly punished.
The Channel Islanders had little choice but to accept the Occupation and suck up whatever was thrown their way. The Allies had their hands full in a hundred other places more

worthy of intervention. Whilst they still waved the Union Jack, it was obvious that the locals were starting to feel isolated and abandoned.

Hitler's interest in the Islands continued unabated and operation Fortress Jersey was enthusiastically initiated with the arrival of tons and tons of steel and cement . Railway lines were being laid in strategic places in order to distribute these heavy materials to where they were needed.

Down in St Helier, in his Green Street home, Bailiff Basil Dechevaux was cradling a glass of brandy. He had already consumed a couple and he marvelled at the rich colour of the brandy as he held it up to the dim light. He had had a tough year, as they all had. Putting aside the food shortages, he felt he had spent a lot of time banging his head against a brick wall with the Germans. His biggest problem, however, had been the odd commando raids that the British had been mounting in an attempt to make the Islanders feel they were not forgotten. The raids were destabilising all the good diplomacy work that he was doing and threatening the population with reprisals. He managed to persuade the War Office in Whitehall , by one means or another, to effectively leave them alone to work it all out. He had every reason to believe that for the time being, they were better off left alone.

He downed the remains of his brandy in one, poked the fire and went to bed.

CHAPTER 28

Total wireless ban

The mild weather of Christmas 1941 gave way to several cold grey days in the new year and the temperatures plunged. On January 13 a couple of inches of snow fell which, combined with the cold, froze hard on the roads bringing the Island to a standstill.
The sand at La Rocque was now covered in pure white snow and the exposed rocks out to sea took on the appearance of icebergs. An easterly wind blew more snow in from France over a period of a week. Schools were closed and the Christmas break was extended into February. The children loved it, as the school holidays stretched to two months. Food rationing became more formalised as supplies started to dry up. With the permission of the Germans, the Jersey authorities were buying goods from France in order to supplement what the farming community were struggling to supply. The black market raised its ugly head with a vengeance until the Germans prosecuted several shopkeepers and suppliers for overcharging. All of these got three months to three years in a French prison for their troubles. The biggest upshot was that all livestock now had to be individually registered and penalties for unregistered beasts were severe. The black market was not restricted to the locals as the Germans themselves weighed in heavily. There was little that could not be obtained for a price.

The cold weather did nothing for Mac's mood. Like most Scots, he was practically immune to the cold and the wet . The last few years in the warmer climes of the Channel Islands had made him soft and, after the initial landscape-changing snowfalls, he became depressed as the mess left after the thaw reminded him of the horrors of the war trenches. He had a large store of dry logs accumulated over several years of

beachcombing. He now felt the need to make his log shed more secure and this kept him busy for a few days. The long and dark winter evenings did not fly by. He could not wait to welcome the first wild daffodils. As the month of March faded, he kept looking skyward, yearning to see the first swallow arrive on its summer migration north. As he reinforced the log shed, he was careful not to dislodge the swallows' nest glued to the underside of the corrugated iron roof. The nest had been abandoned last Autumn as the swallows guided their new fledglings on the long migration south to Africa. It would certainly be occupied again very soon.
Sure enough on April 9 and much to his jubilation, the first swallow of the year breezed in from a south easterly direction and flew over Mac's house. It was one of those moments that define the change of seasons. As Mac scanned the low water scene from his small east facing garden, the unmistakable speed and swoop of the speedy bird caught his eye. It was the bringer of warmer times, maybe happier and more optimistic times and immediately his mood lifted .He waited an hour or two and the solitary bird was followed by another and then another. Within days there was a mating couple building an extension on his wood shed. Spring had truly sprung.

"Welcome, welcome , my little friends. Just rememberrrrr, the rent is due on the first day of the month!!!!"
He roared with laughter and couldn't wait to tell anybody who would listen.

The swallows were not the only visitors who came by air. These early months saw an increase in the numbers of British and Allied aircraft paying visits to the Channel Islands as they flew en route to or from destinations in Europe. Whether this was a direct order from the War Office was debatable, but the odd raid certainly put the wind up the Germans and anti -aircraft batteries were kept busy at all hours of the day and night. The soldiers themselves were under constant training and were kept very busy. Much to their annoyance, even the Luftwaffe Band had to put in extra hours of sentry duty in the more outlying districts of the island.

Buoyed up by this increased activity, a few of the locals had taken to increasingly bold but relatively minor acts of sabotage. Each time a telephone or telegraph line was deliberately cut, the punishments became more severe. Several youngsters got sentences of three months in French prisons for these offences and one wore a five year sentence for distributing propaganda leaflets. This put local government in an embarrassing position .While the stand-off continued, they could all survive. However, in early June, these continued acts of sabotage pushed the Germans into issuing an order for the surrender of *all* wireless sets. The order from the Feldcommandantur, was published in the Jersey Evening Post and immediately sent the locals into shock. Collections and deliveries of wireless sets both small and large were to be organised by the local parishes and the penalty for possession was set at a minimum of six weeks imprisonment and a fine of 30,000 Reichsmarks. Representations were made to the Feldcommandant, Oberst Gruber, by the Bailiff and various committees but all to no avail. The general perception was that the ban also included the German rank and file who would no longer have access to news of losses and setbacks which became more prevalent as the war played itself out. Nevertheless it was a severe disappointment to all and sundry but had to be lived with.
The situation at Mac's house was typical of many that month. He had two wireless sets and decided that only one needed to be declared for confiscation. One was a Roberts and the other was a Decca, both of which received long wave and medium wave transmissions. Both were fairly chunky pieces of furniture measuring about two foot wide by one foot high and deep but the Decca was slightly smaller and more easily taken apart. Mac chose this one to keep and the other he took to the Parish Hall. Here he joined a long queue of like minded

citizens, all extremely cross at this latest prohibition. There was a large table at the top end of the hall with recently surrendered wireless sets of all shapes and sizes stacked up on the stage behind. Each of the twelve island parishes had a central hall and offices which were manned by honorary parish officials. The elected leader of each parish was called the Connetable or Constable and he was charged by the German civil authority or Feldkommandatur to organise the collection.
After about an hour of shuffling forward inches at a time, Mac made it to the front desk and, with a flourish, surrendered his Roberts Radio in full knowledge that he had another set which was not going to make it to the parish hall anytime soon.

"Bring your receipt back after the war and you can claim it back!" said the parish official to Mac.
"Oh,that's verry gud, verry gud!! I willna be holding ma breath!!!"

He tucked the receipt into his pocket and made for the door.

The parish official, Vingtenier Le Brocq, turned to his superior, Centenier Le Brocq , his brother, and whispered,

"....what did he say?"

"Absolutely no idea!" came the reply.

"Bloody Jock!"

Mac's accent had confused them all once again. He was oblivious to it and continued his passage back home by foot, all the time making plans in his mind as to how he could conceal his other wireless. He cut straight down to the coast road from the Parish Hall and then he took a left turn which took him past La Rocque. To his surprise, there were German soldiers everywhere. Lorries were being unloaded, bags of cement were being piled against the sea wall and great reels of barbed wire were being rolled along the pier wall and deposited at regular intervals. Steel rods and mesh were being piled on the walkway. Hitler's direct order for the defence of Jersey was being implemented with extreme vigour. Within weeks, Platte Rocque House, which stood like a sentinel on the higher ground to the land side of the southern slipway, had become a warren of small concrete bunkers and interconnecting trenches. The wall and walkway which went straight out to sea along the pier had now been secured from attack by enthusiastic use of barbed and razor wire. This kind of operation was happening all over the island. There were two main types of defensive positions. The strongpoints or Stutzpunkts were positioned at vulnerable sites and could be bunkers with large coastal artillery or anti-aircraft guns attached. Most of the islands' many bays were covered by fields of fire from camouflaged bunkers, the scale of which was hard to imagine. The second type was the Widerstandsnest or 'pocket of resistance' and this was the type being constructed at La Rocque. The area surrounding the house built on the historic Platte Rocque, where the British had repelled the French in 1781, eventually became home for seven or eight machine gun nests, eight bunkers plus flame throwers and a secret tunnel to the house. The two slipways were blocked and guarded and anti tank devices were positioned on the foreshore.

Mac was shocked at what he saw. He had been busy around his house and had not ventured out for a few days. There was cement dust everywhere and it looked as if the area had been hit by an unseasonal snowstorm. Before he could question anybody , he was politely and firmly moved on. Over the next few weeks, hundreds of slave workers arrived to carry on the job. They were badly treated by the Germans and often worked

twelve hours on and twelve hours off with maybe a twenty minute break for a bowl of watery soup. The Germans themselves had become nervous and jumpy. When they were not involved in defence construction, they were out somewhere on manoeuvres or shooting practice. Prohibited areas were designated by notices in the Jersey Evening Post. Coastal grassy areas, such as the coastal area north from La Rocque to Gorey Castle, were considered vulnerable points of enemy attack and consequently more mines were laid. Hitler was clearly of the opinion that a British attack was imminent . On this score he was totally wrong.
The confiscation of the wireless sets had been a big blow to local morale but those who were brave enough to risk a term of imprisonment in France, did their best to keep trusted neighbours informed of the war's progress. Mac hid his Decca radio within the confines of his shed. He kept Brian and Christine up with the news and impressed upon them the need to be careful who they spoke to. He didn't want a posse of Krauts on foot patrol dropping in on him for a cup of tea and a quick search of his wood shed at two in the morning. Although low water fishing on foot this summer was restricted, he was still enjoying a fortnightly outing with Brian and Peter in Brian's boat. This continued to bring joy to his soul but he was troubled by the thought that this too would soon be banned. And how would they access the boat now that the two slipways were blocked?
He doubled back down the road to visit the Marinelles where he felt sure that Peter would know more. He knocked and Peter opened the door. He had turned sixteen the week before and had blossomed into a tall, handsome young man. They shook hands.

"Hi, Mister Mac, how are you? Haven't seen you for a week. What's been going on? Come on in."

"Och laddie....I've been chopping wood. I'll drop some round

later for yerr Ma. What's happening round the corner?"
"Cup of bramble tea?" Peter reached for the kettle .
"Aye....aye" said Mac.

"Well, according to Johnnie boy's dad, what's happening at La Rocque is happening all over the island. Mass fortifications everywhere. Slave workers, concrete bunkers, golf courses mined, foreshores mined, it ain't looking good."
At that second Christine came through from the garden with Sophie, now three, at full toddler throttle behind her.
"*Aren't*, not *ain't*, son. *Aren't*! Hello Mac, good to see you. Where have you been?"

"Hello, Uncle Mac," said little Sophie, now able to hold her own in conversation. Mac didn't know who to kiss first but he eventually sorted it out.

"Och, lassie. I've just had a wee trip to the south of France. I had a lovely time. Nah, been chopping wood mostly, courtesy of some cargo that got washed ashore in front of ma hoose. I'll wheelbarrow some over later."
"Ah, thanks Mac."
"Fanks, Mac," mimicked Sophie. They all laughed. This family brought such joy to Mac and he berated himself for leaving it so long from his last visit.
They talked for a good hour and Peter filled him in on what he knew. He seemed to think that so long as the boat was registered for fishing and that the three of them remained as registered fishermen, they would still be able to fish as an occupation and gain access to La Rocque via permits shown at the guarded slipway. They were still required to sell a percentage of the catch to the civil authorities and to the Germans. This was becoming less negotiable the longer the war went on. The good news was that they could still get out in the warm summer weather and they would still be able to trade

their catches. Mac's mood lifted further with this news and , after reading Sophie a story, he got up to go.
"Stay for tea, Mac ? "
"Thanks lassie, but I've got things I must do. Better go. Thanks anyway."
He said his goodbyes and walked off past the slipways, observing all the new fortifications as he went. When he got home, he listened to the six o'clock news on the Decca wireless, with a small glass of finest Scotch whisky in his hand. He sank into his favourite chair and looked out of his window towards the rising tide. The shadows were lengthening at the end of another sun filled day.

"Fuck you, Jerry. Fuck you."

He could feel the black dog of depression nibbling at his ankles.
He was annoyed about his wireless set and he had been taken by surprise at the speed of the work being carried out around the coast and particularly at La Rocque . Hitler's orders were being swiftly and efficiently carried out. However, there was one order that still remained buried and that was the one that required the Channel Islands to give up 2000 hostages in retaliation for Churchill's little German hostage- taking foray into Persia. Almost a year after it had been given, it still lay dormant. A meeting in neutral Switzerland concerning prisoner exchanges accidentally brought it chillingly into the limelight in September 1942 when a Swiss delegate tried to arrange an exchange of prisoners and listed possible candidates from both sides. On that list were the Channel Island deportees which immediately brought the absence of action to the attention of the Fuhrer. He railed against his subordinates when he discovered nothing had been done and , after threats of execution, the deportation orders were carried out immediately. A can of worms was about to be opened.

CHAPTER 29

Shock for the band

Life with the Luftwaffe Band had become hectic. The first year of occupation had been a learning process of how to handle the task of dealing with the English people. The locals would have been aghast at being categorised as "English" for, whilst they had pledged allegiance to the British Crown since the signing of the Magna Carta in the eleventh century, the islands were self governing and fiercely independent. Jersey was less than twenty miles from the French coast and its legal system relied heavily on the French language and yet.....and yet....the ninety miles or so of rough sea to the south coast of England had always seemed more worthy of the navigational risks. On balance, Westminster held sway but, despite its influence, the system of government in Jersey was different and decidedly quirky.

Unteroffizier Fritz Doenig was second in command of the Band and had been blessed by having a very mellow and understanding commanding officer in the figure of Major Willy Becker. Becker wore a monocle and was a stickler for discipline. He was in his early fifties and had seen service in the Great War. He realised early on in the piece that his only safe bet was to sign up for the second world war as a musical director. German bands of the thirties had been propaganda machines, playing the sort of military music that the German Wehrmacht could march to and be proud of. This feeling overflowed on to the common people and they came in their droves to hear the bands play. Becker was rarely found at practice, preferring to command from the confines of his comfortable billet at the Mayfair Hotel whilst his number two, Fritz Doenig, exercised almost total control of the Luftwaffe musicians. Becker could easily administer the more formal

agenda of events which included concerts and parades in St Helier and the increasing number of servicemen funerals, both friend and foe. Most of the dead were being washed up on the beaches as a result of naval skirmishes in the adjacent Bay of St Malo, miles to the south. He made sure that the band were well drilled in marching and appearance. The band members were not keen on the marching drills which were difficult enough without having to accommodate cumbersome instruments whilst keeping in step. There were at least four other German bands on the island at that time and all the others belonged to the Heer (Army) and had slightly different uniforms. Becker and Doenig had no doubts that their group was the best.
Doenig's love affair with the Glenn Miller sound that he discovered with the arrival of the radiogram from Government House, continued unabated. The needle ground down the grooves of Chattanooga Choo Choo and he scanned the radio waves for more broadcasts of his favourite artist. His best chance came with the BBC Home Service which had weekly request programmes. Occasionally he was in the right place at the right time and when he heard a new Miller tune, he was ecstatic. He was also having to keep a low profile with the radiogram as he had heard a rumour that the locals were not the only ones to be banned from possessing a wireless. He managed to obtain a pair of headphones from a friend in Signals and with this ruse he managed to convince any interested passer by that he was listening to a record.
Across the Atlantic in America , his favourite composer and arranger was busy too.

Glenn Miller, by all accounts, was a very self contained man. He had spent the nineteen thirties playing trombone in various American bands before turning to the more disciplined skill of arranging the music. He was more organised and less spontaneous than his fellow players. Frustrated by their behaviour but able to gauge their abilities, he assembled his own outfit but quickly discovered that the financial and physical restraints were overwhelming. He had to arrange the gigs, arrange the music and lead a band of hard drinking, badly behaved but talented artists into a well turned out and effective unit. With almost military precision, he weeded out the prima donnas and his own edict of 'anybody who gets out of line, out he goes' seemed to work well. He spent as much time on juggling the cash flow as he did on organising the band. Many times he would find his pockets full of cash, receipts and invoices. As leader he would pay the band members a wage in cash but only after collecting the fee for the night's performance. He was a busy man .

The band developed a sound and in the late thirties broke up once or twice only to reform with different personnel. By 1938 the Glenn Miller Band was making slow progress and almost went broke . Miller was a determined character and weathered the storm. In May 1939, they made their debut at the Glen Island Casino. Glen Island was a holiday resort on an island overlooking Long Island Sound, connected to mainland New York by a low bridge. The Casino championed the Big Band Sound and many a reputation was built upon performances there. The acoustics were also excellent, so good in fact that there was a direct radio link to the National Broadcasting Company. With these successful dates under their belt, the band's success mushroomed and their appearance fees went up tenfold. In one two week period, they performed 140 times. The recording of Chattanooga Choo Choo sold over a million copies and Glenn Miller received the very first ever gold disc. Hollywood came to call and he headed west to make Sun Valley Serenade and , in early 1942, Orchestra Wives.
The outbreak of war in Europe troubled Miller as he knew that, sooner or later, America would be drawn into the fray. The band played on the radio especially for the armed forces and he sponsored a thousand dollars worth of prizes on a weekly basis from his own pocket. The band played on but Uncle Sam started to claim one or two members for the draft. He himself

registered for the draft and, despite being initially rejected because of his age (he was 38), he was accepted to train as Captain. A. Glenn Miller.
It was one of these recordings, relayed by the BBC, that Fritz was listening to. Headphones on, back to the wall in a leather upholstered seat, local newspaper on the table, he was relaxation personified. He was suddenly aware of a kerfuffle in the foyer of the hotel and soldiers were rushing to and fro. He disengaged himself from the headphones and replaced them in the cabinet, locking the small door. He made his way quickly to the foyer where he encountered Gunter Muller coming down the large staircase.

"*Gunter! Gunter! What's happening? Is the war over?*"

He realised immediately by the look on Gunter's face that his humour was misplaced.

"*It's Major Becker, Fritz. He's bloody well shot himself. Blood everywhere up there. What a mess. I was speaking to him at breakfast. He was right as rain. ....*"

Fritz was stunned and found it hard to speak. He made his way immediately up to the second floor where the Major had his room. The medics were carrying a stretcher in. He looked in and saw the body in the armchair surrounded by a bloody mess .There was a letter on the coffee table next to the chair he had been sitting in. Major Becker had put his service pistol gun barrel into his mouth, pulled the trigger and blown his brains out.
Fritz took in this horrific scene with a coldness which surprised him. The room had always looked so neat and tidy when he had meetings with his commanding officer. It was still tidy but the blood and brain spattered books on the shelves along the wall hinted at a story as yet untold. Taking charge, he made sure the

medics carried out their task with dignity and respect. Becker's body was removed and he cleared the room of onlookers. He read the letter that lay on Becker's table .He then blocked off the staircase until the Feldpolitzei arrived a few minutes later. He gave a statement to the investigating officer, then went quietly down the stairs, through the foyer and out into the street. He walked for an hour before returning to the hotel.

At the inquest, two days later, it transpired that the letter held the answer to the reason for his sudden decision to kill himself. His Luftwaffe pilot son, Hans, had been killed on a bombing mission over Portsmouth Docks on the south coast of England. The hand written missive was from Hans' squadron leader and gave details of the raid which had taken place two weeks ago. Hans had been flying a Heinkel He 111 with orders to bomb the docks at Portsmouth. Coming in from the south east over the sea, his plane had been hit by anti aircraft fire and, laden with fuel, exploded in mid air. Becker had already lost his wife in a car accident just before the outbreak of war and this news had been the devastating last straw.
The funeral was a well attended affair as he was a popular man. The German cemetery was in the beautiful churchyard at St Brelade on the south west coast of Jersey. It was a strange occasion . There were a few curious locals standing by the entrance to the cemetery and about 500 German troops and officers, all immaculately turned out, lined the road in neat rows. The church nestled in the western corner of St Brelade's Bay and the view back over the sea was stunning on a beautiful late summer's day. Anti tank structures on the beach and a new anti invasion concrete sea wall reminded those assembled that there was still a war on and that Major Becker was no longer part of it.
After the brief service inside the quaint old Fisherman's Chapel, Fritz gave a superb unaccompanied rendition of Dvorak's Ninth Symphony on the clarinet. It was unaccompanied because the rest of the band, one by one,

crumbled into a useless blubbering mess as Fritz' clarinet soared its way through the tune, better known as "Going Home". Fortunately, discipline returned when the coffin was carried the hundred yards from the chapel to the burial plot in the cemetery to the accompaniment of the German Army Band of the 243rd division. Fritz had asked for their back up and they were only too pleased to provide it. They were billeted just a few hundred yards east along the coast road at the Golden Sands Hotel.

The day was torture and the band were free of duties when they returned to the Mayfair. Fritz collapsed into a chair and tried to gather his thoughts. He just hoped his new commanding officer would be as good as the last one.

He gathered the rest of the musicians in the ballroom and sarcastically thanked them all for their efforts in the chapel. He dispensed a tray load of half filled brandy glasses. They raised them in a toast.

"*Auf Wiedersehen, Willy. Auf Wiedersehen, good friend.*" said Fritz.

With one voice all thirty bystanders joined in.

"*Auf Wiedersehen, Willy. Auf Wiedersehen, good friend.*"

Then they all got drunk.

CHAPTER 30

Deportation begins

When Hitler got wind of the lack of action on his October 1941 order for the deportation of 2000 Channel Islanders, Oberst Gruber, the Feldcommandant of Jersey, had been severely reprimanded by his superiors in Berlin. Whilst pleading ignorance of the original order, his card had been well and truly marked. In order to avoid retribution, Gruber sprang into action and prepared to deliver the official notices within 24 hours . On September 15, 1942, the Germans gave publication to the following.

NOTICE

By order of higher authorities, the following British subjects will be evacuated and transferred to Germany :

a) Persons who have their permanent residence not on the Channel Islands, for instance those who have been caught here by the outbreak of war;

b) All those men not born on the Channel Islands and 16 to 70 years of age who belong to the English people, together with their families.

Details will be given by the Feldcommandantur 515.

Der Feldcommandant Gruber, Oberst.

There was no escape for the Jersey people. The provision of lists of residents by the parishes to the Germans over the last two years had been given freely because most of the information could be gleaned from the Rates List so there was really little point in putting obstacles in the way. For the last few months the population were also required to carry identity cards . The questions were how many people would go ? and how soon?

Both these questions were answered immediately and with devastating consequences.
2000 men, women and children in total were to go to camps in Germany. The first shipment was to leave within 24 hours. The impact of the notice was severe and understandably induced a state of panic. The Germans were quickly knocking on doors distributing notices to unlucky residents to register at the docks the next day .
Many questions were being asked of the local government. What were they doing? How long had they known? Was there any form of appeal? Where were the deportees going? Why was it all so sudden?
Rumours flashed around the island but there appeared to be no chance of rescinding the order. The speed at which it had been delivered and carried out had taken everybody by surprise. The Bailiff, Basil Dechevaux, had been up at College House as soon as he had had a sniff of it. There was lot of table thumping with the Feldkommandant but to no avail. The order would stand. Gruber was adamant. He had Berlin on his case. Dechevaux reminded the Germans of the deal that had been done two years previously.

"In case of peaceful surrender, the lives, property and liberty of peaceful inhabitants are solemnly guaranteed."

Gruber simply reminded him that it was wartime and that '*Befehl ist befehl*' which simply meant that 'orders were orders' . In his heart and mind he knew he was doing a bad thing but there was no way he was going to communicate this to Dechevaux. He had already buried the order for a year and there was little more he could do but finally carry it out.

The fall-out was instant and horrifying. The Marinelles were safe as all were born in Jersey. Brian Le Rouge from the Grenadier was also fine. Mac's name, mysteriously, did not appear on any list. Roger and Eileen Le Ross were not so lucky. Despite living forty five of his fifty years in Jersey, he had been caught in the net by having his place of birth as Portsmouth, England. He had met his wife whilst in the Merchant Navy in Devon. No amount of wrangling from the Jersey Government or the Harbour Office where he worked, could alter the published list one iota. They had a knock on the door on the evening of Tuesday September 15 just a few short hours after the official notice had appeared in the Jersey Evening Post. Roger answered it to find a posse of both German and parish officials standing there. A German sergeant handed him a document which read...

Roger Le Ross 145 Eileen Le Ross 146 John Le Ross 147
Sunny Farm Grouville
In pursuance of the Higher Command, British subjects are to be evacuated and brought to Germany.
You have to appear, therefore, on Wednesday, September 16 not later than 4p.m. at the Garage, Weighbridge, St Helier, wife and minor children.
You have to take with you all papers proving your identity.
It is necessary to outfit yourself with warm clothes, strong boots and provisions for two days, meal dishes, drinking bowl and, if possible, with a blanket.
Your luggage must not be heavier than you can carry and must bear a label with your full address.
You must take with you an amount of money not exceeding RM10 in German notes for each person.
All valuables must be deposited with the banks. Keys of houses must be handed to the Constables of each parish.
Should you fail to obey the order, sentence by court martial shall be effected.

Der Feld Kommandant Gruber, Oberst

"All three of you must report by four o'clock tomorrow afternoon. I'm sorry to be bring such bad news." said the sergeant whose English was good enough to convey the fact that the task he had to carry out was not one that he had undertaken easily.

Roger stood there reading the notice and, after a few seconds silence, he said, "Well, I'm afraid there are only two of us. My son John is dead, a victim of your war, but I'm sure my wife and I would like a nice holiday."

The outside party shuffled uneasily at Roger's black humour and double checked their duplicate lists before a mumbled apology came from the church verger who had been hijacked into accompanying the Doomsday Brigade. "Sorry , Roger. That shouldn't have happened."

"You understand what you have to do ?" said the German sergeant.

Roger glanced up and down the document, then nodded.

"Four o'clock tomorrow then."

"Yawol, mein Fuhrer !" said Roger, clicking his heels together. The sergeant just looked blankly back. He had a miserably thankless task to do and was not in the mood to react.

"I am sorry, Mister Le Ross, but orders are orders. Befehl ist befehl. "

The party shuffled off and Roger stepped back into the house and closed the door. How was he going to tell Eileen? She was clinically depressed after John's untimely and premature death.

They had less than twenty four hours to organise a life change. After a few minutes of reflection, he broke the news to his wife who was sitting in the kitchen. He loved her dearly but she was a changed woman after their terrible loss. She did nothing but weep most of the day .It was now over a year since that terrible day which dislocated their lives for ever. She ached inwardly and it wouldn't go away. The next few hours would be sheer purgatory.
They were not alone in their shock at this terrible order which was delivered like a hammer blow. The wireless surrender, and the indignation that arose from it , paled into insignificance alongside this new order. Families were thrown into panic when they realised there was no escape. Rumour followed rumour as the final destination of the deportees was discussed over the garden fence. Were they really being sent to camps in Poland instead of Germany or if they did finish up in Germany, were they to be used as human shields and housed in vulnerable areas where the RAF would be bombing ? Maybe they were to be used as hostages, ready to be shot at Hitler's whim. The immediacy of the unfolding events and the subsequent uncertainty threw everybody into a spin.

For the unlucky ones, the morning of the next day was spent saying goodbyes to friends and neighbours. At Sunny View, Roger was still consoling Eileen as they collected what possessions were required. Christine, Peter and Sophie were there first thing in the morning to help and do what they could but it was a struggle. Other people arrived and, at an opportune moment when the mood had lightened a tad, the Marinelles said their tearful goodbyes. It was a terrible moment which was being re-enacted island wide. The deportation order was a dagger to the communal heart. The next day, many marriages between young English girls and Jersey boys took place. The girls, by virtue of their birthplace, had to go.

Elsewhere suitcases were packed and transport to the docks

was being arranged. Many chose to check in at one of the eleven outlying parish halls where buses would take them to the Weighbridge Garage for registrations and cursory medical examinations. Three German and three local doctors examined and sent families with young children back to their homes. Mrs Le Cocq, a widow from the parish of St Ouen, was deemed unfit by virtue of the tuberculosis that she didn't realise she had. From two o'clock on Wednesday September 16, crowds in their hundreds congregated near the Weighbridge to give their friends a good send-off and to show the Germans they were not to be cowed . It was more like a football crowd with people shouting and singing. The streets were also lined with German troops who were clearly expecting trouble.
Local government, whilst powerless to effect any change in the deportation order, did their level best to supply a few necessities and luxuries to the unlucky deportees. Refreshments were served. St John's ambulance members were to hand to administer minor medical aid. Eventually from the first eight hundred or so on the list, 280 unfortunates embarked on two vessels bound for France with onward passage to Germany by train. The remainder were charged to return at the same time the next day. There seemed to be no respite from the emotional turmoil. Many of these managed to stay with nearby friends in St Helier but others chose to return to their parishes where they had to reclaim their house keys from the Constables before they could get home.
At ten o'clock that evening, after the boats had left, an officer dealing with the registrations put in a telephone call to the Feldkommandant at College House.
"*This is Major Franz Mollin. Could you put me through to the Feldkommandant himself please. It is important and he is expecting my call......*"

"Yes, Major. This is the Feldkommandant. Is their trouble?"

"Yes sir. There are two missing. Number 145 and 146 from

Grouville parish."

"Okay Major. You know the drill. Contact the Constable of Grouville, knock him up if you must. Then accompany him to the house and find out what's going on. It may be a simple mistake but we cannot afford to let it go. Take Sergeant Schultz and a squad. He issued the original notices in Grouville so he should know the way. Let me know immediately. I shall be up until two in the morning."

"Yes sir."

Gruber felt he had to be absolutely correct as he knew he had gone back on his word to the Jersey people in issuing the deportation order. The delicate balance that existed between occupied and occupier had been upset and he had to tread carefully. However he remained very much in charge and figured he had to do what he had to do.
It took Mollin a few minutes to assemble a squad, a lorry and a motorcycle messenger before collecting the Constable from his farmhouse. At nearly midnight they arrived at Sunny View to enquire of the whereabouts of Numbers 145 and 146 , Roger and Eileen Le Ross. The house was in darkness and no amount of knocking could rouse the occupants. Maybe they had gone into hiding. With the lorry shining its headlights on the front door, it was broken into quite easily and the electric lights were switched on. The squad led by Sergeant Schultz shuffled noisily into the front room and immediately let out a collective gasp. There was blood everywhere.
"*Oh shit.....oh shit!"* said Schultz, looking round the room ,*"what a mess."*

Roger sat slumped in an armchair. There was a newspaper on his lap. The gunshot wound to the back of his head bore

witness to the fact that he had been murdered. Eileen lay dead at his feet with a bullet through the side of her head and her finger curled around the trigger of a British Army issue handgun. They had been dead for a few hours. Major Mollin sent the soldiers outside to wait in the truck until further orders while he sorted the tragedy out with the Constable. He also sent the motorcyclist back to College House with a message for the Feldcommandant.
This left just four people in the room, Mollin, Schultz, Constable John Le Grand and the next door neighbour who had been roused from his bed by all the noise. From this point on, Le Grand took over and contacted a doctor in order to certify that they were dead and get the bodies moved to the General Hospital in St Helier. There was no note left behind and they concluded that Eileen shot Roger in the back of the head and then shot herself . The neighbour, Philip Leyton, who lived fifty yards up the road, thought that he had heard a car backfiring at about 4 p.m. . He said that Eileen had been extremely agitated when he had seen them both in the morning when saying their goodbyes. This was at the same time as the Marinelles had visited.
After a few minutes Major Mollin and Sergeant Schultz left Le Grand to complete the investigation.

"Is there anything I can do, John, while we wait for the doctor. Shall I make some tea perhaps?" said Leyton. They knew each other as old schoolfriends.
"Great idea, Phil, but see if you can find anything stronger. I feel in need of a little sustenance."

The two of them walked through into the kitchen. There were two cups and saucers on the table with a teapot alongside. Philip lifted it and realised it was full. The contents were cold and there was a home made scone on a plate next to the cups. "Good grief, John." said Philip. " She had only just made a pot of tea. Talk about the balance of your mind being disturbed."

Le Grand shuffled round the table. "Yes, it doesn't take long. One moment of madness and it's all over. God knows where the pistol came from. "

"Eileen had been in a terrible state since young John died down by the harbour last year. She couldn't have any more kids after complications with *his* birth and she went rapidly downhill. Roger seemed to be coping alright. Why did she have to take him with her?"

Le Grand was filling the kettle by the kitchen sink. "I guess it's because that was the only way she felt she could be with her husband *and* her son, if they were all dead. Bit bizarre but I have seen it before. You do when you're the Constable. I have to deal with all the sudden deaths in the parish. Just my luck to be doing the job when the war broke out. "
Just then a car pulled up outside and a door slammed . They heard the sound of footsteps on the gravel.

"That'll be the doctor," said Le Grand. "Oh well, Phil, no peace for the wicked. Can you make that three teas?

CHAPTER 31

Goodbyes

The scenes at the docks in St Helier were repeated the next day when 436 people left on a single vessel in the evening. The crowds waving them off began to get unruly and the Germans cleared the roadways around the Weighbridge which stood at the town end of the harbour. The throng of two or three thousand then moved up the hill and found a vantage point on Pier Road which skirted the unhappy scene from some hundred feet higher. On a fine autumn evening the noise they made carried a long way in the still air. Amongst all the heartache, this impotent show of dissent in the face of the enemy was the only way they could find to deal with it.
A second vessel was to have left with a further 300 people on board but, after an inspection by Gruber himself, it was declared unfit and the 300 were told to return in a weeks' time. This caused further problems because households had been locked up and provisions simply given away. Clearly the deportations would continue until the requisite number had left.
On the Saturday, most of the parish of Grouville said goodbye to Roger and Eileen at the tiny church of St Peter La Rocque where just over a year ago, they had buried young John. This time there were no emerging butterflies. Seemingly as part of some sublime message , soon to be departing swallows gathered like a guard of honour perched on the telephone wires which stretched up the lane from the northern slipway at La Rocque. The congregation which could get inside the church sung their hearts out. There were less tears this time. The shock of the deportations and the circumstances of the deaths of Roger and Eileen had somehow numbed the people. They were becoming hardened to the tragedies of war and there seemed to be a funeral every other week. Roger and Eileen's relatives were all on mainland England so the congregation was mostly from Roger's workplace at the Harbour Office and the

surrounding parishes. Mac got there early and reserved seats for Christine and Peter but down the road at St Kitts, the arrangements were about to change.
Christine was getting Sophie ready to go when Peter said,

"Do you mind if I don't go,Mum ?"

Christine stopped buttoning her coat and said quietly,
"Of course not, son........of course not."

She went over to where he was sitting on a kitchen chair and put her arm around his shoulder. She was very upset herself but determined to go to the funeral.
"You do whatever feels right for you. Will you look after Sophie though? "
Peter let out a sigh of relief. He thought his mother would be upset. His best friend's parents were dead and he couldn't change that. In his youthful mind he had suffered intensely at John's funeral and did not want a second dose.
"Okay, ma. I can do that," he said quietly.

He tried to squirm out of the way but Christine managed to plant a big wet kiss on his cheek. He retreated into the back garden to play with his kid sister who was delighted she could stay at home with her hero. She was now four years old and it was only two weeks since she had had her birthday party. Mac had produced a few hard-to-get ingredients from his bartering hat and Christine had produced the finest cake on Sophie's special day. Up to that time, things seemed to be jogging along quite nicely and those with hidden wireless sets spread the more optimistic news of advances by the Allied forces. There was an increasing amount of aerial activity and it was clear that the Germans were spooked into thinking that a direct attack was imminent. However, over in Whitehall, the Channel Islands remained just a few insignificant blobs on the war map and scarcely raised a murmur at Question Time in the House of Commons. The aerial activity was just playful visits by Allied pilots usually returning home from missions with excess ammunition and energy to get rid of. It helped lift the spirits of the Jersey people to know that at least someone had not forgotten them.

Mac and Peter had passed a reasonably pleasant summer when their fishing allowed. Together with Brian from the pub, they were now all registered fishermen with a registered boat. This had probably kept Mac off the dreaded deportation lists but his complete lack of willingness or ability to fill in any form over the last few years had also worked in his favour. The house was still registered on the rates list as being occupied by his late aunt. Her advanced age meant she was too old to be deported but, better still, the seemingly unknown fact that she had been dead for nearly twenty years was the clincher. Mac kept his mouth shut very tight on the whole affair and carried on fishing. With their permits they could gain access to La Rocque Harbour via the northern slip with no problem. There were considerably more troops in the area and the percentage of the catch which had to be donated to the Germans was constantly being increased. Our low water men were up to the challenge and had soon built a false floor in the boat which, by unscrewing two hidden butterfly nuts, could hide what needed to be hidden. If the catch was a good one, most of it was hidden and the boat was trailered up the lane by tractor for "repairs" after the trip. If it was an average or poor day, the boat was simply moored on the beach below the pier and the catch was registered with whoever was on guard at the slipway. The Germans were then responsible for getting the catch to the fish market in St Helier.
There was just the one good day that summer when on an overcast day in July, Mac and Peter hit on a shoal of mackerel a couple of miles offshore. Brian was absent that day with business in St Helier. Hand held lines with feathers were the

order of the day and they caught plenty, pulling in over two hundred fish in the space of two hours. This was what they called a 'trailer day'. It took but a few minutes to pull up the false floor and deposit half the catch in the six inch gap below the deck. Mac and Peter made an odd couple. There were four decades between their respective ages but they were buddies. Peter drew on Mac's experiences and Mac loved Peter for his unfettered youth and his ability to insult the older man without causing offence. Mac was Peter's keeper but was quick to remind him that he was not his father. He could advise but he was no substitute for the real thing. He made sure Peter spoke about his father and they had discussions about where he might be and when he would return.

So life moved on quietly that summer until they were refused permission to trailer the boat up the slipway for 'repairs'. The false deck remained undiscovered but was now ineffective. They continued fishing with the limited amounts of fuel they could obtain.

The Germans worked manically to build Festung Jersey by pouring huge amounts of concrete and steel into the coastline. The equilibrium was maintained until the dreadful day of September 15, 1942 when Hitler's deportation orders had been finally carried out. For those who had been deported to Germany, there lay ahead three years of hardship and cold winters. Whilst not suffering the deprivations and depravity of the so called 'death camps', they were accommodated in internment camps with their liberty denied and the stressful prospect of being used by Hitler as bargaining chips somewhere down the line. Those that remained in Jersey on the deportation list remained like prisoners waiting for the hangman. Over the months of October and November, they had to turn up at the Weighbridge not knowing whether the boat would actually sail or not. If it did, then it was a lottery as to how many would get on board and how many would have to come back in a couple of days. The uncertainty was draining and one or two more suicides were sadly recorded as a result. Nonetheless another 560 people left on September 29. It appeared that the Germans had run out of young non- Jersey born single men to deport as now widows and young single women had now run out of luck. Indigenous Jersey lads also began to appear on the list, mostly repeat offenders found guilty of petty offences. Already the goal posts were moving.

Despite all this, local government continued to govern and its trading committees continued to trade. Subsidies for certain foodstuffs were introduced and withdrawn as supplies fluctuated. The sea link with France was vital as the Purchasing Committee juggled to keep the island fed. However, the dreadful treatment of the slave workers toiling to build concrete bunkers was a constant reminder that things could be a lot worse if the invaders were given half a chance.

CHAPTER 32

October 1942

Mac's swallows left of their own accord in early October. Early one morning, while checking on his woodshed, he looked up at the nest which was muddily glued to the underside of the iron roof. What had once been a squawking mass of greedy beaks was now strangely quiet. The three or four young fledglings had been out and about for several weeks and were now fully independent. Hundreds of swallows had been gathering and twittering on the telephone wires for days, as if collecting their thoughts before the long migration. The restlessness seemed to have got the better of them and today they were no longer to be seen or heard. He looked out to sea and silently said farewell. He was sad to see them go but he knew they would be back in the Spring and they would bring joy to his heart again.

All was not doom and gloom however. Whilst the swallows preferred the warmer climes of Africa, autumn heralded birds which flew in from further north. Varieties of geese would soon be wintering on the rocky shores and other stragglers would sometimes drop in to rest during a storm. Mac was alert to them all. He immersed himself in the seasons and noticed even the slightest of changes.

Things were not too bad despite the fact that he was surrounded by 'bloody Krauts' , all busy working on or building defence positions along the coast. As a registered fisherman, he could gain pedestrian access to the boat on most days to check on the boat. He attempted conversation with a couple of the slipway guards who spoke a little English and managed to find out that the tenants of the offshore towers, Seymour and Icho , had been told to collect their belongings so that the towers could be fortified as extra defence positions. The tenants had leases on the offshore buildings which simply enabled them to stay the odd night for recreational purposes. Mac knew that no-one was using the towers anyway for fear of all the mines that had

allegedly been laid on the foreshore.
"Achtung, minen ?" said Mac pointing in an arc from left to right. He was probing for any bits of information.
The guard looked confused and just shrugged his shoulders as if to say that
he didn't know. Mac left it there but persevered the next time when a more approachable guard was on duty. They met on the sand at the bottom of the slipway and exchanged greetings.

"Good morning, Mac." said Private Klaus Bucholtz.

"Guten morgen, Klaus ."

The guard grinned as he figured this was a breakthrough. Mac was usually pretty gutteral with his expletive-ridden greetings. 'Fuck off kraut' was the very least any member of the Wehrmacht could expect. Klaus couldn't blame him either. He was getting fed up with all the training and guard duties which seemed to go on round the clock day in day out. Nice place as Jersey was, he wanted to be home with his family in Germany and not policing a hostile community while waiting for the Allies to invade.

"Next week we have to guard out there. Is it a good place? " said Klaus, gesturing towards Seymour Tower.

Mac raised his eyebrows in surprise.
"The tower? Are you sure? Well, it's no five star hotel .
But there are mines out there?..........yes? "

"Nein. No. The foot road to the tower is .....er.......empty? The path is ...er...clear. We go this afternoon so if I go boom you can say........ I was ...er....not correct !"

They both laughed and the conversation was brought to an end by a German sergeant bellowing from the top of the slipway. Klaus straightened up and marched back to the road. Mac continued down the sand to the lee of the pier and pretended to check on their boat moorings, all the time assimilating the facts he had just gleaned. It had just turned noon so he decided he was going to hang around until Klaus and his mates took their afternoon march out to the tower. It was low tide in three hours and already the landscape was turning rocky as far as the eye could see.
At two o'clock, the German squad of twenty men assembled on the sand by the southern slip , laden with spades, buckets, garden forks and pick axes. The big sergeant then marched them down to the rocks and past the pier. They then followed a line of sight towards the tower and almost immediately, much to Mac's amusement, they hit trouble. They were climbing over rocks and through gullies with all this equipment and getting nowhere fast. After a few minutes, a single soldier was making his way back. It was Klaus and eventually he called out ,
"Mac, Mac, can you help please. You know the way out to the tower?"

Mac thought about it for a millisecond and headed towards Klaus. He had a golden opportunity to find out where the mines were and what the Krauts were up to. With Klaus interpreting, he set the squad on the right path. For the uninitiated the way out to the tower was not as the crow flies, it was a route that twisted between sand banks and rocky outcrops. Soon they were flying along. The sun was trying to prove that, despite it being autumn, it was still around and with little or no wind about, it was a splendid afternoon. Their army jackboots scrunched on the gravelly sand and just for a bit of fun, Mac started singing. De dee dee dee, de dee dee dee, de dee dee dee dee dee. It was the tune to 'The Happy Wanderer' and within seconds the squad were belting it out in German as they shuffled along. Mac grinned as he knew it would start them off.

Within half an hour they were at the foot of Seymour Tower . A ramp of sand and gravel led to a rusty metal ladder which stretched dizzily upward to the solid front door . The sergeant produced the key and all the tools were taken inside to be stored .
Klaus took instructions from the Sergeant in German and then did a rough translation for Mac.
"My sergeant says thank you for your help. You can....er....go now as we have some work to do. We shall come back in one hour or maybe two."

"Nae problem, Klaus. Make sure you leave here before four o'clock. The sea is very fast." replied Mac, gesturing with his fingers. "It comes fast behind your back."

"Ok. I shall tell my sergeant."

"Right. I'm off. Auf Wiedersehen." said Mac and waved as he turned and set off towards the beach.
Under his breath, he muttered "hope your dogs have kittens and you bloody drown" but his words trailed away into the unlistening air. He took a slight deviation and checked a gully he hadn't disturbed for a month or two. Pulling aside some weed, he stuck his hand into a hole and got it nipped for his troubles. Whatever it was, it wouldn't let go until he yanked it out and smashed it on a rock. His fingers hurt like hell but the one good sized lobster was worth it. He wrapped some seaweed around the dead crustacean and continued the trudge back to the pier. He always loved the 'going out' with its expectation of finding unsuspecting fishy prey. It was the 'going back' he was never keen on. Today was no exception but he kept himself interested by deviating up this gully and that in the knowledge that no mines would have been buried in such tricky terrain. He was right on this score .The danger seemed remote. However,

at that moment, a bullet pinged into the rock about five yards from his head, scattering rock splinters in all directions. He ducked down and then realised that by its trajectory, it had been fired from where he had just been - the tower.
"Bloody ratbags, using me for target practice ! Thanks for showing us the way, Mac. My arse!"
A few more volleys pinged into the same spot and Mac made his way down the gully, using the high walls for protection. He rock hopped his way back, breaking cover only when necessary. Out at Seymour Tower, the big burly German sergeant was chuckling and congratulating himself .

"I really put the wind up that Englander! That'll teach him to dawdle."

He had found his way to the topmost point of the tower from where Mac was an easy target as he zigzagged between the rocks. Mac, naturally, was not amused by the incident and thought later that the 'going back' had at least been interesting. He made his way to shore and was home within an hour. On arrival he put the kettle on the gas stove in order to make a cup of tea. He unfolded his map on the kitchen table and made a few notes in pencil. Cup in hand, he settled with a lurch into his armchair, drank the tea and nodded off to sleep. He was wakened at about seven o'clock by a knock at the door.
"Wake up you Scottish git!" came the voice from outside.

"Lovely to see you too, Brian." he said even before he had opened the door .
"What's up? Have ye run out of whisky? It wouldn't be the first time."

"I am hearing cries from out towards Seymour. Sounds like a couple of Krauts have been cut off by the tide. Come out to your garden and have a listen."

Mac opened the door and they both walked round to the sea side of the little house.
Brian was right, he could here the distant cries.
"Sounds like they are stranded in the direction of Fragile Rock." said Brian.

"What are they doing? It's bloody nearly dark. I suppose we should see if we can help. I'll fill you in on the happenings of the afternoon on the way down to the pier."

By the time they reached the slipway it was dark and there didn't seem to be much action in the way of a rescue attempt. The guard could not understand what Brian and Mac were on about.
" Can you hear their voices. They are shouting for help." Mac cupped his hand to his ear. "Listen...... help,help! Hilf, hilf."

The guard finally realised what they meant and went to the field telephone by the side of the cobbled slip and made a call. Within minutes an English speaking officer appeared.

"There are some soldiers stranded out there. You can hear their cries for help." said Brian.
"Quite so", said the major in very correct English. "We are aware of the situation and we are sending a boat out very shortly. Thank you."

Mac quizzed him further, telling him how he guided them out early in the afternoon.
"Yes, maybe six left a little later than the rest. The first section arrived safely about half past four. Thank you. We can manage."
"Are you sure? Our boat is just down there. We could launch in

minutes as the tide is high enough."
The major thought for a minute and said, "Thank you again. We can manage. Please go home."

Brian and Mac strolled back up to the road. "Should be easy enough. There's plenty of moonlight right enough. Och, leave them to it. Stupid buggers. To think they took some pot shots at me as well. There's gratitude."

"Come back and have a drink, Mac. They can deal with it."

Mac needed no second bidding and within a few minutes walk they were back at the Grenadier Inn and into their first Scotch.

CHAPTER 33

Stupid waste

The dawn brought an altogether cooler change with grey skies and a chilly breeze. Mac's head was fuzzy from the whisky that Brian had poured down his throat last night. It didn't bother him too much as it wasn't as if he was on the early shift down the coal mine that day. However the demon drink always seemed to summon up the black dog and he had endured a rotten night dreaming of flooded bomb craters and muddy corpses.

He made a cup of tea very slowly and took it out to the garden with him. Steam rose like smoke from his drink in the cold air and he shivered before taking his first sip. The tide had gone out and come back in again during the night. He had a few jobs to do, one of which included taking some firewood down to the Marinelles. He decided to drop in on Brian and berate him for his hospitality last night. He also wanted to find out about the marooned Germans but Brian had heard nothing so far.

"It's still early, Mac. We'll find out soon enough," said Brian, but Mac was a little apprehensive about the outcome.

"Can I borrow the van, Brian? I need to shift some firewood to the Marinelles. I'll find out more from the guards on the slipway."

"No problem but I need it back by noon. I need to go into town. Keys are by the door."

Mac was no great driver and he crunched the van into gear .It protested by belching a thick cloud of smelly smoke into the air. He went home and loaded a good stack of wood into the back before setting off towards St Kitts. On the way, he parked up on the coast road at La Rocque and walked to the north slipway. By chance it was Klaus Bucholtz on duty. They

exchanged greetings and Klaus was able to convey to him that no boat had gone out last night . A group of six had left from the tower half an hour after the main squad on the instructions of Sergeant Steiglitz. The main squad had only just made it back to the beach by wading through waist deep water. Last evening they had assumed from the cries of help that the laggards had returned to the tower. They had realised too late that the upcoming tide must have cut them off.
Mac expressed his concern but was pleased that Klaus was safe. He was only a couple of years older than young Peter.
"It is ok, Mac. They are sending another ...army.... out as soon as the tide goes ...away. It is ok."

"Let's hope so, Klaus. Let's hope so."

Mac was not sure at all. He drove on to see Christine and little Sophie at St Kitts, had a cup of tea and then offloaded the wood into the shed in the garden on the seaside of the house. He was hoping that Peter would be there to help him but he was at school in St Helier that day. He craned his neck and could see the west side of the pier at La Rocque but any action that was going on would be on the eastern side.
He drove Brian's van back to the inn and parked it neatly. He put the keys in the letterbox and walked back towards La Rocque.
When he returned to the slipway, the tragedy had unfolded. The search party had walked out with the falling tide, half expecting the missing six to meet them coming back. All they discovered however were six fully clothed bodies in close proximity to Fragile Rock not one hundred yards away from the tower. It was a dreadful, sorry scene. Six young soldiers, all less than twenty five years old, lay lifeless and drowned on the sand banks surrounding the rock. An hour later, a team of stretcher bearers carried the bodies back to the slipway where two ambulances transported them to the mortuary in St Helier.
Mac, together with a few seasoned local fishermen, stood

incredulously near the slipway. Sergeant Steiglitz was issuing orders in his loud voice as he followed the stretcher bearers up the slipway. He caught sight of Mac in the small gathered crowd.
Mac had his arms folded, eyebrows furled and legs astride. They locked eyes and Mac did not have to say a word. Steiglitz knew he was on to him.
"You'll keep. You'll keep.......you prick." said Mac under his breath. He meant it.

The official record at the inquest was that their deaths were caused by their late departure from the tower which, combined with the fast rising tide, had caused them to become stranded on Fragile Rock . The tide had eventually overwhelmed both the rock and the young German soldiers. On a lower tide, they would have been safe as the sea would not have covered the rock.
The unofficial verdict was that Sergeant Steiglitz had made a monumental blunder in assuming they had backtracked to the tower. He had a duty of care to his subordinates and had failed miserably to the point of negligence.
There were further mutterings in the crowd but the sadness and shock of the situation took over and soon a stunned silence fell upon the scene. Mac was furious that his offer of help had been spurned because the dead were all young fellows caught up in a war that was probably not of their choosing. Neither did they die in battle. They died peacefully, but avoidably, as a result of a force of nature. He wondered how their commanding officer would explain this one away to the relatives of the deceased soldiers.
"What a waste," said Mac, as the stretchers came up the slip with their lifeless casualties. "What a useless, stupid waste!"

He turned away and walked slowly back to St Kitts to tell Christine the bad news. He found playing with little Sophie soothed his soul and this was a day when his soul needed

soothing. More tea and cake was consumed until Peter came home on his bicycle, satchel on his back.
He wheeled his bike round the side of the house and came in through the back door.

"Hi Mac! What's up ? Have you been down to the boat today?"

"Aye laddie. I have. And last night. And yesterday afternoon."

He had a lot of news to impart and Peter listened intently. Like Mac, he wasn't sure whether to feel pleased that there were now a few less Germans or sad because it was such a tragedy . The fact that it had all happened in what was their own backyard felt weird to him. It seemed to him that death was around every corner. First Johnny Boy , then John's parents and now this. He was confused. Mac could see he was confused and tried to trivialise the situation by concentrating on the lobster he had caught on the way back and the potshots coming from the tower. He didn't elaborate on the information he had gleaned about the mines, he saved that for another day.
As Mac spoke, Christine stood behind his upright kitchen chair. Despite the intensity of the tale he was telling, he suddenly became aware of her hand on his shoulder. A little shudder ran through his body. He convinced himself that it was nothing but his almost unconscious reaction to her touch surprised him. She withdrew her hand and he forgot about it as he and Peter wittered on into the failing evening light. Eventually, Christine laid the table for supper. Peter suddenly looked up and said,

"What's for supper,Mum ?"

"Why, lobster of course! Courtesy of Mac. He nearly got shot catching this one!"

His face creased into a broad grin.

Within half an hour , the table was laid and the lobster had been boiled from blue to pink. With a lick of mayonnaise and a sip of diluted Muscadet, the war and the occupation were forgotten for a few minutes. At half past eight Mac said his farewells and walked home past the slipways. He waved an acknowledgement at the guards at the entrance to the Platte Rocque defence site which now boasted at least seven concrete bunkers and an array of machine guns and artillery.
"I hope you all die soon, you stupid buggers, " shouted Mac sounding as friendly as he could. He knew no-one would understand.
"Piss off, you stupid Scotchman! " came the reply from the darkness some twenty odd yards away. It took him by surprise but he was quick enough to correct the heckler.
"Let me corrrrect yourr grammaar. It's Scotsssman not Scotchman, you bloody foreigner!"
"Ok......piss off you stupid Scotssssssman!" came the heavily German accented reply.
"That's better!" said Mac feeling that he should have the last word as he had started the conversation in the first place.
"Interesting !" he said under his breath, "a Kraut with a sense of humour. Mmm."

There was a pause as Mac walked on. Suddenly a gunshot rang out and he quickened his pace a hundredfold until he was around the bend in the road. He walked home and lit the fire . A wave of contentment swept over him but in a flash it was gone as quickly as it had arrived.
He stared into the fire and drank whisky from his glass. His mind drifted. Instead of the smell of cordite and decay, he could smell perfume. Instead of the sound of exploding mortar shells , he heard sweet music and the sound of a soft feminine voice. Instead of the sight of muddy corpses, he could see smooth naked flesh and flashing dark eyes. The siren danced before him as he gazed into the fire. The net curtain which loosely lined the black out material of the nearest window

suddenly flicked up and draped itself over his face before sliding back down and returning to the window . It felt like someone touching him. He knew it wasn't real but smiled because it could so easily have been. A face appeared in the glowing embers of the fireplace. It was Christine. Of course it was Christine. He remembered her hand on his shoulder at St Kitts earlier in the evening. He felt intrigued but somehow guilty.

"Och bonny lad. Yer dreamin' just dreamin'......and it won't do ye any gud!"

But all his words and thoughts couldn't alleviate the yearning he felt.

"Och, ye canna go to jail for what yerr thinking!"

With that in mind he took himself , Christine and his imagination off to bed. He couldn't remember when he had last had such a good time.

CHAPTER 34

Leave granted

The tragic circumstances surrounding the sudden death of their commanding officer, Major Becker, had left the Luftwaffe band rudderless. The Mayfair Hotel had become a gloomy place but the twenty eight musicians were still expected to play their marching songs and entertain at the numerous concerts that were organised. Around the islands, the death count continued to rise as activity increased in and over the bay of St Malo. Ships were sunk, planes were shot out of the sky and corpses were washed up all round the coastline. There were more dead Germans now and the Luftwaffe (Air Force) outfit, along with five Heer (Army) and one Kriegsmarine (Navy) band, were called upon to play at the funerals. Doenig was elevated to the rank of Oberleutnant and took over the responsibility of raising the standard and morale of his unhappy fellows until such a time as a new Musical Director could be appointed from Germany. Fritz did not want the job and he missed Becker badly. They had had a great working relationship, Becker provided the structure and Fritz came up with the content. He realised that he had to toe the line and make sure the outfit could play the military marches that German bands were famous for. It was all part of the Nazi package. They had to play waltzes for Government House soirées and sombre tunes for the increasing number of burials. They also had to march in a straight line, a concept that most of the band found alien. They needed discipline and Fritz was first to admit that this was not his forte. It was no longer an easy number as they were now also under pressure to do sentry duties at various defence posts across the island when they were not playing.

To keep the outfit on an even keel, he managed to borrow the services of a drill sergeant for a couple of hours a week . Every Tuesday and Friday, Sergeant Dieter Hankel would appear at seven in the morning and put them through their paces, first without instruments and, after thirty minutes, with instruments. They all hated Hankel while they marched but, out of drill time, he was a pleasant enough fellow with a wonderful tenor voice . As a lad he had been a member of the Vienna Boys Choir so he had a musical background and had travelled extensively. He had also played football for Germany at youth level and was about to receive his first senior cap when the war broke out. Fritz figured he might get him to sing with the band at concert time. The problem was that Hankel was a busy man whose all round talents made him a popular German. The marching with instruments improved and eventually the whole band took pride in their appearance as well as their musical ability.

Leading up to Christmas 1942 they were much in demand for carol services, concerts, recitals and dances. They even did Government House twice , the Kommandant liked them so much. They always came back down St Saviour's Hill happier than when they went up and usually with an extra couple of bottles of Schnapps discreetly hidden amongst the instruments. The radiogram still sat serenely by the small stage in the ballroom of the Mayfair and, at the end of each day, three or four of them would listen to records. Fritz played clarinet, Werner Turner brought his trumpet and Gunter Muller his saxophone and trombone. They would quietly improvise and practise but eventually someone would complain about the noise. The fact was that most of the troops billeted at the hotel were working round-the-clock shift duties. Evenings were not a good time to be making any sort of noise. With the help of Major Brandt at Government House, they managed to move house altogether into a smaller hotel a few yards up the road. The Mayfair , because of its size, had become more of a recreational centre or Soldatenheim rather than a residential billet.
The New Year brought the big move and all twenty eight musicians transferred their kit and kaboodle to the very much

smaller Hotel Bristol. The fittings and facilities were not up to the standard of the Mayfair but at least they were now away from the lingering memories of Major Becker's suicide. The rooms were smaller but adequate.

After a busy spell playing two days on the lawn up at Government House for a visiting dignitary Field Marshal Von Witzleben , Doenig managed to arrange a week's leave for himself and three of the drummers. Arranging leave was always a problem and had to be organised as and when the diary was not too full. On January 4, 1943, the four of them received a message to report at the St Helier docks where the German ship Schottland was due to depart in a couple of hours. It was currently unloading cement and, as soon as was possible, would be sailing for St Malo. A troop lorry was waiting in the road outside ready to ferry any lucky leave takers to the docks when a despatch rider arrived at the hotel on a push bike .
"*Is Oberleutnant Doenig here?*" he asked, without dismounting. Willy Brint, one of the drummers, pointed him out.
"*Message from Government House , Sir. I have to wait for a reply.*"

He opened the envelope. It was from the Kommandant himself.
-
"*My dear Oberleutnant Doenig,*
Field Marshal Von Witzleben is staying an extra night. He has thoroughly enjoyed your performances and has specifically asked for the band to play. Would you please report by 6p.m. tonight. We shall make sure you are all fed and watered .

Oberst Gruber
Kommandant"

There was no choice in the matter. Befehl ist befehl. Orders are orders. He wrote out a brief reply and sent the rider on his way back up the big hill. He sighed and quickly told the three lads he wasn't coming. Also, they were to get on the lorry and have a great time wherever they were going. They all cheered and waved goodbye, promising they would send postcards. The truck took off and disappeared round the corner.

'Oh well, it wasn't meant to be," he thought and he spent the next hour rounding up the band.

They played well that night, just as they always did. The Field Marshal was on his second visit to the island, taking time off from leading the Western Front . He was delighted to listen to them again and sought out their band leader.

"Oberleutnant Doenig....may I call you Fritz.......a magnificent performance. Thank you once again. I hope to listen to you again when we have won the war. It won't be long now. Keep up the good work of the Fuhrer. He very nearly came with me this time. Heil Hitler!"

He clicked his heels and saluted. Fritz returned the salute, thinking what a chicken livered hypocrite he was as his arm raised automatically. Survival was the name of the game and everybody was playing it except the lunatics in charge.

As they were about to depart, Feldwebel Hankel , of drill sergeant and Vienna Boys Choir fame, came running over to congratulate them.

"What are you *doing here, Dieter?"* said Fritz.

"Having a good time! The Field Marshal is a distant relative."

"I might have bloody well guessed. You're going to tell me now that the Fuhrer is your second cousin twice removed and you are flying home for the weekend! Come back with us and have a drink."

Hankel didn't dwell on it long.

"Why not? I assume you are going back down to St Helier. I have just been moved to Monaco on St Saviour's Road. It's a large private house. Very comfortable. "

"Perfect , Dieter. It's just around the corner from us. Come on, let's go!"

He felt particularly chirpy after that little meeting and took pleasure in downing more than his fair share of schnapps on the way back to the hotel. As soon as they got back, out came Big Bertha. This was the name they had given to the bulky radiogram. In between schnapps they introduced Dieter to the Glenn Miller Orchestra's big band sound. Within minutes he applied his trained tenor voice to the lyrics of Chattanooga Choo Choo. Unfortunately his English pronunciation was not as good as his voice but the overall result was acceptable. Out came the instruments and the three musketeers Fritz, Gunter and Werner set about the song, encouraging Dieter to take the megaphone and give it a shot. They had just finished their excellent but slightly tipsy rendition when the shot they were giving it was returned through the window, shattering the chandelier. A shocked silence fell over them.
"*Shut the fuck up, will you! Some of us have got guard duty at 5.a.m.!*"came a voice from the street.
The sound of footsteps faded into the distance and the group burst out laughing.
"*Perhaps he is right. Time for bed.*" said Fritz.
The party broke up there and then.
"*Great night, Fritz. I think I'd better practise my English. Great song, great music. We should do this again, " said Dieter.*
"I hope so, Dieter. Now go home, you drunkard."

It had been a good night but the morning brought news of fresh disasters.
The 1500 ton ship Schottland had left the previous evening in a strong wind and driving rain. Whilst following the slightly smaller escort vessel, the Holland, it had struck rocks and foundered off the southwest of Jersey. News of any survivors was scant and unreliable but eventually, after a couple of days ,it became apparent that 330 out of the original 370 on board had not been accounted for.
Fritz didn't know what to think. He had survived by a sheer

fluke but he had also ordered his three bandsmen to leave on the ship. He got over it . He had come to realise that warfare was just a random collection of extraordinarily random events so how could he be to blame?
He grieved but he still survived and that was the most important thing to him. Eventually he would *have* to put pen to paper and write to the relatives of the deceased. He didn't look forward to that but it still had to be done. Sunday came and the band did the Sunday recital in the Royal Square with a heavy heart. After lunch he grabbed a few minutes to gather his memories and thoughts before commencing his sad but mandatory task of writing to the families of the deceased. The hotel telephone rang and somebody downstairs yelled out.

"Telephone for Oberleutnant Doenig! Oberleutnant Doenig!"
"Ok. On my way!"

It was Military Headquarters at the Hotel Metropole on the other side of St Helier.
"Oberleutnant Doenig, it's Oberleutnant Schmidt here at Military Headquarters. We have some good news for you. It appears your three drummer boys have survived the rigours of a week at sea. They were washed up on a life raft on a group of rocks to the south east. Very lucky boys. Brint, Voller and Klinsmann are yours, aren't they? A bit worse for wear and very cold, they are at the General Hospital. Can I leave you to take over from there?"

"Yes Oberleutnant, they sound like mine. I can pick them up. Thank you for letting me know."

He let the others know the good news and there was a lot of whooping and hollering from all round the hotel. He commandeered a car from the Mayfair Hotel up the road and drove down to the hospital where he was delighted to see his three bandsmen alive and kicking. They were just as delighted to see him. Weak, cold and sea sick after six days in a wobbly inflatable raft, they had finally washed up on the Minquiers reef , just fifteen miles off the south east coast. Out of 370 passengers they were three of just forty survivors . Considering the escort ship Holland was close by, this was a massive loss of life. It took two hours for the ship to go down after it struck the Grande Grune rock, its draft being exaggerated by quantities of cement that had remained in the hold . The wreck lies there to this day, a monument to an avoidable tragedy. Brint, Voller and Klinsmann stayed in hospital for two days before they were happily reunited with the Hotel Bristol.

Fritz Doenig had an early supper and went up to his room . He tore up his draft letters and got on to his bed fully dressed. He was absolutely exhausted and dropped off to sleep in an instant.

CHAPTER 35

Steiglitz confronts Mac

About a month after the drowning tragedy, Mac was still seething about Oberfeldwebel Steiglitz and his dereliction of duty of care. There were occasions when they would pass each other on the coast road or harbour bed when Mac would simply stop with arms akimbo and give him a hard stare. This went on for a few weeks and obviously did not go unnoticed by Steiglitz. It all came to a head one day when Mac and Brian were down at the harbour preparing to lay the boat up on land for the winter months. The nights were getting longer and the temperatures were dropping. Steiglitz , identifiable from a distance by his silver edged forage cap, was marching a squad of a dozen or so foot soldiers down the slipway and out to Seymour Tower for construction and guard duties.
As the squad walked past the boat, Mac picked his moment and said,

"Mind you don't drown that lot, you prick."

Steiglitz brought the squad to a halt immediately and left them at attention before coming over to the Crazy Doris and confronting Mac.

"What did you say?" said Steiglitz in a thick accent.

"I said, be careful out there. It's dangerous." said Mac.

"Take it easy, Mac. I think he means business." interjected Brian, under his breath.

"Do you hate me because I am German?" said Steiglitz. His

English had improved since their last meeting. Mac shrugged but still held his gaze.

"Did you fight in the first war? Is that why you hate me? I have two bruzzers dead in the first war."
Steiglitz suddenly reached for the holster on his left hip and withdrew his automatic pistol. The soldiers stiffened visibly with an audible shuffling of jack boots on sand.
Brian held his breath as Steiglitz confronted Mac who stood firm.

"You would like to shoot me ?" said the German. He activated the cartridge on the Luger side weapon and thrust it butt first into Mac's hand.
".............so shoot me!"

The silence was deafening as the scene played out. Brian couldn't believe what was happening. His mouth dropped open in horror as Mac grabbed and slowly raised the pistol, pointing it between the eyes of Steiglitz . The squad immediately raised their weapons but the German sergeant quelled them with a raised palm.
"Shoot me, Englander. If you hate me then shoot me!"

Mac thought about it for a few seconds whilst everybody figured he would back down. There was a lot of breath holding going on.
"Ah, what the hell !" said Mac suddenly and squeezed the trigger. There was a loud click but there was no other noise, no discharging of the weapon , no other sound.

"Let's have another go then." said Mac, still aiming the Luger between the German's eyes. Brian Le Rouge could not believe what he was witnessing, went white as a sheet and broke out into a cold sweat. He stepped quickly between Mac and

Steiglitz, simultaneously shoving them both gently in the chest. "Now, now children. Mac! Give the gun back to Sergeant Steiglitz. Better still, give it to me and *I* will give it back to him."said Brian, surprising even himself with his assertiveness. He thought to himself that this is no worse than closing time at the pub and besides which , the gun was clearly not loaded. He figured Steiglitz had set it up beforehand in order to test Mac. "Come on, Tarzan, give me the gun."

Mac lowered his aim slowly and handed it, butt first, to Brian who was now feeling a trifle braver.

He hissed at Mac, "You see, it's not even loaded! He's taking the piss out of you!"

As if to demonstrate his theory, he pointed the gun skywards like the starter in an Olympics foot race and pulled the trigger. With an enormous bang and a recoil strong enough to send him off balance, the Luger discharged a bullet skywards, well away from any harm. He nervously regained his composure and offered the butt of the pistol to Steiglitz who accepted the weapon and returned it quickly to its holster .

He retreated slowly backwards a few paces before turning towards his squad and bringing them to attention.

"As you were.Atten.....shun. Quick....march. Left right left right. I love to go a wandering along the mountain track and where I go I love to have my knapsack on my back!"

Brian looked on in amazement and banged his head lightly with the palm of his hand as if not believing the ridiculous sequence of events he had just witnessed and been part of. As the Germans marched out of earshot, he shook his head and turned to Mac. He was livid.

"He's just as fucking mad as *you*. He's just as fucking mad as *you*. He's just as fucking mad as *you*. What have got to say to that, you barmy fucking idiot! Eh? Eh? You could have had us both killed !"

He started pushing and shoving Mac back up the beach. He was beside himself with rage and shock. As Mac moved on ahead to get out of range of the abuse that was coming his way, Brian started picking up pebbles and hurling them at him. The Scotsman took the hint and broke into a trot up the cobbled slipway. The guards stood aside, mystified by their behaviour but realising that intervention could have led to more trouble than it was worth . By the time Brian had reached the van, Mac had already hoofed it out of sight around the corner, heading home. They were both going in the same direction but when Brian drove past , they studiously ignored each other.
"I wonder what's got into him?" thought Mac as the van disappeared into the distance.
Within a month, Mac received an official request from the Kommandantur at College House for an interview to see if he was suitably fit for deportation to Germany. This was a blow he was not expecting as he considered he was flying well below the radar .Most of the required number of deportees had already gone but the Germans were inexplicably scratching round for retired Army officers and various miscreants who had a criminal history. He wondered how he measured up to either category as Corporal Mackintosh would hardly have qualified as an Army officer and neither did he have a criminal record. He guessed that Steiglitz had something to do with it and cursed him every day. Nevertheless he managed to see his GP, Doctor Cameron, and with much coughing and an offer of a quantity of kindling wood, he managed to elicit a medical certificate which said he was suffering from a lung condition brought on by his exposure to a mustard gas attack in World War 1. He took the certificate with him for his interview and once again managed to confuse all and sundry with his finest incomprehensible Scottish accent. The interpreter and the whole Medical Board consisting of three local and three German doctors heaved a collective sigh of relief as he closed the door on the way out. Humorous as this little episode may

seem , quite a few people were warned to prepare themselves for deportation at short notice but were not told their date of departure. It appeared the Germans themselves were none too keen on the whole exercise and even the slightest of medical excuses was sufficient to overturn individual deportation orders.
Mac turned up at the pub a few days later and Brian refused to serve him. The situation remained unresolved for a month until Mac had a piece of good fortune. Winter gales and increased allied activity had resulted in various bits of flotsam and jetsam being washed up on the south east shores. The barge Mazagan had fetched up near Le Hocq due west of La Rocque and had disgorged its contents upon the rocky shores. A particularly high tide had pitched tons of evil smelling black seaweed up by the sea wall near Mac's house and a thorough search amongst the slime-ridden fronds had precipitated a couple of wooden boxes. One contained rotten oranges and ruined butter. The other was altogether a lot more acceptable and elicited a dozen bottles of Cointreau which Mac immediately laid claim to. His find was only twenty yards from his door. That evening he turned up once again at the pub carrying a wicker basket with a tea towel covering its contents. It was a cold Saturday night and the locals were gathering around the open fire.
Mac spotted Brian behind the bar and before he could turn and disappear into the back room, he took a bottle of Cointreau from under the tea towel in the basket and laid it on the bar. "Peace offering, big fella." he said sheepishly. "I'm er.....sorry."

"You're *what* ! Sorry? You're sorry....oh, that's nice. You nearly got us both killed and you're sorry. I'll tell you what....it's going to cost you more than a bottle of Cointreau to get round me on this one."

"Aye, I thought ye'd say that so I brought ye anotherrr five."

Like a magician pulling rabbits from a hat, he put the wicker basket on the counter and pulled out another five trade mark square bottles. Brian looked incredulously at the stash, handling each bottle in turn.
"Well, it looks like Cointreau.........", he hesitated and reached under the counter for a glass. He broke the seal on the first bottle and pulled the cork with a struggle. He sniffed the contents.
"It certainly smells like Cointreau." Mac was shuffling impatiently while Brian poured a hefty tot into the glass and raised it to his lips. He slowly took a swig and swallowed hard. It took him unawares and he spluttered until he was red in the face. He recovered his composure before finally declaring that "it certainly tastes like Cointreau!"
"Well?", said Mac.
"Well what?" answered Brian, thoroughly enjoying Mac's discomfort.
"Ah yes......it's certainly Cointreau. Yes, definitely Cointreau." he said, licking his lips.

They laughed and the rift was healed.

CHAPTER 36

1943 Cliff missing presumed drowned

After a year or two of occupation of the school buildings of Victoria College , the Hitler Youth organisation suddenly upped and went back to the Fatherland. The reasons behind their original presence was obscure. In the early part of the war, the German forces were clearly in the ascendancy and sending young and impressionable *kinder* (youth) into secure captured British territory would have thrown up a lot of good propaganda. Victoria College, with its imposing granite facade perched so prominently on top of a hill overlooking St Helier, reeked of high British educational standards. The fact that the occupying socialist force had ousted the existing pupils so easily and replaced them with their own youth was not lost on political commentators. Leading up to the outbreak of war, the young of Germany were forced to join the Hitler-Jugend which effectively became a paramilitary organisation involved in enforcing the politics of the Fuhrer. After 1940 it performed more auxiliary tasks connected to the war such as fire and medical rescue work. With more action on home territory as the war progressed, they were withdrawn to the Fatherland.

So it was that Victoria College was returned to its pupils and teachers for formal education. The impressive granite building, named and blessed by the presence of Queen Victoria herself in 1852, was cleared and cleaned in readiness for the start of the Spring term on January 21, 1943. It made little difference to Peter Marinelle's world. Classes were back where they had been a year or two ago. As a consequence, he now rode his bike on a slightly different route. Sometimes he would take the coast road to town and use the lower bike sheds before walking the three hundred yards up the steep path around the huge front lawn to school . Other times, he would approach through the many small hilly lanes which connected from the eastern parishes and park in the upper bike sheds near the classrooms.

He loved cycling the three or four miles along the coast in the warm summer months, breathing in the balmy salty air as the sun rose. Every now and again he would take what he called 'the country route' and marvel at the smells and sounds of the hedgerows as he pedalled past fields and farms. School was a good time to connect with his classmates and see what was going on in the rest of the island. He became aware that the town folk were struggling. Rationing was having a severe effect on them and basics were in short supply. Living in St Helier had its drawbacks. The place was crawling with German troops who had cleaned out most of the stock of the declining number of shops. It was illegal for more than five people to congregate and there was constant oppressive questioning by the Feldpolitzei. The townies had little access to the outlying farms whose output was so severely regulated . As time went by, attitudes changed. Hunger and comfort slowly became the drivers. Fuel for fires became harder to obtain. Deliveries of coal became sporadic. Bicycles were commandeered at will and stolen by the needy. All the time, the Allies seemed to be gaining the upper hand on the war front and the situation was dealt with by the hope of liberation before the end of the year.
Peter was turning seventeen in June and was now only attending school to appease his mother. He couldn't bear wearing school uniform and would carry a change of clothes in his saddlebag. He fell in with a couple of class mates who lived at the bottom of Green Street in St Helier and started to kick around with them for an hour or so after school in the afternoon. He started to arrive late at home, much to Christine's annoyance and he had become disrespectful to her on one or two occasions. This was unlike him and she put it down to normal teenage behaviour. She confronted him once or twice and eventually enlisted Mac's help with the result that he pulled his head in just enough to keep them both happy.
Sophie continued to flourish . Born on the day that war broke out on September 3, 1939, she was a living calendar of how

long the war had been going on. She was a delightful three year old, bringing joy to all who came in contact with her.
Christine kept herself busy but was missing having a husband around. She was waiting by Mrs Le Plongeon's shop one day waiting for a bus into town when a German staff car pulled up. The window wound down and a handsome young officer poked his head out. He was in his late twenties and looked like a film star.

"Would you like a lift ? I am going into town. It would be my pleasure."

"That's very kind but I'm meeting a friend on the bus." she replied." Besides which, you are going the wrong way. Town is the other way." Her confidence took her by surprise.

"Yes, I know that but I have a steering wheel. Perhaps another time? "

He flashed her a set of teeth which sparkled in contrast to the suntan of his face. She smiled but did not reply and he drove slowly off in the wrong direction. A little shiver emanated from the pit of her stomach ......and she felt no guilt at all as she enjoyed the moment.
Cliff had been gone for four years now. The letters kept arriving via the services of the Red Cross but they were all heavily censored. All Cliff could say was that he was good and well, *not* where he was or what he was doing. Each letter was heavily laden with 'miss you's' and 'love you's'. She replied in similar vein to each and every one, feeling closer to him as she wrote.

In early April, there was a knock on the door one evening and their world was turned on its head. It was Connetable Le Grand. He looked pretty serious.

"Come in. Come in." said Christine. "Have you brought us more ration books?"

"Hi....... no, it's...er.... not. Look, you had both better sit down. It's bad news. The Bailiff has asked me to deliver this personally."

He pulled an envelope from the inside pocket of his raincoat. Beads of sweat hung on his forehead as once again he steeled himself to thrust a dagger into the heart of another parish family.

"It's a letter from Merchant Navy headquarters sent via the Red Cross. It's about Cliff. I'm very sorry but it appears he is missing presumed drowned. Here......you read it."

The blood drained from Christine's face as she reached for the letter. There was little detail in it except the minimum facts that the Merchant Navy troop ship Possum had been sunk on the evening of March 15, 1943 in the Mediterranean off Algiers with the loss of 396 American soldiers and the crew of ten. There was a ringing in her ears and the world around her was in slow motion. Was he dead? Maybe he survived and would be coming back. Perhaps she was dreaming.
It was so hard to take it all in. In her mind she had always figured that this would be a possibility and thought that she might be ready for it . She stared at the letter and read it four or five times in case she had missed something but the information remained the same. She felt Peter's hand on her shoulder and she passed the letter to him to read. He sat back down again and spread it out on the table. He went through the same emotions as his mother as he tried to take it all in.
"He's only presumed dead, Mum. He could still be alive.....couldn't he?"

"Yes, son. It's a possibility ."

Grief takes people in many different ways. Christine just felt numb. She had been on her own for so long, had guided her son along the straight and narrow and now had Sophie nearly at school age. She had started to feel really alone for a good few months and now she truly was. But she was angry and clenched her fists.

Constable Le Grand went on.
"Is there anyone we can get in touch with to give you a hand ? I've told Mrs Le Plongeon and she said she would drop over as soon as possible. The Bailiff said he would try to find out more but he warned me to say that it was difficult to find out anything these days. He sends his condolences."

"We'll be fine, thanks." said Christine. As she spoke, Mrs Le Plongeon arrived dispensing sympathy and kindness. Constable Le Grand took this as his cue to leave quietly. He went out and closed the door behind him, heaving a huge sad sigh as he walked toward his car. He cursed his job and swore he would resign as soon as the islands were liberated. There had been just too much heartache and he was exhausted with it all. He put his arms on the car roof and rested his head on them.

"Oh bloody hell. I can't take much more of this."
He got in, composed himself and drove off.

Peter gave his mum a hug and Mrs Le Plongeon filled the kettle . Somehow they struggled through the night . Sophie had slept through it all and her joyful presence got them through the next few days. Peter stuck close to his mother not quite knowing how he should behave. The last time he had seen his father was before the Germans arrived, coming up for four

years in July . Memories of his dad's departure on the boat brought images flooding back, images that he tried in vain to banish from his mind.
In the morning, Peter sat on the old chair in the garden, drinking tea and watching the sun rise slowly in the eastern sky .The tide was nearly high and Brent geese were gathering in readiness for their long migration northwards to the Baltic regions.
"Why would you want to leave when it's just getting warmer. Makes no sense to me."he thought. His mother came out from the house and made a circuit of the small garden, checking on any plants that had survived the winter winds. She approached Peter and reached down to put her hand on his shoulder.

" People are very kind", said Christine wistfully, "but now we need to get on with our lives. Bit like those geese, really. " She nodded in their direction.

Peter drank the last of his tea and surveyed the geese.

"Is it ok if I leave school at the end of term, Ma? I want to go full time on the boat ."

She paused but had somehow expected this one to be coming her way.

"We'll do a deal. I hoped you would do another year but I can see your heart's not in it. How about you leave at the end of the Summer term. That will take us up to July. I'll expect a lot more help around the house though and you'll have to earn your keep."

He thought about it for a minute and was a little disappointed to have to endure another term. At least he had a definite date and he was sure he could wing it until then.

"Ok ,Ma. It's a deal."
He kissed her on the cheek .
"Thanks, son."
Sophie had woken up and was standing by the back door in her pyjamas.
"I'm hungry, Mummy, I'm hungry."
Peter ran towards her and scooped her up in his arms. He blew a raspberry on her face and she giggled uncontrollably.
"Well, we'd better do something about that then, eh? Scrambled eggywegg?"
"Yes, eggy weggy weggs." she said between giggles.

Sophie's presence was carrying them along. Soon after breakfast , friends and neighbours started to call.

CHAPTER 37

Lack of purpose

Mac was understandably shocked to hear the previous evening at the pub that Cliff Marinelle had been reported as 'missing presumed drowned'. He had known Cliff only on nodding terms but he was close enough to the family now to know that this would be a terrible blow to them. He had had a few drinks and decided that he would see what he could do in the morning after a good night's sleep. He set off at 9 o'clock the next day not knowing really how he would handle the situation. It was a pleasant Spring morning and the sun felt warm with hints of a good summer to come. As he passed the two slipways of La Rocque, one of the guards waved at him. It was the young soldier Klaus Bucholtz. Since the terrible drowning incident, he had been promoted to Obergefreiter (Corporal) and was now helping in the administration of guard duties on all the defence posts around La Rocque. All the lower ranks had to do construction work which seemed to go on endlessly. They also had to guard these bunkers once they had been completed. It was tiring, boring work. Each night they all did two turns of sentry duty before going off at ten o'clock when the night shift took over. As the year of 1943 unfolded, Berlin felt that the Allies would be invading Europe soon and all of Hitler's Atlantic wall of steel and concrete had been put on red alert. This included the Channel Islands. Hitler still thought that Churchill was anxious to reclaim this piece of Britain and another direct order came to "defend to the last man." Der britischer Kanalinseln (British Channel Islands) were clearly part of the bigger picture.

Not that Klaus was particularly worried that bright morning. He had organised a shift out at Seymour Tower in the afternoon and was looking forward to it. It was a welcome break from the tedium of patrolling the bunkers at Platte Rocque night after night. There was an increasing amount of Allied aircraft

dropping by on their way to and from destinations in France and beyond. When they were spotted, usually at night by searchlights, an intense barrage of fire would take place from defence posts all along the coast. This would light up the sky and result in a shower of shrapnel of all shapes and sizes rattling the roof tiles and roads in the immediate vicinity. These incidents would bring much amusement to the locals as it reinforced the theory that they might *not* have been forgotten by the bigwigs in London. Invariably a brave listener with an illegal radio would provide the information next day that there had been an Allied bombing raid on on some German city and they had dropped in on Jersey on the way home.
Mac waved back and came over.

"Guten Morgen, Klaus. How are you? Has Adolf drowned anybody this week?"
The young corporal knew exactly what he meant.

"No! Oberfeldwebel Steiglitz is away on.....er.....how you say....holiday. He comes back next week. Are you okay? Have you been playing ...er.....how you say.....Russian roulade this week?"
Mac chuckled at this.
"That's very good. Your English is improving but it's Russian roulette.... roulette. I'm verry gud. See you soon."

Mac carried on, not wanting to share the purpose of his journey with the enemy, however friendly they were.
The door to St Kitts was already wide open from the frequent passage of friends and neighbours. He knocked politely on the frame of the door and looked in through the porch to the kitchen beyond where it seemed a small congregation were taking tea. Christine was busying herself by the stove when she heard the knock. She moved quickly to the door to welcome him.

"I really don't know what to say, lassie. After all this time, it's a heartbreaker, a bloody heartbreaker. "
"Thanks Mac, no need to say anything ." she replied. "Just give me a hug....please."

Mac swiftly obliged but disentangled himself before it was witnessed as being inappropriate. Peter came through from the back carrying Sophie and, for good measure, he gave them a hug as well. Sympathisers came and went until the Marinelles were totally exhausted. At about lunchtime, Mac persuaded them to go out into the back garden and enjoy the sunshine while he dealt with any further callers for an hour or two. Christine took the advice and collapsed into a deckchair. She had slept very little last night and she fell into painless unconsciousness within seconds. Peter sat down beside her and swiftly followed suit .Sophie was full of beans and Mac did what he could to keep her occupied in between fielding visitors at the front door. He told them simply that they were all taking a nap and to maybe leave it a day or two before calling again. Mother and son slept soundly in their respective deckchairs . Mac and Sophie found some blankets to put over them. The sun disappeared to the west and the temperature dropped. Sophie got thoroughly impatient and eventually woke them both up. Christine woke, a little refreshed and confused as she fought away the fug of a daytime sleep. Reality struck brutally home as she remembered the situation she was now in. She pushed herself awkwardly up from the depths of the deckchair and pulled her cardigan around her in the chilling air. She gazed out to sea where the fast fading light was playing tricks on the water. Ominous black shapes appeared then dissolved into the light mist as the darkness took over. She cleared her head and saw the craggy Scotsman playing football with her little daughter on the scruffy salt burnt grass at the sandy end of the garden.

"Will you stay for supper, Mac? Please say yes as I don't think I can manage this on my own."
The wall of the dam was finally breached and the tears came pouring out. Christine rushed inside , sobbing as she went. Sophie got upset and Peter joined in for a minute or two. Mac stood in the middle of all this and could do nothing until the storm had subsided. At that moment he would have preferred a few minutes back in the trenches. Eventually some semblance of normality returned and Christine came back downstairs. She was red-eyed but in control.

"Sorry about that. It took me by surprise. Now Mac, potato soup and we have some pork chops courtesy of my cousin. Yes?"
"Aye, lassie, aye. Come on you two, let's lay the table."
The show went on like this for the rest of the week, everybody on eggshells and in their own little world. Peter was convinced his father was still alive and until he was told otherwise, he would carry on with that thought in mind. Christine was confused. She was more matter-of-fact concerning Cliff's fate and figured that he was probably dead. She hadn't seen him for three years and thought, rightly or wrongly, that this was at least a way forward. She had Sophie to raise and her three year old was her immediate priority. Peter, with guidance, would be able to take care of himself and little Sophie didn't have a clue what was going on anyway.
Was Cliff really dead or did he survive the glide bomb attack by the Germans on the troop ship he was working on? The question was just another detail in the fog of uncertainty that ensued on the islands. Lack of information gave way to overactive imaginations which visited folk in their quieter moments. Mac wasn't the only one being chased by the black dog. Lack of purpose was beginning to drag like an anchor in a gale.

CHAPTER 38

The summer of 1943

Early in the year, the Germans had issued an order banning boat fishing. They did this from time to time only to rescind the orders two or three months later. All fishermen were invited to attend the German Harbour Office at the Pomme D'or Hotel in St Helier where they individually had to sign a declaration. It read like this.

"I hereby declare, during the time of fishing, not to commit any acts prejudicial to the interests of the German Army. I bind myself not to tolerate nor to favour any espionage nor any secret attempt to escape by the use of my boat.
I understand that any act or outrage against the rules of fishing shall be severely punished and that all my possessions shall be confiscated, and my family shall be held equally responsible."
When Mac read all this in the Evening Post, he laughed out loud.

"Aye, they'll be wanting a pint of blood as well as most of the fish. Now they are asking me to hang myself as well! Bloody nerrrve!"

They had no choice. The Germans were increasingly jumpy and were determined to maintain security. That meant restricting all coastal movements. All small craft had to have identification numbers and were registered . Checks and inspections were frequent as a number of small craft had been used in escape attempts. The Germans eventually took to accompanying the larger vessels of over 25 feet with an armed guard. The Crazy Doris fell short of this requirement but Mac thought "it won't be long before the buggers will be coming with us."

A further worry for Mac and others was the persistent search for illegal wireless sets. Another amnesty had been granted the previous summer but now they meant business. Heavier punishments were meted out and prison sentences went up to three years. A further order had been issued to warn of further repercussions. The Allies were gaining in confidence and the waters between Jersey and the French coast became increasingly hostile. What had previously been a quiet crossing for cargo and troop ships was now becoming dangerous. The consequence was that the only link for food supplies was now being slowly strangled. Coupled with the fact that the Channel Islands were now firmly on the strategic map, many a night was disturbed by coastal guns firing off at passing stray bombers who were not averse to firing back.

During the Easter school holidays, tragedy struck at Greve D'Azette beach where a group of fourteen year olds were doing what fourteen year olds did. Hanging out on the beach just to the east of St Helier and on Peter's bike route to school, the group had been scouring the beach for war treasure. A number of ships had floundered recently, some by accident and some by force of war, coughing up all sorts of bounty on the shores. Amongst all these were hundreds of detonator mechanisms which had slowly come ashore from the wreck of the Diamant a few months earlier. Detonators were magnets to the boys as they could explode them without too much difficulty. They were like fireworks on Guy Fawkes night but with a force of explosion which was considerably greater and in this case, lethal. The poor kid took the full impact of the device and died as a result of multiple injuries. It was particularly tragic incident which was not lost on Peter. He knew the boy in question and thought it a stupid waste of life. He had exploded detonators himself and thought it a pretty risky business despite the end result of a loud bang plus a hole in the ground. He and John Le Ross had let one off one day behind some rocks on the beach. It had exploded prematurely before they could retreat to a safe distance. They both had a ringing in their ears for a couple of hours and then realised how lucky they had been. Every piece of shrapnel and surrounding stone had missed them completely. They laughed about it but knew not to do it again.

Peter went back to school after Easter and every day became purgatory. Bored with book work and longing for fresh air, it took about a week to start bunking off school. He would set off on his bike from La Rocque and simply see what the day had to offer.

Invariably he would get checked off the register at school and then surreptitiously retrieve his bike from behind the bicycle sheds and freewheel down the hill into town. He would then turn left down Green Street and out on to the beach at Havre des Pas where the open air swimming pool was. It was familiar territory to him as swimming was his sport of choice in the summer term. He would spend time twice a week lapping up and down after school.

On sunny days, the German troops would be there too. They were billeted in the many hotels and guest houses that bordered the beach down there, just a stone's throw from the middle of town. They loved to sun themselves on the rocks and the elaborate terraces of the swimming pool. Peter could smell the suntan lotion that they used from a hundred yards away as it drifted on the sea breeze. He crossed the raised planked walkway which led from the pavement at a height of about ten feet for a distance of eighty or so yards out to the pool across the sand. This was to allow access when the tide was high. Peter would pause on the walkway and study the people below. The pool itself was magnificent and large, allowing lanes to be put down for school swimming races. It had a low springboard and a separate selection of high boards for the more accomplished divers . It was always full of seawater except when they opened the sluice gates for winter cleaning.

The Germans had imported a number of French prostitutes who

were living at the Victor Hugo Hotel a few hundred yards to the east. Most of them had seen better days but the fact that they were all indulging in sexual intercourse was a constant source of fascination to Peter. Their days off were many (as theirs was mostly a nocturnal trade) and when the sun shone, they were brought out by the extravagantly well endowed Madam for a walk, always in single file. Peter stood and watched as they walked past, awarding each one a number of points out of ten. One poor olive skinned soul with a scab on her lip rated a generous solitary point. Times were clearly hard for them and it didn't look like much fun. Each pasty face told an unhappy story. A local lady on the nearby pavement said rather loudly in French, "Elles ont vues les meilleurs jours." *(They have seen better days.)*This precipitated a barrage of abuse from the ladies of the night making her wish she hadn't made the comment. Peter laughed out loud from the safety of the walkway.

"Oi," said a voice from behind. "You didn't mention you were bringing your girlfriends!"
He turned round and was met by two of his ex-classmates who seemed to be on a similar mission. Paddy and Tintin were both townies and Peter was in awe of all the mischief they seemed to indulge in. They both lived in Roseville Street which was not more than a couple of hundred yards away. It was a street populated with beautiful granite faced guesthouses, half of which had been taken over to provide accommodation for the Germans. They knew the area well and were street savvy in the way that townies were.
The beach and the open air pool were their playground.

"Want to see some fun?" said Tintin. "Come back to the beach with me and witness this spectacle from a safe distance."
Tintin and Paddy led the way back to the promenade and down the steps on to the beach where they unrolled their towels on a dry patch of sand fifty yards or so from the overhead walkway.
"In a few minutes, Sergeant Sheizenhausen will be cycling

along to take his daily dip in the pool. He will leave his bicycle leaning against the railings on the overhead walkway and he will retrieve his swimming togs from his saddlebag. He will continue on into the pool area. Then the fun starts."
Peter couldn't wait. This was fun. So much better than school. As they waited, pretty girls started to drift on to the beach. Some were German girls who worked for the occupiers . There were also one or two French girls who had been seconded into administrative jobs. There were also local girls who liked to fraternise with the enemy. The sunbathing soldiers couldn't wait to offer them cigarettes and the opportunity of cheeky conversation. Most of the Jersey young men had left in 1940 to join the Forces so legitimate male company was in short supply. Eventually and naturally, the barriers became blurred and the older folk had no hesitation in labelling these girls 'Jerrybags'. Criticism was unforgiving and many a local girl had to bear the barbs and arrows of an older generation.
While they waited they fell into the brutal conversation of callow teenagers. The townies bragged,
"I bet she shags!"
"If I give you half a crown, will you pull your knickers down."
"See that girl over there. She does it for a potato."

And so it went on. Peter was used to all this as it went on at school. Raw and sexist as it was, Peter thought it great fun. His hormones were racing in a puddle of post puberty confusion.
"Here he comes," said Tintin.
Sergeant Scheizenhausen alighted from his gleaming bicycle on the promenade pavement and pushed it onto the raised walkway close to the pool gates.Scheisenhausen wasn't his real name but it was a well-earned soubriquet much used by the locals. He propped the machine up against the railings and retrieved his swimming togs from the saddlebag. He took out a thick chain and passed it through the bicycle frame and around the railing before securing a chunky padlock to the ends. Satisfied that his pride and joy was now secure, he walked off.

Tintin was already in motion, climbing the stone steps up to the promenade. Cool as a cucumber he walked the fifty yards to the bicycle and carefully slid the railing out from the securing post thereby releasing the padlocked chain which was now hanging freely round the frame. He carefully slid the railing back into the post and shoved the excess padlock chain into the saddlebag. He then grabbed the handlebars before wheeling the bike in the direction of the pavement. He walked it confidently along the road , crossed to the other side and up Roseville street to his parents' guest house three hundred yards away. He pushed it round the side alley to the back garden and closed the gate behind him. There was a large shed in the far corner which had been built on blocks. He pulled it around the side and concealed it under the shed amongst old bags of fertiliser and soil.

Tintin was back on the beach within ten minutes, albeit sweating profusely. Another half an hour elapsed before Scheizenhausen returned to the fold, his hair slicked back all seawater wet and shiny.

He searched along the railings for his treasured bicycle but all to no avail. Finally he exploded in a mass of whirling arms and foreign expletives, questioning all and sundry as to the whereabouts of his property. Nobody had seen it go and if they had, they weren't telling. An opinion poll would have had him down as an obnoxious sod. He was a pompous cruel man and was even disliked by his own side.

The boys were hugely amused by the behaviour of Scheizenhausen which lasted a good hour before he admitted defeat and wandered lost and forlorn back to Military HQ at the Hotel Metropole, ironically positioned at the top of Roseville Street not far from Tintin's place.

Whilst Tintin was cocky and brave, he was also not noted for his good looks. He got many a knockback from the girls on the beach but Paddy with his handsome face and charming ways would invariably pick up the scraps from Tintin's table. Both

boys had been asked to 'leave' school which was a polite way of saying they had been expelled. Not being able to get a job could be put down to lack of effort but they nonetheless enjoyed the freedom of doing nothing. Who could blame them but the problem was, how long could they hang on to it ?
Peter was freewheeling, not sure of where he was in the world, and quickly fell under the spell of the two others. For the first three weeks of the summer term, he bunked off two days in three and on those days he fell in with his townie friends. They chatted up the girls, stole bicycles, smoked cigarettes and drank rum from Tintin's guest house. One day the conversation turned to the prostitutes who worked at the brothel in the Victor Hugo Hotel. It transpired that Paddy had bet Tintin that he couldn't get into the place and steal a pair of French knickers from one of the rooms without being caught. Cocky as Tintin was, he chose a time during the day when the ladies were out promenading by the Bathing Pool and succeeded quite comfortably in his task. The hotel backed right on to the seawall and he was able to climb over from the beach and gain access through a sash window. It was so quiet in there that he sauntered in and out of a dozen rooms before he made his exit with a pair of French knickers in his pocket. All the occupants were out in the fresh air.
"Do you fancy a go, Pete, or are you too chicken? said Tintin.
'Yeah, bet you can't. I reckon you're a virgin anyway. You might get lucky." chipped in Paddy, winking at Tintin.
"Or unlucky!" said Tintin." They all look pretty shagged out to me. All you have to do is grab a pair of knickers . I'll show you the way in. It's easy when they are all out down here. Can you do it or are you too bloody chicken?"

In a few minutes of madness, Peter found himself climbing the gently sloping granite wall that led up from the beach to the back of the Victor Hugo. Tintin climbed the few feet with him and, as arranged, showed him the sash window before leaving him to his own devices. Trembling with excitement, Peter pushed the sash window up and hauled himself inside. As forecast, it was as quiet as a mouse and it smelt divine. Cheap perfume filled the air, nylons and knickers lay on the double bed and a bra lay draped over an old wooden chair. He quickly grabbed the pair of knickers and stuffed them into his pocket. 'Mission accomplished', he thought.

The excitement was overwhelming and he couldn't resist the temptation of exploring further. This was too easy! Tintin was *so* right. He moved towards the door and just as he put his hand on the doorknob there was an audible rustling sound behind him. He turned to see a figure emerging from the little annexe where the toilet was situated. He heard the sound of the toilet flushing and then tried to focus on the figure that came towards him. She must have been about thirty, totally naked and definitely female. In the two seconds it took to digest this information, he was off towards the window to make his escape. His feet, however, would not move and his gaze returned to the form that stood before him. She had long shiny red hair which contrasted starkly with the paleness of her skin. Her ample breasts were picked out by the sunlight coming through the window. His eyes fell upon the red triangle of pubic hair which glared back at him from between her legs. She opened her mouth.
"Have you paid Madame, Monsieur ?"
He stood there, dumbstruck, but fully aware of the incredible stirring in his trousers.
" You have paid, yes? "
Peter nodded, more in panic than as a result of any conscious decision.
"You are tres jeune........er... very young."

She reached out with her slender fingers and touched his face.

"Are you a cherry boy?" She asked as if she knew already.

He made as if to say something but his throat was too dry. A sort of whimpering squeak passed his lips. He was studying her skin and the contours of her breasts. He had no time for conversation.
"Suivez-moi. Follow me." She led him by the hand into the little annexe and ordered him to take off his shirt. She gently unbuckled his belt and one by one, undid the buttons on his trousers which fell silently around his ankles. She pushed his underpants down and, dextrously avoiding the upward movement of his erect penis as it broke free from the shackles of his clothes, rendered him totally naked.
"You *are* a cherry boy. Oh la la! This is so special."
She drew some water into the sink and sponged his erection before drying him with a towel. She knelt down before him and cast the towel aside. She looked up to his face, opened her mouth and sucked him in. He was long and hard. He felt no control whatsoever as his body took over from what little train of thought he had left. His joy stroke arrived in less than twenty seconds as he ejaculated down her throat. She gagged, coughed and grabbed for the towel. She rose and spat into the sink before swallowing the last few drops. He stood there, embarrassed and spent. He couldn't help noticing the hard, tight curves of her bum cheeks as she leant over the sink. He moved the three steps to stand behind her and stroked her back, marvelling at the marble smoothness of her skin. He suddenly broke away and made to get dressed. She made out to restrain him and grabbed his arm.
"Not finished yet, cherry boy. Ce n'est pas finis."
She wiped him down with the towel before leading him to the bed. She lay down and guided his mouth on to her nipples. She clutched him to her breasts, engulfing him as he sucked hungrily. Rising for breath, he explored her white belly before reaching down to her wet red triangle. The feeling of disappointment and sadness that comes with male orgasm was leaving him as he felt her wetness with his awkward fingers.

She reached for his semi erect cock and coaxed it back to life. Before he knew it, she had straddled him . In a trice, she had opened her red patch and sucked him right in. She rode him like a jockey, urging him on until he came again, her delicious breasts moving up and down in rhythm with her thrusts. He was totally spent but she rode on, grunting and growling. His loins were in turmoil, it was wet and slippery and he wanted to stop. Their pubic hairs grated audibly as she ground her pubis into his . With a huge gasp , she pulled up and away from him. An enormous wave of urine poured out of her in spurts, over him and over the sheets. He was as shocked as any young man would have been confronted with the same circumstances. It all ended dramatically when suddenly there was a knock at the door and a male voice outside said ,
"Are you ready, my darling Antoinette ?"
Panic set in.
Peter reacted instantly. He pushed her off, leapt across the room, grabbed his pile of clothes and, still naked, climbed quickly but carefully back out the window. Throwing his clothes to the ground, he closed the sash window behind him. There was a narrow pathway all round the back of the hotel where he quickly dressed himself before clambering over the wall. He sniffed in the smell of Fifi's discharges and wretched. Tintin and Paddy were sunning themselves at the bottom, grinning like Cheshire cats.

"Well, how did you get on ? Did you get the knickers?" teased Paddy.
"Yeah, did you get the knickers?" chirped Tintin.

Peter was still quite flustered and , understandably, out of breath. He scrabbled in his trouser pocket and pulled out a pair of scrunched up silk knickers.
"Let's have a sniff," said Tintin, snatching them from his hand. He sniffed them long and hard before passing them to Paddy who also took his fill before handing them back to Peter.

"Did you go into the other rooms along the corridor? You were in there a good half hour. We thought you might have taken a nap on one of those big beds."

Under a barrage of further questioning, Peter finally surrendered and told them,
"Look, I went in through the window, found the knickers and then this gorgeous red haired lady came out from the back room, totally naked. She stripped me of my clothes and then we had a shag. It was fantastic. That's it."
His bald statement was met with total derision by the other two. They fell about laughing.
"Yeah, right. ....and then another one came in the door and you shagged her as well."
"You little liar! "
The two doubters rose from the sand, satisfied that Peter had stepped up and completed his task. There was no further questioning and he felt he was now officially part of the gang. He was also in shock. In the space of a few minutes, he had lost his virginity. The world was going mad and so was he. Everything seemed out of control and incredibly exciting. They strolled back towards the Bathing Pool and discussion, to Peter's relief, had turned to other things. The tide was coming in , the sun was warm and it was time for a swim. They crossed the walkway to the pool and undressed in the mens changing room. As they walked down the steps to the water, they all noticed the strong smell of urine. Tintin was first to trace the smell to Peter.

"Cor blimey, Pete, you smell of piss. That's 'orrible!" said Paddy. Tintin sniffed him too.

"You've pissed yourself, cherry boy. That's truly foul."

Peter ran the last few paces to the edge of the pool and dived in. He felt the cool sea water closing around his body and immediately felt cleaner. Even under water he could smell her perfume. He was a good swimmer and he settled into his rhythm, rolling and stroking, rolling and stroking and kicking until he reached the far wall. It was a distance of two hundred yards and when he got there, he couldn't remember any of it. He grabbed the bar and took a deep breath. His crotch was sore with all her grinding but it gave him a pleasant memory which would stay with him all his life. He felt triumphant and, at the same time, almost deflated. He rubbed himself all over to remove all traces of his unexpected moments of madness. He smiled to himself and set off in the direction of his floundering mates. Manhood had overtaken him.

CHAPTER 39

Life beckons

Manhood may have accidentally overtaken him but he couldn't help remembering that Tintin had called him 'cherry boy'. The more he thought about it, the more he thought that he had been set up. He never got to find out. His mother got a call from school to the effect that his attendance had been erratic and she reminded him of the deal they had struck. He was still coming to terms with the loss of his father and his first sexual experience . He himself felt he needed to pull his head in and was happy to take his mother's advice and went back to complete his education, albeit for just two months until the term ended. It also transpired that his excellent Australian crawl was in demand for the school swimming sports. Mr True, his housemaster, had been very supportive of his situation and gently encouraged him back into full attendance.

Only a few days later, he got some more bad news. Tintin , Paddy and a few friends had found a complete light calibre shell which had washed ashore just to east of the Bathing Pool. They all stood around studying it until one of the group attempted to remove the fuse. The shell exploded , killing Tintin and Paddy outright and seriously injuring two of the others. The news of the tragedy travelled fast. Where details were sketchy, people were happy to make it up. Tales of body parts being found hundreds of yards away were unfortunately true but the fact of the matter was that it was a terrible tragedy and two young lives had unnecessarily been brought to an end. Tintin and Paddy had taught him what it was like to be a townie and it wasn't lost on him. Their behaviour had been crude and boorish but they had been good friends. He thought of them often.

Peter was devastated and became withdrawn. He drew solace from his swimming training at the Bathing Pool. The school had a booking for the competitive lanes twice a week and he took full advantage. There was no other swimmer who could come close. His mates used to check to see whether he had grown gills and scales. This was something he could do well. Water held no fear for him. While he was swimming, he could think. His mind would soar into unknown territory , travelling down pathways he could never realise in real life. He could swim for miles and not know how long he had been in the water. He turned seventeen on June 15 and celebrated the next day by winning all the races he was allowed to enter.

Christine was pleased that things were back on an even keel and Peter was back in the fold. Curfew hours were changed and nobody was to be out after 10p.m. or before 5 a.m.. More items of food were rationed down further and Mrs Le Plongeon at the local shop carried on complaining about her workload with the ration books. The fact that supplies were thin on the ground was attributable almost solely to the Allies presence on both sea and in the air. Locally there was little reason to suspect an attempt would be made to liberate the islands but all the peripheral activity in the lead up to a full scale invasion of France was having an increasingly profound effect.

Peter's end of term school service was held in the first week of July and was combined with Prizegiving Day. Peter was due to receive his Swimming Colours for his outstanding performance in the swimming gala. It was to be a special day and Christine had asked Mac if he would come along for a bit of moral support. He gave her short shrift.

"Och, lassie, I would rrrather stick pins in my eyes. Dressing up amongst all those toffee nosed brown nosers would give me a pain in ma arrrse! Not even for you, lassie."

He was stubborn and he hated any sort of formal occasion. However he did promise to drive them up to Victoria College in Brian's van on the day and when it came, he didn't let them down.

Christine had chosen to leave Sophie with her next door

neighbour and spent the morning getting herself ready. She chivvied Peter into looking respectable on his last day at school and, to his credit, he scrubbed up well. He was happy to endure this last farcical piece of pageantry by realising that, as from tomorrow, he was free at last. Christine looked her usual immaculate self. She had rehemmed an old but pretty dress in a more modern style and, with a minimal amount of fuss and effort, looked a million dollars. How could Mac even have thought of denying her his presence?

At one o'clock there was a loud and persistent honking of a car horn outside which , frankly, did not sound like Brian's van at all. Peter opened the door and looked out. His jaw dropped as he observed the car. It was a massive black 1938 Vauxhall 16, polished to a mirror like shine, and behind the wheel was Mac. He was grinning like a Cheshire cat. He wound down the side window.

"What d'ye reckon, laddie. Wee bit better than the van, d'ye ken ?"

Peter walked around the car, running his hands along the smooth lines of the body.

"Where on earth did you get it? It's immaculate!" said Peter.

"Aye, I did a deal with a wee farmer friend. It's on loan for the day.....and I bought some petrol off an auld friend who works for the other side."

"All above board then Mac?"

"Indubitably. Is your mother ready yet? "

"About ten minutes I reckon. Sophie is with Mrs Chambers up the road. Come in."

The car door swung open and Mac alighted with some

trepidation. He was in full Mackintosh tartan kilt and evening wear. From his bowtie, white shirt, waist coat and short jacket to his kilt, sporran, knee socks and brogues, he was the very epitome of a Scotsman.
"What d'ye reckon, laddie. Will I do? D'ye reckon the lassies will be after me now?"

Peter was lost for words. After a minute or two , he said.
"Why are you wearing a skirt, Mac? I'm not going if you are coming dressed like a girl. No way. No....way. " He went back inside.

Mac followed him into the house. Christine came half way down the stairs and stopped in surprise when she saw Mac in his Scottish regalia.
"Wow!" she said. "That looks pretty impressive. Are you wearing anything under that kilt?"
Mac's face reddened under the onslaught.
"I'll not dignify yerr question with a response. You dinna look so bad yerself, lassie. Now just so you ken, my capacity today is as a chauffeur and nothing more. I'll no be sullying the archways of Victoria College Great Hall today. I'll drive you both there, I'll open the door, you get oot and I'll wait until you're finished. Then I'll drive ye back. Savvy? Come and have a look at my van."
Peter heaved a sigh of relief at this and made Mac promise not to get out at any stage when they got to school.
Christine stepped outside and gasped at the Vauxhall.

"I'm ready. Peter, go change into your school shoes and then we're ready to go."

Peter disappeared inside. Christine closed in on Mac.
"Won't you come up to the hall for prizegiving, Mac? "

"No, lassie. It wouldna be right. It wouldn't be appropriate. Your husband's missing in action and tongues would wag. Rightly or wrongly, it wouldna be right. I'll be waiting in the car until you both come back. "
Christine hadn't give it a thought but could see Mac's point of view.
"Okay," she said thoughtfully and put her hand on his arm. "Okay. Thanks, Mac. where would I be without your common sense."
Mac smiled and opened the rear door for Christine.
"You look lovely," he said very quietly and this time Christine blushed.
He closed the door with a clunk. Christine slid on to the leather seats and snuggled down. The front door of the house slammed as Peter came out and climbed into the front passenger seat. He felt the leather and stroked it.
"Now, young fellow, this is the plan. I drive you there to the front door of the Hall. You get oot and go around to the other side .You then open the door for your ma and escort her inside. I'll be waiting for you at the finish. Okay?"
"Okay, Mac. It's a deal. Just make sure nobody sees your skirt."
"It's a kilt, laddie. It's a kilt. Right now, everybody happy ?"
He crunched the lever into gear and drove gingerly off. It took them fifteen minutes on the open road , eventually driving into the College grounds through the upper gate at 1.40p.m. He drove through the archway, past the statue of Sir Galahad and turned right in front of the main door. The big Vauxhall turned heads. Because of the petrol shortage, most people had arrived by public transport or even horse drawn carriage.
Peter escorted his mother inside and across the annexe to the bottom of the main granite stairs to the Great Hall. He took her arm and they climbed the steps to the hall. At the door they parted company. The pupils were arranged in their four 'houses' across the hall north and south. The parents sat at the eastern end while the western end was occupied by a large elevated

stage. During term time, the school choir would sit on the stage and sing out of key . The headmaster would pontificate from a lectern in front of them. The stage led off northward into the library which connected to the main door via a short wide passage.
Prize-giving droned on and, in the warmth of the afternoon, a few people dozed off. Prayers were said. Announcements were made and the Head gave a speech. While this was going on, Mac had parked around the back of the Great Hall and got out, searching for the toilets. He went in a side entrance and discovered the changing rooms straight away. When he had finished he turned right instead of left and found himself at the bottom of the main staircase. He was immediately spotted by the porter Lewis who was hovering at the turn of the stairs. Lewis had worked as an assistant at the school for twenty years and was all blue serge and peaked hat. He had already run a practised eye over Mac's immaculate appearance. What Lewis didn't know about the workings of the school was not worth knowing .

"This way, Brigadier" he said and beckoned him up. "I've kept you a place at the back with his lordship."
Mac was a bit confused but decided to pick the ball up and run with it.
"Okay......er..thank you." He followed Lewis up the stairs, turned right into the passage through to the library. Unbeknown to Mac, he was now about to be guided onto the main stage to sit with the bigwigs. Lewis slipped him up the steps to the stage, out of view of the people in the Great Hall and into a chair at the front of the gaggle of high-ranking old boys who had been especially invited. His arrival was unnoticed by everyone. The Headmaster droned on . Eventually he awarded a table full of prizes. Blah blah blah....it went on.
"Best swimmer of the year.............Peter Marinelle!"
A cheer went up from his mates as Peter rose from the ranks of Sartorius House and made his way up the steps of the stage to

shake hands with the Headmaster and the Chairman of the Board of Governors. As he turned to walk back down, he heard a stage whisper which caught his attention.
"Well done, laddie!" was accompanied by a thumbs-up as Mac half rose from his seat before deciding a bit more discretion was in order and sat back again. Peter blinked the blink of a disbeliever and took a long hard look. There was a pause.
"Off you go, Marinelle, and good luck for the future."said the Chairman of the Board of Governors.
Peter nodded and descended the steps back to floor level of the main hall. At the far end, Christine shed a tear. It was a big moment. She had guided Peter through eleven years of schooling. Her daughter would be starting school next year if there was one to go to. Her husband was missing in action. There were so many questions that only time and the departure of the invaders would answer.
The event broke up at four o'clock and Mac picked them up by the front door as arranged. He was quick out of the blocks and was at the head of the queue in the Vauxhall. Christine and Peter were waiting . Mac drove slowly up and braked. He was just about to get out but he remembered his promise to Peter. A figure darted out from the annexe. It was Lewis, all blue serge and peaked hat.
"Allow me, madam, " he said as he opened the rear door. Christine smiled and eased herself in. "Marinelle, you can get in round the other side. Off you go. Don't hang about."
Peter did as he was told. You didn't mess with Lewis.
With a grin from ear to ear, Lewis saluted Mac and said, "Nice to see you again, Brigadier. Same time next year?"

"Oh yes. Definitely. Wouldnee miss it for the worrrld."

"What was that, sir? Do give my regards to her ladyship, won't you." replied Lewis, but Mac was already on the move and the words were lost in the grating noise of the gearbox.

"Brigadier? Brigadier? What was that all about,Mac." said Christine from the back seat.
"Tell you over a cup of tea." said Mac , laughing uncontrollably.
Peter was grinning from ear to ear. He had officially left school. Life beckoned.

CHAPTER 40

Fritz goes home and wishes he hadn't

Oberleutnant Doenig managed to arrange five days leave in early March. Being officially in the Luftwaffe, he managed the outward trip by hitching a ride on one of the few remaining aircraft left at the Airport in St Peter. Most of the Air Force were needed elsewhere in Europe and the Mediterranean. Fritz figured it would not be long before his cushy number in the British Channel Islands would be at an end. The train trip across France was dangerous as the risk of being strafed by Allied planes rose in proportion to the number of bombing raids that were taking place over western Germany. That was exactly where he was heading, back to Essen to see his widowed mother. He zigzagged his way into his home land and witnessed the start of the destruction of West Germany. The Krupp factories were producing armaments in and around Essen but they were now subject to a bombing campaign. When he got home, his mother had already left for her sister's house in the Bavarian Alps where it was safer but colder. His father Ernst had died from lung cancer the year before war had broken out, a premature end brought about by too many cigarettes and a deep felt disappointment in the way his country was heading. Fritz collected the house keys from the Niedermeyers, their family friends who were still running the corner shop. A quick catch-up with them revealed that one of his school mates Willy Brecht had been killed on the Russian Front. A vision of Willy dashing round the playground when they were six year olds flashed across his mind. Willy was a hard little nut with endless energy. How could he be dead? He bought some groceries , said his goodbyes and told them he would return with the keys in a day or two. He went back to a freezing cold house and lit the fire that his mother had left in case he returned. He cobbled together a meal and broke out a bottle of Reisling from the pantry. He glanced around the walls

at the framed photographs of his mum and dad, cousins and grandparents . An old school photograph caught his eye and yes, there was little Willy Brecht in the back row. His face was blurred.
"*How typical! The little bugger could not stand still for a minute.*"
He fell asleep in the armchair in front of the dwindling fire only to be woken by the sound of Wellington bombers overhead at two in the morning. The distant 'crump' of bombs was evidence that the Krupp factories were the target of the Royal Air Force that night. He made a bed under the heavy dinner table and grabbed a couple more hours of interrupted sleep. At first light he wrote his mother a long letter in vague terms as he knew that , even here, they would be censored. At least the information he had given the Niedermeyers about his own situation would be passed on without too much interference. At midday he went down to the corner shop and discovered the full extent of last night's air raid. There were at least fifty dead, two factories obliterated and one whole street completely gutted by fire. The shop was busy and news was dire. An old man shuffled in and Fritz recognised him. He was an old friend of his father.
"Hello, Mister Dietermeyer. Remember me ? Fritz Doenig. Mathias' son."

The old man looked up with a smile of recognition and shook his hand.
"Young Fritz.....well, you're a sight for sore eyes. Oberleutnant ? I see you've done well. Not many young men left around here. All gone to war. Most of them dead. Glad to see you are okay. You'd think we'd have learnt from the first war. Bloody stupid."
He lowered his voice to a whisper.
" You can shove all that Nazism right up Adolf's arse. Hasn't done us any good at all. How's your mother?"

Fritz chuckled. "*She's fine according to the note she left me although I haven't seen her. Took off last week to Aunt Eva's in the mountains. She should be safe there.*"

The old man bought some bread and made to go.
"Give my best to your dad. Haven't seen him for ages. I'll look out for him at the football ."
Fritz's face registered surprise but he felt he couldn't spoil a forgetful old man's day by reminding him that Mathias was long gone.
"Okay Herr Dietermeyer. I'll tell him when I see him. Have a good day. Nice to see you again!"
Another hour catching up with people in the shop and all the news was bad. He had made a list of people to visit but he felt it would be a pointless exercise. Practically all of his old school friends were in the forces and scattered over Europe and beyond. Older relatives and friends had fled the danger area. He decided to leave as soon as he had secured the house. He cleared the fireplace and washed up the dirty crockery. As he closed the curtains he looked out through the window to see that it was snowing hard. He felt cold and a wave of depression went through him as he slithered along the now icy pavement to leave the house keys with the Niedermeyers. An overwhelming sense of foreboding filled the air in the shop as they all said their goodbyes.
*"We'll see you soon,"*said Mrs Niedermeyer. *"Hopefully all this nonsense will be over soon and we can get on with our lives."*
He nodded in agreement. *" I hope you are right. Sooner rather than later, I hope."*

He waved and closed the shop door behind him. As he did so, the bell on the door made a loud solitary clang which resonated and seemed to be recording a point in time. The moment was not lost on him and he hesitated as the sound fell away. He cast his eyes over the peeling paintwork which surrounded the shop windows and was suddenly hit by an icy wind which broke his pattern of thought. He pulled the collar of his great coat up around his ears and shivered.

"Farewell, Essen. I have a feeling I might not be back for a while."

The trip back by train across France was quiet but he still felt anxious as he huddled in a corner seat looking out of the window. He changed trains in Paris and had ninety minutes to kill before his next connection. He decided to stretch his legs and find a nearby cafe. He sidled down the Rue Guillaume and wondered how everything could be so normal. The pavements were busy with people going about their business and there were well dressed patrons in all the restaurants. The sun was out but it was still cold. A few leather coated German officers had braved the weather and were sitting at the outside tables of the Cafe de Londres. He steered clear of that one as he wasn't in the mood to 'Heil Hitler' anybody. He crossed the road , carefully avoiding an old Citroen travelling down the road at a reckless speed. He had just reached the other side when there was an almighty squeal of brakes as the car pulled up sharply in front of the Cafe de Londres. A machine gun barrel poked its nose ominously out of the back side window and in the space of ten seconds had sprayed a deadly hail of bullets into the gaggle of German officers previously enjoying their coffees outside. Three lay dead and another limped away inside the cafe. The Citroen did a loud wheelspin as its tyres tried to catch up with the leaden foot on the accelerator pedal. It fishtailed out of sight.

Fritz needed no second bidding. He was gone, melting away into the chaos and screaming that followed. He was back inside the train station within two minutes and sat down on a bench close to his platform. He pulled his lapels up over his face with one hand and with the other he caressed his Luger pistol inside the front of his coat. His train could not come soon enough and he didn't feel any safer when it did.

He reached St Malo a couple of hours later . He had been warned there would be no planes available to take him back to Jersey so he headed for the docks. As he did the wind started to increase from a light to a moderate breeze and the skies darkened.
The boat trip back was horrendous. He managed to board a smallish 1500 ton cargo vessel which was clearly not built to carry passengers in comfort. There was a large swell running and as the ship departed, Fritz felt sure that it would turn back if it was too rough. He spent the next three hours throwing up and if he hadn't been stuck inside, he would have willingly thrown himself overboard in order to swim ashore. The boat finally arrived at St Helier Harbour and threw itself against the jetty in relief. The crew thought it was great fun. All of the hundred or so passengers had been sick. Fritz found a wooden bench on the quay and cleaned himself up while he recovered his senses. There was no immediate transport. It was dark and it was raining. He was miserable as he started staggering the mile or so back through town to the Hotel Bristol. He arrived at his billet about half an hour later. He was hungry but at least he no longer felt sick. He had managed to walk off his nausea. It was ten o'clock and everyone was in bed. After raiding the kitchen for food and water, he got to his room, undressed and threw all his clothes in a corner. He clambered unenthusiastically into the shower and braced himself for the cold water. He washed the day's events from his skin, dried himself with a tea towel and dived under a mass of blankets on the bed. It had been a day to forget and conversely a day he would always remember for its brutality and sorrow.
He slept for twenty hours and surfaced at 6p.m. the next day. It was still dark and he felt totally disorientated until he realised the length of his sleep and the events of the previous day. He got up, shaved, dressed and tottered down the stairs towards the dining room. Gunter Muller was first to greet him at the bottom.
"Oberleutnant Doenig! Good to have you back, Fritz. You're

back early. Did you have a good time? "
Fritz hesitated. *"You wouldn't believe me if I told you, Gunter. Am I glad to be back. This is so much better than home. I'll tell you all about it over supper. Let's grab the window table."*
The pair were soon joined by Werner Turner who had been taking band practice earlier in the afternoon. One of the brass players was also a chef and he volunteered twice a week to cook for the thirty or so members. Usually the food was carried in hotfoot from the large kitchens at the Mayfair but tonight was Bierkeller night with sausages and sauerkraut. Fritz was delighted to be amongst friends again. Goodness only knew where the beer had come from and he wasn't going to ask.
It took him half an hour to describe his horrendous short leave. Werner and Gunter listened intently, horrified at what they were hearing.
"All that ties in with what we are hearing on Big Bertha. The BBC reported a massive bombing raid on Essen and it must have been the bombers we heard flying over a couple of nights ago. We seemed to be firing off a lot of AA flak. Not that we ever seem to hit anything. They are usually way out of range." said Gunter.
Fritz then described his adventure on the Rue Guillaume in Paris when he could so easily have been in the firing line.
"I'm pretty sure they were SS officers. They were sitting ducks. Last time that happened, they executed fifty of the locals. Just took them out , put them up against a wall , pulled up a couple of motorcycle machine gunners and shot the lot. They'll do a hundred this time, for sure. I tell you, my good friends, without fear of this being repeated, we aren't so badly off on this little island. We would do well to keep our heads down and our noses clean."

CHAPTER 41

Mackerel seas and skies

In early July 1943 the Germans celebrated their three years of occupation. They held a march past in St Helier when it took two thousand or so soldiers a full fifteen minutes to pass the Feldkommandant as he stood on a dais by the Town Hall . Two German Army bands combined to play military marching tunes and the propaganda division had a field day with their movie cameras. The local population showed a lack of interest by ignoring the whole charade as best they could. One little old lady chose her moment to dart across the street in front of one particular unit of infantry, spilling the contents of her shopping bag on the road as she tripped theatrically over her own feet. The unit was marching at top speed and she definitely wasn't. They broke ranks and had to reassemble as best they could further down the road. Madame Le Bas gathered her goods and continued on her way to change her ration books, leaving the chaos in her wake.

The summer weather had been good with lots of sunshine and not much rain. Without the war, this would have been a bumper season for the little island. The hotels and guest houses would have been full of happy sunburnt tourists. Instead, they were full of unwelcome soldiers who would not be paying the bill when they left. Their departure was vehemently desired by the locals and the sooner the better. The volume of overhead and naval allied activity , coupled with general good news gleaned by the illegal wireless listeners, finally gave rise to increased optimism about an early end to hostilities. This short term happiness was unfortunately tempered by decreasing food supplies, caused by the very activity that the locals were advocating. Supply ships were being harassed, machine gunned and bombed off the route from France. But still the garrison of over ten thousand troops remained at roughly the same number. A similar situation was going on in the sister island of Guernsey just a few miles to the north west. There, another ten thousand or so troops guarded a population just a few hundred less than the forty thousand on Jersey.

Peter Marinelle was now free to pursue his new career in fishing and a glut of mackerel saw the Crazy Doris loaded to the gunnels on two or three occasions at the end of July. A new German order requiring a guard to accompany *all* fishing vessels came into effect . This was to stop all escape attempts of which there was an increasing number as the war dragged on. These were mostly sixteen to eighteen year olds who were becoming bored and disaffected by the lack of any sort of pattern to their lives. Their efforts were fraught with danger. If the Germans didn't see your canoe or small boat leaving the coast and use you for target practice, then the dangerous seas between the islands and England were only too willing to swallow you up . If you were unlucky enough to be caught in the act or assisting the act, then you could expect a court martial and a year or two in a French prison. The Germans were ruthless in interrogating any suspects involved in failed attempts. Relatives and friends of would be escapees bore the full brunt of the Feldpolitz and their brutal methods.

Much to the relief of both Peter and Mac, it was the newly promoted Corporal Klaus Bucholtz who managed to wangle himself a trip on board the Crazy Doris. It was he who was responsible for setting the guard rosters and it was he who thought he was the best equipped for the job. He was a clever lad, inquisitive and knowledgeable. Klaus had just turned 21 and was pleased that his new promotion had given him just enough authority to take advantage of the surroundings that he found himself in. He was a farmer's boy from Steinkirschen in northern rural Germany when he found himself conscripted into the Wehrmacht at the tender age of eighteen. After a few weeks of training, he found himself on a train to the Western Front soon after Hitler had advanced through France to the Atlantic. He had felt his life was out of control until it returned to some semblance of structure as he settled into the routine of 'befehl ist befehl' or 'orders are orders'. His world was still rural and he would spend time improving his English and chatting with the local farmers about this crop and that. The sea was new to him and he loved it. With his promotion, he could at least distance himself a little from the boring duties of the common foot soldier.

That day on the slipway at La Rocque, he made sure he checked all the relevant paperwork regarding the Crazy Doris with Mac and also their licences which they had obtained at the start of the year. This was more to demonstrate to the rest of the Defence Point La Rocque (known to the Germans as der Widerstandsnest) the procedure that was to be followed. His English was improving rapidly and he explained that the new rules meant that all registered fishing boats had to be accompanied by a guard to prevent any escape attempt. Everybody knew this but 'befehl ist befehl', so he thought it best to explain to all concerned. The sun was shining and the tide was nearly high when he decided to have a bit of fun. He told both of the crew of the still moored Crazy Doris that Sergeant Steiglitz had been assigned to them and would be down in a few minutes.
Mac's face turned to thunder and he spluttered as he fought for words.

"Yes, Mac. He will not be long. Just two or three minutes and he will be here with his ... er.....Luger."

Peter had been standing behind Mac so his face could not be seen. He was trying to stop himself from laughing and his shoulders were convulsing. Mac turned round and wondered what was going on. The cat was out of the bag.

"I'm sorry. I am having.....how you say......a joke with you. Yes?" said Klaus, smiling.

Mac recovered quickly and, more in relief than acknowledgement, he laughed too.

"Verrry gud. Yes, verry gud. I suspect young laughing boy here set me up for that one!"

Peter was beyond a meaningful reply as he was spluttering too much.

"Come on then, laughing boys. Let's catch some fish before the tide changes its mind."

Klaus went back up the slipway to retrieve his knapsack and returned, armed with his rifle. The Doris was afloat by this time and the three of them waded out and climbed aboard, using the new little ladder at the stern. A few minutes later they untied themselves from the mooring chains and fired up the motor, slipping out leaving the pier on their right. Peter looked up and saw a gang of Todt workers rolling out and fixing barbed wire to the ladders and railings of the pier. He nudged Mac and pointed upwards towards the construction work. Mac gazed in wonder and turned to Corporal Bucholtz.

"Do you *really* think that the Allies will attack Jersey, Klaus?" said Mac.

"I hope not," replied Klaus after careful consideration. His English was much improved but he still had to think before he spoke.

"........but *befehl ist befehl* and Berlin .....er..says that the islands will be....um....defended until the end."

"Let us hope that it won't be necessary. Maybe one day soon you will all leave so we can bloody well get on with our lives." said Mac, realising as he spoke that it wasn't really Klaus' fault. Klaus was taken aback but took it well. He paused before he replied. He looked Mac straight in the eye and said,

" Yes Mac......I understand......I understand. I also want that." He looked wistfully towards the horizon and fell silent. Almost as an afterthought , he said quietly,
"I also want to go home."

The atmosphere became decidedly gloomy until the warmth of the sun began to lift all their spirits. They headed silently straight out to sea way past Seymour Tower. Two miles to the north the mighty Mont Orgueil Castle shouted its massive presence and glared down over the long bay of Grouville. It would have looked even more impressive in medieval times as it would have been painted white to deter prospective invaders from France and Spain. 130 ships of the Spanish Armada would have passed the islands on their way to England in 1588, albeit a few miles to the west. Even in those days the English Channel was a busy place. To the south the more modern late eighteenth century Icho Tower made much less noise. Along with Seymour, Icho Tower was also part of the German defences. After an initial period when both towers were manned, they were now just checked once or twice a day to make sure no commando landing force was hiding there. No-one could accuse the Germans of being less than diligent in this respect.
They had about twenty lobster pots to check and rebait. Mac and Peter were well drilled as to their positions, each one being marked with a single white buoy. It was quite a physical effort

to haul each wicker basket up the six or seven fathoms they were lying in. On a good day they would expect three or four lobsters and the same number of crabs. On a bad day there would be nothing and they might lose a pot or two to a westerly gale. Klaus was happy to help and he trusted both of them not to throw him over the side. As soon as he had got on the boat he had stowed his rifle in a tarpaulin next to his knapsack. Further out to sea he had removed his army blouse and singlet to catch a bit of sun. Mac was impressed by that and the way he mucked in with the hauling of the pots.

"You had better be careful, Klaus. Ma gud buddy Steigy might be watching you through his binoculars. He'll have you on a charge," Mac joked and Klaus grinned.

"I think I am okay this week. He is on ......er....holiday....no..how you say.....leave?"

"Happy days. He might get blown up on the way home," chirped Peter.

After four hours of leisurely hauling pots, they all felt comfortable with each other and anchored up at two o'clock for a late lunch. Peter pulled a wooden box out to make a table and the three of them sat around the benches at the stern, enjoying a well earned break on a very pleasant day. There was no swell at all as Mac and Peter tucked into their fish paste sandwiches. Klaus produced some fried potato cakes and, much to their amusement , informed them that these were kartoffelpuffers.
"Have some. ......please. My mutter makes these when I am small. Now I make them in the kitchen of the guest house. Potatoes, flour, cheese, onions, salt, pepper. Please try."
Both Mac and Peter declared them completely edible and spent the next few minutes practising saying 'kartoffelpuffer'.
"These are very very nice, Klaus. You'll make someone a lovely

wife!" said Peter.
They bantered their way through lunch and dozed off in turn, rocked to sleep by a combination of the hot sun and the gentle movement of the boat. Mac became conscious of a faint clunking sound coming from over the side. It became more insistent and slightly louder before he decided to investigate. He struggled to his feet and looked overboard. His reaction was instantaneous.

"Holy shit, it's a bloody mine. Stay where you are and don't rock the bloody boat."
It was a massive floating Polish mine, a great six foot black metallic sphere with horns sticking out of the top. It was bumping malevolently up against the side of the boat, waiting to blow them all out of the water as soon as one of the horns was disturbed sufficiently. Mac gently grabbed the broom which was tucked under a bench near his feet. Gingerly, he grabbed the wooden handle and manoeuvred the bristly end towards the mine. Peter thought Mac was having them on but as he stood up , he realised that he was telling the truth.
Mac started to push the mine away from the sides but it was proving a tricky process. Each time he pushed it, the sea pushed it back. Eventually he managed to jiggle it towards the bows and ,with the lightest of shoves, it broke free of the boat . Seemingly relieved, it drifted with the current for a few yards and then stopped as it scraped on a submerged rock.
Peter and Klaus raced towards the anchor chain at the front and began pulling it up while Mac yanked at the starter cord of the engine. Six pulls later, it reluctantly kicked into life and Mac quickly steered the boat away from danger. The mine was designed to sink much heavier craft and they had been saved quite simply by the shape of the Crazy Doris' hull. A heavier swell might have triggered the deadly horns into detonating but calm seas had been their saviour. They beat a hasty retreat out to sea and slowed down only when they were half a mile away. In the meantime the mine had escaped the clutches of the

submerged rock and drifted on to find its final resting place on the Petit Bidou rocks. Here its horns engaged with a more sympathetically shaped recipient whereupon the mine obliterated a natural navigational mark which had stood proudly on the printed chart for more than a hundred and fifty years. Small pieces of the Petit Bidou rained down on the Crazy Doris, chipping the paintwork of the cuddy where Mac, Peter and Klaus were sheltering, waiting for the shower to stop. Mac immediately noticed that the Petit Bidou was now a mark of the past. At first he thought he might be mistaken and had miscalculated the height of the tide. However it should have been there but now it clearly was not. He turned the boat round and headed back to investigate. His suspicions were correct. The rock had been smashed to pieces. Peter was first to notice what else was going on. As they circled the now non-existent mark, he shouted,

"Will you take at look at that!"

To port and starboard, stunned and dead fish emerged from the depths to pierce the surface of the sea, already disturbed by the explosion. All around it was like a boiling cauldron of cooking mackerel, their iridescent colours being picked out by the sunlight.

"Bloody hell!" said Mac.
"Scheisse!' said Klaus.

"Mackerel! Hundreds of 'em. It's Johnny boy. Johnny sent them! Woohoo!"

Peter's life had been a whirlwind in the last year and he had managed to come to terms with the loss of his best friend. Time had healed the recurring nightmare of that tragic day. This seemed to Peter to be a little reminder from his best buddy that

he was still around.
The force of the explosion had sent a shockwave through the sea to a distance of a hundred yards, killing or stunning practically all the fish in that area. A large shoal of mackerel had been feeding around the Petit Bidou when the mine detonated. A few large green pollock appeared followed by a massive ten pound bass. Peter stripped down to his underpants and dived overboard, grabbing the bass before it could disappear. Mac produced a landing net and between the three of them, they reaped the harvest. Peter grabbed the largest fish and pushed them into the landing net, Mac swung them overboard and Klaus found a storage space for each one underneath the seats. When the big ones had been hauled aboard, they started on the mackerel. There were hundreds . Their timing was perfect. They had been at sea for nearly eight hours and the tide was now coming in to carry them back to La Rocque for seven o'clock. It stayed light until just after the curfew hour of ten o'clock that evening.
There was a lot of fish and with the aid of Klaus filling out all the relevant paperwork, Mac and Peter managed to keep everyone happy. A good amount was sent straight to market as was their legal requirement by the German authorities. Klaus was happy to take some prize specimen fish as recommended by the skipper and first mate. He was also quick to point out that he would not be inspecting the boat before it was trailered back to the farm for 'routine maintenance'. He ordered the slipway guards to let the tractor, trailer and boat through.
Mac had had a wonderful day. Peter had connected once more with his late friend. Klaus had had the best time ever but was sunburnt and hurting. The sun had shone and the warmth of the day would stay with them until tomorrow. Mac and Peter reached the Grenadier Inn where Brian was waiting by the front door with his arms folded, glass of Calvados in hand and his omnipresent wheelbarrow by his side.

"How did it go, boys? Lobsters as thin on the ground as ever?"

said Brian.

" Well, laddie," said Mac from the height of the tractor seat. He thought for a bit and then said,
"I think you're gonna need a bigger barrow!"
The story unfolded and Brian was beaming. Everyone was happy.

CHAPTER 42

Jersey looks a mess

Brian Le Rouge bypassed his wheelbarrow and filled his van three times that evening, each time distributing the catch to outlying farms in exchange for potatoes, tomatoes, carrots, tobacco and pork. His exchanges flowed back to Mac and Peter to supplement their diets. They were the lucky ones. These extras came their way by the advantages of their trade. They had goods to barter and farmers to barter with. Conversely, in town, exchanging a bicycle tyre for a pair of old shoes wasn't going to feed anybody. Not all the farmers had their customers' best interests at heart. One was given two months in prison for deliberately ploughing in an acre of potatoes which should have been lifted. This was usual practice in peacetime when the price was uneconomically low, but under current circumstances it was unforgivable. Frequent checks by the Germans precipitated unregistered pigs and cattle for which the usual sentence was a fine of twenty five pounds. Dairy farmers were fined for 'milk adulteration' which was a polite way of saying the milk was watered down. One or two publicans were fined for watering down tots of spirits and shopkeepers prosecuted for selling sugar above the recommended price. Goods came sporadically from France and all were rationed. You could buy only on production of the coupons in your ration book.

Obergefreiter Klaus Bucholtz knew all this was going on as his own Sergeant was also involved in the black market. Steiglitz was stealing petrol from the depot and exchanging it for milk and eggs with a local farmer. He was sure that this was just the tip of the iceberg.

After his fishing trip, it was the last thing on his mind. That evening he was hospitalised after complaining of dizziness. It was a simple case of dehydration. The doctor didn't need more clues than the redness of his sunburnt skin . With rest and the intake of fluids, he was back in action within two days.

However , his new extra- curricular guard duties were curtailed when an order was issued by the Feldkommandantur to the effect that boat fishing was now banned completely until further notice. After such a good day out, this came as a disappointing but not unexpected blow to Klaus. His Defence Post overlooking La Rocque harbour had been in action two or three times a week at the end of July. A couple of R.A.F Hurricanes returning from a mission over France had taken an interest in the area around the Bay of Grouville. Their curiosity satisfied, they were about to fly off north back to England when a couple of Kriegsmarine patrol boats in the bay opened fire at them. The Hurricanes were clearly piqued by this show of aggression and returned to strafe both vessels with the result that one was completely destroyed by fire and the other limped back to port. The anti-aircraft guns at La Rocque were in use most nights as they fired ineffectively at numerous overflying aircraft. There were also numerous target practices during the day and night when general warnings were put out for civilians to stay indoors. Anti-aircraft guns, machine guns, field guns and rifles would all add to the noisy mayhem and shrapnel rained down on the countryside. Festung (Fortress) Jersey was clearly in a state of nervousness.

The Feldpolitzei had become paranoid in winkling out illegal wireless sets and sentences for possession were increased further . The order had been extended to include their own troops as the news from Europe got worse. An announcement on the BBC radio at 7p.m. on 8 September 1943 told of the unconditional surrender of Italy. Despite the threatened penalties for wireless possession, this information found its way into the homes of all islanders within minutes directly or by word of mouth. This was the best news they had heard for three years and many a bottle of brandy was retrieved from its hiding place in order to celebrate. It was bad news for the Germans and the morale of their troops started to wilt.

As the end of the year drew close, it became apparent that law and order was starting to fray at the edges. The cause was hunger. Numerous slave workers, constructing bunkers and railway lines for the paramilitary Todt organisation, already half starved by a miserably cruel diet of cabbage and soup, began to break out of their badly guarded camps at night and steal whatever food they could from whoever they could. They were a desperate bunch of badly treated, badly fed and badly clothed unfortunates who had been captured by an enemy who showed little humanity towards them. A mixture of Russians, French, French colonial North Africans , Spaniards and others made up the workforce . The locals had witnessed their cruel treatment at the hands of the Todt and did what they could when visited at night by these wretchedly underfed prisoners. The island was looking a total mess at year's end. Makeshift narrow gauge railway tracks randomly criss crossed fields, roads and private gardens in order to shift quantities of sand, cement and steel to their construction sites. At certain places there was so much dry cement dust lying around that it looked like a ski resort.

An outbreak of diphtheria enforced the cancellation of many social events in order to avoid the spread of the disease. The Feldcommandantur tolerated places of entertainment such as cinemas and theatres. The Germans enjoyed 'making show' as much as the locals. Pantomimes, plays and musical recitals could go ahead but content was carefully monitored. The iconic Forum Cinema in St Helier was now essentially a German cinema showing German films and understandably biased newsreels. The troops lapped it up. Outlying Parish Halls were also harnessed by choirs and Dramatic Societies , basically to alleviate the increasing boredom. The various bands played on, both local and military. Fritz Doenig and the Luftwaffe Band were much in demand playing weekly recitals in the Royal Square in St Helier but the increasing number of funeral appearances was sapping their morale. Casualties at sea manifested themselves as corpses washed up on the beaches, every one of which had to be buried and given a respectful send-off, whether they were friend or foe. Things had changed markedly from the time they had marched in and taken over. The ban on fishing boats was lifted a month after it was made and all boats and fishermen had to be registered again. Unregistered boats of under 14 feet now had to have a large visible number painted on them and those lying neglected on harbour beds had to be lifted and lined up on the quayside. The Crazy Doris went out again weekly until October when cold weather and a lack of success forced them to take the boat out of the water. It overwintered at Roger and Eileen Le Ross' old house .The house and land had been left in the trust of Roger's lawyer ,Terry O'Sullivan, who lived miles away at St Peter in the west of the island. Terry was happy to lease it out for a small rent for the duration of the war to an old school friend Michel Le Gros. Michel had assumed the soubriquet of 'Big Mick' owing to his short stature. Nearing fifty years old, he was as wide as he was tall. In the dark he resembled a barrel but what he lacked in height he made up for in strength. The property at Sunny View was a fine old traditional granite farmhouse which had a huge barn and a few outbuildings nearby. The farmland had been sold off before the war leaving just two acres which Eileen Le Ross had previously cared for. Mick had quickly flattened the area and planted a variety of vegetable crops. He was a sociable fellow and quickly made his presence felt at the Grenadier. It was during a conversation with Brian and Mac that he made the offer of the barn and yard to house the Crazy Doris whenever needed. Like Brian, his wife had left for England before the Germans arrived but , *unlike* Brian, he didn't miss her at all. He was having the best time. There was no-one to nag him, no-one to denigrate him and no-one to order him about. He was happy to offer the fishing fraternity a secure undercover place to work on their boats in the winter and enjoyed the to-ing and fro-ing that went on. Mac and Peter spent many hours sanding and painting and even little Sophie went along once or twice.

It was on one of these occasions that Christine had decided to go into St Helier to have lunch with her old school friend Anne-Marie. She was waiting for the bus a few yards down the road from St Kitts when she unexpectedly found herself climbing into the back seat of a recently requisitioned large black Rover 14 car driven by the same good looking officer who had offered her a lift some months ago at the very same spot. She had spurned his first offer but at the time she had been surprised at the little tingle she had felt in the pit of her stomach. She made her mind up not to spurn a second offer if indeed it ever came and there she was, doing exactly that and thoroughly enjoying the thrill of it. Hans Stich was a Lieutenant in the Kriegsmarine and was on his way back from Gorey Harbour to his billet at the Grand Hotel on the seafront in St Helier.

"So you finally are having the courage to accept a ride into town. I don't bite, you know." he said. He spoke English well, without the usual harsh, guttural edge that English-speaking Germans have.

"Well, it's not really socially acceptable to be seen fraternising with the enemy.....but, as the bus is late by nearly an hour, I thought I might take a chance. You don't look too dangerous, except you are driving on the wrong side of the road." Christine couldn't quite believe the words that were tripping so easily off her tongue. Starved for years of any meaningful flirting, she found herself off and running at a speed that scared her. She was a pretty woman in her late thirties and since the uncertainty of her husband's "missing presumed dead", she was now faced with her own uncertainties over where she went now. Would she simply shut up shop or would she submit to the embers that still burned within her ? She missed the physicality of her relationship with Cliff and now she had a choice. She could just get used to the present state of affairs or she could pursue the feelings that stirred within. As yet, she hadn't quite made up her mind.

"To us Germans, this is the right side of the road and it's the *right* side of the road. I am driving back to the St Helier harbour but I can take you to where you are going....." said Hans, "where are you going?"

"Snow Hill would be good. My friend lives in Bath Street so I could walk from there. Thank you." said Christine.

"Are you visiting your boyfriend?" he said, his tongue firmly in his cheek.

"No." she said tersely, not wanting to divulge anything more about herself. She was beginning to feel uneasy about the direction the conversation was heading and now wished she had never accepted the lift.
"I am sorry," said Hans. "I should mind my business. I didn't mean to be rude. I have a wife and two small children in Berlin. I have no news for four weeks now. It's very worrying."
The conversation then turned to more mundane subjects such as the weather and, as they clattered and bumped over yet more railway lines, the state of the roads. The big Rover 14 continued on its way until they stopped at Snow Hill where Hans got out from the driver's seat and opened the back door to let her out. Christine slid down off the leather seat on to the pavement , ignored the hand that was offered and thanked him.
"It was my pleasure. My name is Hans Stich."
She said thank you once more and walked off down towards Bath Street.
Snow Hill was a major intersection of small roads leading down to the main streets and it was a busy meeting place for friend and foe alike. She looked round and saw a dozen pairs of eyes surveying her disapprovingly. A scruffy man with baggy trousers tied around his waist with a piece of string looked her in the eye and spat on the pavement at her feet. The atmosphere felt oppressive.

"Bitch!" said a voice from behind her. She didn't look round to see where it was coming from but set off quickly , her heels clacking on the pavement as she quickened her pace.
When she arrived at Anne-Marie's house and told her what had happened, she got little sympathy.

"Big flash requisitioned car. Good looking German officer in smart uniform gives you a lift and drops you off on the busiest spot in town ? What were you thinking, dear ? You're a Jerrybag."
"A what ?" said Christine.
"A Jerrybag. A person of the feminine persuasion who consorts with the Germans. Don't worry about it. You just got out at the wrong place. Most of the gossips hang around Snow Hill looking for things to criticise. They'll have forgotten it by now. You country bumpkins are so out of touch. Cheer up. Tea? Real tea?"

Despite what Anne-Marie had said, she was astonished and upset at the snide remarks that had come her way at Snow Hill. She resolved to do better .
"I'll get him to drop me off in a side street next time!" she said, more in jest than bravado.
"That's my girl ! There's going to be a next time then?" replied Anne-Marie, pouring the tea. "We'll make a new woman of you yet!"

CHAPTER 43

Big Bertha brings comfort

Fritz Doenig had every right to be full of indignation and fury when he discovered that Major Becker's grave had been desecrated. The band had been playing at yet another German officer's funeral at St Brelade's Church cemetery and , after the service, he assembled his musicians in the road below while he walked the hundred yards or so to briefly pay his respects at Becker's headstone which was some way from today's burial. When he got there he was astonished to find the headstone lying face up and a large coffin-sized hole in the ground. After his initial shock, he retraced his steps to the assembled band and made sure that the promised transport was waiting at the end of the road. He despatched his men on the troop lorry back to town and walked back down the road to the vicarage to investigate the mystery.

He walked up the grass pathway to the wooden door and rang the bell. The Very Reverend Basil Austin answered the knock , immediately acknowledging Fritz. They had met on many occasions and were on nodding terms without ever having a conversation of any length. Fritz got straight to the point.

"Good afternoon, Reverend. I am sorry to trouble you .Can you tell me please what has happened to the grave of Major Becker up in the German Cemetery. The monument stone has been knocked over and the grave has been dug up."

Basil Austin could see that he was upset and asked him to come inside so that he could tell him what he knew. He led him into the large front room. The afternoon sun was filtering through the net curtains which swayed in the breeze coming through the open french windows. There were three or four large leather sofas scattered around. It was obviously a room where a lot of talking had gone on.

"Please sit down......... I'm happy to say it has nothing to do with me and I could never , ever condone such behaviour as I

have seen this week. A squad of soldiers arrived last Wednesday with orders from Oberst Gruber that the coffin of Major Becker was to be relocated to the Stranger's Cemetery in town. They could not tell me why, so I telephoned the Oberst to ask for an explanation. I got through only to his office where Colonel Muster took my call. I protested most vehemently that these orders were an outrage, whatever the reason. He told me to calm down and accept that this was an order from a much higher authority. There was nothing to be done except go along with it. I pressed him for a reason and finally he gave it. On the orders of the Fuhrer himself, *any deceased soldier of the Motherland.............. who had committed suicide and by doing so had shown a dereliction of their loyalty to the Fuhrer..........could no longer be buried in a German war grave...... and those that already had been buried thus would be exhumed and reburied somewhere else.*
I told him straight away that this was ridiculous and an outrage against decency and the Christian religion that both of our nations follow. All he said was .....befehl ist befehl. Orders are orders."
Fritz shuffled in his seat. He was beside himself with anger and frustration. Reverend Austin could see his reaction and went on explaining.
"Believe me, if I could have done anything, I would have. They threatened me with rifles in the end. I stood over them and at least made sure they did it with respect. Thankfully I think they all felt the same way as I did. Befehl ist befehl is all they ever seem to say. Nobody protests!" The vicar was getting a head of steam up. He continued.
"You are all like sheep heading towards the edge of a cliff. The trouble is you are hell bent on taking us all with you. Why did you ever come here? We don't want you here."

The friendly priest surprised even himself with his fervour and indignation.
Fritz finally spoke.

"I also do not wish to be here and I am sorry. I play music and organise a band. I have a rifle but I do not wish to fire it. I find myself in a foreign country far from my home land. It should be my choice but it is not. You are right when you say we should protest more but we do not. Protest and you get shot by your own people. You are right when you say it is an outrage. Willy was a good friend. He did not kill himself to be dishonourable. I am sorry. I have said far too much. Please keep this conversation to yourself."
Austin smiled and nodded. "Of course. That's what priests do. I understand your predicament. Maybe I shouldn't have said all that...........but.... I can see you are a thinking and sympathetic man...... and it's best that I do. The situation with your friend's grave is absolutely ridiculous. Will you stay for some tea ?"

"Nein danke, Reverend. As you can tell, I am very......er........disarranged ?. Please forgive my bad English. I must go back to St Helier. "

"Your English is excellent.' Disarranged ' is a good description. I like that. Well, good luck and don't despair. Come for tea next time you come here to play. You would be very welcome. God does not differentiate between nations and besides which, my wife Muriel makes a very nice Stollen cake."

"Ah...Stollen. Yes, that would be good. Oh....one more thing , Reverend. Could you see that the stone of the grave is safe ? I can bring some men to move it to the Stranger's cemetery."

"Of course. I will tell Thomas to look after it and store it in one of the gardener's sheds. Come back when you like, Fritz. It's always good to see you, even though you are the wrong side."

He smiled and led Fritz to the door. They shook hands and Fritz disappeared left and then right along the road through St

Brelade's Bay past the Soldatenheim at the Colleys' hotel. He quickened his pace until he reached the hill at the other end when gravity took over and the steepness of the incline stole his breath. His anger was subsiding but his thoughts were random and without form. He continued walking, happy in his 'disarranged state', mile after mile until he arrived exhausted at the Hotel Bristol. His thoughts were now a lot calmer and certainly clearer. He was wondering how he could protest.
It was late in the afternoon when he opened the door to the dining room and felt the thump of Big Bertha's deep bass tones riffling his trouser legs. Glenn Miller's Moonlight Serenade was playing . He walked in and, by virtue of his rank, immediately claimed the comfortable chair.
Werner got up and put a glass full of brandy in his hand. *"You look like you need this, my good friend."*
"Yes. Thanks Werner. I do. Please give me a few minutes while I listen to my favourite band. Turn it up!"
Werner obliged and as Moonlight Serenade filled the room with sweet music, he sank deeper into the comfy chair, deeper into his brandy and deeper into his thoughts.

On the other side of the Atlantic, Moonlight Serenade was filling a lot of rooms as Glenn Miller's distinct Big Band Sound took America by storm. The invasion by the Japanese at Pearl Harbour had forced the Americans to officially join in and Miller signed up for the draft. Captain Alton G. Miller was initially in the U.S.Army but before they realised who he was, he was transferred to the Air Force. After months of misguided manipulation by his superiors, he assembled a fifty piece band. He managed to persuade the doubters that his musicians could improve the morale of the troops wherever they played. By the end of July 1943 he was hosting a series of money raising 'war bond drive' programmes on the radio and his music filled the air waves. At last he had the ears and hearts of his superiors. And so it was that Big Bertha, the cumbersome mahogany radiogram, was receiving one of these relayed radio

programmes at the same time as Fritz collapsed, disheartened, into the comfy chair at the Hotel Bristol in the German occupied Channel Islands. Inadvertently, the Glenn Miller Sound was touching the hearts of the enemy as well.
After supper, he told the band what had happened with Major Becker's grave and the reason given by the Kommandant. Like Fritz, they were extremely unhappy.
Werner spoke first.

"*Can we at least locate the new grave? Always assuming there is one, of course. What a terrible thought!*"

"I shall make enquiries up at Government House in the morning. The Reverend Austin at St Brelade's Church was very helpful. He was as pissed off as I was and gave the gravediggers a hard time. He is storing the headstone for us until we can decide what to do......anyway, we can't do anything more tonight so I'm off to bed!"

He said his goodnights and wearily climbed the stairs, shattered by the events of the day. He had some enquiries to make in the morning.

CHAPTER 44

D-day approaches

The island government's Purchasing Committee was still doing a good job importing foodstuffs from France and keeping up a subsistence diet for the hungry population. Every week or so there would be 'extras' such as 1/2 pound of macaroni or a jam or sugar ration. Bread was baked at communal ovens mostly in the main town of St Helier. The gas supplies became intermittent and hours were limited to an hour in the day and an hour at 6 p.m. Potatoes and tomatoes were grown in abundance along with other catch crops but quantities were regulated at to who they were sold to and at what price. At the end of the day, the Germans could simply step in and commandeer exactly what they wanted. Mostly the system was policed by the Germans and prosecutions handled by the local judiciary. For instance, in April 1944, a farmer who sold 15 hundredweight of potatoes to the Germans without a licence was fined fifty pounds, another 30 pounds for possession of an unregistered pig and a third was fined three pounds for an unlicensed sale of tobacco to a German soldier. However it was impossible to stop people from bartering what they had and many fortunes were made as market forces took over. It was clear that both sides were of the opinion that to regulate what supplies were available was the best option. Unfortunately the importation of foodstuffs by sea from France was becoming ever more problematic and as 1944 dragged on, the population grew correspondingly thinner. Playing fields and lawns were ploughed up to grow potatoes and wheat. However the Germans were so twitchy from fear of an impending Allied advance that they were just as likely to cut down a field of ripening wheat in case invading soldiers were hiding in there. Even 'Big Mick' Le Gros, at Sunny View , was surprised one day when he discovered a squad erecting pylons on his two acres of crops. The pylons were supported by wires and had explosive charges on top, presumably to deter parachutists as they dropped to earth. Large three dimensional triangular metal structures , well over head height, began appearing on open beaches such as that between Seymour Tower and Gorey Castle. These were anti-tank defences and again had explosive charges at their apex. The sandy beach sloped up to the golf course so the original sea wall was of no consequence to an invading force. This also resulted in the golf course, which previously had been mined over half its acreage, becoming totally out of bounds with additional ordnance being laid. The golfers had been expecting it. They were running out of golf balls anyway. Before the war , if you lost a ball then you lost a ball and put a new one down. This option was now out of the question . At least the members could still use the clubhouse but there was to be no more staggering home across the course after curfew. There were now also two types of bunker on the course, the traditional sand bunker was now joined by the German concrete bunker - both types to be avoided!

Mac had no time for golf and even less time for the hierarchy at the golf club. To him, they represented the snobbishness and class distinction that separated the English from those north of the border in Scotland. Hadrian's Wall divided the two nations geographically but it might just as well have been a cultural chasm a hundred miles across. He had quickly grown sick of the 'hooray Henry' officers who regularly sent their men over the top in World War One. He counted himself lucky to be an engineer in that conflict and his historical dislike of the English had not waned in the intervening years. He found Jersey to be a breath of clean air, not quite English and not quite French, and he regularly thanked his late aunt for bequeathing him her house and her lifestyle. The black dog that followed him now , although bad enough, was not the same menacing, slavering creature that would turn him into a whimpering wreck on his return from the Somme. Military leaders sitting at their desks in Whitehall wanted nothing to do with shell shock (or post

traumatic stress disorder as we now call it) and preferred to shoot their own men for what they suspected to be cowardice under enemy fire.
It was still cold that Spring and Mac had no inclination to be launching the Crazy Doris anytime soon. Light flurries of snow kept dusting the landscape but at least the days grew longer. Soon the swallows would be returning and the Brent geese departing, all of them still oblivious to the conflict around them. The winter had been a great provider for Mac as numerous shipwrecks yielded their cargoes upon the eastern shores of the island. Living as he did just a footstep from the beach, he was always first to spot the flotsam that came in with the tide, spilled from the bowels of a wrecked cargo or navy vessel. There had been plenty recently, either storm driven or bombed out from above or beyond. Aside from the copious amounts of timber that washed up , another crate of spirits washed up. This time it was 24 bottles of Glenfiddich scotch whisky. The smallish heavy wooden crate was like a homing pigeon, seeking out the only Scotsman on that stretch of the coast. It bumbled in on a spring tide and Mac swore later that it had his address on the side. With the speed and skill of a pickpocket, he was out there at first light weaving his wheelbarrow the hundred yards down the seaweed strewn beach to the high tide mark. Just as swiftly the crate was hauled back up the beach and into his wood shed. There he split it open already in jubilation because the label on the side was telling him it was Glenfiddich and lots of it. He felt sure that he would have been spotted by the guards who manned the newly armed old Jersey round tower, a few yards along the road from his house, so he was quick to hide his stash in the secret space he had made behind the book shelves in his front room. He had enough bits of useless flotsam lying in the shed to fool any suspicious German patrol into thinking his beachcombing had yielded little of value. Sure enough, within minutes there was a loud thumping on the front door. He left it for a few seconds before yelling out, "Hang on. Hang on!"

He opened the front door and there was his old friend Sergeant Steiglitz standing there with a patrol of six foot soldiers. They didn't stand there long for they swept past Mac, rifles at the ready clearly searching for whatever Mac had found on the beach. This wasn't the first visit Mac had received from Steiglitz and his minions over the last year. As they thumped and searched, Mac said,
"Will you all be staying forrrrrr tea and cake? Shall I put the kettle on?"
He was totally ignored as they opened doors and cupboards. The search was thorough , diligent and not too intrusive.
"Vot was in der vooden box?" said Steiglitz, fixing Mac with a gaze that would have rendered lesser people petrified.
"Just spoiled fruit and useless china. Have a look outside."
He held the back door open and pointed at the opened crate, a collection of china plates stacked to one side amongst some mouldy oranges. Mac had set the scene well. After a quick search of the lumber in his shed, the squad retreated. Steiglitz, the veins at the side of his shaved head throbbing in apoplectic rage, was still staring at Mac as if expecting him to break down and confess to something. Mac was having none of it.
" Tea?" he hesitated then continued, " Oh! Have ye drowned anybody lately ?"
There was no reply and they left as quickly as they had arrived.

"Thank you for calling.Come again soon. Stay longerrr next time. "

The patrol left and Mac closed the door quietly.

"Bastard! "

He put the kettle on and made a cup of tea. The whole day was still ahead of him and he had 24 bottles of Glenfiddich hidden away. He had got one over Steiglitz and a sudden wave of

contentment swept over him. He was half way through his boiled egg when his breakfast was interrupted. Suddenly a bullet shattered one of his seaside windows, passed over his head and embedded itself in the ceiling. A puff of white plaster fell like snow and glass from the window showered the room. Mac ducked down on the floor and crawled to the back door which was still open. He peeped out, still crouched down. There was Steiglitz, on his own, down on the beach some eighty yards away .He had his rifle to his shoulder, still pointing it at the house. He stood there like a statue, clearly wanting Mac to see him. After three or four minutes, he lowered the rifle and set off along the beach towards the golf course and out of sight.
"I wonder who's rattled *his* cage," Mac said under his breath. All that day, he watched a succession of Allied planes passing overhead to the north and heard the crump.crump,crump of bombing coming on the still air from the coast of France. About four weeks earlier, an American pilot had crash landed some three miles inland in the parish of Trinity. Before the airman was picked up by the Germans, he managed a long chat with the farmer who was first on the scene. His perception was that the Allies were ready for 'the big push' and it was just a matter of time before the Germans were on the back foot. Nuremburg had recently been bombed and Allied aircraft were now targetting north and west France in a effort to test the German defences. This piece of news was immediately disseminated on the bush telegraph and morale soared sky high. At last something was happening.

Mac was buoyed by the sight of so many planes heading in the right direction. After lunch , he took himself off on his bicycle to see the Marinelles.

CHAPTER 45

Christine gets into trouble

Mac was surprised and disappointed to discover that Christine wasn't at home. When he knocked at the door it was the four year old Sophie who let him in through the porch into the kitchen. Peter was sitting at the table.
"Hello Mac. How are you?" said Peter and got up to shake his hand. Sophie had already attached herself to Mac's leg but he carried on walking stiff legged. She roared with laughter and clung on.
"Mummy's gone into town," said Sophie.
"Good afternoon, sweetheart. And to you, big man. Oh, has she now, and has your big lazy brother been looking after you?"
"Yes,Uncle Mac. We've been painting. Look!" She showed him some newspapers daubed with painted stick men.
"Oh, that's very nice," said Mac and Sophie retreated to carry on at the table.
"What about you, big man? What have you been up to?"

"Not much. Getting a bit bored really. Done a bit of swimming training at the Bathing Pool with the club . Water's still cold though. Cleaned up the back garden after the last storm, fixed up my bike, caught a small bass off the seawall, babysitting, cooking. You? I did hear you had a small find."

"Ha! that'll be big mouth Brian Le Rouge who told ye that. Did he also tell you that Steigshitz took a potshot at me from the beach?"

Peter looked up in surprise, then chuckled. "No way! What happened?"

Mac told him the whole story and Peter could not stop

laughing. While Sophie carried on painting, the odd couple chinwagged for an hour. Peter made the tea while Mac mused some more.
"Aye, twenty four lovely bottles of the finest scotch whisky........I'll let ye have a wee dram on yer birthday !"
Mac went on, changing the subject.
" I suppose, as we are officially fishermen, we should at least get the Crazy Doris back on the mooring. Although ye can bet yerr boots the bloody Krauts will issue a no fishing order as soon as we do, and we will probably have to register again at the Kriegsmarine office..... ....Where's your mother gone?"
" She's gone to see her new best friend Anne-Marie in town. She's been two or three times in as many weeks. I don't mind. Sophie's no trouble. She stops me from getting bored..........don't you?" He turned and stared theatrically into her face.

"Oh well, be sure and give her mae best when she gets back. I'd best be off, Steigshitz will be missing me! He'll have a patrol out."
He got up and made for the door.
"Have ye got a wee kiss forr me, Sophie? Uncle Mac is going now."

"Don't go, Uncle Mac. Don't go, don't go!" Sophie was insistent but Mac was on his way. He pecked her on the cheek and promised he would come again soon. As he strolled back towards the harbour he felt sorry he had missed Christine. It was still mid afternoon and the late Spring sunshine burned his face. It felt good. He got as far as the south slipway when he was stopped by a road block which was just being set up.
He saw Klaus Bucholtz who was organising his men.
"What's going on, Klaus?"
"Oh sorry, Mac, we are having a live ammunition practice in fifteen minutes. Go through and if you get stopped further up, just tell them I gave you permission. They can always ring

through."
"Thanks, Klaus."
As Mac manoeuvred past the roadblock a large black Rover 14 driven by a Kriegsmarine officer, nudged past him heading in the same direction. Oberleutnant Hans Stich had just dropped Christine Marinelle off a few hundred yards short of St Kilda but Mac wasn't to know that. He got home and poured himself a large glass of Glenfiddich. He slumped into the armchair just as the first shell was fired by the anti-aircraft batteries at Platte Rocque. The bombardment quickly reached a crescendo and Mac was immediately in trouble as the shrapnel dropped onto the roof tiles and the ground shook menacingly. He dived under the kitchen table and pulled it into a corner, covering himself with a rug. There he sat, anxiously remembering the horrors of the trenches. The practice lasted an hour and he could hear the jackboots of passing German troops on the road outside as they hurried to intercept some imaginary enemy. The all clear siren was sounded and silence, at last, reigned.

The Marinelles were a similar distance to the west of Platte Rocque and suffered the same noise as Mac had. They were not too worried as this was all new to them and really quite exciting. Christine, on the other hand, was also feeling as anxious as Mac but for a far different reason. She had been to see Anne-Marie alright but the outing had been a little more proactive than a chat over a cup of tea. Anne-Marie was an outright flirt and had few scruples about engaging with the enemy . She was slowly drawing Christine into her web. She had somehow turned the morning tea meeting at the Belle Etoile cafe into drinks at the Blue Yacht near St Helier Harbour. The Blue Yacht skirted the docks and was run by an Italian family who had been stranded in Jersey at the outbreak of war. Because Italy had aligned herself with Hitler, they had been bundled into a makeshift Jersey prison camp for a couple of months early in 1940 only to find themselves fortuitously on the other side when the Germans invaded. They were released

and quickly went back into the restaurant business at the Blue Yacht. With its proximity to the harbour basin and the Kriegsmarine boats and administration offices, it was, to put it bluntly, a good place to meet a sailor! However these sailors were no ordinary folk. The Blue Yacht was a meeting and eating place for German naval officers from the Hafenkommandant Kanalinseln (Harbour Commander) headquarters a few yards away at the Pomme D'Or Hotel. Christine followed Anne-Marie into the saloon bar at about noon and within a couple of minutes they were the centre of attention or rather, Anne-Marie was. There were only six or seven officers there and Anne-Marie seemed to know all of them. Very quickly Christine had been introduced to everybody. One of them was none other than Leutnant Hans Stich, her chauffeur of a month ago. They all looked so clean and immaculate in their white summer jackets with gold buttons. This was a world away from the fishermen of La Rocque! The smell of their cologne wafted round the bar, drowning out the stale stench of cigarettes which usually clung to the curtains. When she saw Hans she smiled and cursed herself for showing her hand too eagerly. She was drawn immediately but warily into his aura while Anne-Marie chatted away with the rest of them. Drinks turned into lunch at one of the long tables in the restaurant and Christine floated amiably on air as Hans led the conversation at their end of the room. The fruits de mer , the moules marinieres, the fresh baguette and bottles of Muscadet all went down with enthusiasm. Where did they get this kind of food from? There was supposed to be a war on. It was two o'clock when she remembered she had told Peter she would be back just after three. She looked at her watch and caught Anne-Marie's eye across the table.
"Gotta go." she mouthed but there was no way Anne-Marie was leaving this early.
Hans came to the rescue with an offer of a lift in the Rover 14. "I have to go out to Gorey Harbour this afternoon to drop some orders off . It would be my pleasure to take you home."

"Well, if you're sure..." said Christine, desperately trying not to sound too enthusiastic. Her heart was racing as she acquiesced meekly. Where was all this leading to? This man was handsome, courteous, intelligent, attractive but was also German and married with children. She herself was also married with children, but her husband might be dead and there was a war on. She felt that she was walking into a minefield but for the first time in years she felt alive and totally on the edge of something momentous. The pair of them made their exit and said their goodbyes. Anne-Marie winked at them and Christine hated her for it. Hans held the door of the Blue Yacht open for her and led her away around the quay to where the car was parked inside a large warehouse which had been requisitioned from a timber merchant.

She put her hand on his arm as if to pull him up.

"You realise I can't be seen with you, don't you? Perhaps I should just catch the bus. The bus station is just up the road."

Hans stopped and turned to face her in the dim shadows of the warehouse.

"I understand.....but maybe I could drop you close to your house but in one of the country lanes where nobody will see. Yes? "

He suddenly reached out and ran the back of his hand down the skin of her upturned face. Just as suddenly he pulled away.

"I am so sorry....." he said, genuinely embarrassed ."I didn't mean to offend you."

Christine blushed but instantly felt more in control.

"You didn't, Hans. You didn't."

She gently grabbed his offending hand and put his palm back on her face. Their heads moved closer and there were no more words as their lips touched , gently at first and then harder as mutual passion took over. She realised immediately that she had crossed the river . Just then another car appeared at the doors of the warehouse and drove in. They quickly backed away from each other and got into the Rover, Christine in the front passenger seat alongside Hans. They both sat there in a bemused silence as they regained their composure.

"Do you think it would be better if you sat in the back, Christine?"
She smiled at him and said, " No, I'm fine. This will do!"

Hans was the perfect gentleman and dropped her off on a deserted country lane where Christine had directed him. By this time they had both come back to the reality of the situation and parted company quickly, a little embarrassed at what had taken place. She had five hundred yards or so to walk home but she felt she was flying as she made her way back. Her heart was still racing as she tried to come to terms with the surprise events. She opened the door of St Kitts and Sophie flew into her arms. She was glad that she was home.

At about the same time, Brian Le Rouge was just returning to the Grenadier Inn . He had been in town delivering black market eggs to the kitchen at the back of the Blue Yacht just before noon. Whilst waiting for payment, he had glanced leisurely through the cooking fug of the kitchen into the restaurant area.
What he saw going on took him completely by surprise.

CHAPTER 46

Becker reburied

It only took a couple of phone calls from the Hotel Bristol to Reverend Austin at St Brelade's Rectory to discover where Willy Becker's remains were now buried. On the pretext of visiting Government House, Fritz took a walk through St Helier and up the hill at Queen's Road to the Strangers Cemetery where he had arranged to meet the Church Warden. Joe Le Fevre was tasked with maintaining the records of all burials and at the request of Reverend Austin, he informed Fritz of the whereabouts and circumstances of the new grave. Seventy five year old Joe was not the friendliest of churchwardens and rarely spoke two words when one would do. Taciturn was a word that made him sound exciting. Not surprisingly, he was quite brusque in his dealings with Fritz. He pointed to the southern end of the large cemetery.

"That section down the end. Row C is three back and it's the fourth grave in. His name is marked on the wooden cross. Be quick about it, eh!"

His accent was that of a dyed-in-the-wool Jerseyman, part French, part English but sounding almost South African.

Fritz raised his eyebrows in surprise at his surliness but did not rise to it. He set off in search of Willy's resting place. The whole affair filled him with sadness and anger. How could his suicide be judged as being dishonourable by a despot sitting in Berlin ? Hitler's orders for disinterring suicides from war graves was inhumane and cruel. Fritz felt he should be protesting about the whole regime. His thoughts were sidetracking him from the task in hand and he quickly located the fresh grave with its makeshift white wooden cross. He said a few words to Willy as he stood on the nearby pathway. The view was magnificent. The graveyard was perched on yet another high point overlooking St Helier and the Bay of St Aubin to the south and the west. The weather was fine and the distant sea bristled in the breeze. A few minutes later he arranged a date and time with Joe to reset the headstone.

"Doesn't matter what time to me. You bloody Jerries will come when you like anyway!
We don't want you here. I wish you were all in the bloody cemetery. Six foot under!"

Fritz could see his point but did not take time to argue the case and left quickly.
When he returned to the Hotel Bristol, he arranged for the immediate transport of the headstone from St Brelade to St Helier .The headstone would then be repositioned on the Thursday and a service would be held at 7 a.m. on the Friday. The Reverend Basil Austin had agreed to conduct a short service. The headstone was heavy and with the help of a couple of heavy lifters in the band, they hoisted it onto a lorry and transported it to the new resting place. He impressed upon his men the need for discretion as he wasn't sure how this would be interpreted by his superior officers.
At 6.30 a.m. on Friday morning, all of the band piled into a troop truck which then made the five minute journey up to the Strangers Cemetery. Despite the previous assurance of the surly church warden that the gates would be open from 6 a.m., a brand new chain and padlock around the large wrought iron gates told a different story. The lorry pulled up and Fritz jumped down to see if the padlock was open. It was not and he returned to the cab, taking down a large sledgehammer. After three blows, the padlock disintegrated to the applause of his men. The chain was unravelled, the gates opened and in they went. A few minutes later, the Very Reverend Basil Austin arrived in a rusty old Ford and at precisely 7.a.m. he conducted a brief service over Willy Becker's new resting place. The congregation was respectful and quiet, Fritz played a clarinet solo and the job was done. Fritz was still angry and felt he should have taken more time . He marched his men back to the

truck and then accompanied Reverend Austin back to his car.
"Thank you, Reverend. You are very kind to drive all this way so early in the morning. It was a nice service."
"I can't really say it was a pleasure ," he replied,..." seeing as it was a funeral, but it was certainly no trouble. Any time, Fritz. Any time. Be sure to come and see me next time you come to the church."
At that moment, a very irate churchwarden came scurrying down the path from his office near the entrance gate. He was waving a broken padlock in his hand and was apoplectic with rage.

"You vandals! You vandals! I'm going to report you to the Feldcommandant for this! It's a bloody outrage !"

Without missing a beat, Reverend Austin summed up the situation and rescued the day.
"I'm so sorry, my good man. I got here early and I couldn't leave these people to wait outside now, could I ? I smashed the lock with my carjack.....made a bit of a mess, didn't I? You carry on, Leutnant Doenig and I'll sort out the damage with Le Fevre. Go on, old boy, push off."
Fritz could not resist a quiet smirk at the genius of the man. He brought the men to attention and the air fizzed to the sound of twenty odd pairs of jackboots clattering on the tarmac. He saluted his friend and marched off behind the band.
Austin grabbed the churchwarden's arm and guided him towards the office.
"Would ten pounds cover your trouble, Joe ? You don't mind if I call you Joe, do you? It seemed so very rude to keep them waiting and I felt responsible."
He extracted two fivers from his wallet and shoved them into Joe's outstretched hand.

"Now then, we'll hear no more of this or your boss will get to know of your black market shenanigans. Do I make myself clear?"

At this, Joe's not very righteous indignation subsided into acquiescence. His initial look of surprise took on a more guilty expression and he nodded his affirmation. Not that Reverend Austin knew anything at all about his 'black market shenanigans', he had taken a stab in the dark and come up lucky!
Joe Le Fevre walked away with his tail between his legs and the Reverend was left by the gates looking at the empty wallet in his hands.

"The Lord giveth and the Lord taketh away," he mumbled under his breath. "I'll get it back from the Sunday collection."

He reached inside the window of his car and opened the door from the inside. The old Ford was in bad shape. He started it up with a handle shoved through the hole above the front bumper. Two turns and it fired up. He left a cloud of acrid smoke in his wake as he grazed the gates, deliberately some would say, on the way out.
Hopefully, Le Fevre would keep his mouth shut.

CHAPTER 47

D-Day

Eventually Mac got accustomed to the almost continuous drone of aircraft overhead, the practice shelling drills of the anti-aircraft guns and the clatter of jackboots on the road outside as squads of young and frightened German soldiers went on manoeuvres, awaiting the arrival of an Allied attack. Earlier in the year a direct order had been issued from Hitler to the effect that the Channel Islands had 'fortress status' and as such were to be defended until the last man. The Feldcommandant was anxious not to place too much emphasis on it as he was hoping that it would not be necessary and he certainly had no desire to be that last man. At the time of issue, the order was buried under a plethora of other orders and assumed no significance whatsoever. The immediate threat to the Germans was coming from the south east of England where their intelligence suggested that an attack on the mainland of France by the combined forces of the Allies was imminent. Hitler was still convinced that the British would dearly love to liberate the Channel Islands but nothing could have been further from the truth. They hardly got a mention at the War Office in the planning of the D Day landings. They were there in the Channel below the Cherbourg Peninsula, they were heavily defended and it would take a huge amount of effort to free them. Despite Hitler's attraction to this little part of Britain, the islands now had little strategic value and it was questionable if they ever had.

The summer of 1944 started officially on June 1 and Spring said goodbye with a few hot days. Mac's swallows were busy reproducing in the eaves of his wood shed and the Brent geese had long gone. The wisteria on the sheltered road side of his house had blossomed and shed purple petals everywhere. The Crazy Doris was laid up once again as the jittery Germans banned boat fishing one more time.

At the other side of La Rocque, St Kitts was flourishing, despite the shrapnel from the defence position tinkling on the slate roof at regular intervals. Sophie continued to delight and Christine had developed a contented flush brought upon no doubt by her nascent relationship with the German lieutenant. Peter has started to feel a little twitchy with the inactivity of it all and had taken to cycling the three or four miles along the coast to the Bathing Pool in St Helier. He had been reluctant to go there since he was unwittingly robbed of his virginity, fearing the redhaired lady who had committed the felony would recognise him and demand money . This particular episode affected him greatly until he began to see the funny side of it. Once he had recovered from the shock of it, he decided he couldn't wait for the next time he could have sex, but hoped it might not be so brutal. The area itself brought back the horror story of the deaths of his two pals. However the French lady had long since gone and the last four years had been about survival as the war unfolded in places across the world . Losing friends seemed to be part of his life, he knew no different and he got over it all. Familiarity eventually healed the wounds and he became a star member of the Jersey Swimming Club, his Australian crawl drawing admiration from his contemporaries, particularly the female ones. He was a sensitive soul and could not accept praise too easily. His self confidence was growing and he was beginning to feel more comfortable in his own skin. The end of May leading up to the Whitsun holiday saw the thermometer soaring. The days were getting longer and the sun was overhead as he hopped down over the garden wall onto the sand. There was no evidence that the beach in that area had been mined. There had been a lot of foot traffic with the building of the defence post at La Rocque and a lot of sand had been taken from the foreshore to mix with cement for bunker construction. It was clear from this that the area was safe and Peter confidently headed between the rocks in the direction of Icho Tower. Icho was another coastal tower built on a rock, half a mile due west from Seymour and five hundred yards south of

St Kitts. The tide was not a particularly high one but was dropping leisurely down the shelving sand. His intention was just to have a quick swim . The warm still weather of the previous week had left the water as clear as gin and he slid easily into its welcoming arms. The air temperature may have been warm but the sea was still chilling. He was accustomed to the shock of the initial plunge, the Bathing Pool was his normal stomping ground and that was an open air sea water facility. By the beginning of autumn the sea temperature would peak at around 20 degrees centigrade and that was Peter's favourite time of year. Today he bore no grudge against the weather and swum out with the current towards Icho Tower, revelling in the feel of the water as it cleansed his mind and body. It was so different to moving through fresh air. Air had the ability to flick at his skin, it could be moody when it was strong and gusty but water was all embracing. It enveloped Peter instantly and soon he was duck diving to depths of ten feet in order to explore the sea bed before the tide left it high and dry. The currents that ran between the rabbit warren of rocks and sand could be quite vicious when weather and tide had a mind but they bore no threat today. He surfaced and started swimming strongly along the shore line, marvelling at the visibility through the water beneath him. Swaying fronds of bladderwrack waved back at him from below. Soon it would be uncovered by the falling tide and it would cry out as it dried in the hot sun. Amongst the seaweed he spotted a solitary spider crab and, as he swam out a bit further, a few more. The squad turned into a platoon and the chances were that , further out, it would turn into an army. The false serenity of the day was then betrayed by the arrival overhead of Allied bombers. The drone of their engines grew louder until suddenly the anti-aircraft guns opened up from the defence position at La Rocque, barely five hundred yards from where he was. He trod water for a few seconds and then struck out for the exposed rock called La Coniere which he scaled before finding a comfortable sitting place on the sea side. From here he could watch the fun. The

Wellington bombers were high in the sky and well out of range of the guns which fired more in anger than any hope of hitting anything. It was unusual to *see* the bombers rather than just *hear* them passing at night. Events were clearly hotting up. The planes disappeared in the distance towards France and the gunfire ceased. Peter felt quite safe and that was synonymous with the peculiar position that existed in the islands. The sun was out, the tide went back and forth, and yet they were occupied by a load of foreigners who didn't seem too hostile but insisted on subjugating the people who enjoyed this idyllic lifestyle. Peter knew no different. This Occupation had blighted his teens. The last four years had been a heartbreaking adventure but , at the end of it, it was *still* an adventure and he was living it through wondrous eyes. He stood up and found himself a flat rocky ledge three feet above the water. He launched himself into a dive and splintered the glass that was the surface of the unruffled sea . Surrendering himself once more into the chilly depths, he swam back to shore against the outgoing current before fetching up in front of St Kitts. The tide had receded a fair distance and the walk back up the beach was much longer than the walk down. He decided to dry off and cycle round to Mac's house to discuss a low water spider crab expedition.

Mac was still hiding under the table when he knocked on the back door.

"Who is it?" yelled Mac from the kitchen.

"It's *me*, Mac. "

"Who's me?"

"Sergeant Steigshitz. Who else?"

Mac abandoned his hidey hole and opened the door. He beckoned Peter in.

"Oh, do come in Sergeant Steigshitz. Pull up a chair and shoot me, why don't ye. How you doing, young Peter? What's new?"

"Spider crabs, Mac. Hundreds of 'em. Spotted them just now. Tomorrow would be a good day."

"So long as the krauts don't start popping off at high flying

pigeons like they did today, then I'll be up for it. The tide's no' great but if the spiders are on the march then maybe we could encourage them to walk right up to the back door. D'ye fancy a wee dram, young fella? Matured on my estate?"
Peter was a bit reluctant as he was no drinker and had had little opportunity, given his age. The occasional sherry with his mother was the only experience he could muster. However, the sun was going down and it seemed rude to refuse. They went outside and sat on shabby deckchairs overlooking the beach. Mac's 'wee dram' burned his throat and sent him into a coughing fit almost the second it hit his throat.
"Och, ye bloody big jessie. It takes a Scotsman to enjoy a good scotch. Dinna worry son, I'll make you a cup of tea instead. We don't want your ma smelling your breath and thinking you've been drinking, do we ?"
Peter coughed his answer.
Mac went back inside to put the kettle on. Peter recovered his breath and rested his head back on the top bar of the deckchair so he could look straight up. Squadron upon squadron of aircraft were again flying eastward, way up high. The Allies were certainly up to something big and it was more a question of 'when' they would invade France than 'if' they would. The anti-aircraft guns from the coastal defence positions nearby opened up but soon stopped when they realised it was a wasted effort. They were way out of range. The early months of 1944 saw a lot of false dawns as the Allies sought to deceive the Germans . The most logical place to attack would have been around Calais as it was the closest point to England. The Germans had already constructed the Atlantic Wall from Norway down to Spain (the Channel Islands was part of it) and they had the option of whistling up troops wherever they were needed. They therefore concentrated their efforts into reinforcing the area around Calais, in the knowledge that Allied troop numbers were building up in south east England. The Allied plan was to mount military operations in order to trick the enemy into believing the inevitable invasion was about to

begin. This meant the Germans had to have contingency plans for half a dozen potential sites and in the event of the D-Day landings on the Normandy beaches, they were undermanned in the vital area. The high level of aerial and naval activity around the islands in the early months of 1944 was a result of these plans.

The odd couple never did get to go on a low water expedition the next day as the Germans issued an order for an exclusion zone on all beaches except those near St Helier. Exactly one week later on June 6 , the D-Day landings began. In the early hours all hell broke loose island-wide as every defence position opened up at the hordes of overflying aircraft . The big 8 inch naval gun at Les Landes was also brought into action , firing at shipping, and even though La Rocque was miles away from its position in St Peter, the ground shook as if there was an earthquake. The news was quickly disseminated by those with a concealed wireless and the expectations of the population finally turned into reality. The reality was that the action was taking place just fifty miles to the north east of Jersey across the Cherbourg peninsula. The distant rumblings that could be heard were the crucial battles taking place on the beaches of Utah, Omaha, Gold, Juno and Sword. The days that followed tipped the balance of World War Two and inevitably the toll on human life was immense. Over four thousand Allied troops were killed before the beach head was achieved at the end of that week.
The population of the Channel Islands mourned the losses but celebrated the news. They could be sure that liberation would come soon. But they were wrong.

CHAPTER 48

Peter turns eighteen

The Allied Forces eventually broke through the German defences in Normandy but made slow progress towards Paris over difficult terrain. The mood in Jersey and Guernsey continued to be one of total optimism. The Germans maintained their discipline and in the days before and after D-Day, they were still clearly expecting the enemy. Ambulances were stationed near all defence posts, guards were doubled near all billets and soldiers generally slept at their posts. The telephone service was hijacked to stop communications but the good news still got through. The corresponding bad news for the German soldier was manipulated accordingly by the propaganda machine. Defeats in France were turned into heroic rear guard actions but the stark truth was delivered to them by the locals. Hitler's army was on the retreat .

As the days of June passed, it was clear that there was to be no immediate battle for the Channel Islands and the order banning fishing boats from putting to sea was rescinded, but you sailed at your own risk. A state of high alert still existed and Allied planes flew over in numbers which did not abate until late August. Every night was accompanied by the drone of propellers overhead and the sounds and flashes of explosions on the French coast a few short miles away.

Despite the tides being unfavourable - it being a neap or 'nip' slow tide- Mac and Peter were raring to go. Today was Peter's eighteenth birthday and he couldn't think of a better way to spend it. The high winds of the previous week had given way to a gentle offshore zephyr and summer sunshine embraced the island like a long lost friend. There was barely enough water to float the Crazy Doris but float it did and they drifted out on the gentle breeze. They only had a quarter tank of petrol so they

wouldn't be going far today, probably out to Seymour then east to Icho with a swim in the lagoon between and a bit of rod fishing thrown in for good measure. Christine and Sophie had been pencilled in for the day out but it was deemed too dangerous for them. There was the risk of mines and always the chance of an Allied plane mistaking them for Germans. Sergeant Steiglitz was also an ever present threat, although he had not been seen recently.
The odd couple had no success in Crab Alley and soon drifted over the La Rocque Lagoon. This was a large sandy area devoid of any rock that was so prevalent everywhere else. Generally it was uncovered at three quarter tide but the tide today was not being pulled fast in any direction and the lagoon remained steadfastly between six and ten feet deep. Peter was quickly diving overboard to the sounds of Mac's encouragement.
"Come on, Johnny Weismuller. Show us yerr style. Show us yerr Australian crawl. Show us yerr gold medal ! Go find some crabs !"

Peter smiled in mid air and was quickly into his chosen element as he kicked his way to the bottom. The sun was bright and the sea was so clear that he flirted with his own shadow cast upon the sand below. He burst back up through the surface, took a breath and was gone again.
"That kid is turning into a fish!" Mac smiled. He was proud of his young friend. He thought how wonderful it was to be that age , full of energy and hope. Then he realised that, like Mac himself, Peter's life had been blighted by a world war. At least the futile carnage of Mac's war had not been repeated in the same horrific way but nonetheless it was something neither of them should have had to endure. Down below the water, Peter's adventure continued. He was bursting with the joy of his activity, his muscles did what they were told and he could hold his breath for ages. Soon he surfaced with a large spider crab and the expedition was officially under way. Mac dropped

anchor, cast a fishing line into the distance , selected a large wide brimmed hat from a chest, set up his deckchair and surrendered himself to the midday sun. The crabs kept coming until Peter tired of it. He climbed up the ladder at the stern and flicked the water from his hair all over a dozing Mac.
"Och you dirrrty wee bugger ! "
Peter grabbed a towel and dried himself off.
"Is it time for lunch, Mac? What we got?"
"Well, wee laddie. I have managed to obtain.... at great expense..... some bread and a tin of finest caviar."
Peter looked up in surprise and said, "And what's caviar when it's at home?"
"Och, ya bloody sassenach. Ye haven't a bloody clue, have ye ? Ye've no lived if ye've neverr eaten caviar ."
"Well then, what is it?"
There was a pause.
"Well, to tell you the truth, wee laddie, I haven't got a bloody clue either. Brian told me it was fish eggs or something similar. He got the tin in exchange for some tobacco. I'm sure it'll be fine in a sandwich made from Mrs Le Plongeon's finest bread. "
As the crew of the Crazy Doris sat down to lunch, Christine was sitting at the kitchen table at St Kitts. The back door was open and she could see their boat just five hundred yards out from where she was. Sophie was up the road with a friend from play school. A Red Cross letter lay unopened in front of her. She made herself a cup of tea , then drew a kitchen knife under the flap of the envelope and pulled the letter out. It was from Cliff and was dated March 8, 1943, over fifteen months ago and exactly one week before he went missing, presumed drowned. Red Cross letters had a habit of getting sidetracked due to some wartime calamity. The envelope on this one had been stamped , opened and resealed several times. The letter was in Cliff's usual 'love you,miss you' style and Christine was quickly reduced to tears as the tragedy of his demise hit her once again. It was over a year ago and now this message from the grave. Her insides were stirred up again as once more she

had to confront her feelings. Today of all days, she thought, the birthday of their first born. She felt absolutely numb and after staring at the wall for the best part of an hour she came to the conclusion that this changed nothing. He was dead before and he was dead now. The kids were her reminders and she had to get on with it all. She carefully folded the letter back into the envelope and placed it carefully in the bottom of a well packed drawer, covering it up so it would not be accidentally discovered. She closed the drawer silently and determined to carry on as before.

The sounds of heavy gunfire a couple of miles to the south east interrupted and eventually curtailed the Crazy Doris' day out. Distant land based naval guns fired off a couple of shells and the air seemed to shudder under the load of the noise.

" Bloody hell ! Here we go again. Best we up anchor and get back to the beach. We don't want to be part of the action," said Peter.

"Aye, I think yerr ma is preparing a wee birthday treat for you, as we speak, so it's a good time to quit. We've got nearly twenty spiders which should be easy enough to sneak past the guards. They'll be busy firing their pop guns anyway. "

Mac fired up the motor and it coughed reluctantly into life. Fifteen minutes later they eased back into the same spot as they had left by the pier. The tide had hardly moved at all and they ran the boat aground next to the mooring buoy.

"Perfect timing," said Peter as he tied up. Within ten minutes, they were wading through the shallow water carrying all that was needed in two hessian sacks, including their spider crabs. Mac had been right about the guards or rather, lack of them. They got a whistle and a wave from Klaus who was up on Platte Rocque looking down on the slipway. They scrambled over the barrier and up the slipway before turning left towards St Kitts.

Christine was impressed by the catch as well as the fact that they had arrived back on time at three o'clock. This had been

more by luck than judgement and neither of them felt it necessary to tell her the truth. A quick glance between the two fishermen was evidence of their complicity. The table had been laid for afternoon tea and , from many different sources, Christine had conjured up the ingredients for a birthday cake. Peter was put in charge of the tea and today they had real tea, not some ersatz mix of blackberry leaves and nettles but a lucky find mixed up in some flotsam brought ashore in the previous week. There had been a fine harvest of cargo finding its way on to the east coast, much shipping had been sunk but also many lives had been lost. Dead bodies were in abundance and beachcombing had become a macabre business. Despite all the deteriorating circumstances, the birthday party went well. Neighbours dropped in at regular intervals and to Peter's delight, a posse of fellow swimmers from the Bathing Pool had cycled out from town. They abused and embarrassed him in front of his mum but he gave as good as he got. He was particularly pleased to see amongst them the stunning girl Melody Jones whose statuesque beauty was overshadowed only by her diving ability. When Melody was on the high board, the pool would stop and hold its breath in awe. What Peter didn't know was that when *he* was swimming up and down the roped lanes, it was the seventeen year old Melody who was holding *her* breath in awe. Eventually they might get together but today wasn't the day. Afternoon turned into long summer evening when the cyclists said their goodbyes. Peter waved them off one by one. Melody was last in the queue and a bit wobbly as she pushed the pedals to get going. She made a total mess of it and collapsed sideways into Peter as he stood waving on the pavement outside St Kitts. He caught her and held her up on the bike while she gathered herself.
He was immediately overwhelmed by her softness and sweet smell. She snuggled into him and whispered,
"Happy birthday. See you at the pool Saturday?"
Peter struggled enthusiastically for breath, his throat dry with excitement.

"Yes..........." His brain wouldn't let the words out.
"Is that it?........." she came straight back at him.
"Yes.......I mean 'no'." Peter was now squirming with embarrassment.
"I mean 'yes', I'll see you Saturday."
Melody cocked her head upwards and kissed his neck. She broke away and cycled off to catch the others up, leaving him redfaced but ecstatic. She congratulated herself on making her loss of balance on the bike look like an accident. He floated back into the house , grinning from ear to ear. Mac had been watching him through the open door and had witnessed the whole episode. He feigned innocence and said,
"What you grinning for, big man?"
"Nothing, just having a good day Mister Mac......just having a good day."
Mac laughed out loud and beckoned his young friend through the house into the garden where the party continued into the fading light. Big Mick from up the road had turned up with some bottles of home made cider for the birthday boy but didn't stop for long. Sophie flaked out and was put to bed where she slept soundly. While Christine attended to her, Mac and Peter pulled their deckchairs further down towards the beach end of the sandy garden and got stuck into the cider. A warm glow fell over both of them as they watched and listened to Allied planes passing overhead. A German anti aircraft gun a mile or so to their north fired off a few shells before realising it was a pointless exercise. Intermittent gunfire and explosions could be seen and heard from the coast of France as the action headed southwards. It surely couldn't be long before they were liberated.
Mac filled up Peter's glass once again and staggered back to his deckchair.

"You were getting a wee bit close to that Melody girlie before, weren't ye big man? I got the feeling she likes you. Can't see why, mind you."

Peter blushed and then realised Mac couldn't see his red face as it was getting dark. With a couple of pints of home brew cider inside him, he was overcome with Dutch courage.
"Yesh Mac," he slurred," I think I'm in love!"
Mac was taken aback. Peter was normally so shy about his feelings. Mac started clapping and said,
"You're priceless, big man, absolutely priceless!" They both laughed out loud.
Just at that moment Christine sashayed down the garden path, her gorgeous figure silhouetted against the light from the kitchen. Mac squinted through the alcoholic haze and the moment he saw Christine, his heart raced .
"He thinks he's in love. Well, me too big man, me too!" said Mac, under his breath but a little too loudly.
"What's that, Mac ?" she said, holding out her empty glass.
"I was just saying that you probably need another drink. Here, sit here. I'll fetch another chair."

And there they sat, all of their problems unresolved. All around them, the war went on. It was like Guy Fawkes Night with all the fireworks going off. It was a warm, balmy evening and they drank some more. A thunderstorm had been moodily edging up from the east and the air felt electric and heavy. The atmosphere was breathless but the storm refused to break. It rumbled and growled, spitting random hailstones that tinkled on the galvanised gutters of the house. The lightning fizzed intermittently through the air and the thunder cracked in response. They laughed because they were tipsy and couldn't tell the difference between the thunder and the gunfire. A few heavy drops of rain disturbed the sand and dust by their feet and bigger hailstones clanked more noisily on the tin roof of the little shed. The sweet smell of summer rain filled the air as they sat there unmoved by the increasing dampness all around. The spell was broken by Sophie's cries from indoors and they all raced inside.

CHAPTER 49

The war passes them by and supplies dry up

While the Germans prepared for a visit from the Allies, the Luftwaffe Band had to leave their instruments behind when their jobs were expanded to include various guard duties around the island. The threat of British commando raids was very real and every sentry on duty in the more remote parts of the island had the extra incentive to stay awake. Oberleutnant Fritz Doenig was tasked to provide three men for each of seven defence positions for the night shifts. He knew it was coming and it really wasn't a problem for him or his men. Being part of the Luftwaffe, they were all trained in the use of arms and anti aircraft weaponry. Fritz made sure that each three man squad saw service in different defence positions and organised transport to and from the venues, usually before 9p.m.for the start of the shift and 8a.m.at the end. They would all sleep at the Hotel Bristol until 3p.m. and convene at 7p.m. for an evening meal before setting off to do it all again. Fritz got to check out personally most of the defence positions on the south and west coasts of Jersey and was himself surprised at the extent of the work that had been done by the Todt organisation . While he hated their methods of using and abusing slave labour, the results were impressive. He took to travelling shotgun on the transport lorry when he was free from other administrative duties. The lorry travelled from Gorey south to La Rocque, then on to St Helier Harbour and followed the coast road west along St Aubin's Bay, up the hill and left at the top to Noirmont Point . From the headland you could look back east over the bay to St Helier. From here they passed the church where Willy Becker's grave had been desecrated and then moved on down Route Orange to the south western tip of the island where the Corbiere lighthouse had stood sentinel for a hundred years or so. The seas here had fetched up from the wild Atlantic Ocean driven on by mighty westerly winds. To

the north stretched the white sands and huge breakers of St Ouen's Bay where Hitler had stood nearly three years earlier, studying the lie of the land and giving advice. There were bunkers everywhere, their fields of fire covering every conceivable angle along the coast. For a month, Fritz enjoyed these rides in what they called 'the tourist bus'. The evenings were long and the weather was warm. Each day they chased the setting sun to the west. Each day they prayed they wouldn't be sent to the Eastern Front. The night duties for the men were quite nervous occasions as they were led to expect attacks from any direction at any time. Fritz took to meeting all the commanding officers of each defence post they visited. He was fascinated by the extent of all the bunkers.
It was at the La Rocque defence post that he was introduced to Obergefreiter Klaus Bucholtz who had been delegated to take him on a tour of the surrounding structures. Despite the difference in rank, they got on well. While Fritz was quizzing him about the two offshore towers and the castle at Gorey, Klaus was just as inquisitive about the band .
"How old is the big castle? Do you have to guard the towers out there? Do the locals still fish from her? "
" Where did you learn to play? How long have you been here? Have you heard the Big Band Sound from America? Do you like it?"

All questions were answered by each in turn. Walking down from the high point at Platte Rocque with the intention of gaining access to the pier, a pair of de Havilland Mosquitoes came into view from out to sea at a height of about a thousand feet. Before Klaus had had an opportunity to identify whether the aircraft were friend or foe, the defence post was already on the case and a barrage of anti-aircraft flak flew noisily over their heads.
"*Whoops! Let's go, Herr Oberleutnant.*"
The pair raced back to the bunkers and the Mosquitoes kept coming. They were British bombers back from a specialist

mission to bomb a Gestapo HQ just south of Rennes. As soon as the ack-ack guns opened up on them, the pilots of the aircraft knew they had a target for the two spare bombs they were carrying . Lining up the nest of bunkers that boasted the guns that were firing at them, they flew side by side and unleashed a bomb each before peeling off in opposite directions. Fritz and Klaus dived into the nearest trench and crawled into a bunker. Both bombs missed their target but ploughed into unoccupied houses on the coast road behind Platte Rocque, ripping the roof off both, shattering windows and scattering debris over a wide area. The Mosquitoes left as quickly as they had arrived, banking to the north and disappearing over Gorey Castle. Their near misses had caused some collateral damage but good fortune meant that no lives were lost. All the houses nearby had their windows blown out and the occupants didn't hesitate in relocating into other unoccupied houses further inland .The activity in the Platte Rocque defence post was attracting too much attention from the Allies. Geographically, La Rocque was poised on the south east corner of the island , a likely target for any aircraft returning from France to England. Four years earlier, it was German bombers coming from France that had picked out La Rocque as their first target. La Rocque just couldn't buy a trick.

Fritz helped in the clearing up exercise and when he felt the time was right, he said his goodbyes.
"Got to go, Klaus. Wouldn't mind having a look at those old towers out there another time."
" Any time you like, Oberleutnant. It's been a pleasure to show you around." replied Klaus.
Unusually, they shook hands instead of the usual Nazi salute. Neither of them felt like a parting Heil Hitler. The war was grinding them down.

As Fritz walked away , he called out,
".......and when you are in town, drop in to the Hotel Bristol.

It's next to the Mayfair Soldatenheim. There will be a schnapps with your name on it !"

Fritz had borrowed a car for his trip out and was dismayed to find the windscreen had been smashed by a rock in the air raid. He cleared the sizeable stone from the front seat , brushed the shattered shards out of the car and was back on the road within minutes in the newly air conditioned Peugeot, the rush of warm air blowing his cap off on to the back seat. He wondered how he would explain the damage to the car pool mechanic who he had done him a favour by loaning him the car in the first place. As he drove back to town, his mood lifted and he started whistling the tune to Glenn Miller's Chattanooga Choo Choo, tapping out the rhythm on the steering wheel with his fingers. On the other side of the Atlantic Ocean, Miller himself was driving, albeit with a complete windscreen, to the recording studio. His 50 piece Army Airforce Band was once again playing and recording. He had battled with his superiors to convince them of the benefits he and the band could bring to the war effort. Finally winning this particular argument and raising thousands of dollars for the war effort with his sponsored radio request programmes, Miller felt that they should get where the action was and he pulled strings to get the band overseas to Europe . In June 1944, they boarded the NY8245 en route to London,England. The NY8245 was military speak for the mighty ocean liner, the Queen Elizabeth. They would not be slumming it en route.
The London they discovered was a battle torn city still recovering from the Blitz. There were bombed out buildings everywhere and the threat of the self guided V-1 bombs was ever present. The air raid sirens went off at regular intervals and the population were still jumpy. A lot of American military personnel were based not far from the King's Road in Chelsea. The band's billet in Sloane Court was right in the middle of all this . On July 2, after Miller had had a premonition, he ordered

a move up to Bedford some 45 miles to the north. It turned out to be a timely move as on July 3, the very next day, a V-1 bomb dropped on Sloane Court killing 74 U.S. military personnel and three civilians. Even today, a plaque in the wall between Sloane Court East and Turk's Row commemorates this tragedy.
Glenn Miller constantly had gloomy feelings of events that were unfolding. He told his friends back home that he felt he would not be coming back from this trip. In spite of this, he drove the band on and the sound reached out over the air waves over a wartorn Europe where both sides of the conflict were reaching out for better times. The Allied troops could not get enough of him.

CHAPTER 50

Revelations

The long days of June stretched inexorably on . The Germans remained nervous but at least had stopped wasting ammunition at high flying aircraft. There was plenty of intense naval action to the east as the Allied advance spread slowly down the French coast. The food supply chain on the sea route to Jersey was becoming increasingly fragile. Many an escorted convoy of cargo boats was sent back to port or sunk by Allied gun ships. The supply route was close to being cut completely but the mood on the island was still one of expectancy and optimism that the Germans would soon be on their way. However, even as close as St Malo, twenty miles to the southeast, it became apparent that Hitler's orders to 'defend until the last man' were being adhered to. The old 'befehl ist befehl' maxim was to blame. For weeks it was possible to see the fireworks on the French coast from the seaside gardens of La Rocque to Gorey.

Christine kept the family close to her as she recovered from the jagged shock of Cliff's letter from the grave. A week after Peter's birthday, Mac called round one evening to take him to the pub. She was pleased to see them disappear . Sophie was asleep in bed and she had time for a moment of quiet reflection in the kitchen. She made herself a cup of tea and while the kettle was boiling, she retrieved a letter from the drawer where she had hidden it some weeks before. She took it out of the envelope, carefully straightened out its folds and laid it out on the table. While sipping at her mug of tea she read it for the last time . She then struck a match and set fire to a corner. Holding it carefully so as not to burn herself, she placed it carefully in the fireplace and watched it go up in flames. It was her moment of closure to the feelings that had been plaguing her for the last few days. It was a symbolic moving on. She had made up her mind before she received that letter and her hand was still firmly on the tiller. There was to be no turning back. She went back to the drawer and retrieved a second letter, this one as yet unopened. She slid a kitchen knife under the flap of the envelope and slit it open. She unfolded the handwritten letter and read it. It was from Hans Stich.

"Dear Christine,

It was lovely to see you recently and I am sorry not to have kept in touch. I am struggling with my conscience as to whether we should maybe meet again. As you know, I am married with two small children and you also have children and a husband who we hope will return when this war has finished.

My problem is that I have serious feelings for you which I am finding hard to overcome. You are always in my mind and I find this disturbing. I also have a premonition that I will not survive this war. I hope you understand these words as I am finding it hard to write down my thoughts. Please believe me, I am a truthful man.

I have to leave it to you as to whether we should meet again. Perhaps you should tell me to simply go away.

I would find that difficult.

Please tell me I can see you again.

Kind regards,

Hans x "

She stared at the letter and read it again. She smiled , blushed and said out loud,

"Yes, Hans Stich, ...you *can* see me again."

Up the road at the Grenadier Inn, Mac and Peter were sampling some of Brian's home brewed cider. The usual suspects were there playing darts, dominoes and crib, chewing the cud and each giving his or her opinion as to when the war would end. An acrid blue fug of cigarette smoke clung stickily to the air. The linoleum on the floor was wearing thin and stuck to the soles of their shoes as the customers trod the same furrows to the bar. Life was moving on as before. They were all just breathing in and waiting. Peter got sucked in to a game of darts and Mac chatted to Brian over the counter.

"You still in love with Christine, Mac ?" said Brian, as casually as he could. He sounded serious.

Mac reddened up but managed to bluff it out. He couldn't remember when, or even if , he had confided this information to Brian.

"Of course I am. Nothing will change my undying affection for that lassie. In the nicest
possible way, of course. Why do you ask?"

Mac was waiting for the punchline but it never came. Brian remained serious but strangely silent.
"Come on , laddie. Spit it oot! "

"Well," Brian said," you ain't gonna like this and I don't really know if what I saw has any significance whatsoever so just hang on to your hat."

Brian moved his head closer to Mac, as if he was about to impart a secret. He *was.*
"Well..... a couple of weeks ago I was delivering some eggs to Gino at the Blue Yacht in town. I slipped in through the back door as usual - I wasn't exactly there on legitimate business - and was striking a deal in the kitchen - and I had to wait while Gino came up with the cash. I happened to look into the dining room because I knew it would be full of Krauts stuffing their fat faces and who should I see but none other than your Christine in *very* close conversation with a very flash German naval officer. It looked like they had been there a while. There

was only the one long table full of a dozen Kraut officers and two girls. That Anne-Marie Tonton was there too, making as much noise as she always does. It looked like they had all had a very long lunch by the number of empty wine bottles on the table. I stayed talking to Gino for as long as I could while still clocking the party over his shoulder. About ten minutes later she left with the Nazi sailor and they were all over each other. But the time I had slipped out the back and come all the way round the building to the pavement, they were gone. I haven't told a soul until now, but I thought I had better tell you."

Mac had been listening intently and was dumbfounded by these revelations. It was a while before he looked up.

"Are ye sure it was Christine?"

"Yes, Mac. There was no mistake. On thinking about it and giving her the benefit of the doubt, she was maybe there with that Anne-Marie. Isn't she her cousin or best friend or something?"

"Aye, I think so. She's maybe a bit of a wild one. Blimey! " said Mac. He was finding it hard to take in.

"Well, there is quite possibly a completely innocent explanation for it. After all's said and done, I was also doing a deal with the enemy, but since I've known Gino for ten years or so, he's hardly the enemy despite him being one of Mussolini's mob."

At this point there was a customer shouting for a drink down the other end of the bar and Brian broke off to serve him. Mac was quite pleased he did as he felt lost for words and quite miffed at Brian's account. He wanted to get away from the pub to gather his thoughts but Peter was still involved in his game of darts.

"Ah, he's big enough and ugly enough to find his own way home tonight. It will be light for a long time yet, " he said to himself.

He caught Peter's eye and shouted,

"I'm away to ma bed, big fella. Your ma will be wanting you home before ten."

The darts players all jeered as one but Peter acknowledged Mac and gave him a thumbs up before throwing a double eighteen to end the game. The players jeered some more as Mac turned for the door. He caught Brian's eye over a gaggle of waiting customers standing at the bar.
"See you, Brian......and mum's the word. Okay?"
Brian nodded and tapped his own nose with his forefinger in affirmation.
Mac's head was in a spin and when he got home, he poured himself a Glenfiddich in order that he could assimilate the news.
He sighed and collapsed into the big brown leather chair by the window looking out to the south. The sun had already set but the day had left its colours in the sky. He didn't really know how he felt. Did he feel jealous? At first he didn't think so. She had never shown anything towards him that came anywhere near any sort of attraction other than that day he had felt her hand upon his shoulder. No, he was imagining something that wasn't there. He was assuming things that didn't exist.....and yet, yes, he *did* feel hurt but couldn't explain why. What was to be done? Nothing. What was the point? She had her own life but he had somehow become a part of it, keeping an eye out for them all. And this is what he got in return? No, that's not right. He didn't have a problem with any of this until a year ago when Cliff had been declared 'missing presumed drowned'. That's when it changed. He was at least fifteen years older than this lovely girl that he frequently dreamed of and some of the dreams he'd dreamed had not been the dreams of a gentleman. He smiled and laughed at himself. You dirty old bugger. You dirty old bugger. The whisky had hit his brain and his mind was racing. The net curtain waved towards him on the strengthening breeze and covered his face, trailing away like......yes, it was Christine's hand again.
He looked east towards France and saw the dimming red light of a noiseless explosion.
Time for another whisky. He started to sing. "Campbelltown

Loch I wish you were whisky, Campbelltown Loch och aye."
He jigged around the room.
Hearing the sound of distant aircraft, he moved out into the garden and looked up.
"Same old, same old. Time you came and rescued us all."
He manoeuvred himself clumsily into a deckchair, spilled his drink and passed out. The passing out was to become a recurring event.

CHAPTER 51

Political situation after D-day

Bailiff Basil Dechevaux, as head of the Jersey government, had been ploughing a tricky furrow in dealing with the German administration. He trod a fine line between legitimate protest and civil disobedience. The basic fact that the islands had been occupied by force of arms could not be denied and it was within this framework that both sides had to work. The Germans enforced a quota on the local growers and could hijack anything else on an ad hoc basis. The government had been given permission to import goods from France and the Department of Essential Commodities had worked diligently to keep the local population fed. However , as the Allies forced their way to Paris and down the French coast , they also captured all the sea ports that Jersey supplies were being shipped from. The War Office in London were aware of this but were happy to maintain and promote this situation . Regrettably they were also starving the indigenous people. The food situation in July and August deteriorated. The sea link to France became more and more dangerous as the navies of the Allies sought to close it down. By the second week of August, St Malo to the south had been liberated after a defence to the last man had finally been negotiated down to a surrender. This fine old walled city had been burnt to the ground by a combination of allied bombs and fire raisers. The German defending garrison, numbering barely one hundred, had destroyed anything of use to the enemy in the city before retreating into the deep cellars of the chateaux. They had also sent over 300 hostages onto the Fort National as a further bargaining chip. Built on a tiny island , Fort National was reachable at low tide from the beach at St Malo. There were German guns still firing from another island, Cezembre, which was further out to sea. On two or three occasions, Cezembre was visited at night by supply boats of the Kriegsmarine based

on Jersey and Guernsey. These were dangerous missions but kept the Germans fed and watered . Eventually the war moved on towards Germany. France was liberated but the Channel Islands were still on their own under German rule. The islands then became a refuge for enemy troops who had become stranded on the French coast. There was no other port of call for their escape and a bucket brigade of boats, carrying fit and wounded, struggled into St Helier Harbour. The Germans who had been captured by the Americans in France had been well treated. Many of the Americans themselves were of German extraction anyway so there was no great animosity towards them. It was the Europeans who had borne the brunt of the sadistic cruelty that Hitler had unleashed. It became glaringly obvious that over twenty thousand Wehrmacht troops had effectively become marooned on the Channel Islands. The German Supreme Commander of the Channel Islands, Oberst Von Schmidt(Gruber's boss who was stationed in Guernsey) , then announced that they had completed a survey and had estimated that current stocks would not run out until January 1945. This came as quite a shock to Dechevaux who knew full well that they could barely survive one month let alone five or six. And so the stand-off continued with both sides not knowing what even their own superiors had in mind.
The German troops were were mostly sleeping at their defence posts, the anti-aircraft guns fired the odd obligatory shell at a distant aircraft and practice firing days were held every week. These were noisy days and involved the movement of troops along the coast roads with rifle target practice on the beaches. In town, the Feldpolitz were trying to prove a point, presumably that life was going on as before, by hassling pedestrians for identity cards and being generally unpleasant. House searches still revealed illegal wireless sets and those caught with them could expect interrogation followed by a six month jail sentence at the least. Young lads just being cheeky and disrespectful could expect a beating and a jail term. A small group of pseudo Gestapo personnel had recently arrived and

were billeted at the Silvertide Guest House near the Bathing Pool. They made themselves extremely unpopular around St Helier, their methods of investigation and interrogation being a lot more violent and intrusive than the rank and file of the Wehrmacht.

The Todt construction organisation still stood alone and their slave workers were fed even less as the food situation worsened. Many of these workers would break out of their prison camps at night, foraging for food in and around the outlying farms. At La Rocque, Big Mick Le Gros found himself the unknowing host to a large Russian slave worker called Grigor who had apparently been living in his hayloft for the last eight months. Farms were searched on a regular basis in an attempt to round these prisoners up but generally the locals were able to move them on to another safe house when the risk became too great. As the food situation worsened, law and order started to break down. Crops in the field would be dug up by thieves in the night causing farmers to patrol their acreage armed with sticks and knives. The thieves would most likely be the slave workers on the run or on a night out but they were joined , as the weeks passed, by local miscreants. Night time became increasingly dangerous in the countryside as a state of anxiety took over. Some of the soldiers were called upon to do solo guard duties protecting greenhouses in vulnerable areas. They hated this as there was nowhere to hide or cover. They had to stay awake with their rifles in one hand and torches in the other.

As liberation became increasingly certain, the waiting became intolerable. Those youngsters, like Peter, who were boys at the start of the Occupation were now young men, eager to get on with their lives. They were bored and became keen to get away from the island .It no longer meant an almost impossibly dangerous journey across the sea to England. Now that France had been liberated, that twenty mile stretch of water was like a magnet. It was just over there. All manner of craft were used. Small pedaloes used just a few years ago by holidaymakers having a good time, rafts, canoes and small dinghies were all put to use and mostly launched from the south and east coasts of Jersey. Unfortunately their enthusiasm was not usually matched by their navigational skills and they were often beaten back by a combination of weather, adverse tides and equipment failure. Failed attempts triggered the inevitable interrogations for them and their relatives with prison sentences following for the guilty ones. The Newgate Street prison became full to overflowing and sentences were postponed until there was space. The Germans could easily have built a less well appointed enclosure but Gruber was conscious of the fact that when his war had ended, he did *not* want to be held responsible for any action which could be construed as inhumane. Dechevaux brooded over the impasse but urged his government to try harder. He urged the Department of Agriculture to keep planning and policing. He encouraged the Department of Essential Commodities to continue trying to get supplies in from Guernsey and France. He was about to appeal to the Protecting Power (Switzerland) for help but he needed permission from Gruber to send the message and the word of the War Office not to intercept any such possible mission. The Allies had come across the problem before when the Red Cross was involved. It was not thc fault of the Red Cross but usually the supplies fell immediately into the hands of the enemy. He had to persuade both the Germans and the Allies to give permission for a shipment and he had to elicit an undertaking from them both not to interfere in any way. Time dragged on and the weeks passed.

CHAPTER 52

Christine's denouement

It was only a few days before Hans Stich received Christine's hand written letter at his Grand Hotel billet and he was delighted with her response.

My dear Hans,
Thank you for your letter and for being so frank about your feelings. I shall be visiting Anne-Marie in town next Wednesday . Perhaps we could meet at the Blue Yacht at midday?
Kind regards,
Christine Marinelle

It was deliberately formal and non-committal. She had written it out at least five times before putting the final version in an envelope and nervously posting it. The red pillar box was outside Mrs Le Plongeon's shop. She was as nonchalant as she could manage before she slipped the instrument of her nascent adventure into the lap of the postal service. The deed was done. She had rolled the dice.
Peter had agreed to look after his sister for the best part of that day. Christine tried her best *not* to look her best, she didn't want anybody to even *think* she was meeting anyone special. She always looked good so this was really no problem. She paid the bus driver and as she passed over the money, she realised her hand was shaking. The thirty minute journey along the coast road seemed to go on longer. Did she want time to go more slowly so she could change her mind? Did she want time to go quicker so she could play out the adventure sooner? She didn't know and she didn't care. The bus arrived at Snow Hill soon enough. Anne-Marie was waiting for her , unaware of any arrangements that were already in place. She assumed they were having tea somewhere and was quite surprised when

Christine suggested they go to the Blue Yacht.
"Blimey, you're keen," said Anne-Marie as they linked arms setting off the few hundred yards down to the harbour.
"No, not really. It's just that the food was good last time."
They both exploded with laughter like a couple of schoolkids. The quality of the food was not at the top of her list.
It was ten past midday when they got to the Blue Yacht and the same crowd of officers were there as last time. Hans looked superb in his white Kriegsmarine officers' uniform and beamed as he greeted Christine. After that, the restaurant could have been torpedoed and she wouldn't have noticed. Hans had declared his interest in her and , whilst not declaring hers, she had not turned him down. She had somehow managed to clear the decks in her mind and was happily engaging in the unfolding scenario. The conversation flowed like the wine and by two o'clock they had flirted their way to a point of no return to the almost total exclusion of their fellow diners. The party broke up and Anne-Marie wandered off to the bar with two of their number. Hans offered Christine a lift home but, as she had the afternoon free, she accepted his second offer of further drinks and conversation back at the Grand Hotel where he was billeted. They linked arms to set off towards West Park but she quickly realised this was a big mistake. Heads were turning everywhere. Handsome Hans in his white Kriegsmarine uniform was standing out in the bright sunshine like the Corbiere Lighthouse and she, *she* was hanging on to him like a leech. The alcohol that had loosened her inhibitions suddenly drained away and common sense took over. She turned to Hans.
"Look, this is silly. I had better go. I had forgotten about all this fraternisation nonsense. That lot over there will have me down as a Jerrybag for sure," said Christine, looking across the road at some elderly people waiting at the bus stop. One of them was the old La Rocque fisherman Gaston who, despite his look of total disinterest, had already identified and judged her in his mind. A smelly Gauloise cigarette clung stickily to his lower

lip. He nodded a greeting which she pretended not to notice. She immediately pulled away from Hans but the jury had already returned their verdict of 'guilty' and the tut- tutting from the small bus queue was audible even across the busy street. Hans wasn't quite so concerned and simply suggested that they separated, he would walk back into town and go the long way round back to the Grand and she could walk along the seafront and meet him in the foyer.

With a dozen or so pairs of eyes tracking her every move, they set off in opposite directions trying to look as nonchalant as possible. Christine was so flustered she had trouble putting one foot in front of the other. She soon turned the corner onto the Esplanade and immediately felt more secure. She crossed the road and walked past the granite Abattoir building. The road itself was a mess . The raised heels on her shoes were no help as she hopscotched across the sunken railway tracks onto the seafront. There was no doubt it was a lovely day and the cooling summer breeze tugged at her dress. She began to be plagued by doubt. What had promised to be a watershed day had been compromised by those busybodies at the bus stop. The doubts increased in direct proportion to the decrease in the effects of the wine. She started walking faster and within ten minutes she stood facing the impressive facade of the Grand Hotel. There was a massive German bunker on the seaside of the road, the slipway to the beach had long since been blocked and the place was alive with troops coming and going.

"Should I go in or go home?" she said under her breath.

"Well, I may as well be hanged for a sheep as a lamb. They've already got me down as a jerrybag. Let's go and earn the certificate."

With her mind seemingly made up, she weaved her way back across the road and up the steps to the foyer of the Grand. Hans was standing outside and guided her in through the revolving doors. The reception area was large and impressive and very busy. They slipped unnoticed into one of the sitting rooms facing out across St Aubin's Bay. The afternoon sun was

grilling them through the large windows and it was uncomfortably hot.
"It would be cooler upstairs?" said Hans. It was a statement and a question. Christine knew exactly where this was leading . She nodded and followed him out to the carpeted staircase leading up from the foyer. She looked at her hand and saw that it was still shaking. Her whole body was alive with nervous expectation. She had finally reached the fork in the road that had been causing her so much angst. She knew that all she had to do now was take it and see where it went.
Hans unlocked the door and led her in. The spacious room overlooked the park on the west side of the building, a view that was quite mundane compared with the sea views from the front of the hotel. She stood looking at the children playing on the grass below across the road. Hans had unbuttoned his formal Kriegsmarine jacket and thrown it on the settee. He came up behind her and stood very close, breathing on her neck. She twisted her head back like a cat being stroked and reached behind while still facing forward. Her hand settled accidentally but immediately on the front of his trousers. He could not disguise his erection and surrendered to her touch. His tongue traced a path from her neck to her ear and his hands reached around her sides to gently feel her breasts. His touch was electric. She tried to turn around but he held her firmly, now gently nibbling her ear. Suddenly her dress was up around her waist and his hand was reaching down the back of her knickers. His middle finger traced the slippery crease between her buttocks and reached down before settling upon her quivering vagina. She could not disguise the dampness that she felt and curled her backside up like a cat on heat. He withdrew his hand and gently tugged at her knickers until they were spiralling down her legs to the floor. This was all too quick for her but she just let it roll. Her nerve ends were jangling and this was no time for a debate on the morality of the situation. With one hand stoking the fire between her legs, he quickly unbuttoned his trousers with the other and shuffled them and

his regulation underwear downwards to join her pants in a puddle of lust on the carpet. She was now leaning forward over a small table with her hands hanging over it on to the window frame. She watched the trees in the park while the storm built inside her. She felt his warm hard cock rubbing between the cheeks of her bare backside and a light cool breeze played upon her naked flesh. She spread her legs wider and felt completely and utterly exposed. She breathed in his cleanliness and smelt his cologne. With a deft touch Hans adjusted his stance and slipped his cock inside her. She felt it slide comfortably in followed by the warmth of his thighs as they pressed upon her skin. She pushed back and he pushed forward. He grunted and she pushed harder. He moved his hands around to her breasts and felt the hardness of her nipples through her clothing. They were both building towards a climax to the accompaniment of rattling furniture when he whispered urgently in her ear,

"Katarina, Katarina, Ich liebe dich. Ich liebe dich."

An alarm bell sounded in her head. Maybe that's the German for Christine, she thought. The rest of it she couldn't understand. Her eyes flashed to the side and she scanned the picture frames on the chest of drawers. One was a wedding photograph and she could just pick out the writing underneath. "Hans and Katarina Stich June 1936."

Her reaction was instant and brutal. She twisted round with such force that it knocked him backwards into the armchair. He yelled out in pain and sat there wincing with his shirt in disarray around his chest, his erection like the target on a hoopla stall.

"I am so sorry. I am so sorry," he said. He was close to tears not sure whether his pain was physical or emotional.

Christine quickly straightened her dress, picked up her knickers and shoved them into her handbag. Leaving him in an ungainly heap in the armchair, she marched out and found the ladies toilet at the end of the corridor where she cleaned herself up. She put her knickers back on, brushed her hair and raced downstairs to join the mayhem that was the hotel foyer. The revolving door was no obstacle to her and she left it spinning wildly in her wake. She elected to turn right and swept down the wide pathway from the hotel and right again on to Peirson Road. She needed to walk and walk and walk in order to shuffle her thoughts into some semblance of order and dissipate the anger she was feeling. She crossed through the small triangular park, smiling at the small children enjoying the grass and the sunshine. The large People's Park lay across the way. Pre-war it had been a proud grassy area , big enough for four or five football pitches and enjoyed by the townsfolk. Massive gardens cloaked the western terraces. Now they lay untended and growing wild. The grassy area had been ploughed up to grow potatoes and a few huts on the south east corner heralded a community of underfed slave workers. Her anger boiling inside her head, she climbed the steep hill behind the gardens. Breathing heavily she passed the bowls club, its lawn no longer in the pristine condition of former years. The hill steepened and eventually she was rewarded for her efforts by the fine views of the bay of St Aubin which unfolded before her . She leaned against the railings and regained her breath. The breeze riffled her hair and blew on her bare legs. The sea was down below and half a mile away, sparkling and moving with the wind and tide. Unseen to her, there were concrete bunkers all around and further up the hill, large field guns could be fired at any attempt at a landing in the bay. She heard the sounds of jackboots on the road behind her. She turned to see what was happening and a squad of six German soldiers were struggling up the incline. She acknowledged them as they passed and each one politely smiled and called out "Good afternoon." The sweet smell of their cologne clung to the air. She thought it would be much

easier if they could be a little less polite.
None of her thoughts helped the turmoil she felt within. There was still a fire burning between her legs.
She continued walking to the top of the long hill and then returned down Queens Road back in to St Helier. The last bus to Gorey left town at 5pm and she was home at St Kitts by six. Her mind was working overtime and she felt glad to be home. She knew she needed some sleep.
"Hi Mum," said Peter as she walked in through the porch. "Have you had a good day?"
Before she had time to answer, Sophie came running in from the garden, shouting
"Mummy, Mummy, Mummy!"
Christine embraced her gorgeous little daughter and gave Peter a hug. Peter noticed she was flushed and upset.
"You okay, Mum?"
"Yes, yes. I'm fine. Bit of hay fever. Just got a bit of a headache. Can you put Sophie to bed, son. Think I'll have a lie-down .Okay?"
"Cor blimey. I've gotta do everything round here," Peter whinged lightheartedly.
He watched her shuffle off towards the staircase.
"Pissed again," he said under his breath.
"I heard that!" she replied but she was happy that was *all* he was thinking.
She went to the bathroom and washed away the remnants of the day. She was done with crying, she was hurt and tearful, and she was thankful to be back with her family . She slept for twelve hours. As the early morning sun worked its way through the cracks in her black-out curtains, she knew that she had been stupid and that she should have come straight home after lunch instead of dallying at the Grand Hotel.
A small part of her also acknowledged that the day had been wildly exciting and that she had enjoyed every second of it. Her emotions simmered for days.

CHAPTER 53

Pianos and swastikas

The promise of a schnapps with Fritz Doenig was not the guiding force to Klaus Bucholtz' visit to the Hotel Bristol in late July. One of the band had been on evening duty at the La Rocque defence post and had inadvertently left his rifle in one of the bunkers. This was a serious military offence but before anyone could make a song and dance about it, Klaus had hidden it away and made it an excuse for a trip into town. He got to the hotel late afternoon knowing this was a good time before their stints on guard duty in the evening. All places of troop residence had had sentries since well before D-Day in early June and the hotel was no exception. He had little trouble gaining entrance and asked one of the men if he could see Oberleutnant Doenig on a matter of some urgency. He waited in the dining room and saw the well-used piano in the far corner. He went over and sat down on the piano stool. He thought for a minute. He spread his hands wide, rested them on the keys and started to play the tune he had last played as a sixteen year old in the schools music competition back in Germany. It was Beethoven's Fur Elise and as he stumbled through the opening notes, he could imagine all the faces of the family and friends he missed so much, listening to him play . His fingers took over from his brain. He watched them skimming over the keys, surprised that he could remember any of this. He stopped when he heard a shuffling of feet behind him and turned round instinctively to see Fritz standing and listening.

"Not bad, Obergefreiter! We could use a piano player."

Klaus rose quickly to his feet and apologised for his intrusion.

"I am so sorry, Oberleutnant. I got a little carried away. I thought I was back at the school music competition."

"You never told me you could play the piano, Klaus. You'd be better than the sausage fingered Schultze that plays dance

music for us now. Is it too early for a schnapps, my friend?"
"Well, possibly, Oberleutnant. Officially I came to return this rifle which I think belongs to one of your crew. Normally my Sergeant would have been on the case, breathing fire and threatening a court martial. In the circumstances, I took the appropriate action ."

Klaus reached for the weapon that he had propped in the corner. Fritz looked perplexed.
"Thank you, Klaus. That was very considerate of you. I shall have the culprit shot in the morning! "
Klaus raised his eyebrows in surprise.
"Just kidding, Klaus, just kidding. I shall have him tortured first ! How are things at Platte Rocque? Any more low flying aircraft dropping bombs on your arse?"

Klaus laughed out loud. He could feel they were kindred spirits. Fritz beckoned him to the small bar in the corner of the dining room. He took out a key and opened the drinks cabinet.
"The benefits of rank ! Schnapps, my friend? ....and then you can tell me where you learned to play piano like that."
Fritz held two small glasses in one hand and expertly poured out the Schnapps. They downed them as quickly as he had poured .
"I learned to play from the age of ten. I passed all the exams but then the Fuhrer intervened. I was all set to go on to the Institute when I received my call-up papers."
"Great pity but hopefully you can return to it after this has finished," replied Fritz. He waved his glass around to indicate 'all this'.
"Not much chance of that! I had a scholarship to the Dusseldorf Institute of Music. It got obliterated last March. Nothing left of it. Not much left of anything by the news I am getting."
"Really ?A scholarship, eh?I'm impressed! What a shame. Yes, you're right about the news. I reckon we'll be cut off completely

very soon. When was the last time you went home?"
"Over two years since I saw my family and now that all leave has been cancelled, who knows? It's a mess and the sooner we surrender, the better............oh, I'm sorry, Oberleutnant. Perhaps it's dangerous to be giving my opinion."
"No, Klaus, you are quite safe here although it's best to be careful who you are speaking to. There are one or two of the Feldpolitzei around who are not keen on the truth. One of my lot was hauled in for an interview and a thumping last month for suggesting in public that the war was not going too well for the Fatherland. I managed to get him released but not before he got a black eye. Anyway, enough of this depressing talk......have a listen to Big Bertha!"
Fritz moved to the side of the cocktail bar to where the mahogany gramophone was standing. He plugged it in and switched on. It hummed benevolently into life. He unlocked another cupboard behind the bar and withdrew an illustrated cardboard sleeve containing a long playing record. He put the record on the turntable, moved a lever or two and the music of Glenn Miller filled the air.
Klaus was beaming......
"I know this one, I know this one. Don't tell me........In the Mood ! Yes?"
"Ah, you know your music, my friend. You've been listening to the British radio, haven't you? Don't worry, if you look closely at the tuning dial on this machine you will see that most of the time it is pointing to the BBC Light Programme. We put a piece of sticky tape over it in case of a visit from the Feldpolitzei. They still think it just plays records!"
They both chatted while listening and talked about their choices in music. Klaus was unaware that the band of the Luftwaffe played so many open air concerts in and around St Helier.
"Yes, we don't just play the marching songs for marching troops......" said Fritz... *"for which I am thankful. You try teaching a collection of uncoordinated musicians how to put*

one foot in front of the other in unison whilst playing an instrument. The bass drum player dropped his bloody drum last week! We were going downhill at the time, he could have killed someone. Field Marshal Rommel should put us in the front line. We'd be dangerous!"
And so it went on. It all changed after about ten minutes the turntable slowed to a halt and so did the music.
"Oh shit," said Fritz,*"...another power cut. They are becoming a regular occurrence. Have another schnapps. It should come back on in a few minutes."*

"No thanks Oberleutnant, I should be getting back. My sergeant is expecting me back by 6.30pm and he wouldn't take kindly to me being drunk AND late. Thank you for your hospitality, though. You have been most kind."
"No,Klaus, it is you who have been kind. One of my boys would have been in all sorts of shit if you hadn't looked after that rifle. I appreciate that. And if you ever feel like a change of uniform, you would always be welcome here."
"Thank you, Oberleutnant. Unfortunately the piano is my only instrument and I can't see myself pushing one down the road when you are marching on parade!"
"No, I suppose not. Good thought though! You can always come and play here, you know. Sunday night is usually best. We practise all sorts then. We've even got a singer now. He was our drill instructor for a while. Turned out he was in the Vienna Boys Choir. Although his voice is a bit lower now.........."
They both laughed.
Fritz saw him out on to the street and they shook hands before parting.
"Sunday, Klaus ?"
"Yes, why not? Sunday, it is , Oberleutnant. Thank you."

Klaus walked back to the Weighbridge where he had a lift waiting. Although the war news was disappointing, he felt

elated that he could still play the piano. Like riding a bicycle, he knew it was something he would never forget.....but even so, he was pleased with himself. A small victory in what was turning out to be a rather large pile of crap. He returned to Platte Rocque for another night of total boredom. About midnight, while listening to Allied aeroplanes droning overhead, he flexed the fingers of both hands like a concert pianist ready for a performance. He was certainly feeling more optimistic. There seemed to be less planes tonight but the men were kept busy manoeuvring the searchlights and sounding the warning sirens. At least they hadn't fired any guns tonight. That could all change, however, but that would be the responsibility of the night shift. There was plenty of moonlight and he decided to march his men back to their billet at the Bon Voyage Hotel which was a mile towards town on the land side of the coast road. The sound of jackboots on the road became a familiar sound at the same time every night. Tonight was a bit different however as one of the soldiers at the front of the squad suddenly broke off , raising his rifle and challenging a shadowy figure standing in a garden on the seaside of the road. The squad of ten bristled with raised rifles and shuffling feet. They were terrified and understandably nervous Was this a British commando? Were there others around, eager to slit their throats? They fanned out , peering into the gardens of other houses nearby.
"Hands up! Hands up!" shouted the soldier.

After a very robust shake-down it was discovered that it was the old Frenchman Gaston Guillaume, clearly drunk and staggering home, he claimed, from the Grenadier. He was swearing in his native tongue, "Salope, salope." was all he said. He was out after curfew so it was going to be a couple of months in the Gloucester Street prison. Klaus ordered someone to double back to Platte Rocque to arrange transport for the prisoner, left two men to guard him and then marched the remainder back to their billet. Peace returned to the south east

corner of the parish of Grouville.
In the morning, Peter discovered a pot of black paint and a paint brush lying by the porch. He thought nothing of it except that it might be Mac who had left it there. Paint was in short supply and he may have received it as part of some dodgy deal.
It came up in conversation at the pub the next night. There was Brian, Mac and Peter chewing the cud by the long bar at the Grenadier.
Peter was first in.
"Was it you that left a pot of paint and a brush outside the house last night, Mac? Are we painting the boat again? "
"Nay ladee, it wasnee me. Last night was a bit of a blank though." said Mac.
"Then that's a bit of a mystery. I think it's my shout. I'll have two pints of your best fizzy water, please landlord ," Peter called to Brian who was coming out from the backroom to serve at the bar.
"Can't even do that tonight, young Pete. I can do you two teas though. Oh, you too, you'll love this! Old Gaston got arrested last night near your place, Pete, after midnight. I spoke to Klaus this morning and he reckons the old goat was pissed and staggering home from here when they picked him up. They've banged him up in Gloucester Street for the time being. He may just get three or four months this time. I shan't miss him. I reckon he's rotting from the inside. Bit strange. He may have been pissed but he wasn't on his way home from here, that's for sure."
None of this information registered too deeply with Mac who had gone a bit quiet since Brian had imparted the information regarding Christine's dalliance with the German Kriegsmarine officer at the Blue Yacht the other week. He had come to terms with it and hoped it was not true but Brian was a pretty reliable witness and a good friend. He was also very good at keeping his own counsel for which Mac was thankful.

The next day, the feisty Scot had cause to check on the Crazy

Doris which lay idle at La Rocque Harbour. The Germans had issued four conflicting orders regarding fishing from boats over the last two months. You can, you can't, you can and just last week, you can't. It was all quite amusing, not that anybody minded as you stood a good chance of being shot at by both sides if you did venture out. Klaus was just coming out of the Platte Rocque post and shouted a greeting to Mac as he was going down the slipway.

"Morning, Mac. How are things?"

"Morgen, Klaus. Hungry as ever. We're starrrting to witherr away. Any new orders this week? "

"No, my friend. It's all......how you say......very dull. Although we did arrest Gaston the old Frenchman a couple of nights ago. That was the most exciting part of the week. I don't understand him. He was in the garden by a house along the road . He was...how you say.....up to no good. He kept shouting the same word.'Salope, salope'.

I think he is maybe not right in the head. We locked him up. He will have three months in the prison."

Mac looked puzzled and suddenly said,

"The silly old bugger wasn't carrying a pot of paint, was he?"

It was Klaus' turn to look puzzled.

"How did you know about the paint? His hands were covered in it. We think he put a big swastika on two houses near the golf course....but that is.... how you say...... a secret. Every time a swastika appears, ten ' V' signs follow. So we scrub them off. What did you say about a pot of paint?"

"Och, nuthin'. He's a bloody nutter. Lock him up for ever, I say."

"What is 'nutter', Mac ?"

Mac tapped his temple with his forefinger.

"Aaaaah, yes. Nutter. I will remember this one." Klaus smiled as he spoke.

"I'm sure you will, Klaus. I'm sure you will. See you soon," said Mac, smiling as he moved away.

" Yes, see you later."
The tide was out and Mac walked down the sandy beach, through the sticky mud near the pier. He heaved himself aboard up the stern ladder and sat down with a sigh on the back bench. He felt deflated and tired. With his elbows on his knees, he held his head in his hands and stared at the deck at his feet. He felt confused and sad. He had put two and two together and come to the conclusion that the little shit of a Frenchman, Gaston Guillaume, had been in the act of daubing a swastika on the wall of St Kitts when Klaus' patrol had chanced by. The daubing of a large swastika on the sides of houses had become the favourite way of identifying local girls who were suspected of consorting with the Germans. Even Mac knew the English translation of 'salope' was 'bitch'. None of the surrounding houses was occupied so it was a bit of a stretch of the imagination to think that St Kitts wasn't his target. How much did the little pisshead know ? There was only one way to find out. He knew Peter was going to swimming training tomorrow evening and wouldn't be back until late so he would strike while the iron was hot.

CHAPTER 54

Showdown

Mac knocked on the door of St Kitts at six o'clock the next evening with a small bag of fresh vegetables he had traded on the black market.

Christine opened the door and, although he didn't show it, he felt strangely hostile towards her. Feeling angry would help him confront her.

"Staying for supper, Mac? Peter is out and Sophie will be in bed soon. I could do with some company. Please ?"

"Ah well, hen. Seeing as you put it so nicely. As it happens, I've got a wee bottle in ma bag! I need to talk to you about something."

"Ooooo, that sounds ominous. Let me feed Sophie first and get her off to bed. You may have to read her a story, though. Are you up to that ?"

"Aye, of course , lovey. Of course I will."

And so it went on for a couple of hours until the time was right. Sophie was asleep and the table was cleared, just leaving a half empty bottle of white wine and two full glasses.

Christine pulled her chair up to the table, "Fire away, Mac."

Mac downed his glass of wine and served first.

"What I have to say is a wee bit tricky, lovey." Mac had the Scottish habit of calling people 'lovey' when a conversation had serious undertones .

"And you must remember that I only have your best interests at heart."

He hesitated.

"Well, come on. Spit it out, man."

Christine had no idea where all this was leading.

"Okay, lovey. This is really hard.......You've been spotted at the Blue Yacht dining very closely with the enemy. To be specific, a Kriegsmarine officer in a very smart white uniform."

There followed a stunned silence. The blood drained from

Christine's face. At first she was angry.
"What? What? *Who* saw this? Who was it? It certainly wasn't me. It couldn't have been."
After her initial outburst, she realised that she had clearly been found out and it would be wiser to discover the truth.
She leaned forward. "Who was it, Mac?"
"It doesn't matter who, hen. The fact is that he is a reliable witness and he came to me in confidence and left it with me, knowing I was a good friend of the family..........."

Mac could see Christine was severely rattled. He went on.
"I'm telling you this for your own good, lassie. In St Helier, they are ganging up on jerrybags. They get insulted in the street and some have even had their heads shaved by force. I don't want any of this crap to happen to you. God knows, this war here on the island bears no resemblance to what we suffered in the trenches. We seem to be living in a weird dream. It isnee real."
"Is that what I am, Mac. A jerrybag? Is that what you think of me?"
At this stage, Christine lost her composure completely and broke down into floods of tears. Mac thought it best for her just to cry it out. He still felt angry and had no desire to put a protective arm around her and go "there, there".
When the tears had subsided into an occasional sob, Mac went on.
"Were you serious about the jerry in the white uniform?"
"Yes....yes I was. He offered me a lift into town when I was standing at the bus stop out there one day. I refused the first time but it put my life into focus. I've been living with the probability that Cliff had been drowned and felt I deserved one last chance. After all, I'm nearly forty. The next time he offered, I got in.....and that's when it started."
Mac was doing his own drowning at this point. He really didn't like what he was hearing. He felt betrayed. He really wanted to believe that it was a case of mistaken identity and everything

could go on exactly as it was before . So betrayed he was that he suddenly blurted out,
"Have you been shagging him?"

Christine was quite taken aback but Mac's harsh question opened up the discussion .
Mac tried to recant his question.
"Och, I'm so sorry, pet. I really didn't mean to say that. It isnee ma business."
"Since you ask so nicely as whether I was having a meaningful physical relationship with Hans, the answer is 'no'. But I have to admit that it hasn't been for the want of trying."
She was lying .
Mac was going down fast with all this information that kept coming. He had had better days on the Somme. He had asked a stupid, candid question and now had to cope with the feelings her answers would stir up.
Christine continued.
"Hans and I came out of the Blue Yacht arm in arm early last Thursday afternoon after a lovely lunch. As we turned the corner, we were in full view of the people in the bus queue across the road. You should have seen the looks on their faces. That smelly French fisherman was there with that silly beret and he was the worst, his cigarette practically fell out of his mouth. I was mortified. I think at that moment I realised how stupid I was being. I ran off and caught the bus home. I won't be seeing him again, Mac."
Christine realised that this was not the entire truth but, as the end result was the same, she felt no shame in ending the story at that point.
"I'm pleased to hear it, lassie. It must be hard for you what with Cliff and everything. You and your kids are beautiful and I would hate to think of you all being the target of gossip."
They both then sat there at opposite ends of the table in complete relaxed silence. Both of them had tackled emotions that were troubling them and both felt relieved to get it out

there. The fact that Gaston had indeed spotted her in the street with the Nazi naval officer was more troubling. He wasn't sure whether he should tell Christine that the Frenchman had been arrested for daubing swastikas on houses and St Kitts had been his next target had it not been for the intervention of the German patrol. After another drink, he decided to keep that information to himself. He would deal with the Frenchman personally.

Nonetheless they talked on into the light evening until Peter returned home, grinning like a Cheshire cat. Swimming training had been fun and Melody had been teaching him a few things about diving. He was besotted with her. Mac was happy for him. Christine made him drink one for the road before she saw him off. She gave him a big hug on the doorstep but he was in no mood to reciprocate this time. He shuffled unsteadily off towards La Rocque slipway. The evening was long and light. Curfew was still an hour away.

He growled quietly to himself. "You fucking big prick, Mac. Why did ye have to blurt it oot? Are you shagging him? What a stupid fucking question. Ya big fucking purple headed prick!"

An anonymous voice replied from the bunkers of the defence post at Platte Rocque, now just a few yards away.

"Goodnight, Jock!"

Mac was up for this. He shouted back in annoyance.

"I am not fucking Jock, Jerry!"

There was a silence of about ten seconds.

"And I am not fucking Jerry, Jock!"

It sounded like the voice of Sergeant Steiglitz but, in his semi-drunk emotional state, he couldn't be sure. He staggered on and a bullet fizzed past his left ear. Yes, it was definitely Steiglitz. One up to me, he thought. Not even looking back, he waved his arm in total disdain.

The black dog followed him home. Tonight, for a change, he would not be sleeping with Christine. Tomorrow he would square things with Brian.

CHAPTER 55

Swim time

As July 1944 played out, the amount of activity around the Jersey skies and harbours continued to react to what was going on some twenty miles across the sea in France. Against this backdrop of unchallenged overflying Allied aircraft and intense naval activity, life on the islands simply carried on in a fashion that wavered between patience and boredom. They patiently waited for what was thought to be an inevitable German surrender, but when it didn't materialise, boredom set in for both friend and enemy. The squeeze on food supplies took its toll on the general well-being of everybody except German officers. People were more susceptible to minor infections and the scarcity of medicines exacerbated the situation. Digestive systems were put to the test . Many a sermon at St Peter La Rocque was punctuated by the gut rumblings of the congregation. These 'Jersey rattles' were funny at first and then they became part of normal life, eventually going politely unnoticed.

All of this passed Peter Marinelle by. He was living on the fruits of love. Melody and he were inseparable. He was never home. Forever hanging out at the Bathing Pool, he was living in a euphoric daze. Life for him could get no better. Mac hardly ever saw him and Christine had to read him the riot act as to the hours he was keeping.

The awful weather of June and early July had finally given way to a more acceptable summer as August swept in.

"When are you going to bring Melody home to see us all, Peter ?" Christine asked one rare night when Peter was home.

"Whenever you invite her, Mum. Whenever you invite her."

And so it was on the August Bank Holiday weekend that Christine gathered up all the odd bits and bobs of food she had squirreled away in the pantry and put together a lunch that would at least fill their bellies. She had to admit that Melody was a lovely girl and she never once had a thought that this slip of a girl was taking her son away from her. Peter needed a normal life. It was bad enough that he had no father and in that respect, Mac had been her saviour. Mac may have been a tad feisty at times, especially after a whisky, but he had been a rock these last few years. He had looked after all of them , fixing the house and keeping them fed. She hadn't seen him since the night of her confession but hoped he would drop in after she left a note in his letterbox inviting him to drop in on the Bank Holiday. She hadn't heard from him and he hadn't shown up by one o'clock so they started lunch without him in the back garden. The lazy nip tide edged slowly back and forth and sparkled benevolently in the background. Over the last few days, there had been a general relaxation of the rules regarding civilians on certain beaches. This was a rare concession and had more to do with the fact that the occupiers were now no longer on 'full alert'. This was the only stand down they had been allowed since their arrival four years ago. No longer did the foot soldier have to carry arms wherever he went. This was an extraordinary turnaround and was tantamount to the Germans officially acknowledging that the islands had been bypassed by the Allied advance. They were no longer expecting an attack. The locals took full advantage of the situation and clambered over barbed wire and barriers to get on to the sand and swim in the sea. La Rocque was no different and after lunch, Christine, Sophie, Peter and Melody slipped down on to the beach intent on a much needed swim. Not many locals were aware of the lagoon that existed between the two towers of Seymour and Icho. Peter was keen to show Melody but Sophie was demanding his attention. After a few minutes, Christine took over baby sitting duties, allowing the two young swimmers full rein to explore . The sea was as benign as it was possible to be, flat calm with little or no current to deal with. Christine watched them go and they were soon out of sight swimming around some exposed rocks. How good it was to see them, a happy pair of human dolphins in the prime of their youth. Cliff would have loved to have seen them too and she realised it was the first time he had sprung into her mind for a month or two. She had two beautiful children , each one a reflection of their happy times together. In that moment she resolved to do better. She felt instantly happier. She heard a shout from the garden some 100 yards behind her and she turned to see Mac waving . Sophie's face lit up and the two of them walked back to greet him.

On the other side of the pier at La Rocque, one or two families had meandered down the slipway on to the sand by the seawall. Klaus had cleared an entrance through the barricade for this purpose and was off the two hundred yards down to the water's edge to check on some wreckage that was being washed up. He carried no rifle or side arm, despite being in uniform. There was a good reason for this as Klaus was anxious to go for a swim in the hot weather. He was also on duty. After ostentatiously checking that the flotsam was harmless, he ducked behind a large rock and stripped off to his underpants. He quickly found a spot where the water was deep enough and dived underwater. Although he was a country boy, he had taken to his new seaside existence with relish. He was short of time and after a quick splash around, he scuttled surreptitiously to where his clothes were piled on a large rock. He could dry out here without being seen and within minutes he was ready to resume his military duties. A few months ago he could have been put on a charge for dereliction of duty with some serious consequences but in the current atmosphere it felt appropriate to take time out. A raucous seagull dropped a shellfish onto rocks nearby and dived back down to see if he had done enough damage to expose the meat inside. Out of the corner of his eye, Klaus saw a flash of iridescent blue as a secretive kingfisher skipped through the air to its nest in a grassy bank close to the pier. Bloodsuckers, limpets and bladderwrack above the tide level creaked and grumbled as they dried out in the hot sun. A solitary egret looked nervously on from a safe distance, ready to move away. The happy shrieks of children playing near the seawall filled the still air. This was the rush hour at La Rocque. Klaus stopped and looked around, sucking up the sights and sounds.

"This is good...... but now........... I want to go home," he said out loud. He hadn't seen his family for two years . He had two younger brothers who were coming up to military age. If the war went on past Christmas, there was a good chance they would be conscripted.

He felt suddenly melancholy and set off back to Platte Rocque , his jackboots dragging in the gravel . The sea water dried on his skin leaving tell tale trails of salt on his sunburnt face. The figure of Oberleutnant Fritz Doenig was waving and beckoning from the slipway. Klaus was pleased to see him and quickened his pace. They shook hands.

" A fleeting visit, my friend, as I have to be in town in half an hour. Band practice tomorrow evening from six o'clock, Klaus. We are also celebrating the end of our sentry duties so be prepared for some schnapps drinking !"

*"Brilliant,"*replied Klaus and he theatrically stretched his fingers out as if readying himself to play the piano........*"and welcome to my world. Not bad, eh?"*

He nodded in the direction of a shimmering sea and a lowering sun.

"Yes, you're certainly doing it tough out here. See you tomorrow?"

"Absolutely!"

Fritz sauntered back to his car at the top of the slipway, its engine still running.

Life continued for both sides in this crazy situation. As the Allied grip tightened over France and onwards to Berlin, less and less planes were in evidence and shipping came to a near standstill. By the end of August, with the arrival of more of the retreating enemy, the German ranks in Jersey had swelled to sixteen thousand including six hundred casualties whose presence put further pressure on medical supplies. The unluckiest of the new arrivals were some Americans who had been captured on the Cherbourg peninsula during a raid initiated by the Germans in Guernsey. They found themselves imprisoned in their own secure hut in St Helier at the top of Pier Road with a fine view over the harbour. The situation was becoming more complicated by the day.

Christine and Sophie soon reached Mac on the sand below St Kitts. Sophie grabbed hold of Mac's leg while Christine gave him a big, meaningful hug.
"Thanks , Mac........thanks. It's good to see you."
"Thanks for what, lassie?"
"Thanks for looking out for us all. Thanks for stopping me..... make a fool of myself."

He grabbed her shoulders and pushed her gently away. There seemed to be a tear in his eye but he managed to croak out, very quietly,
"You know I love you, don't you? You people are all I've got."
This was *so* unlike Mac, a man who had always kept himself to himself. He *never* expressed his emotions to other people. Christine looked totally surprised but the moment that stood still, moved swiftly on when a small voice floated up from near Mac's knees. A little smiley face was beaming up at him and a little hand was tugging at his shirt.
"Do you love me too, Uncle Mac?"
He plucked Sophie from the ground and swung her in the air.
"Oh, yes my little lovey. I love you the *most* of all and I've got a wee present for you up at the house. Let's go! "
Mac and Sophie rushed back up to the garden hand in hand and Christine was left to ponder on Mac's words.
Minutes later, the sound of a penny whistle filled the balmy summer air as Sophie tried unsuccessfully to coax a tune from Mac's gift. Within an hour the two human fish returned from the lagoon, sunburnt and still dripping. Peter carried a large

rusty tin which was full of cockles.
Mac was first in.
"Ah, you little genius. I taught ye well. Usual place?"
"Yes, but the sandbank was still underwater. Lucky the tin was lying around. There's a good feed there! Shall I put the saucepan on the stove, Mum?"
"Yes, but you two can stop dripping on my clean floor first!"
"Sorry Mrs M ," said Melody.
"Yeah, sorry Mrs M," mimicked Peter.
"Yeah, sorry Mrs M," mimicked Sophie.

Mac was just about to open his mouth and complete the sequence when Christine glared at him.
"Don't ....even think about it, Mac !!"

They all burst out laughing. Family life had returned.

Mac had recounted to Brian the saga of Christine's involvement with the German naval officer . She had promised that that was the end of it and Brian had given his word that it would go no further.
Later that evening, Mac had a quiet word with Christine to reassure her secret was safe. The whole episode had hurt him deeply and it took quite an effort on his part to tell her all this.
Back at Platte Rocque, Klaus was marching a squad back to the guest house as the shift ended. He had been inducted as a guest player into the band and was off to another practice as soon as he had eaten. Fritz had promised him a spot up at a Government House recital in a month's time.
Life for all on the islands had become a series of little plans which barely stretched beyond a few weeks. A stalemate existed. The Germans, in their isolation, would not shift and the Allies had bigger fish to fry. As supplies dried up, the autumn months passed by and the weather worsened. They would soon be entering what was to be called 'the hunger winter'.

CHAPTER 56

Klaus' first band practice

Klaus hitched a ride into town on Sunday afternoon. He had been waiting at the bus stop outside the Bon Voyage when a lorry full of naval ratings en route to town from Gorey Harbour ground to a halt. He knew the driver and held out his thumb as it slowed.

The driver, Carlos, yelled out , *"Klaus, you old cherry-picker you. I'm going into St Helier to the Weighbridge. Hop in beside me, if you dare!"*

Carlos and Klaus were pre-war acquaintances of a similar age. Carlos' family were potato farmers who lived in the next district to the Bucholtz' cherry farm.

"Thanks for that, potato head. Good timing! How are you? "

"I'm well and good apart from all this shit. You?"

"Same here."

And so the conversation went on. Eventually they got to discuss food and its scarcity.

"I heard from a good source the other day that our food stocks will run out in a month. What happens then? Do we run up a white flag and surrender ?" said Carlos.

Klaus moved his head a little closer towards the driver and replied,

"Well, maybe that wouldn't be such a bad idea, my friend. Maybe I'm just saying what other people are thinking."

"Yes, you're right. It would be good if we were home for Christmas but I don't think there is much chance of that."

Carlos dropped him off at the town end of St Saviour's Road and he had a bit of a walk to the Bristol.

He sniffed the warm air and breathed in honeysuckle scent from a nearby garden. He watched some butterflies dancing round the purple flowers of a buddleia bush and listened to some bees who were lazily collecting pollen from the flowers of some hollyhocks. A thin old lady struggled rheumatically in the garden, fighting a losing battle with a weed that steadfastly refused to yield. He paused just as she stopped and looked up.
"What do you want?" she said, rather too aggressively for his liking but he was used to it.
"I am sorry. I was just admiring your garden. I can smell the ....honeysuckle?"
"Well, the only thing I can smell is bloody Germans! Now bugger off!"

For once, this touched a nerve and he walked quickly on. For a moment then he had been transported back to the gardens of Steinkirschen and home comforts. The old lady could have been his grandmother. The plants, the bees and the butterflies were the same back home except there were more cherries there. He quickly pushed aside the feelings of homesickness but not before they had stabbed him one more time. This was crap. Let's go and play piano. He walked round the corner and noticed this time there was no guard at the entrance to the Hotel Bristol. He walked into the dining room unchallenged.
Fritz welcomed him and sat him down at the piano before he even had time to take his army blouse off.
"Quiet everybody.....please. Can I introduce to you all to Obergefreiter Klaus Bucholtz. Some of you will have met him down at Platte Rocque on your guard duties which incidentally we are no longer required to do (cheers from the audience) *....and he makes an excellent cup of tea ......(*cheers from the audience)*.....but he also plays the piano........ which he will now demonstrate !*

Klaus looked a bit sheepish being put on the spot but he rose heroically to the task but not before he had replied to Fritz.

"Sir, sir! Thank you for your welcome but I must correct you. It's now ***Feldwebel*** *Klaus Bucholtz.*(a theatrical 'oooooooo' went up) *I do play piano but not for a while so please forgive me."*
From his little speech he moved seamlessly into a dire off note version of 'chopsticks' to the laughter and jeers of the fifteen or so members of the band who could be there today. They loved him already. His spirits rose and he glided into Fur Elise, his fingers and brain in renewed harmony. He watched his hands in amusement, he was cruising, it was all inside his head and his fingers did the rest. He finished to cheers and a schnapps appeared on top of the upright piano.
Fritz was obliged to make them practise all the parade ground music that was the major part of their day to day routine. He then moved on to more orchestral pieces that were reserved for the recitals in the Royal Square and Government House. Today was a more special day as they were celebrating the cessation of the unloved guard duties. He felt they needed a break. They were all homesick and confused. The music took their minds off it all. By seven o'clock Klaus was into his third schnapps and coupled with the current lack of food, he felt a little light-headed. Seven or eight of the band were dismissed and they had another drink. Big Bertha's valves lit up but dimmed prematurely to their groans as another power cut ensued. Werner Turner came to the rescue with his trumpet.
"Come on." said Werner.*"We can do this ourselves!"*
Raising the trumpet up, he licked his lips and blasted straight into the opening bars of "The boogie woogie bugle boy from Company B", a 1941 Glenn Miller classic.
Werner's trumpet playing was faultless and, through the ensuing alcoholic haze, Klaus recognised the song. He assumed rightly that no-one would be able to sing the long and complicated lyrics , they would be hard enough for an Englander in his own language. He leaned forward over the piano, belched loudly and proceeded to fill in the vocal bits with what can only be described as his first attempt at boogie

woogie piano. He was a natural and Fritz beamed with pride at his discovery. One by one the rest joined in, Fritz on clarinet, Gunter Muller on saxophone, Rudi Klinsmann on slide trombone and Willi Brint on his drum collection. People started gathering at the door of the dining room. Dieter Hankel, their ex Vienna Boys Choir vocalist, slipped in through a side door and started clapping out the rhythm. After fifteen minutes hammering the keys, Klaus could take no more and he passed out, striking his head with a discordant note on the piano keys as he slid off his piano stool. The music stuttered to a halt as they realised their star player had become tired and emotional.
"Shut the fuck up, will you!" an irate German voice could be heard outside. At the same moment , a bullet fizzed through the open window and sheered the last remaining link of chain that fixed the chandelier to the ceiling. It came crashing down in the middle of the dining room's parquet floor with a noise that marked the end of the impromptu concert. The small crowd dispersed in a hurry.
"That's a lot better. You guys couldn't play "Three Blind Mice". You're shit!"
Klaus wouldn't have known it but it was the unmistakeable voice of the trigger happy Oberfeldwebel Steiglitz who was now billeted nearby. He was now in charge of a defence position on Westmount overlooking St Aubin's Bay and was even more flakey than when he was terrorising Mac at La Rocque.
Klaus was put on a sofa for a couple of hours to recover while the band partied quietly on. They returned him home by troop lorry at about midnight. His head was banging the whole of the next day.

CHAPTER 57

December 1944

The food supply situation grew gradually worse and quantities of rationed goods such as bread and meat were adjusted downwards .A general lack of direction began to set everyone's nerves on edge. Out of the blue in early October, the Germans put out a statement in the Jersey Evening Post acknowledging that the Islands had been effectively cut off since a month before D-Day and that existing stocks and ongoing harvested produce were not enough to maintain the status quo.

"The Supreme Commander of the Channel Islands (Oberst Von Schmidt) has informed the German Government of the situation and is intending to take the matter up with the Protecting Power. Any action the Protecting Power may decide to take is beyond the control of the Occupying Authorities."

The Protecting Power was diplomatic speak for a third party who was capable of mediating, in this case it was Switzerland and the Red Cross. The Red Cross would be capable of alleviating the food supply situation to either side of the conflict depending on the circumstances. The Red Cross had been delivering mail to both sides already.

Most people realised that little would happen quickly but at least the process had been set in motion. What was more worrying was that the Germans also stated that they had no intention of leaving.

A month passed by without any action or acknowledgement . Remembrance Day on November 11, commemorating the dreadful losses in World War 1, seemed to elevate the urgency of the matter and more discussions were held between the Bailiff and German officials. Bailiff Dechevaux questioned the fact that no reply had been received from the Protecting Power and the Germans were equally at odds with that fact. He pressed them to send an official message from himself and that was transmitted in German on the evening of November 13. A

month had been lost. The situation was deteriorating and even the German soldiers were declaring that they were 'hungry'.
Boredom set in for everybody as the situation limped along. Fishing from vessels was allowed again but the lack of fuel combined with the foul weather meant there were few takers. Mac managed to prise Peter away from Melody a couple of times in early Autumn and they harvested all they could with bumper crops of hand netted prawns beyond Seymour Tower. On one occasion they took Klaus as a thank you for all his help with their permits and he had a great time. Earlier in the occupation, they would not have countenanced his company but the situation was now becoming ridiculous. It was every man for himself or you would starve. Klaus in return made sure that they had unlimited access to the beach at all times which was not the case for the rest of the population.
Escape attempts became more brazen. Late one evening, four young lads appeared at the sea wall near the Bathing Pool with two canoes and, unchallenged, carried them down to the water's edge. They paddled off east a couple of miles into the twilight but it quickly became apparent that their canoes were not fit for purpose. Within minutes of believing they had cracked it, the canoes were overwhelmed , became waterlogged and sank. All four drowned and their bodies were washed up a day later. The Germans issued a warning, revealing that they would no longer attempt to rescue any visible escape attempts but would certainly open fire instead. No sooner had they issued the order than another party of five teenagers humped a rowing boat over the wall near Anne Port just north of Gorey Castle. Hearing the noise , a nearby German defence position sent up some flares and exposed them in the light. They refused to stop until an order to open fire was given. One of the lads was shot dead and the others carried his body back up the beach into the arms of the waiting soldiers. It was an avoidable tragedy but it confirmed that the war was still on. Better organised escapes originated from closer to home just up the road at Sunny View where Big Mick helped a number of young people store all

manner of small boats and dinghies until they were ready to make their attempt. The weather leading up to Christmas was not conducive to rowing or paddling and many efforts ended in tragedy. Young lives being lost added to the awful feeling of desperation and hunger that pervaded the island. Gas supplies ran out when no more coal was available . Electricity became unreliable and was switched off and on at irregular times.
There was unrest in the German ranks and arrests were made in cases of insubordination. An unusual daily visitor to the island was an Allied aircraft which would fly over around midnight and drop leaflets designed to unsettle the occupying army. They were written in German, would land in random areas and soldiers were immediately deployed to collect and destroy them. Combined with the propaganda emanating from the wireless sets and all leave being cancelled, this resulted in an undercurrent of dissatisfaction amongst the common soldier. It was clear to the commanding officers that discipline was becoming harder to maintain.
At last on December 6, the Germans notified the civil authorities that a Red Cross supply ship was due to leave Lisbon in neutral Portugal bound for the Channel Islands. Dechevaux was overjoyed. Things were finally on the move.

CHAPTER 58

Christmas Fayre looms

Brian's meeting with Klaus was a fortunate coincidence. On his way to the parish hall on his bicycle, he dropped into Mrs Le Plongeon's shop to ask if she would put one of his hand-made posters in the window.

"Good morning Brian," said Mrs Le Plongeon, squinting at him over her glasses. "Have you lost your way?"

"Very funny, Mrs Le Plongeon. Everyone's a comedian these days. Any chance we can put one of these up in your window?"

"Seeing as I am on the Christmas Fayre Committee and we agreed that I would at the last meeting - you were *there*-I guess it will be alright. Can you put it on the door?"

"Of course you were. Of course you were. Yes, on the door. Splendid."

It took Brian a good half hour to put the poster up. Every time he went to stick the poster on the back of the glass panel on the door, a customer came in. First it was Christine.

"You lost your way, Brian ?"

"No, my dear. I'm attempting to put up a poster proclaiming to the world that the Christmas Fayre is at the parish hall this Saturday. Starts about two o'clock. We've got carol singing and the usual stalls, hoopla, roll a penny, cakes and stuff . All in aid of the parish fund. We are hoping to put on a meal Christmas Day for the hungry poor.....................that's you and me......depends on whether the Red Cross gets here in time. You coming? "

"Yes, I hope so," said Christine, "Sophie will enjoy it as well. Is Father Christmas coming?"

"Ah, Christine, if the chimney is big enough he will be there. You're wonderful. I can see what Mac says about you is all true. I didn't believe him until today!"

"Do you want a clip round the ear, Brian?"

"Ooooo yes please, Christine."

Just then the door opened and interrupted the banter that Brian was so good at.
It was Klaus on a mission from Platte Rocque. As always, he was in full uniform which in normal circumstances would have brought any conversation to an abrupt halt. Shopkeepers could not refuse to serve the Germans but subservience was generally not on the agenda. However, despite being the enemy, Klaus was well known in the district as a polite young man and was treated as such.
Brian stood up and came theatrically to attention .
"Sergeant Bucholtz! Good morning."
"Ah Brian. Good to see you. Are you lost?" said Klaus in his German accent.
Brian rolled his eyes as Mrs Le Plongeon and Christine laughed out loud.
"Everyone's a bloody comedian. No, I am not lost. I am distributing posters advertising our Christmas Fayre on Saturday at the parish hall. We are having Christmas carols, all sorts of stalls just to get everybody in the mood for the festive season. It's all for charity, we are hoping to give a few people a good meal on Christmas Day. Simple as that."
"Ah...good....good. I hope it...er.. went....er no .....goes well."
Brian said his goodbyes and ducked out of the door into the road. Meanwhile Klaus had managed to buy a small amount of milk from Mrs Le Plongeon and was out through the door before Brian had got on his bicycle to continue his journey to the parish hall.

"Klaus, do you think you could get your friends in the band to play on Saturday afternoon? That chap Fritz is a friend of yours, isn't he? Mac was telling me."
Brian was pushing his luck and he knew it but he was a bit bored with organising the Christmas Fayre. He had not been met with much enthusiasm in the parish. He felt the proceedings needed a lift.
The question took Klaus a bit by surprise but he thought for a

moment and replied,
"I can ask. I shall see him tonight at practice . I ...er....shall....can ask him then. "
"Practice? Practice? What's that all about?" said Brian inquisitively.
"Ah! I cannot tell you all my..er...secrets but I play the piano..... a little bit. Fritz wants me to help with the recitals they do at Government House for *der grosse Nummer*.....the big cheese. I can tell you tomorrow morning. Good?"
"Thank you, Klaus, that would be excellent ."
Brian straddled his bike and, ringing his bell, pushed off down the road.
"Play the piano, eh? That's a new one. The man is full of surprises. You'll be fine. There's a piano at the parish hall. We'll see if you're any good."
As he accelerated in the standing position, the chain slipped on the cog, precipitating him swiftly downwards and delivering a painful collision between crotch and saddle.
"Aaaaaaargh !" he yelled in pain.
Klaus winced in sympathy as Brian continued painfully up the road. The front tyre was nearly flat and the inner tube was a patchwork of repairs. The rear wheel was slightly buckled and rubbed on the brake pads as he pedalled. He would not be winning the Tour de France on this machine. This was the cross they all had to bear. The lack of bicycle tyres, shoes, warm clothing, chocolate, fruit, petrol, coal, gas, medicines , you name it, all had a grinding downward effect on the fabric of life. The arrival of the Red Cross ship could not come soon enough but it was doubtful that bicycle tyres would be listed on the inventory.
Brian got his answer the next morning and was very pleased to get a positive response from Klaus, although he still had to run it past his fellow committee members. As far as Fritz and Klaus were concerned, the band would arrive by lorry at about 3.30pm on Saturday December 16 at the Parish Hall and play a selection of Christmas carols for an hour.

After catching up with his three cohorts on the Christmas Fayre Committee, he got an unenthusiastic approval for the German band and was pleased to get back to the pub by mid afternoon. What had started out as a mild December day with weak sunshine had deteriorated into a blustery melange of cold mist and rain. It would continue over the weekend.
That evening at the Grenadier Inn, the mood was one of muted joy as Brian read from the Jersey Evening Post to a small audience of regular customers huddled round the open fire. The wind and rain battered against the many windows making him raise his voice.

"Listen up all you Jersey boys........and of course......." nodding at Mac, " the Scotchman."
Mac was theatrically outraged.
"I'm no a fucking Scotchman! I'm a SCOTSMAN and bloody proud of it."
"Don't worry, Mac," said Brian. "There'll be a boat soon and you can piss off back to Glasgow!"
The ten or so regulars cheered loudly and Mac grinned mischievously, knowing he had stirred up a hornet's nest. There was not much else to do than stir them up. They loved it.
Brian continued,
"For once, there is good news in the paper tonight! I shall read it to you.....
"Supplies of food, medicines and soap are to be shipped to the Channel Islands.(cheers) The German government had approached the British government with a view to sending supplies and they have decided that it was right to send additional supplies of medicines, soap and food parcels. Final arrangements had not been completed but it was believed the ship would be ready to sail next week. She is a Swedish vessel sailing from Lisbon. It was hoped a representative of the Red Cross would sail also in order to investigate the conditions prevailing in the islands and arrange extra supplies. Signed Basil Dechevaux, Bailiff. 13/12/1944."

"Anyway, whatever you think," said Brian." That's got to be good news. At least something is on the move although from what I hear, the Germans are intent on staying. There'll be no surrender by the sounds of it."
After a brief discussion, the crowd dispersed to play the games that had kept them going for the last four years. The dartboard was showing signs of distress, the bristles dropping out like dead flies on impact with the darts. One of the dominoes' sets was now two pieces short - quite where or when they had disappeared was a mystery that no-one could solve. The holes in the crib board were filled with the grime of fishy fingers which refused to be dislodged with a simple tap on the bar counter. The pub had looked seedy before the war but right now it looked dead on its feet. What fabric remained was held together by the bonhomie of the drinkers.
Eventually Mac caught Brian on his own at the end of the bar. It had been nearly four months since they had discussed Christine's little adventure. Mac had filled him in straight away. He explained how Christine had realised the implications of it all and that she had finished the relationship before it had really started. He had also filled him in on Gaston's involvement with the swastika daubing. The Germans were happy to give Gaston an eight month sentence, given his being caught with paint on his hands. He would be out of prison after March and they would have to lean heavily on him to keep his mouth shut. Whereas the serving of a lot of prison sentences for lesser offences could be postponed, there was no way Gaston would be released early. His daubing offence was a serious one for which Mac and Brian were thankful.
"We'll maybe have to be a tad careful when the smelly little bugger gets out of prison."
said Mac.
"I think you'll be able to manage that, Mac. There was never any love lost between you two, was there?"
"Nope. He's a shifty little bugger. Anyway there's Christmas to

get oot the way first before he's a problem. Talking of Christmas, let's hope that Red Cross ship gets here in the next week. That's if it exists, of course. Are ye opening over the festive season?"
"Yes," said Brian."I've got a load of sloe gin coming up for consumption over the next week or two and my special Calvados should be good too. The apples that Big Mick were growing have been excellent for it. Are you coming on Saturday ?"
"What's happening Saturday?" replied Mac.
"Oh, come on Mac. Have you not seen the posters ? We are having a Christmas Fayre on Saturday at the parish hall. All the usual stuff except there won't be so much of it as usual. There will probably be the usual cake stall but this year cakes without sugar or eggs. Second hand clothing, hoopla, all the fun of the Christmas Fayre. And this year, Klaus has managed to talk the Luftwaffe Band into playing some carols late afternoon. Did you know he plays the piano? You've seen him with his mate Fritz who just happens to be the leader of the band. Their lot used to do guard duty under Klaus at Platte Rocque. You coming?"

"Oh aye, as if I *need* some second hand clothes. I think I'll stay in and watch some paint dry!" said Mac, despondently. "Is that a good idea to have the Krauts playing carols ?"

"I don't know yet but apparently, Glenn Miller and his band can't make it. I just happened to mention the Christmas Fayre to Klaus and he said he might be able to help out with the entertainment. He was certainly true to his word. I know what you mean though. We'll get the odd moaner but this war could end tomorrow. I'd rather have a German band than no band at all. They do pretty good Christmas carols by all accounts. It's a big thing with them."
"Och, if it's such a big bloody thing, they can piss off back to Germany and play their carols back there!" Mac replied. He

was clearly not in a good mood and went on,
"Well, Brian, as a matter of principle, I will not be there!"

Brian felt a bit deflated as he was having trouble selling his enthusiasm for the Christmas Fayre. As Mac climbed off his stool, Brian gave it one more shot.
"Christine said she would come. She's bringing little Sophie and Peter's bringing his girlfriend."
Mac had lost interest and was already moving towards the door. He was feeling down and didn't feel the need to share it. He turned to speak as he opened the door but a gale force wind blew cold air and leaves into the bar to the accompaniment of derisive shouts of those huddled round the fire. "Shut the bloody door!"
But Mac was in no mood to respond . He left the door blowing violently on its hinges and tilted his body into the wind. He felt despair of the blackest nature and walked the country lanes for miles in the foul weather before the rain finally penetrated his coat and started dripping down the inside of his trousers. He regarded this as a personal insult and decided to go home. He was shivering when he got through the front door and immediately stripped all his clothes off and left them in a pile on the floor. He dried himself off with the towel that was waiting to be washed and threw himself despairingly under the bedclothes. It took the best part of an hour before he stopped feeling cold. It was a long dark depressing night the like of which he had not seen for a long time.

CHAPTER 59

Friday December 15 1944

Flight Officer John Morgan was struggling to discover his aircraft's position . The impenetrable fog that had enveloped them since their take-off from RAF Twinwood Farm near Bedford seemed to be worse and the needle on the compass spun crazily. Even the altimeter was reluctant to give a reading. His passengers, Lieutenant Colonel Norman Baessell and Major Glenn Miller, grew increasingly apprehensive .

"Do you know where we are, Morgan?" said Baessell.

"Not really, sir. Regrettably the compass is all we've got but I can estimate by the time we have been flying that we have come about 150 miles but not necessarily in a straight line. The last land we saw was Beachy Head but since then, nothing. I shall try to get underneath this garbage to get some idea of where we are. Sorry I can't be more certain. Once I get a visible on the ground, we should be okay. We'll be very close to the French coast, that's for sure."

Miller caught Baessell's eye and raised his eyebrows in consternation. The engine was very loud and conversation was hard even over the radio headphones. Morgan pushed the controls forward and slowly reduced height. The fog refused to shift. At least the altimeter had burst into life showing a healthy height of three thousand feet. This was real seat of the pants flying and he felt totally disorientated with no observable horizon. They had enough fuel for a six hour flight so he figured there was lots of leeway. They had set off at two o'clock hoping to get to Paris before dark but the fog was bringing a premature dusk. He had to assume his magnetic compass was right most of the time, despite the needle's volatility. Just then,

the noisy Pratt and Whitney engine started to misfire. He fiddled with the fuel mix and after a few long minutes it returned to its previous healthy drone. Miller and Baessell began to sweat profusely but felt relief as soon as the engine resumed its former regular rhythm.
"I figure we are over France. We flew south south east over Maidenhead and then turned over Beachy Head towards Dieppe but this was all flying on the heading given by the compass. I shall assume my navigation is correct until we get a sighting."

They flew on into the fog and the single Pratt and Whitney R-1340 engine droned enthusiastically on. Unbeknown to them, however, the compass was giving an unreliable reading and they were effectively flying in a circle over the bay of St Malo about twenty degrees west of Morgan's estimated course. Miller looked at his watch. It now showed four o'clock and their blind journey was starting to weigh him down. All he could see through the window was white mist.
"Is this how it's all going to end," he thought."I should never have stepped on to this wood and paper aeroplane." Miserably, he poked a finger into a small hole in the canvas fuselage.

Morgan slowly brought the plane down to one thousand feet and through the fogbanks he could finally glimpse that they were over the sea. This was a disappointment to him as he still had no point of reference. He checked the compass and flew on towards what he hoped was France. The low cloud then enveloped them once more.

"We have plenty of fuel, sir .It's better to be safe than sorry so I will maintain this height until I know we are over France." Unfortunately whereas the height was right, the direction was wrong. They described a large circular course and still they were over water. At about 4.45 pm the engine spluttered and

Morgan fiddled with the fuel mix. He knew that things could quickly resolve themselves but he was running out of time, it was almost dark . He needed to see where he was flying. He took the aircraft down another five hundred feet and after another fifteen minutes flying time, the engine started to splutter again.

"Shit, that's all I need! The carburettor is playing up again. Bugger!" said Morgan.

Just then he thought he could pick out the whiteness of a shoreline on his starboard side. He banked right sharply. Miller and Baessell were sweating behind him, sharing every scary moment. The engine was doing them no favours but Morgan persuaded it to do one last left turn so he could line up the beach which was fading in and out of sight as the mist blew along. They glided down through the fading light and mist, bumping and rolling in the wind and waiting for that final inevitable violent moment when their lives would be snuffed out.

CHAPTER 60

Rescue

Mac's depression showed little signs of lifting and he had been housebound by the weather all day that Friday. It was still cold, wet and miserable outside. He had done a few chores in the morning but by about two o'clock he was ready to stoke the fire up and spend the rest of the day reading a book in front of it in his armchair. His wood supply had not dwindled even though he had given a lot away to his needy friends and neighbours. Living next to the beach had its compensations. As yet , no more bottles of Cointreau or Glenfiddich had made their way to his back door but he lived in hope. Christmas was coming and another year loomed in captivity. This last few months had been awful. Little was getting through and Churchill's 'dear Channel Islands' were wilting.

At least there was hope on the horizon. The Red Cross ship the ss Vega was expected to arrive soon from Lisbon with much needed food supplies. Mac was not so sure.

He had long since drifted off to sleep when Peter knocked on the door at half past four. He welcomed him in, sat him down in a chair and went outside to fetch some more wood from the shed. It was late afternoon but it was already nearly dark. On his way he heard what sounded like a misfiring plane approaching. The noise receded and was followed by a muffled crashing sound. He strained his eyes to see through the swirling mist when he heard a muffled explosion coming from the same direction. The fire that ensued glowed for half a minute before it was extinguished, then all went quiet again. By this time Peter had joined him as he too had heard the misfiring engine from inside the house.

"Wow! Sounds like that plane has come down." said Peter.

"Fancy going out to have a look........ the krauts won't be

bothered and visibility is pretty poor plus it's cold and wet and getting dark. Tide is low and I've got spare waterproofs. Coming?"
"Yes, why not," said Peter .
" Let's go. Might be Adolf Hitler."
"Hope he's got some spare sandwiches!"
"We'll grab the tilley lamp on the way out."

The odd couple togged up and set off over the garden wall straight onto the beach. The mist turned to rain and back again and the gloom faded into a damp blackness. It was a miserable evening and Mac very nearly turned them back when he discovered his boots had sprung a leak. Their pathway was relatively easy as coming from this direction, they could bypass most of the rocks. They could both do it blindfold. It wasn't long before they heard the scrunching of boots on rock and gravel and intermittent cursing in an American accent.
"Oh Jesus it's cold, Norm . I can't feel my toes."
They edged closer to the noises and figured they didn't represent too great a threat.
"Over here! Over here, my American friends. Come this way. I'll light the lamp."
Mac quickly lit the lamp with some difficulty and turned the wick down low before moving towards them. Suspicious at first, it soon became clear to all four of them that they were friends and not enemies.
"Boy, are we glad to see you guys!" one of them said, "Where are we?"
"Listen,"replied Mac, "you are in the German occupied British Channel Islands, just off the coast of France. The coastline is heavily defended by German troops and we should get off the beach as soon as possible. Firstly we need to turn down this lamp so as not to attract any attention from the krauts on the coast. We can talk as soon as we get back to my hoose. In the meantime stick close and keep as quiet as you can."
With that the odd couple led the Americans skilfully back

through the gullies and within minutes they were all back in Mac's front room and nobody was any the wiser.

The two Americans were cold , wet through and clearly in a state of shock. Mac stoked up the fire while Peter made sure all the curtains were drawn tight. Their uniforms were wrung out and hung up by the fireplace to dry . Within minutes, towels, blankets and whisky were the order of the day.
"I'm Mac and this is my young friend Peter."
"I am ...er.. Norman..... and this is ….Major...er.....the Major."
The Americans were in shock and still not sure of their surroundings or the identity of their rescuers. After loosely identifying himself, Norm went on.
"We were on our way from England to Paris, heading for..er... the Major's unit. Our plane got lost in fog and then seemed to run out of fuel. I'm afraid our pilot was probably killed on impact and if he had been still alive the explosion and fire would have got him. We were hoping we had landed in France."
"Well, you were a wee bit unlucky, Norm. You were only fifteen or so miles short but you have landed in German occupied Jersey.....one of the Channel Islands abandoned by the British over four years ago now........ but we'll no go inta that noo. We heard your engine spluttering overhead, then the noise of the crash followed by the dimmest red light of the fire coming through the fog."
Peter was sitting at the table, drawing a map with pencil on a piece of brown wrapping paper. The two American officers got up and stood over him while he outlined the island and its proximity to the French mainland.
"Can we get to France from here? I need to get there as soon as possible. It's very important." said the man Norm had called 'Major'. Peter looked to Mac for an answer.
"Well, my friends...." said Mac , warming to the task,...."*that* is going to be tricky. That fifteen miles of sea between here and there," he pointed to the coastlines on the makeshift map, " is

and has been a most treacherous journey at this time of year. You might do better to sit out the final few weeks of the war."

It wasn't the answer the Americans were looking for. They were still in shock and had difficulty understanding Mac's Scottish accent.

A couple of whiskies all round brought an altogether more mellow discussion.

"First we'll need to find out if the Krauts are on to you. You were lucky that we happened to be in the garden when you crashed so let's hope they maybe didnee hear or see it. The incoming tide and the rain will have washed away all of our tracks by now. Depends how much debris is left and how much will have been washed away."

"The fire was pretty intense and the plane was made out of wood and canvas. All I had was a small leather bag stashed up front and that would have burnt well . It all happened very quickly so we didn't retrieve anything" said the Major.
Outside , a westerly wind had blown the mist out to sea . A cold driving rain had set in and battered against the roadside windows. The wind forced its way through every gap. It was a foul night.
"Don't think even the Krauts will venture out on patrol from their bunkers tonight." said Peter.
"Maybe, maybe not. They are all as jumpy as hell. They see British commandos round every corner . They will run their patrols as per usual on the hour every hour so we had better hide you here for the night. Your kit will be dry by morning. You'll have to kip on the floor tonight but I don't think you'll mind so long as it's warm and dry. We should really move you tonight but it's pissin' doon oot there and no very nice."
The Major looked at Peter quizzically.

"He means it's raining," chipped in Peter acting as translator. "We'll find you a safe house in the morning. Mac's right though, if it wasn't for the weather we should move you tonight."

Just then a huge gust of wind battered at the doors and windows with audible ferocity. The rain beat against the windows with renewed force as if to say 'this will make your mind up'. It did and the visitors made themselves comfortable on the floor . Peter put his waterproofs back on and said his farewells before heading back to St Kitts. Mac told him to go home and not say a word to a soul. In order to beat the ten o'clock curfew, he took Mac's bicycle . The gale force wind was right in his face and he would have made better progress walking. He cursed the weather but pedalled on into the pitch black darkness with just a small light on his front forks to guide him home. In the end he got off and walked the last half mile. As he passed La Rocque there didn't seem to be any signs of panic and he didn't encounter any German patrols.

It was still raining at first light and the gale had abated. The beach returned to its wintry monochrome. The good news was that the plane crash had not raised any suspicion at the German defence posts. There had been a great deal of allied aerial activity over the last year as D-Day came and went. Last night was a bit different as visibility was so poor but it seemed that only Peter and Mac had heard and seen the crash through the murky twilight. After a stormy night of high seas, all that was left of the aeroplane was an engine which was already half buried by shifting sand. The canvas fuselage had been broken up and blown ashore to join the rest of the debris of the last five years of warfare.

Norm and the Major had slept fitfully and uncomfortably on the floor of Mac's front room. Despite their miraculous escape,

the taller American still felt gloomy and sensed that escape to France would not be on the agenda this side of Christmas. At first light, Mac managed to convey to both of them exactly where they were. The Major seemed amused by the fact that the place they had randomly crashed into was called Jersey. Mac's priority was to get the two visitors moved as soon as darkness fell again. That meant that they would have to hide out all day and he persuaded them to hole up in the padlocked woodshed while he went off to arrange their transfer to Big Mick's at Sunny View up the road. He left them food, water and maps and disappeared for a couple of hours. He returned with clothes for them and the three of them waited for nightfall while huddled in front of a roaring fire. As soon as the light had faded, the three of them scuttled across the coast road and threaded their way across hedged fields until they reached Sunny View where Big Mick was waiting to receive them.
After the handshakes and introductions, Mick showed the two Americans up to their makeshift room in the hayloft. Part of a huge shed, the ground floor was home to an array of boats all laid up until summer or liberation, whichever came first. The Crazy Doris sat on a rusty trailer awaiting more attention from Mac and Peter. The weather had been so cold and wet that even working inside the shed had become a chilly and unwelcoming task in the few hours of daylight that were available leading up to Christmas. There was a staircase up to the loft which took up half the area of the floorspace and a rope and pulley ran down from the loft to the ground at the rear. Mick showed them the layout of the property in case they had to make a rapid escape but one of the Americans was twitchy and inattentive.
"Is there any way we can escape to France from here, maybe from Mac's place? We need to get away as soon as possible."
Big Mick was sympathetic but advised against it until the weather improved.
"Have a look at the loft first and then come over to the house. We can discuss it in depth this evening," replied Mick before he turned to Mac who had climbed aboard the Crazy Doris a few

yards away.
"Are you staying,Mac?"
"Aye," said Mac. "I could. Nothing else on the agenda. Pub's nae open the nicht."
The Americans looked questioningly at Mick, presumably seeking a translation.
Mick answered their gaze by saying,
"No, haven't a clue either. The Scotch are a mysterious race. They used to speak English but not so much these days."
"Scotch? Scotch ? Ach, yer bum's oot the windee, ya sassenach bassa! Scotch is fer drrinkin!"
The Americans remained mystified.

CHAPTER 61

Christmas Fayre Saturday 16 December 1944 Parish Hall

Together with a band of willing helpers, the committee had spent the week decorating the hall and had done a fine job. There was no shortage of mistletoe, Christmas trees or pine cones and the hall was a splendid sight. Candles were in short supply but a rich elderly parishioner, being ill and believing she was about to die, had recently donated an extraordinary amount of carved candles. It was a crying shame to have to light them as they were clearly show pieces but she was adamant that they be used for the Christmas activities. The Constable was to make a speech and give permission for them to be lit at about four o'clock.

On Saturday morning, the parish hall was a busy place with volunteers working feverishly to set up a number of stalls. The kit for the coconut shy had seen better days. You had more chance of flying to the moon than knocking a wooden coconut substitute from its seat on top of a pole. The hoopla competition remained an enigma. Most of the parishioners were convinced the circumference of the hoops was questionable but prizes were definitely won. The refreshment stall would be a success owing to the imagination of the Bridge Club. The giant teapot was still blackened from last year's efforts. The Knitting and Sewing Club had done their best to produce things to sell and most of the wool they were using had been recycled from old garments. Brian had donated a quantity of home made non alcoholic wine which he had produced from a concoction of wild berries and he had persuaded Mac to give up one of his bottles of Scotch as a raffle prize.

The second hand clothing stall had been set up in the centre of the hall as this was likely to be the most popular. Over the last year or so of deprivations, people had lost weight and got smaller . Many a belt had to have an extra hole punched in it to accommodate a smaller waist and it was a good opportunity to pick up something that actually fitted. Prices were set deliberately low in order to benefit the most needy. Weird and wonderful things were donated. A dilapidated beehive rubbed shoulders with a rusty bucket and broken umbrellas. The parish community had once again come together but this year there was something clearly missing. Despite all the camaraderie of pulling together for a common cause, the mood matched the weather. It was dark and wet outside and people were fed up with feeling hungry and cold. Worst of all, they felt used and abandoned- used by the Germans and abandoned by Churchill. The prospect of a fifth Christmas in captivity was a depressing thought for most of them and enthusiasm for the festive season was waning.

The doors opened to the public at two o'clock and the usual scrum down for the second hand clothing stall was less manic than usual. The crowd swelled as the afternoon played out. Even if you didn't spend any money it was still a great time and place to catch up with friends and family. Mrs Le Plongeon persuaded Christine and Peter to help sell raffle tickets. Klaus appeared in uniform and was immediately advised to at least remove his jacket and look a bit more casual. Brian caught his eye and pointed to the front of the hall where the parish piano was positioned just below the stage.

"Over there, Klaus. I think it's a good one. They use it for choir practice. Have a look and I'll bring you over a cup of tea and a cake."

"Thank you, Brian. I'll take a...err......look."

While the hall was buzzing with chatter, Klaus tinkered with the Steinberg upright. He was joined quickly by little Sophie who was fascinated by the sounds and size of the piano. Klaus enlisted Sophie's help and sent her off to Brian to fetch a pair of pliers. After a few minutes adjusting hammers and wires, Klaus declared it playable. Sophie stood next to him and watched,

mesmerised, as his fingers danced along the ivory. Christine joined them and said hello to Klaus whom she knew by his association with Peter and Mac. They both liked him and that was good enough for her.
"Can you play Silent Night, mister?" said Sophie.
"His name is Klaus, Sophie. He is practising for the concert later. Best not to bother him just now," said Christine.
"No, it's okay," said Klaus, "I can play it. We sing this in Germany too."
Sophie looked up, her little angel face in innocent surprise. "Are you a Kraut? Are you going to shoot me?"
Christine and Klaus froze as one and caught each other's eye. Somehow her question brought the whole conundrum into focus. Christine let it run. He *was* a Kraut after all and he had no business to be here .
Klaus quickly replied,
"Of course not. You sing first and I will play the piano. Ready?"
At this point Christine was called away to help on the refreshments stall and felt confident enough to leave Sophie happily singing for a couple of minutes. Klaus was enthralled with her voice and encouraged her along. Amongst all the hubbub of the hall, she happily sang the song she had learned at the creche she attended most mornings of the week while Klaus accompanied her quietly and expertly.
"Do you think you could sing that a bit later when the band arrives?" said Klaus as Sophie skipped away back to her mother. He got no reply but there was no reason to suggest that this confident five year old wouldn't do it.
The winter light began to fade and the Constable gave the order to light the festive candles. One by one they flickered into life, casting dancing shadows on the gilt frames surrounding portraits of previous incumbents of the office of Constable. They looked a fearsome lot and did little to add any levity to the occasion. The winter winds found the gaps in the casement windows and did their best to blow the candles out to spoil the

fun. Constable Le Grand stepped up onto a table to welcome all to the Christmas Fayre.
"Order! Order!" Brian shouted, "Let's have a bit of hush....for our Constable.....George Le Grand.....who has kindly volunteered to say a few words!"
"Hardly volunteered, Brian. Hardly volunteered. I'll be brief."
There were ironic cheers from the back of the hall.
"Can you hear me at the back? Right, then listen up. I know times are hard but hopefully things will improve. We should hopefully raise a good amount today for our community Christmas dinner . However......however......I have just received a message from the Bailiff to inform us all that the Red Cross ship the Vega will not be here until after Christmas and possibly not until early January."
There were gasps and murmurs of disappointment and cries of "no!"
Whatever goodwill that was in the hall had drained away with the bad news.
The Constable continued, "Yesterday marked the winter solstice, the shortest day of the year with the least amount of light. Our distant ancestors would be celebrating this as it meant the worst of the winter was over. Let's look at it in a similar vein. After the darkest, shortest day things must surely improve. We must therefore make the best of what we have today and try not to be too disappointed because when the ship does arrive, I shall be buying the drinks! Now come on, enjoy yourselves!"
There were a few desultory cheers but the mood had hit rock bottom. The wind and rain continued to batter the hall and cries of "shut the door" were frequent.

The band arrived by lorry in the pouring rain and was greeted by Brian and Klaus at the side door. There were eight of them in total which Fritz thought was sufficient for an informal carol service. The stage had been out of action for a couple of years after a fire had damaged it so they set up just below it close to

Klaus' piano. It took only a few seconds for several parishioners to notice the German uniforms in their midst and register their disapproval by booing vociferously.
"Piss off back to Germany, Krauts!" came a voice from the back.
Fritz looked worried but not unduly perturbed. The protests became noisier and eventually an old shoe was lobbed from the rear. This seemed to mark a tipping point in the proceedings. Fritz could have quite easily and justifiably withdrawn but what happened next took everybody by surprise. Fritz took a good look around and climbed on to the table only recently vacated by the Constable.
Resplendent in his jackboots and Luftwaffe uniform, he faced down the crowd. He spoke loudly.
"Please listen. Please listen. I am Oberleutnant Fritz Doenig and I am, how you say, the Obermeister of the band. We spend...er.. we have spent the last five years playing marching songs and concerts in the island . Some of you may have heard us in the Royal Square. These days.....unhappily.... we play many funerals, some for the Allied soldiers and some for the German fatherland. We treat with ...er...dignity.....both sides of this....."
He hesitated and looked sideways at his worried fellow bandsmen. He knew how they all felt and he continued. He felt it was time for him to cross the river.

"We treat with dignity both sides of this ….stupid.....stupid war!"

The noise quickly abated and the heckling fell away as he continued. His German accent seemed to lend gravitas to what he was saying. A hushed crowd hung on his words.

"I will tell you this. On the evening of December 4 this month the city of Heilbronn in south west Germany was attacked by three hundred Lancaster bombers of the Englanders. I think they call it...er... carpet bombing. They dropped thousands of bombs leaving over six thousand people dod.....er....dead. One thousand of these were kinder ...er .....little children under ten years old. Little babies too. This is not propaganda. I know that this is true..........I know that this is true."

There was an audible gasp from the upturned faces of the parishioners below him.He paused before repeating himself once more.
"I know that this is true ......One of my men, Obergefreiter Carl-Heinz Schmidt, is a good musician. He plays the accordion. He comes from Heilbronn and was made to join the German Army in 1939 at the same time as most of us. This morning.......this morning.....this.......morning......I had the sad, sad task of informing him that his beautiful wife Eva and his three beautiful children, Jurgen, Rudi and baby Helga, had been killed in that air raid, along with his mutta....er his mother."
Fritz hesitated and the crowd of some three hundred people fell deathly silent.
"How do you tell someone this news?....... What words can I find to comfort him? What has he left?................. We find ourselves in this mess all together. I know you cannot forgive us for being here and I understand that. But.......but....I also.. cannot forgive what happened in Heilbronn!"

The wind that was fighting to burst the windows open suddenly abated. A total stunned silence ensued. Fritz went on.
" Many friends of yours and mine have been killed in this stupid war and the one before. Words cannot replace what we have all lost. I suggest we try to forget our differences for an hour or two and pray that we can all live in peace again."
And with that, Fritz jumped off the table and back on to the floor. His audience looked shocked and crestfallen.
Off to the side of the hall, Klaus was sitting at the piano, equally shocked and pained by Doenig's speech and the terrible

news of Carl-Heinz's family. Little Sophie tapped him on the shoulder.
"Can I sing now, Klaus?"
Klaus hesitated for a second and said,
"Yes, of course. That's a good idea. I think it might help."
Taking advantage of the silence, he led Sophie into their version of Silent Night. Her little angelic voice split the air like the tolling of Christmas bells. So sweet was it in contrast to what they were all feeling, a lady on the knitting stall immediately started to cry. The awful noise of her anguish swept through the onlookers. One by one the dominoes started to fall. Hearing the sobs , Mary Le Masurier burst into tears . She had lost a grandchild of Sophie's age, killed in a German air raid over Portsmouth where her own children had sought safety before the outbreak of war. Eileen de la Mare wept over grandchildren in France that she had never even seen. She hoped they were safe.
The Knitting and Sewing stall was awash with tears. Grown men dabbed at their eyes.
Sophie's five year old crystal clear voice filled the hall with innocent joy and everybody felt it so deeply inside. Everybody in that hall had a reason to be sad.
Brian lifted Sophie up on to a large empty table so they could all see as well as hear her. She was so good, her little blond curls dancing in the candlelight. While she sang, Klaus sang the descant quietly in German. His mind too was drifting home, building snowmen and ski-ing to Aunt Sylvia's house, yule logs, Stollen Christmas cake and playing football with his kid brothers in the garden. He had a hard job seeing the piano keys through the tears in his eyes. The crowd shuffled nervously forward to hear better, most of their faces wet with the emotion of the last few minutes. Brian started what happened next. Very quietly and respectfully, members of the parish moved amongst the other members of the band and linked arms around shoulders while still gazing at this little angel, this gorgeous unspoilt child on the table, singing her tiny heart out.

".......all is calm, all is bright.....round yon virgin, mother and child........holy infant, so tender and mild...."
The duo continued to the sound of men and women weeping and sniffing until finally and almost thankfully they finished. The audience applauded loudly and cheered but they were happy to have a moment to dry their eyes and pull themselves together.
Within a minute or two, Fritz and his men had set up their instruments. After much pursing of lips and practice blows from the trumpet, trombone and saxophone players, the Christmas concert got under way with a rendition of 'Good King Wenceslas.' By now the parishioners were determined to join in and they sung lustily - much to the chagrin of the vicar who always had trouble making a reluctant congregation open their mouths at all when it came to singing psalms and hymns. Nobody in that hall was untouched by the torture of the last few minutes. Brian got back to the kitchen where he started to prepare his special Christmas mulled wine. Unfortunately he had no cloves, cinnamon or oranges but what it lacked in spices it made up for in warm red wine which in itself was an achievement as there wasn't much to be had. He and Mac had somehow contrived to exchange something for something else somewhere along the line sometime. That was the nature of the game and on this occasion the benefactor was the Christmas Fayre. Fifteen minutes into the band's playlist of Christmas carols, Brian came out from the back with a tray laden with cups of hot red wine for the musicians. Given the weather outside and the improvement in the mood inside, they guzzled them down in quick time before firing up again. Jingle Bells assumed a more robust tempo and the congregation grew more enthusiastic with their singing. During a break, one of the band slid out through a side door to retrieve two bottles of schnapps which were smuggled back inside an instrument case. Their army blouses had long been discarded as they worked harder to entertain the parish.

CHAPTER 62

Concert

At Sunny View, the sounds of a band playing Christmas carols came drifting between the gusts of the westerly gale. The sound was so incongruous and out of place that they instantly turned their heads towards the large open door of the huge shed. The parish hall was over a mile away but Mac was first to realise what it was.
"D'ye fancy a wee trip to the parish hall, boys? Today is the Christmas Fayre. Brian told me that all were welcome, and it sounds like they are having a good time" said Mac thinking that Mick would say it was too dangerous. He was wrong.
"Why not?" said Mick. "I can squeeze a mile or two out of the van. What do you reckon, guys? Not much else we can do except have a good time."
There were smiles all round as they piled into the back of the old Morris van that Mick had nurtured back into life with the aid of his mechanical knowledge and a pint of petrol he had siphoned from a German staff car. There was only one headlight and the one windscreen wiper on the van had trouble coping with the rain that was driving across the countryside. Mick took his foot off the accelerator in an effort to avoid the granite walls on both sides of the road and give the wiper time to do its job. Within minutes they had arrived , parked up and run inside.
The Luftwaffe band were in full flow. Jingle Bells was on its third repeat and its umpteenth chorus. The public had found Brian's font of free mulled wine and the mood had definitely lifted. Mac had a quick word with Peter and Brian to make them aware of the two Americans who quickly merged into the background. They were both dressed in traditional knitted fisherman's jerseys which had previously seen service on the Crazy Doris. Now paint smeared and battered , the jerseys leant an air of authenticity to the Americans. They were in no danger

unless there was a visit from a German patrol and that was unlikely given the weather . The only reason the Krauts would have to enter the hall would be to join in the fun.
Norm and his sidekick overcame their initial fears which were few considering that neither had had occasion to be in occupied territory before. Neither had they seen a German soldier in the flesh until now and these ones seemed pretty harmless. Mac quickly located the mulled wine and made sure their guests were looked after.
At about six thirty, Fritz announced that it would have to be the final carol as they had to be up at Government House in an hour to perform for the Kommandant and his guests. At about the same time, Feldwebel Dieter Hankel arrived hotfoot from Government House with a hand delivered message.
" Oberleutnant Fritz Doenig. A message from the boss. He is in bed with a case of food poisoning .The concert is off and you've got an early night! "
Fritz wasn't too disappointed .
"Thank goodness for that! How do you feel about singing a couple of songs for us?"
"What? You know me. I love an audience!"
"Okay, we'll give them a traditional German song...O tannenbaum? Just don't sing in that stupid high voice you had when you were in the Vienna Boys Choir!"
Dieter laughed out loud and Fritz announced the reprieve to the cheers in the hall.
More mulled wine arrived and Dieter oiled his throat before fronting the music. The crowd had grown to four hundred as word got round the neighbourhood of the concert. Dieter gave them his rendition in his beautiful tenor voice but it was clear that the audience wanted something a bit more uptempo.

Fritz had a quick discussion with his fellow musicians to the effect that it was time to launch their own particular version of the Glenn Miller Sound to the general public. They were only nine musicians but they gave it their best shot and nearly took

the roof off.
"*Eins, swei, eins, swei, drei, fier...*" and off they went belting out the first few bars of In The Mood. If ever a bunch of slightly inebriated musicians were 'in the mood' then this was it. In musical terms they were tight and together. Just quite where and when Mr and Mrs Le Sueur had learnt to jitterbug so well was a mystery but they set the parquet floor alight to the amazement of the onlookers. It wasn't long before they were joined by some others and the party was under way.
Norman nudged the Major as the band shifted through their repertoire.
"Not bad, eh ? Glenn Miller is famous in *old* Jersey too!"
"I guess they must have been listening to the radio. There's no other way they would be familiar with that song!" replied the Major.
Just then, Mac appeared next to them both with a couple of glasses of Brian's Original Calvados, a brew that had been maturing in the cellars of the Grenadier Inn for twelve months or so.
"Smell it first, gentlemen, then sip it gently. It's apple brandy and it'll knock yer wee socks clean off !" said Mac. "Pretty good band, eh? For a bunch of Krauts anyway."
This was praise indeed from Mac who couldn't abide any music which didn't have bagpipes playing it.
He held his glass up for a toast.
"Slainte Mhath !"
The Americans let this one go , rightly assuming it was some obscure Scottish salute.
"Down the hatch," said Norm and downed the liquid in one. He spluttered momentarily but managed to suppress his surprise at the burning sensation in his throat. The Major was more circumspect. He drunk very little, preferring to be in charge of all his actions and tonight was no different. He still felt anxious and was desperate to get to France as soon as possible. He felt obliged to move in closer and skirted the hall until he was right up close. Within a minute, he was waving his hand

and conducting surreptitiously. Norm followed him and could not hide his amusement.
"Gee, you princess. You can't resist it! Are they any good ?"
He saw Norm's lips move but couldn't pick up what he was saying. He smiled and took a small sip from his glass. The Calvados was not unpleasant and warmed him inside.
Fritz led them into the 'Boogie Woogie Bugle Boys from Company B' which to the amusement of the crowd was sung in German into a megaphone by Dieter. Unfortunately there was no such thing as a 'W' in the German alphabet and Boogie Woogie still came out as Boogie Voogie in his thick accent. The mulled wine kept coming and so did the Calvados. Norm was now clearly ticking and jinked his way through the throng to where the band had stacked their instrument cases. Spotting a spare trombone, he was on to it straight away. He lifted it and carried it over to the Major who recoiled in horror.
"Put it back, Norm. You'll get us all shot. Musicians are a bit protective of their instruments. For Christ's sake, put it back."
At about that moment, the music stopped as Little Brown Jug came to a close and the band took a short break. Fritz had seen the trombone being carried away and rather than cause a scene he yelled out, "Hey, you think you can play? Come and join us, we need an extra trombone. We have only one and two would be good."
He was joking of course and didn't want to cause a scene. He just wanted the trombone back.
Norm however was not to be deflected.
"I can't play but I know someone who can!" His American accent immediately drew a few gasps of surprise.
"Shut up, Norm. For God's sake. Just leave it!"

But it was one of those moments in life where things spiralled out of control.
Fritz could see the funny side of it and thought he would have some fun.
"Come on then, come play with us. It's Christmas. Anybody ?"

By now the trombone had been thrust into the Major's hands and there was no backing out. Initially thoroughly embarrassed by it all, he decided the best policy would be to go along with it all. He wet his lips then pursed them, blowing through the mouthpiece and moving the slider back and forth, hamming it up as if he knew what he was doing. Fritz however had moved on past caring and announced their version of Tuxedo Junction and counted in Gunter Muller to start the opening bars on *his* trombone. Gunter, however, was in the middle of swigging down some gluwein and was in no position to start playing. It was the Major who opened, albeit shakily, to the surprise of Fritz who, through an escalating alcoholic haze, took a closer look at his new bespectacled trombonist and nodded his approval. Fritz thought he looked familiar but the thought was buried as he came in on the clarinet. The American's lips relaxed but he was clearly out of practice and was happier when Gunter joined him. Just quite when the Major stood up and started conducting the now tipsy band of German musicians was debatable but it didn't take long before they all realised that he knew what he was doing. What was worse was they all started winking at each other and calling him Glenn. This amused him no end as he realised that they were clearly having fun at his expense. He was happy to go along with their little joke but was also impressed with their musical ability. 'Tiger Rag 'zipped along at breakneck speed with Klaus ripping it up on the piano. Willi Brint was trying to keep up on his makeshift drum kit when his bass drum reacted to his aggressive style and rolled away from him into the crowd. The number ended to laughter but the Major immediately filled in the gap and took Fritz and his men totally by surprise when, adjusting his glasses, he spoke to them in German.

"How are you guys with Moonlight Serenade? Can you handle the change of pace?"

Fritz and his men roared with laughter but were too far gone to grasp the reality of the situation.

"Well, boys, there's a challenge." said Fritz." *Can we handle the change of pace, Mister Miller? I think we can. Okay boys?"*

And off they went. Fritz' clarinet soared as the mood slowed. Their new conductor was impressed and encouraged the other horn players into better things while he kept the rhythm with his hand. The number ended but he gave them no respite.

"What about Chattanooga Choo Choo? Can you do that? Remember, it don't mean a thing if you ain't got that swing!"

And off they went again, this time with Dieter Hankel singing all the words in German. It worked well and those who could dance got up and danced and those who couldn't dance just shuffled their feet. The band were clearly impressed with him but still thought it was an elaborate joke. In the middle of 'Pennsylvania 6-5-000', Norman managed to catch his eye and gestured to him that they were about to leave. With the crowd on a high, they slipped away to the back of the hall where Big Mick and Mac were ready to go back to Sunny View.
Brian was busy organising what was left of his stock of home made cider. The mulled wine had been finished off by an enthusiastic clientele and he had covered his outlay by charging a shilling a glass. Mac looked across and realised Brian was under pressure. At that moment he decided to stay and give him a hand. He apologised to Big Mick and the Americans and he said his goodbyes before retiring to the hall kitchen to help with the washing up. The calvados was having an effect on him and he was feeling quite mellow. Brian , in his capacity as leading committee member for the Christmas Fayre, had everything under control.

CHAPTER 63

The American escape plan

The journey back to Sunny View was just as eventful as the journey there. The rain swept down on them again, testing the dodgy windscreen wiper once more. In less than ten minutes, the two Americans had climbed the ladder to the hayloft where they had planned to spend the next night or two. Both were feeling a little better about their plight after their evening out. The Major had thoroughly enjoyed his bizarre connection with the Luftwaffe band.
"While you were up there pretending to be Glenn Miller, I had a very interesting conversation with one of the locals ," said Norm. " He told me there were quite a few boats moored up at Gorey Harbour which would be capable of doing the trip to France. Now, I've checked the maps they've given us and Gorey ain't so far as the crow flies. I reckon it's not beyond our capabilities to make our way up there and have a look."
His travel buddy smiled in anticipation. "Go on, Norm. Show me."

Norm spread the brown paper map out on the small table between the swails of hay.
"Take a look........there's a main road that runs along the coast from near here and pitches up at the harbour . Exactly where we want to be!"
At last he was met with a bit of enthusiasm.
"That's the best news we've had tonight! When do we go?"

The question hung in the air as they heard Mick at the bottom of the ladder.
"Not so fast to get away, lads! I've got some hot drinks for you. Come down and I'll go through the maps with you while you taste my finest ersatz coffee!"

They climbed gingerly down the ladder. Both were now feeling more optimistic .
Michel outlined the situation for them.
"Gentlemen.... the biggest thing in your favour was that the Germans have absolutely no idea you are here......that is until this evening when you both stepped into the spotlight at the parish hall. One thing you don't know is that there are a couple of dozen American prisoners locked up in a prison near the harbour in St Helier. They were captured near Cherbourg ten days ago during a German raid which was sent out from here . This is common knowledge so anybody there tonight , locals or Krauts, who picked up on your accents will be questioning whether you are escaped prisoners or some such thing. Either way, somebody is going to smell a fish. "
"Gee, Mick," said the Major, "I guess I kinda blew our cover, eh?"
"Yes, you did but that crowd tonight thought it was worth it. However, I reckon your best plan is to lay low for a couple of days until we can find out if anybody is asking questions. We can move you round to other safe houses as and when. Bear in mind also that anybody caught harbouring you is likely to be subject to some serious shit. "

This went down like a lead balloon to both of them. They became anxious again. Neither of them wanted to hang around any longer than they needed .
"Okay Mick," said Norm. "I know where you are coming from and don't think we are unappreciative for all the help we've had. Perhaps if we sit on it tonight and hatch a plan tomorrow. The sooner we go the better....... before, as you say, more questions are asked. We don't wanna become hot potatoes for you. "
The Major interjected,"Yes, thanks Mick. We really appreciate what you've done for us, and Mac and Peter too."
The three of them sipped their hot drinks until Mick yawned .
"Sorry guys. It's been a long day. I'm off to bed. Sleep well. I

suggest you pull the ladder up behind you when you're ready to sleep. Take the bucket with you in case you need a pee in the night. Goodnight and I'll see you at first light."
"Yes, thanks again, Mick. See you in the morning."
The Americans finished their drinks and carried on talking into the night. Outside the wind had dropped out and it had stopped raining. They opened the barn door slightly and looked out. It was pitch black and the clouds had cleared to reveal a sky full of stars.
"Gee, would you believe it, Norm. The storm has passed. What say we go now?"
"God, you're an impulsive impatient bugger. You've maybe got a point though."
And so what had previously been idle chit chat suddenly turned into a solid plan. Within an hour they had raided the surrounding laid-up boats and had secured two dark coloured heavy overcoats. Mick had already given them a big supply of biscuits and water, surely enough to last them the few hours it would take to get to France. They found an old army haversack hanging on a peg and stuffed their supplies into it. They donned their ill fitting overcoats and shuffled out into the night through the side door of the barn. The rain had stopped but it was wet underfoot as they made their way back towards the beach and the coast road via the adjacent fields. Visibility was poor and progress was slow. As soon as they got to the coast road, they decided to stick to the bitumen and take their chances. If a German patrol was out and about, the probability was that they would hear the Krauts first and take cover over the low walls that skirted the road. In the event, they encountered not one person and pitched up at Gorey Harbour an hour later. There was a small amount of lighting around the harbour but by keeping to the dark patches, they easily avoided detection by soldiers who were now becoming less diligent as the cold weeks went by. The tide was going out and practically all of the scruffy armada of abandoned craft were stuck fast on the mud of the harbour. On weighing up the situation, Norm

remarked that 'they wouldn't be leaving any time soon.'
All was not lost, however, and they skipped over the sea wall. They wearily trod their way through the mud and made their way towards some larger craft a bit further out. There were several laid-up German coasters on their moorings which provided cover for them while they assessed the surroundings. The moon poked its spotlight between some scudding clouds and picked out a cabin cruiser about fifty yards away. This was afloat in waist deep water and they quickly decided that it could be what they were looking for. The water was excessively cold but once they were wet, there was no turning back. The Major found the anchor chain and hauled himself aboard. He made a quick inspection and hissed at Norm to come aboard. They quickly realised that there was no fuel, no motor and furthermore no means of using this particular boat to get them away. It was also clear that the tide was still going out and the craft settled gently onto the harbour bed. Down below there were some serviceable oars and a few rusty tins of corned beef. They realised that the tide, or lack of it, meant there would be no escape attempt that night and they would have to come back at dusk the next evening. To find an escape craft was therefore a priority and, while the tide was out, the two of them took a couple of hours to scour and reconnoitre the harbour mud for a boat large enough to take them both which could also be rowed. They would use the oars which were down below on their cabin cruiser.
Their choice was very limited as the Germans had made sure that all small boats were registered , taken ashore and then secured so as to avoid them being used in escape attempts. However there was but one which sat about fifty yards away and, following a slow slog there and back through the sticky mud, they declared it suitable. They then returned to the cabin cruiser and settled down on the damp musty beds below decks. The Rose Marie had seen better days. Pre-war she had hosted a lot of trips to France and back but now she lay abandoned, her owner dreaming of her from the bowels of a tank heading east

across France.
"What do you reckon? Should we make our way back to the farm or sweat it out here during daylight?"
"Well, Norm. It would appear nobody knows of our whereabouts so let's keep it that way. Not even the guy at Sunny View knows exactly either. I reckon we should stay here and risk it. There's a few supplies here and the water we brought should last. It's less than twenty miles to France which is no distance at all. I say we stay. Yes?"
Norm, however, was not as keen as his companion to be rowing a small dinghy across a few miles of rough sea and he said so.
"Don't you think the small row boat is a tad risky?"
His words fell on unlistening ears as the Major rooted around the large lockers below. He broke the lock on a door and peered into the blackness within. He lit a match but immediately extinguished it when he read the word 'petroleum' on the side of four five gallon sealed metal drums.
"Shit, Norm. There's at least twenty gallons of fuel in there! Mick told us there was none left anywhere."
"Well, my friend, even I know that petrol is no good without an engine. Maybe you'll get lucky again and find one in the other cupboard."
He was already on the case. He ripped the door off another locker and felt inside, finally hauling out a heavy package wrapped in an oily tarpaulin. Peeling back the folds of the tarpaulin revealed a fair sized outboard engine.
"I think we just did, Norm. There's just enough light from the pier. It says Daimler Benz on the side. Will ya take a look at that ! This is our ticket out of here."
"Well, now you're talking. All we do now is find out where it fits. Let's hope it's an outboard as opposed to an inboard engine."
At last Norm added some enthusiasm to the conversation. This was his area of expertise. As a young lad he had spent many hours motorboating on the lakes around Salt Lake City and had worked in his school holidays for a boat hiring company

keeping the engines up to scratch in the workshop.
"Sorry, Norm .You've lost me. What's the difference?"
Norm explained and instantly they both felt more confident. On inspection he discovered the engine was an auxiliary outboard motor which had clearly belonged to another smaller vessel. There was no way it would power the cabin cruiser to France.

"No dice, " said Norm. "It's doesn't belong to this boat. The shaft is way too short. It probably belonged to a smaller boat they maybe used as a tender to get to and from the mooring."
They thought for a moment.
"What if we fit the engine to the rowboat we looked at. Is that feasible ?"
Norm's face dropped at the thought of the smaller boat but he had been asked a question and was obliged to answer in the affirmative.
"I seem to recall that the transom was pretty sturdy so we should be able to fix it on. At least we know the boat doesn't leak, it's been sitting in the water for a while. Let's just see first if we can get this motor going. The fuel pipes may be missing, let's have a look."
It was difficult working in the dark and they decided to try and get some sleep. At first light , the two Americans would assess the situation.

CHAPTER 64

All systems go

A cold drizzly dawn broke over the harbour. Once again the weather drained the colour from the landscape. Norm was first to take a careful peek above the deck. At first his attention was drawn to the area of shore they had set out from. There were concrete bunkers everywhere and he was surprised that they had managed to get as far as they had. He let out a sudden low whistle as his head swivelled to take in the enormity of the massive granite castle that rose vertically to the north. Built on a promontory two or three hundred feet high , Mont Orgueil, better known as Gorey Castle , was a monstrously impressive and impregnable building which had stood for nearly a thousand years as a defence against all comers. The Germans had not been slow in realising its potential . It had a natural elevated field of fire which covered the whole of the east coast and they were quick to add more modern defence positions to it. Surprisingly to the locals, they were not unsympathetic to the history of its fabric and onlookers were hard pushed to see what they had built. The harbour that nestled below bristled with bunkers and one or two of these had windows and doors painted on them to make them blend in, clearly to disguise them and confuse the enemy. An outsider, however, could be forgiven for thinking that the Germans themselves had nodded in the direction of European history and done their best to preserve what they could in this tiny part of it. It was not the same story in the rest of the world.

The Major joined him at the portside window and confirmed Norm's low whistle.

"Gee, you don't see many of those back home!"

They spent an hour observing the scenery and the comings and goings of the Germans before they returned below to investigate the engine dilemma. It was such a still day that it was difficult to keep noise to an acceptable level without

arousing suspicion from the guards on the pier. It was also very cold and they were thankful that they had dried out their clothes from last night. Their newly acquired overcoats were proving extremely effective. There was also a hatch door they could close which sealed off the lower deck from the weather outside. Making the minimum of noise, Norm cobbled together all the bits necessary to propel a small dinghy the twenty miles to freedom.
The hours of daylight raced along as they prepared the plan of action.
"Well, we've got all the bits and I can piece them all together but we need to start and run the engine here below decks before we go any further. As soon as we do that, we'll be discovered because of the noise. I don't see how we can get away with that one."
They both thought for a moment.
"There's bound to be some boats leaving the harbour at some time. Maybe we could wait and fire up using their noise as cover."
They didn't have to wait long. An old German fishing trawler now used as a gunship was preparing to leave some three hundred yards away. Its engines idling loudly, it made enough noise for Norm to be able to pull the starter cord without fear of being overheard. After a lot of swearing and sweating, the twenty first pull elicited a gurgling sound and the engine burst into life. It also elicited a lot of smoke which they were not prepared to vent via the open hatch for fear of discovery. He cut the engine and they both coughed and spluttered as the noxious gases found an alternative route out. This sequence of events was repeated four or five times as the trawler idled noisily nearby. Each time the engine fired up, the smoke displaced more oxygen down below until they struggled to breathe.
"Okay Norm. I guess that's enough. Are you happy with that? I've got a headache."
"You gotta love that German technology, " replied Norm," that

Daimler-Benz engine has been lying there for five years maybe and it kicks into life pronto. Now all we've gotta do is work out how to get *it* and the fuel cans and rucksack down onto the mud and into the rowboat."

After much muted discussion, they decided that, when it was dark, at a certain stage of the upcoming tide both vessels would be afloat. The dinghy was further out so would float first. At the right moment it would be possible to shin down the anchor chain of the Rose Marie into a couple of inches of rising tide. One of them would wade out from where they were , release the mooring rope and pull the smaller boat back and tie up alongside. They could also tie the dinghy up on the seaward side of the Rose Marie to minimise the fear of detection. It would then be a straightforward business to drop the supplies down, then the fuel, the oars and finally the engine. The engine was heavy but could be manhandled from one person to another with a degree of difficulty which would depend on the movement of both boats in the water.

They ran the plan through their heads, realising that after they had successfully accomplished all this, they would have to wait another couple of hours until the tide had turned as the advice from the old fellow at the parish hall had been to float out on the outgoing tide. This would get them out past the pier whence they could start the engine and head for France.

They would get lucky with the tides. The clouds never dispersed during the daylight hours and darkness fell at five o'clock which was about the time Norm climbed overboard and retrieved the dinghy some fifty yards away. Like leading a horse on a rein, he gently eased the boat back to the Rose Marie and tied it up next to the anchor chain. As the tide rose, the boats started clanking together until Norm managed to secure the smaller one, using the anchor chain as a restraint. The two of them quickly transferred the knapsack, oars and food , followed by three metal cans of fuel. They had also managed to unscrew a rather heavy compass from the cabin furniture and that was throw down as well. Neither was looking forward to transferring the heavy engine but the swell was minimal and they managed it with ease in the darkness. So far it had all gone according to plan . They then had the task of fixing the engine to the transom. Again things went well. The vice type fittings secured the engine strongly and neatly . Norm made sure the screws were extra tight, made everything secure and scrambled back up the anchor chain.

It was still bitterly cold but the sky seemed to be clearing revealing an intermittent full moon. This was not good news as it increased the risk of being spotted and captured. This was something neither of them were prepared to contemplate. They were not going to sit the war out in a prison in Jersey.

They then sat by the galley table and waited for time and tide. A tin of corned beef was found in the galley pantry and they set about engaging the metal key and opening it. They were both hungry and despite the fact that the tin was celebrating its sixth birthday, neither of them resisted the urge to fill their stomachs before the journey. It tasted a bit metallic but it did the job and both felt fully prepared to execute their plan as soon as the moment arrived.

They had to wait nearly four hours before the tide turned and the current reversed to hopefully float them out to sea. The wind had started to increase from the west and the moon quickly disappeared behind the clouds. Throwing their overcoats into the boat first, they shinned down the chain and got dressed again.

"Well, this is it. Good luck, good buddy. We should be in France by morning."

"Let's hope so, Norm. Let's hope so. The boys will be worried they won't be getting their pay checks."

With these words, he slipped the rope that attached them to the Rose Marie. The outgoing tide lifted them gently and with the aid of one of the oars used as a tiller, they headed slowly east towards open sea and France. It seemed to take for ever and all the time it felt like they had twenty pairs of eyes following their every move. They could just make out a German soldier

lighting a cigarette at the end of the pier.
How could he not see us?, they both thought . But their luck held and within an hour they had rowed far enough out to risk starting the motor. By this time the weather was deteriorating quickly. Unbeknown to them a massive depression was creeping up from the west pushing into an anticyclone that had produced the low temperatures of the day. As the two masses of air met, it produced an angry blizzard of biblical proportions which broke just off the east coast of Jersey.
The two Americans watched in terror as the seas rose in fury around them. From almost flat calm , conditions had changed to a tempest in half an hour. The snow swept down on them in all directions and the boat started to be tossed like a cork. The engine started on the first pull but the turbulence was so intense that the propeller spent more time overspinning in fresh air then below water as the dinghy bucked up and down. Norm cut the engine to idling speed to avoid burning the motor out. They pressed on uncontrollably eastwards before the rising wind . They would have been safer nose to wind or even anchored but there was no way they could stop the boat barrelling downwind. They were also soon being swept north eastward towards the reef of sand and rocks known as the Ecrehous. At least if they fetched up there, they could sit the storm out. They were also shipping water and soon their feet were immersed and quickly numb. They were also suffering from the first effects of food poisoning brought about by the infected corned beef they had consumed three hours earlier. Soon they were both violently ill and hallucinating. A massive wave hit them from the side and the boat overturned, pitching them both into the icy water.
The dinghy floated in an upside down position and eventually was swept ashore on the Ecrehous where it broke up, leaving splintered waterlogged planks which ebbed and flowed with the tide until they were used on a weekender's fire many months later.
The two Americans were never found.

CHAPTER 65

Who would miss them?

Mac had a bit of a headache the next morning but it wasn't the skull splitter he had been anticipating. He and Brian had been clearing up until well after midnight so the alcohol had had every opportunity to work its way out of his system. He made himself a mug of ersatz coffee and contemplated the high tide from the garden. The gale force winds of the previous day had abated and the temperature was dropping fiercely. The steam from his drink spiralled upwards like smoke from a lit cigarette. He gazed along the shoreline and his eyes came to rest on what looked like a small satchel being pushed about by the tide. Leaving his coffee on a small heavy wooden table, he hopped down onto the shingle to investigate. It was indeed a small leather satchel now seriously waterlogged. He could just make out some indiscernible initials on the closing flap before he gingerly picked it up and drained the sea water by holding it at an angle. There was a bit of movement along at the German defence post so he retreated the few yards back to the garden and the wood shed. There he undid the satchel straps and looked inside. It was full of sheets of paper which had all melded into one sodden lump. At this point he lost interest and put the paper mess back into the satchel, to dry out in the shed. He went back inside and gave it no further thought.

Up the road at Sunny View, Big Mick was surprised when he couldn't raise his house guests for breakfast. He shinned up the ladder and quickly realised that they had disappeared. He searched around for a couple of minutes.
"Bloody hell! They haven't even left a note. "
Mick soon realised he was in a bit of a quandary. Would they be coming back? Were they lying low somewhere else? Have they already made their escape? He thought the most obvious

scenario would be that they were lying low and would resurface soon. Late that morning, he cycled down to the pub to tell Brian who in turn told Mac and Peter in the evening. The mystery deepened by the day as no further news came about. The parish was agog with the gossip surrounding the Christmas Fayre but the conversation was more about Sophie's singing and the lads from the Luftwaffe than two strangers with American accents. Oberleutnant Fritz Doenig was keeping a low profile and also trying to keep a lid on his fellow musicians. He was worried in case word got back to the Kommandant at Government House that the carol concert had got slightly out of hand. After his table-top speech he would then be in line for a charge of treason and an appointment with a firing squad . Despite the jokes the band members made about "Glenn", he made sure there were no loose tongues outside the Hotel Bristol . They all knew very well that two mystery Americans had been up to no good but bringing attention to it would have simply drawn more investigations into their alcohol fuelled performance. The drive back to town from the parish hall that night had been eventful to say the least and they had left a trail of destruction along the main road. Fritz had let their official driver go home early and Willi Brint had volunteered as he seemed to be the most sober one standing when the lights went out. Willi was a good drummer but he was no driver and the troop lorry crunched and lurched its way back to town, taking out two gateposts on the way. Neither would their identity have been in any doubt , given away by their drunken carol singing in the back of the lorry. All songs sung in excellent German, of course.

Luck was with them, however, as Christmas overtook the islands and anticipation of the impending arrival of the Red Cross ship reached fever pitch.
Feldwebel Klaus Bucholtz was coming to the conclusion in the bunkers at Platte Rocque that the Parish Hall gig had possibly not taken place at all as his memory of it was somewhat

sketchy. When he explained to his fellow soldiers that Glenn Miller had made a guest appearance, they laughed so hard that he felt obliged never to repeat the story to them. He came across Brian at the post office a couple of days later and all Brian could do was slap him on the back. The other customers in the shop were all over him as well.

"Well, I must congratulate you ,Klaus. That was a hell of a party. I can safely say that was the best Christmas Fayre we have ever had. The Constable was ecstatic, two Centeniers got drunk , two Vingteniers needed revival and Mrs Le Gresley laddered the new stockings that she's been saving for the last four years. You and little Sophie had them crying in the aisles. All in all, that was a great evening!"

Klaus smiled a little sheepishly but he listened carefully so that he could fill in all the bits he couldn't remember. He was getting a good idea of the bigger picture. It also wasn't a good time or place to mention the two Americans, he would leave that for next time.

Brian noticed that , like most people except German officers, he had lost a bit of weight.

"Have you not been well, Klaus, or are they not feeding you?"

" No, I am quite well...er...thank you. But..er....like you, we do not have enough food and we are bored with eating potatoes and rice. We have been collecting.....er how you say.....'limpets' from the rocks. They are so hard to shift."

Brian sympathised with him and made a mental note of his predicament.

"Blimey, Klaus. Limpets! The poor man's scallops. You'd need hundreds of those to fill your belly. I'll see what we can do......"

Brian was true to his word. The Christmas Fayre had produced a large surplus of income over expenditure due mostly to his own enthusiasm and generosity and he was in a position to buy goods that were on the black market. At two o'clock on Christmas Eve afternoon he met Mac at the pub as arranged. A few minutes later, Big Mick arrived in the car park, driving a horse and cart. The horse Atlas looked a bit uneasy and eyed

them all suspiciously, scraping its hooves on the gravel in an act of defiance. The cart was soon loaded with boxes and sacks to be delivered to the needy of the parish. They were just about to set off when Peter arrived on his bicycle.
"Better bloody late than neverrrrr, big man !" said Mac.
"Brian told me half past two. Have I got the wrong day?" said Peter in fake innocence.
"Climb aboard the sleigh, Peter. We're off to the North Pole! It's certainly bloody cold enough!" said Mick. At that moment Brian appeared at the pub door with a tray of steaming mulled wine.
"One each, to warm us up before we start our deliveries!"
Mac proposed the toast.
"Slainte Mhath! " said Mac but, as usual, it sounded a tad obscure.
"What does that mean?" said Brian, finally asking the question that he had spent years trying to ignore.
"It's a verry auld Scottish toast." replied Mac.
"What does it mean?" said Brian.
"Nae bloody idea! Let's try another one then. 'Lang may yerr lumb reek!"
"What does *that* mean? " said Brian, not in the slightest irritated by Mac's ignorance.
"It means..... may yerr chimbley reek ferr a lang while."
"What did he say?" said Mick looking at Peter.
"No idea whatsoever." replied Peter.
"You bloody sassenachs.....you're just winding me up. Merry bloody Christmas!................ D'ye underrrstand that one !"

They downed the warm red liquid and all laughed out loud.

"Ok, Rob Roy, it's bloody freezing. Let's get going!!" said Brian, and soon the caravan of good people was clip clopping up the road, delivering welcome supplies to the neediest families of the parish. It was hard work unloading and climbing in and out of the old carriage but, as there was no

petrol to be obtained for Brian's van, they had no choice. Everybody was pleased to see them . Optimism abounded and hidden stocks of alcohol were being broken out. Oiled by the ongoing liquid welcomes they were receiving from all and sundry, the afternoon became more erratic but they managed to deliver to everybody on Brian's list by six o'clock when it was well and truly dark.
"One more delivery to do, my good friendsh." said Brian, now three sheets to the wind.
" We need to find Feldwibble......sorry.....Feldwobble........ oh bugger, FeldWEBEL Bucholtz. I think we owe him one. Without him, we'd have had no band the other night and without him, we'd have never heard little Sophie's singing...............I've still got a tear in my eye just thinking about it."
"Och, dinna set me off again, Brian. The wee bairn sings like an angel. Unlike her big brother here who sings like a foghorrrn in labour."
"That's a bit harsh, Mac." said Peter, feigning hurt pride and downing another glass of mulled wine. "I *was* in the school choir, you know."
The mood remained upbeat and, on Brian's instructions, Mick pointed Atlas in the direction of the Bon Voyage Guest House which was half a mile from where they were. He knew Klaus was not working that evening and would in all probability be at his billet. The war had gone seriously and fortunately off the boil and sentry duties were no longer doubled. In consequence Klaus' workload had decreased and his shifts were less arduous.
Just before Mick guided the horse out into the middle of the road in order to get Atlas around a large pothole in the road, they had to wait for a big black Rover 14 which was coming in the opposite direction. It was being driven by a German naval officer.

“Nice wee car,” said Mac, keeping up the banter.

“Shame about the prick driving it!” replied Brian.

The face of the driver was just visible, being lit by an internal light. Brian thought his face was familiar but didn't give it another thought as he figured it was just another German officer in a requisitioned car. The Rover disappeared round the bend towards La Rocque and, unknown and unseen to them, pulled up right outside St Kitts. Leaving the engine running, Oberleutnant Hans Stich got out, pushed an envelope through the letterbox, got back in the car and drove quickly off.
The horse and cart eventually turned through the entrance of Bon Voyage and pulled up on the gravel. Buoyed by the confidence inspired by the alcohol they were consuming on empty stomachs , launched into a pseudo German version of 'The Happy Wanderer'. They soon had an audience of inquisitive German soldiers who filed out to listen. Eventually Klaus emerged through the front door to cheers from the horse drawn carriage. It was freezing cold and the crowd quickly dispersed back inside.
They quickly pulled Klaus aboard where he drank the obligatory mulled wine.

"A toast ! To Klaus, good friend ......and enemy. " said Brian . They all raised their glasses and Klaus felt a little uneasy.
"As a token of our appreciation for your help with the Christmas Fayre, Klaus, and the fact that you are looking a little thin , we have a Christmas present for you. All you have to do is eat it or drink it !"
Peter peeled back a small tarpaulin to reveal a couple of plucked chickens, a huge chunk of pork, a stash of vegetables, a jar of honey, some jam, some soap, and a bottle of Schnapps. Klaus blinked, not sure of what he was seeing or the sentiments he was sharing. Peter chipped in,
"...and what is more, Klaus, my mother has made you a special cake. She says she hopes you like it and that you will soon bugger off home to eat it ! "

Peter had said this in jest and the humour was not lost on Klaus. He chuckled, paused, saw the cake, took a sharp intake of breath, bit his lip and suddenly a tear dribbled down his cheek

"I'm sorry." he said wiping it away. " It's a Stollen cake, my favourite. My mutta would be making one just like this right now .....how you say.....er..back home. And yes, I would like to ...er...how you say....bugger off home to eat it!"

Klaus quickly recovered and went up another notch in everybody's admiration of him.

Santa and his elves then unloaded the last of their deliveries and carried the goods into the kitchen of the Bon Voyage. Brian had to get back to the pub as Christmas Eve was traditionally a busy evening despite the shortage of alcohol . The intermittent electricity supply was also becoming a problem and many nights were spent drinking by the light of the open fire.

They managed to persuade Klaus to come back to the pub with them for a Christmas drink. He was reluctant to go as he was in a difficult position. He was not quite an enemy and not quite a friend. Balancing between the two was quite a juggling act. He resolved the situation by agreeing to accept a lift in their carriage and walk back in an hour as he had non-uniform duties to attend to at the Bon Voyage at eight o'clock. Another mulled wine was downed and Atlas set off once more like a reluctant schoolboy on the first day of term. It was still freezing cold and as they made progress back along the coast road past La Rocque to the Grenadier Inn, it started to snow. Peter also had duties at home and persuaded Mick to drop him off at St Kitts. There were mock howls of protest from the rest but their remarks fell like water off a duck's back. He climbed down from the cart, opened the front door and yelled for Christine and Sophie to come and look at Santa's sleigh. They came to the doorway and laughed out loud. After a quick rendition of "We wish you a Merry Christmas", Atlas registered his disapproval by walking smartly on towards the pub.

"I guess we're going!" said Mick to more laughter.

"See you tomorrow, Mac?" said Christine.
"Aye, lassie. Peter has a piece of pork for you. About midday?"
"Oh God, not you for Christmas again!" chirped Peter.
"Think yerrself lucky, young fella!" shouted Mac as they disappeared into the driving snow.
Christine, Sophie and Peter waved them off and went back inside. Christine had an envelope in her hand.
"Another Christmas card, Mum?"
Christine coloured up and turned away.
"Er.......yes. From Auntie Eileen."
She squirreled it quickly away in her pocket. She had food to prepare.
The snow continued and Peter and Sophie ventured out to the back garden to take a look. It was hard to tell who was the more excited. It didn't snow very often in this southernmost of the British Isles and it was always a source of wonderment. They looked out towards the beach and , even in the dark, the whiteness of the settling snow threw out a magical light.
"Will we see Father Christmas out there, Pete?" said Sophie.
Peter thought about it for a few seconds.
"If we are very still and watch very carefully, we might be lucky."
It looked and felt so beautiful out there that he almost believed it himself.

Later that night Christine finally went to bed, drew the blankets around her and by the light of a small candle, she opened the envelope. She had already recognised the handwriting. At that moment she realised her heart was nearly jumping out of her chest......and it wasn't from anger.
Back at the pub, Brian was sweeping the linoleum floor behind the bar counter and thinking how tatty and worn the place was. It reeked of booze and cigarette smoke but he could no longer smell it as , after years of the same, his senses no longer registered it. He leaned on the broom and suddenly remembered the big black Rover 14 which they had seen on the

coast road earlier. He thought he had recognised the driver but couldn't put a name to the face at the time. Now it came back to him. It was the same naval officer he had witnessed with Christine when he was spying from the kitchens of the Blue Yacht. He felt pleased that his memory was still in working order. The next time he saw Mac he gently dropped it into the conversation.

CHAPTER 66

Drinks at the pub

When the horse and cart arrived at the Grenadier Inn, Mick, Brian and Mac looked like the leftovers from an expedition to the Arctic. The driving snow had got heavier and Atlas was finding it hard going. Brian and Mac got down and Mick set off quickly for Sunny View before the snow got any deeper and before Atlas got too tired and cold.

It didn't take long for things to warm up at the Grenadier. The open fire was stoked up with driftwood and the regulars mooched in. Most were the usual suspects but there was also an influx of people who would only come in at Christmas and Easter. Mick returned from Sunny View an hour later to join in the fun . Mac and Peter took Klaus into the kitchen at the back as it would have been uncomfortable for all concerned to drink with him in the main bar, particularly as he was in uniform. Klaus was their secret and the friendship they showed him was clearly reciprocated.

Brian had left a bottle of 'sloe gin' on the table and told the boys to tuck in. Sloes were small dark berries which were harvested from the hedgerows in Autumn and added to the gin he had brewed earlier. The resulting drink matured over months and years, each year's sloe gin being carefully labelled with the date it was started. This was a young one, a 1944, and no less potent for its youth. The sweetened gin eased its way down their throats and they were quickly into the topic of the week.

"What a night!" said Mac. "Seems like yesterday. What with the Oberleutnant's speech, Sophie's singing and your performance with the.... what do you call it?.....the swing band ? It was all too much to take in for an auld Jock like me!"

"Ya", said Klaus, "little Sophie has a beautiful voice and I think Fritz was maybe very upset. He would ...er...as normal....walk away. I was surprised when he got on the table. But he was correct.....this war is....very bad for everybody."

Brian came through from the bar at this point and joined them at the table.
“The Luftwaffe Band excelled itself. I've never seen Mrs Le Plongeon so excited. You guys should do it for a living. You could start your own Glenn Miller band!”
There was a lot of laughter at this. Klaus thought they were in on this elaborate joke but he couldn't have been more wrong.
“Who were the two Americans?” asked Klaus , trying to summon up an innocent look.
“Do you know, we haven't the foggiest idea.”said Brian.
Both Peter and Mac only knew the two Americans as Norm and the Major and had certainly made no connection whatsoever. Their conversations with them had been guarded and circumspect and what little they did know they were going to keep to themselves. There was no point in stirring up a hornet's nest with loose talk. Klaus was a friend but this was still wartime. Klaus, however, would not let it go.
“The Luftwaffe boys are sure that one of them was Glenn Miller.”
There was more laughter.
“From the pictures I have seen, he looked the same. He knew things....yes....he knew things. I think maybe you boys know things too! Yes?”
“No,” replied Brian,“we know nothing! We know nothing!” And then almost as an afterthought he added, “ Best to leave it, my friend. ”
What little they *did* know was not going to be broadcast. The facts were that two American soldiers had turned up near Seymour Tower, Mac and Peter had rescued and hidden them overnight, their names were Norm and 'The Major', Big Mick had given them a 'safe house' at Sunny View, taken them to and from the Christmas Fayre , they had disappeared overnight and no-one had seen them since. Everything the low water men had done would attract the death penalty if discovered. As far as they knew, the Germans had not seen any explosions through the fog that night and the only Americans they knew about

were tucked up and accounted for in a prison in St Helier. The two strangers at the Parish Hall had disappeared without trace . Neither was Oberleutnant Fritz Doenig about to launch an enquiry because to do so would precipitate the fact that he had made a treasonable speech that evening which would also incur a dawn meeting with a firing squad. It was in the interests of them all to put a lid on the Christmas Fayre and at last Klaus got the message. There was no more talk of Glenn Miller that night and he later walked back to the Bon Voyage with the warmth of the sloe gin to keep out the cold and the snow. He cursed the snow as all it did was remind him of home.
At the Grenadier Inn, the customers toasted the imminent arrival of the SS.Vega and the speedy departure of the Germans.
Back at Sunny View, Mick went to check on Atlas but was horrified when he opened the stable door. There was blood and guts everywhere. Poor Atlas had been killed and butchered in the last hour by persons unknown. On a bed of straw, his severed head was all that was left. This was a carefully plotted affair. There were several sets of footprints in the blood that was smeared on the flagstones. There was a good chance that the culprits were slave workers on the run but he could not rule out the Germans. Also desperately short of food, they were not averse to raiding farms and outhouses in their search for food. One or two locals also sprung to his mind. There was little to be done but report it to the Constable in the morning. The Krauts would clearly be feasting on fresh horsemeat tomorrow. Mick was furious and upset. Atlas was as stroppy as a Guernsey donkey but he didn't deserve this violent fate. He set about the sad task of burying what remained of Atlas and then washed away the entrails that dotted the stable floor. He got to bed well after midnight, worn out and emotionally drained.
The death of the horse highlighted the risk that all farm and domestic animals faced. Such was the shortage of food that many a cat or dog would disappear never to be seen again. Cats were particularly vulnerable. Many were simply picked up and

put into a handy sack. The sack would be swung round and dashed hard against a nearby wall. The cat would then be skinned, cooked and eaten. Things could surely not get much worse.

CHAPTER 67

Liberation comes slowly

The Germans had not helped increase the festive spirit and a lot of raids were made on farms like Sunny View, ostentatiously looking for unregistered pigs or cattle but, in reality they were unofficial visits from individual units who just took what they could find. One of these raids could have resulted in Atlas being butchered but there was no proof. Law and order was still on the brink of a meltdown. Food was being stolen by friend and foe alike and the farmers did not know who to blame. Supplementary rations which were normally released on special occasions were noticeably non existent. School holidays were extended through to the end of January as there was no means of heating the school buildings. However the island people were buoyed through Christmas by the thought of the arrival of the Vega which eventually and triumphantly sailed into St Helier at 5.45pm on Saturday, December 30.

An editorial in the Jersey Evening Post put it in a nutshell. "...only those who have knowledge of how many of the poorer inhabitants have lived over the last few months can imagine what this will mean. Medical supplies, foodstuffs, soap, all urgently needed, are being provided and a commission will decide what other supplies are required. So the year ends on a brighter note and we enter the New Year in the knowledge that, although there may still be hard times ahead, our position is less serious than it might have been..."

Two hundred and fifty tons of Canadian packed goods were unloaded the next day, enough for two parcels of chocolate, biscuits, tea, butter, sugar, milk powder, jam, corned beef, salmon, prunes, cheese, soap, pepper and salt to be distributed at the parish halls for each islander.

The Germans organised the labour and security before the parishes took over the transport to their respective parish halls with the use of horse drawn carriages. Red Cross officials had accompanied the vessel and after meetings with German and Jersey officials it was decided to continue deliveries at the rate of one a month to include specific items which were out of stock. The evacuation of serious medical cases was also discussed as was the possibility of supplying American and French Colonial prisoners with food parcels. Deliveries of gas coal were also on the agenda. Gas coal would provide gas for cooking and coke for fuel. It appeared that the maintenance of an electricity supply remained problematic. The really good news that was precipitated was that the ss Vega was to be afforded a safe passage from Lisbon to the Islands and back again. The promise of supplies was virtually guaranteed by the Protecting Power (the Swiss Red Cross officials) and the Belligerent Power (the Germans). This was clearly a step in the right direction.

The supply and future promise of ongoing supply of foodstuffs and essential goods meant that the black market all but disappeared for a few weeks. Brian was particularly pleased as it meant he could get back to running the pub full time instead of scurrying around the parish doing deals. There were also one or two black marketeers who were not particularly pleased to be holding stocks of previously hard to obtain items such as butter and tea.

The situation for the Germans was desperate but still they clung on. The German Kommandants of both Jersey and Guernsey, along with their boss. the Supreme Commander Oberst Von Schmidt were fully aware of the "Fortress, no surrender" status that had been bestowed upon them by Adolf Hitler in February 1944. They had all successfully buried the order but there was trouble on the horizon in the shape of Vizeadmiral Friedrich Haufhaus who had joined the hierarchy in Guernsey as adviser to Supreme Commander Oberst Von Schmidt. Haufhaus was a card carrying Nazi Kriegsmarine (Navy)officer and disliked the Supreme Commander's 'soft' approach with his essentially military administration. The Kriegsmarine(Navy) and the Heer

(Army) were traditionally at loggerheads and the atmosphere at the Supreme Command in Guernsey was a breeding ground for the conflict to continue. Nicknamed 'Pinball' by his subordinates, his soubriquet was well earned for his inability to avoid navigational marks when in command of a ship. And yet....and yet, he was a Nazi idealist from the thirties and had a lot of friends in Berlin who were more interested in his politics than his navigational skills. Von Schmidt began to feel the pressure and after the Red Cross deal had been finalised, he officially played a 'medical grounds' card and relinquished his position two months after Christmas. His departure was swift and secretive. A four engined Focke-Wulf FW 200 Condor aeroplane touched down in Guernsey on a cold clear evening in late February 1945. Von Schmidt was gone and took with him nearly five years of Channel Island history. Unofficially Haufhaus had gone over his head and had him removed. Perhaps here was the pivotal reason for the behaviour of the Germans during the Occupation. Von Schmidt was a member of the 'old school' military and had little time for the fanatical fascism of Adolf Hitler that reared its head in Germany in the 1930's. At the outbreak of the second world war, he was a high ranking officer in the Heer and had no choice but to follow orders. Perhaps the Channel Islands turned out to be a comfortable option that kept him and his cohorts out of the line of fire. With Haufhaus now in charge, it was possible that the 'fortress status, no surrender' would be enforced in a final tragic showdown. The existing German administration railed at the possibility of this outcome. The situation was not apparent to the local government and the optimism that abounded at the turn of the year simply turned to impatience as the Allies drove relentlessly across France towards Germany. At least the regular visits of the SS Vega ameliorated the feelings of abandonment that the population of the Channel Islands had had to suffer since the outbreak of war in 1939. What happened however was that the Vega got delayed more than once. There was a major shortage of flour and the Germans persisted in requisitioning bread on a whim. Bread was an essential commodity and it angered Bailiff Dechevaux and his government that, after all the negotiations with the Germans and the Red Cross, they would still requisition a foodstuff that was absolutely essential to a people who were already under-nourished. To cap it all, the Germans demanded an excessive increase in the amount of milk which had to be delivered to them weekly. This Dechevaux negotiated downward to a more acceptable level. And still they came in hard.

Anne-Marie Tonton, Christine's sister-in-arms at the Blue Yacht, fell foul of the regime when she got innocently caught up in a tangled web of deceit and desertion. There was a lot of dissension within the ranks of the Kriegsmarine with sailors frequently fighting in the streets of St Helier and generally going absent without leave. One of these turned up at Anne-Marie's house in St Helier one evening, claiming he was a friend of a friend and could she shelter him for the night. Foolishly she took him in and he was still there three days later. In the early hours of the morning on March 4, the Feldpolitzei arrived in force looking for the deserter and took both of them into custody in Newgate Street prison. This was a serious matter as the Germans had already threatened the population with the death sentence for harbouring deserters and escapees. It was no surprise when, after a brief trial, they were both sentenced to death by firing squad. Poor Anne-Marie was forced to watch the poor sailor being shot, knowing full well that the same fate awaited her, albeit in a few days time. Given the circumstances it was a cruel and unnecessary episode but the German occupiers were determined to maintain discipline, law and order.

Fortunately in this case, Bailiff Dechevaux was quickly on the well trodden warpath up to see the Kommandant and managed to get Anne-Marie's sentence commuted to life imprisonment. The warning bells were still ringing and life under the Germans remained grim and fearful. Anne-Marie understandably had a total breakdown and never really got over

it.
Christine got through Christmas and the New Year in the knowledge that she could take up again with Hans when and if she chose to. She had a few guilt feelings which she assuaged by paying extra attention to Sophie, Peter, Melody and even Mac had a bit of mollycoddling over the next week. They all said goodbye to 1944 now safe in the knowledge that they had at least been saved from starvation by the arrival of the Red Cross ship Vega.
With Sophie in bed and Peter and Melody at a nearby party, Christine once more spread Hans' letter on the table.
"My dearest Christine,
You see, I spell it right. I am so very sorry about our meeting at the Grand Hotel. I was completely overcome by the situation and everything I did was as if I was dreaming. I have no excuses and I am sorry if I called out my wife's name in a moment of passion. Believe me when I say it was passion as I have such feelings for you. It has been driving me crazy for many weeks. The fact is that I love you and want to be with you.
I also love my wife and children but in a different way. My parents always expected Katerina and I to be married and so it was. Soon we had two children and I was off to war.
I don't know if I will ever see my wife and children again and I have not seen them for two years now. There is no prospect of going home and I wish the war would end soon. I do know that I love you and hope you give it another chance before it is too late. Please let me see you again so I can explain better.
I have moved to the Pomme D'Or hotel at the Weighbridge where the Kriegsmarine Headquarters are. If you can bear to see me again, Friday January 5 at two o'clock is good. I shall be in the Officers Bar which is on the corner of the Esplanade and Mulcaster Street. No need to explain if you do not wish to come. If you are not there, I shall understand perfectly.
My love, Hans.xxx "

Every time she read it, her insides turned to jelly. Here she was, a grown woman in her late thirties being pursued by a beautiful younger enemy officer who told her he was in love with her. She could surely not reciprocate his approaches. She was married and had two children. He was a sworn enemy of Britain and she stood to suffer reprisals if she was found out. It would be an act of treason , after all was said and done. On the other side of the coin, life was feeling very precarious despite the end of the war being on the horizon. The last five years had changed everybody's perspective on time. She sighed and folded the letter back into the envelope. She put the envelope back in the usual place at the bottom of the kitchen drawer.
"Absolutely no way." she said quietly to herself.
"Presumptuous bloody Kraut." She surprised herself with the vehemence of her little outburst.
She changed her mind on Tuesday, again on Wednesday and once again on Thursday. Sophie was staying over with a friend on Friday night and Peter was staying with Melody and her parents in town for the weekend. Without doing anything in particular, things were stacking up for a clear day on Friday. She had a clear choice of yes or no. Either would be easy.
And so it was at ten o'clock on Friday, Christine found herself alone in the kitchen at St Kitts with her best skirt, blouse, shoes and winter coat on, deciding whether to catch the bus into town in fifteen minutes. She went out through the porch, locking the door behind her. She turned her collar up against the icy wind and walked the few yards to the bus stop. Once again, her heart was racing and once again , she knew she could change her mind at any moment. She waited and waited but the bus never came. This in itself was not unusual as with fuel of any kind being in short supply and parts practically unobtainable, a regular bus service was unsustainable. The question was....how long could she wait in the cold.
Her question was answered at ten thirty when the bus came into view from the direction of Gorey and stopped to let her on. This one was powered by gas and the smell of it made her feel

queasy but she persevered and sat by a draughty window where the air was cold but at least fresh. The trip was not straightforward. The bus broke down twice and eventually reached Snow Hill in St Helier three and a half hours later at exactly two o'clock. She now knew what she had to do and she walked from the bus station down Mulcaster Street until she reached the corner of the Esplanade where the Officers Bar was located within the massive Pomme D'Or hotel which also doubled as the Kriegsmarine headquarters. Without hesitating, she pushed the door open to find an empty bar room, devoid of any staff . Dish cloths covered the glasses on the bar top. It was clearly not open. There was an envelope on a table propped up by a salt cellar. She could make out the name
' Christine' . She went over and opened the envelope.
"Dear Christine,
I have a small job to do and won't be back until three o'clock at the latest. If you come and I hope you do, please make your way to my quarters in room 303, the key is in the envelope. It is easy to get lost so follow the map on the back. Love, Hans."

She turned the page over and studied the directions. Three minutes later she had climbed three flights of narrow stairs when she heard someone coming up behind her. It was Hans and they reached the top step together and stood on the landing facing room 303. They kept their distance from each other, each a bit wary. Hans spoke first.
"Well, you have the key, Christine. We can't get in without it."
Suddenly she realised this was probably the last moment she could escape the exquisite danger that was presenting itself. As she gave the key to Hans, time froze and then seemed to move on frame by frame. Click went the chunky key in the lock (she would always remember the sound of that key turning in the lock) and Hans pushed the door open, standing aside to let her go in first. She hesitated, gave it one last thought and took the fork in the road. She stepped inside.
The suite of rooms was luxurious and had panoramic views

across the Weighbridge to the harbour and beyond across St Aubin's Bay.
“Things are much better here,” said Hans. “ Take a look round. I have a bathroom with hot water. Have a look and do take your coat off. The radiators are on so you will find it comfortable. There is a bath and a shower in there with real gold taps! I really didn't think you would come . I was waiting at two o'clock and there was no sign of you. I had to take some documents to the Town Hall so I wrote out a note and left it on the table. When I came back I followed you up the stairs. Please , come and sit by the window. Would you like a drink? ” He paused to take a breath.
“It's really nice to see you.”
Christine smiled and walked to the chair, easing herself into the welcoming cushions. She looked up , mentally admiring his white Kriegsmarine jacket that reminded her so much of their previous liaison at the Grand Hotel. The surroundings here were so much nicer .
“It's good to see you too and I only just made it myself as the bus broke down twice. I really shouldn't be here.......... and I have to meet a friend at four o'clock.”
She was lying through her back teeth and she knew it.
“Look, Christine. I just had to tell you to your face that I am sorry about our last meeting. I cannot take back what I said at that moment. It just come out of my mouth. I think what I wrote in my letter is what I think. I am not so good with words. I hope you believe me. I usually tell the truth.”
“Usually?”
“Well, this morning I told my commanding officer that I wasn't feeling well and would have to miss the afternoon orders. That wasn't the truth, was it?”
Christine laughed.
The smell of his cologne wafted her way and she breathed it in. He was staring at her.
“You look so beautiful. Please stay. Every minute is precious.”
Once again she felt herself falling headlong down the abyss. He

leaned over and caressed her face with the back of his hand. They kissed a kiss that left them both breathless and from that point on there was no turning back. Their dangerous liaison was sealed in a few whirlwind hours of rising mutual passion. This time, he got her name right. Again and again and again and again. At ten o'clock she got out of bed to go to the bathroom. She sat down on the toilet and looked around. There really *were* gold taps. She opened the shower door and turned the taps on. Beautiful clean hot water rained down on her from the huge shower head. She turned to face the wall where the soaps were stacked on a glass shelf. She helped herself to the Eau de Lily and unscrewed the top. She suddenly felt she was being watched and so she was. Hans had snuck in and was sitting on the edge of the bath. Her immediate reaction was to cover up what she could with her hands but she quickly realised this was ridiculous and gave this idea up as quickly as it had arrived.

" You don't mind if I watch. You look so beautiful."

If Christine had been a cat, she would have purred. She felt sore and sated but still turned on by the relentless passion that was coming her way. His eyes were sucking her in and she knew it. He stood up and moved slowly across the tiles and got under the shower with her. She turned like the same cat on heat and clung on to the gold taps, angling her backside towards him in a brazen act of invitation.
He was quickly inside her. They were at it once again and she absolutely loved it. The hot water rained down over them as they drained the final dregs of energy out of each other.

Hans dropped her back home very quietly just after midnight. They were both shattered and very happy. Christine went straight to bed and fell asleep in seconds.

With the car's heater on full blast , champagne in his belly and a smile on his face Hans headed back along the coast road back to town. He started to think of all the complications that they had just generated with their risky behaviour. He also mused about what a wonderful evening they had just had. On a stretch of straight road, he nodded off to sleep with his foot firmly on the accelerator and piled into a massive, immovable granite gate post, sending him through the windscreen. He struck the same gatepost with the top of his head and died instantly. It was half an hour before a nearby local home owner opened his front door to discover the carnage a few yards down the road. A fractured radiator pipe was hissing steam and there was a smell of petrol wafting on the cold January air. The Kriegsmarine officer Oberleutnant Hans Stich was slumped over the bonnet, his white tunic stained with blood. The Constable was telephoned and the Germans informed. A German ambulance arrived but the medics quickly ascertained that he was dead and removed his body to the town mortuary. A few lines in the Evening Post the day after marked the tragic event but did not raise much concern. It was one less German. Mac sat by the fire at the Grenadier Inn and read the newspaper . There was a half page obituary of the American band leader Glenn Miller who had now officially been declared 'missing presumed dead' after his plane disappeared over the Channel the week before Christmas. Mac paid little attention to this news as his eyes were focussed lower down the page at the local obituary column.
Since a conversation with Brian, he was familiar with the black Rover 14 involved in the tragic accident and he knew exactly who Hans Stich was.

CHAPTER 68

Heartache for Christine

Christine heard the next day that there had been a car crash in the next parish but hadn't paid much attention to the news. She was floating on air and never quite took it in until the evening paper was delivered to St Kitts. When she read the name, the blood drained from her face and she rushed to the bathroom where she spent the next half hour vomiting in terrible distress. She was inconsolable and Sophie couldn't comprehend what was going on.

“Mummy, mummy, why are you crying?”

Poor Christine was absolutely blitzed by the shock of it. She realised poor Hans had died just five minutes after they had kissed goodbye. She was glad Peter was away for the weekend because she'd have found it hard to explain why she was so upset. Sophie eventually accepted that 'mummy was feeling sick' and after a few minutes Christine pulled herself together. She had a dreadful gnawing pain which had no specific origin except the realisation of the tragedy that had unfolded.

What was she going to do? Who could she tell? These were easy questions as she was going to do nothing and say nothing. Nobody knew anything anyway. She would be a mess for a few weeks and only she would know why. She would overcome it. She was forgetting one thing though. Mac knew of Oberleutnant Hans Stich and it didn't take him too long before he was questioning the proximity of the crash and the fact that there had been nobody at home at St Kitts that evening when he had dropped by twice on the off chance of giving the Marinelles some coffee he had received in a Red Cross food parcel. In the meantime , her stomach churned constantly and she found it hard to eat. She would cry herself to sleep every night but she had to muddle through for the sake of Sophie. Black circles grew around her eyes and she lost more weight. She had no one to talk to. Anne-Marie would have been the only one who would have understood but she was now in prison. She was glad Peter was away most of the time pursuing his relationship with Melody and, for reasons unknown, Mac hadn't been round so much lately. The weeks passed as she tried to recover from the brutal shock of the events that January day.

It was therefore quite a surprise when one evening in late March, Mac came knocking at her door. She forced a smile and gave him a brief hug.
“Can I come in, lassie? Can you put the kettle on. I've brought some real coffee. Is Sophie in bed?”
Christine forced a weak smile and nodded. “Sit down, Mac.”
He did as he was told but knew he should be leading this conversation and he stepped right up to the mark. He had been brooding over this for the last few weeks.
“What's the matter, pet? Those dark circles under yerr eyes are telling me that it's not just lack of food that's ailing you.”
She sat down with a sigh, put her head in her hands and said, “It's nothing ,Mac. It's just this ruddy war. I've had enough of it.”
“Aye, well, that's gud to hear. There was me thinking that it might have had something to do with the death of Oberleutnant Hans Stich of the Kriegsmarine in a car crash a few weeks ago.”
Mac couldn't believe he had just blurted that out.
Christine looked as if she had seen a ghost and Mac was mortified at his own outspokenness.
There was complete silence as they struggled to come to terms with the remark.
“Look me in the eye, lassie. Come on. Is all this to do with him? I canna help ye if yerr not straight wi' me.”

The tears burst from her eyes. She couldn't hold them back any longer. Five minutes of sobbing followed before she could speak.

“I couldn't help it , Mac. We fell in love with each other. I was feeling very vulnerable what with Cliff dead and everything. I'm not apologising for it . What Hans and I had was something good. He was an honest person, more honest than me. I'm sorry I lied to you before. I'm so sorry.......”
She sobbed again and she was clearly in a lot of distress.
Mac was also in distress mainly because the object of his affections had lied to him and he was having trouble coming to terms with that one. He had managed to detach himself from her over the last couple of months and felt better for it but now it came charging back at him like a herd of buffalo.
“I'm sorry you lied to me too . You know he was married and had kids, don't you?”
“Mac, there's not much I don't know about him. I loved the man. And I've got kids too, but there's a war on. There's been so much death and disappointment, I just thought I would take the chance and grab the tiger by the tail. Believe me, I thought long and hard about it.”
She didn't add that the risk involved with the relationship is what drove it on. The thought of their liaison still turned her insides to jelly. She now wasn't sure whether it was the risk or the love that she missed.
They talked the evening away and Mac felt better now that she trusted him with her secret. He was also glad that the Oberleutnant was dead but he wasn't about to share that one with her. Christine felt better too now that she had offloaded her grief. They had forged a new alliance and a calmness prevailed between them. She talked it out until they both had nothing left. A few minutes easy silence was broken when Mac spoke.
“Changing the subject....is the big jesse that calls himself your son likely to be around over the weekend. Its Easter Sunday on April 1 and as an April Fools joke I thought it would be a good idea to do the old traditional 'let's all freeze and lay a net down at low water for Easter'. I'll be seeing Mick at Sunny View tomorrow as he has all our nets stored in the barn. Could you

mention it to Peter? We'll be laying a net from Easter Friday..... How's his romance going? Is he still loved up and under the thumb? We don't see him down the pub anymore. I miss the big man."

"He's good, Mac, and for once in my life, I can honestly say he is better off away from me at present. I don't want him to see me like this as I can't possibly tell him why. He said he would be back tomorrow some time so I'll tell him."

She paused and continued,

"Look Mac, I'm really sorry for not being straight with you in the first place but now it is what it is. Hans is dead and I'm not. Life goes on. Now you can either stop being my friend or we can get back to where we were before. What do you say?"

Mac gulped down the dregs of his coffee and reached out for her hand.

" I'll always be your friend, lassie......always. I know I'm a crusty old bugger but so long as I'm still breathing, I'll be watching your back."

He bridged what could have been an awkward moment by quickly saying,

"You just make sure the big jesse is ready to help us with the nets on Friday. It's a good tide. It may be a tad chilly but I've a feeling in my water that it could be worth it."

Christine squeezed his hand. "Thanks, Mac. I'll get him to call round as soon as he gets back."

Mac got up to go and replied, " ...aye, if I'm not home I'll be in the pub."

"Now, there's a surprise, Mac!"

They both laughed, both feeling at ease once more with the other. They said their goodbyes in the porch and Christine watched him walk off towards La Rocque.

When she knew he was well out of earshot, she said very quietly to herself,

"I haven't told you everything , Mac. I haven't had a period since Christmas."

CHAPTER 69

Easter Friday Bonanza March 30 1945

Mac's 'feeling it in his water' about the Easter fishing expedition was not met with overwhelming enthusiasm at the Grenadier Inn.

"Too bloody cold!" said Brian.

"There'll be less fish than ever! It's still bloody winter !" said Big Mick.

"Och ye bloody lily-livered crapauds. Dinna look a gift horse in the mouth. It's a racing certainty. I don't get these feelings very often. There's been a lot of movement in the water on the high tide this week. How about if I crack out the Glenfiddich before and after."

There was a universal cry of "I'm in!" and the expedition was officially on.

"Okay," said Mac. Here's the plan. We meet at Mick's place at Sunny View early tomorrow morning to collect the 'magic carpet' and transport it to the south slip . It's a big spring tide which peaks at about seven. Shall we meet at 9 a.m. at Mick's? It'll take an hour or two to set up near the slipway and then we can follow the tide down."

There was a general murmur of agreement and the traditional first fishing trip of the year was in place............. war or no war.

Peter lurched out of bed the next day and cursed agreeing to go on this cold and foolhardy expedition. The air temperature wasn't extreme, in fact it was fairly mild. He knew however that the sea temperature lagged a couple of months behind the weather which meant that any body parts below waist level were in danger of losing all feeling as they waded in the chilly sea through the gullies. Neither his mother Christine or sister Sophie had surfaced . His mouth was dry from last night's session at the pub. Reluctantly he shaved , dressed and forced himself out the front door on to the road and off past La Rocque where the tide was lapping the sea wall. On a rock next to the pier about a hundred yards out, a man in black was fishing deeper water using a long bamboo fishing pole and a small hook baited with his own secret mix of bread and fish guts. In a well practised movement like that of a magician, with his right hand he yanked a snared grey mullet from the water into the air and with an equally deft movement of his left hand he caught it in a hessian sack. The trick was to get a good purchase on the mullet's first bite before its soft lips gave way and released the small hook. It was a perfect still day to catch one of these 'slippery ghosts'. Peter almost applauded before moving on to Sunny View.

The team of low water men numbered four, Mac, Peter, Brian and Mick. Although they hadn't applied for a permit to take the net down through the checkpoint on the slipway, there really wasn't any need as they were all well known to the unit. They chirped at each other on the way down towards Seymour Tower before fixing the net on one of the most productive gullies and returning to the slipway by 3p.m.. It was a huge tide and best of all, none of them got very wet. They would return after midnight to collect their catch and reset the net for the next tide. The night session was cold and almost completely unproductive except for two small bass. They reconvened at ten a.m. on Easter Saturday morning, enthusiasm waning fast. It was still cold and grey and they struggled to keep their spirits up as they followed the receding tide. Mac's timing was perfect and they arrived at the gully just as the net was exposed. What they saw took them all by surprise. This was the big one that they all aspired to. The net was bustling and bulging with wriggling fish of all description. Bass, mackerel, pollack and mullet were in abundance. Their problem was how to get it all back to shore. The solution was simple and they rigged the net up with the fish in and doubled it over for strength before humping it back. In all they returned in a pool of sweat with over 500 pounds of fresh live fish, safe in the knowledge that the net would not be relaid any time soon and they would be spared the disappointment of another fruitless and cold night

march.
They were ecstatic with their catch and most of it was bartered away, the last hundred pounds finding its way, via German hands, to market in St Helier. As they sat in front of the fire in the pub that night, Mac put it succinctly,
"We'll nae get another catch the ken of that, my friends. I think that's the last net I shall lay for a long while!"
As sad a statement as it was, the other three agreed wholeheartedly.
"I shall miss the numbness in my legs," said Peter.
"I shall miss being bitten by angry conger eels," said Mick.
"I don't like fish, anyway," said Brian.
How they laughed as they downed Mac's whisky.
"Slainte Mhath!," said Mac.
"Slainte Mhath!," they replied in unison.
They had clearly been practising. Mac beamed .
"Yeah, Slainte bloody Mhath!! Bloody sassenachs."

It was a long and happy evening.

+

CHAPTER 70

Early May 1945

The weather improved after the Easter weekend and very soon Mac had welcomed back his family of swallows. This year however he felt less optimistic. Christine's affair had disappointed him and he derided himself for his emotional involvement. There was no denying he felt let down and somehow things would never be quite the same again. Peter was still 'loved up' and was sailing along on a cloud of desire in the company of Melody. She was a lovely girl from a good church going family. Despite her overt flirtatiousness, the gap between cuddles and full on sexual intercourse had not yet been bridged. Every moment they were alone was a battle between her religious upbringing and his overwhelming desire to get inside her pants. It was an age old dilemma which would only be resolved by marriage. It was a wrestling match in more ways than one. He didn't need Mac any more, he was pushing on under his own steam and Mac was happy for him. Mac should have been content in his isolation but his old demons were coming back to haunt him. His imaginary night time obsession with thoughts of Christine had been soured and images of the trenches had returned with a vengeance. The whisky was still a comfort and he placed more and more reliance on it to take him to comfortable oblivion. Waking up each morning became a disappointment to him.

Back at Platte Rocque, the German defence position was in limbo. Rumour had followed rumour and up until the end of April there was a possibity that they would have to stand and fight until the last man. This filled them all with dread. They were hungry and afraid but they still had to follow orders. There were still boring guard duties to perform which did little to keep their minds off home and family.

Klaus was organising rosters one morning early in May when he had a surprise visit from Oberleutnant Fritz Doenig who had dropped by on his way back from a big administration meeting at Gorey Castle.

He parked a very delapidated troop lorry at the top of the slipway and hailed Klaus from a few yards away.

"Good morning, Klaus. Good to see you. Are you going on your holidays soon?"

"Ah, Oberleutnant. I am afraid I have used up all my leave. Remember I was in Hawaii for two weeks just before Christmas!"

"Good to see you haven't lost your sense of humour."

"Have you got a few minutes, Fritz? Remember I said I would take you out to the tower? Well, now's your chance, maybe your last chance. I have to do a routine check on some wiring out there."

Fritz looked at his watch, thought for a second and said,

"Why not? I feel like a tourist. I have just had a small tour of the big Gorey Castle. Let's make a day of it. I have some good news but I will tell you when we are away from all this."

He gestured towards the defence position.

It was nearly midday and a waning spring tide had sucked the water from the landscape, racing eastwards towards the French horizon.

The two German soldiers then strolled down to the sand, their uniforms as bland as the background of black and brown rock and shingle. Klaus led the way. Just like his feelings towards the land his father grew cherries on, the low water backdrop now beckoned him like an old friend. He felt at ease with it all, he could recognise rocks and gullies. The sun was early summer warm, warm enough to make the exposed bladderwrack gasp and creak.

"What's the good news, Fritz? I know the Fuhrer is dead so you had better come up with something more original than that."

"Yes. The good news is that the boss, Herr Oberst, up at

Government House is ready to surrender and sign anything so we can all go home. The bad news is his new boss in Guernsey, the Supreme Commander of all the Channel Islands Vice-Admiral Haufhaus, has the final word and it seems he wants to carry on until the last man. Seems he was right up the Fuhrer's arse in the thirties in the days of the blackshirts. You'd think with his best buddy Adolf being dead that that would be it. All over! But no, this idiot stands between all of us and a final suicidal battle. Let's hope he sees sense. Anyway, how have you been? Have you seen Glenn Miller again lately?

They both laughed out loud at this. They had discussed the mystery Americans on more than one occasion at the odd band practice they had had as the war ran itself out.

"We may laugh, Fritz, but one of my men gave me a magazine he had confiscated. It was a year old and had a full feature article on Glenn Miller with a full page picture of him on the cover. Our visitor bore a remarkable resemblance to him! I have asked around discreetly but nobody knows who they were and no-one is telling anyway."

As they neared the tower , Fritz marvelled at the view to the north across the exposed sand and rock towards the castle that he had just come from.

"Like you, I'm convinced it was him.....although there's no way we can prove it and now he is dead, we'll never know. All I know is that it looked like him and he just knew what he was doing. As a musician, you can tell, you just know. Why would we need proof anyway? We were there and so was he and he disappeared that same week in a light aircraft somewhere over the English Channel."

They climbed the few stone steps to the rock where the corroded ladder started and climbed up to the front door. Klaus

produced the key and they struggled over the threshold. Most of the several small windows of the square tower were broken and a cool welcome breeze blew through. It felt damp but not unpleasantly so. Klaus checked that everything was in order and then briefed Fritz on the history of the island's coastal towers. After five minutes he finished his talk.
"....so you see, the British built these round towers to keep out the French and what happens? Us bloody Germans walk in ! I hope also that we are about to walk out as well."
Fritz laughed but the mood was one that mirrored the increasing uncertainty of the situation. "*If they are round towers, why is this one square?*"
Klaus pondered the question as he hadn't realised either but he cobbled together an answer.
"Good question! This is obviously the exception that proves the rule."
"Good answer, Klaus. You are so full of shit. It's a good job you can play the piano!"
"Thank you very much, Fritz. So many compliments. I hope to play it again soon back in Germany ," replied Klaus, looking wistfully out through the door at the geography that had seeped into his soul.
"*.....but on the other hand, I will miss all of this. I can't say we've had it bad."*
Fritz was impressed by his knowledge and replied thoughtfully,
"I just hope bloody Haufhaus sees sense and surrenders .Otherwise we shall be in for a bunfight!"
Klaus completed his check list and pondered if this would be his last visit. With an impending surrender to the Allies, what would happen to us all. Would they send us all back to Germany? Would we serve time as prisoners of war? Would there be some form of retribution? The future looked bleak and uncertain.
"What will become of us, Fritz ?"
"Your guess is as good as mine, my friend. Hitler has left the whole of Europe in ruins and we'll obviously get the blame for

it. It doesn't look good."
Klaus had been rooting around in the cupboards near the sink when he exclaimed,
"Aha! I thought that bastard Steiglitz had stashed something out here. He always came back from his lone patrols smelling of booze!"
He crouched down, reached in and pulled out an as yet unopened bottle of Schnapps.
"Well, would you believe it! God knows where he stole this from. Probably from a private house. He would give Hitler a run for his money! Apparently he finally flipped last week and went AWOL. He'll be facing a firing squad when they get him."
"Perhaps, Klaus, but perhaps the end of the war will save him. Probably his worst nightmare. Wasn't he the shit who finished off our chandelier that night?"
"Yes, I'm pretty sure that was him," said Klaus. *"You might like to take this bottle back with you to the Bristol........for the benefit of the Glenn Miller Orchestra ?"*
They climbed back down the rusty ladder and back onto the shingle, sand and rock that stretched out below. About two hundred yards away to the north, amongst the wreckage of old iron boats and anti-tank obstacles, the remnants of over five years of conflict glinted in the milky sunlight.
"That looks like the remains of an aircraft engine." said Fritz. *" Can we take a look?"*
A propeller blade and a portion of an engine poked its nose above a shifting sandbank.
Fritz inspected it and said,
"I knew my Luftwaffe training would come in useful one day. This is a Pratt and Whitney R1340 Wasp engine. Probably American. You're impressed, aren't you ?
"Yes," replied Klaus. *"...your knowledge of aircraft engines astounds me."*

"What a mess though. All this crap, all these lives lost.....and for what? We voted for change in the early thirties to gain back

our national pride, we voted for a charismatic leader and what did we get. A maniac with a hidden agenda. We'll all be paying for this, you mark my words!"
"Has the sun got to you, Fritz ? You're turning into a politician and there's no coming back from that one! Come on, let's go back. We might find the war has ended while we've been down here."
He took a good long look around him before continuing.
" I'll be sad to leave this place. Very sad."

A comfortable silence descended between them as they both grabbed the moment. They walked slowly back to Platte Rocque, enjoying the surroundings but pondering anxiously over the future. They shook hands and said their goodbyes.
"Good luck, Klaus . Look after your those hands."
"Thanks, old friend. Look after those lips."
They looked each other squarely in the eye.
"Piss off, Fritz. Get out of here."
"To be correct, it's piss off... Oberleutnant."

Fritz smiled , turned , walked back to his lorry and was gone. They would not be seeing each other again for many years.

CHAPTER 71

Freedom at last

Vice Admiral Haufhaus, the Channel Island Supreme Commander , was preparing for the final showdown. He had over 25,000 troops at his disposal to protect a group of tiny British islands which were heavily and professionally defended with steel and concrete. Every point of landing was covered at every conceivable angle. There would be huge loss of life if an invasion force was mounted by the Allies. Haufhaus was adamant that ' befehl ist befehl' , the Fuhrer had given him no choice and he would defend until the end.

His ideological intransigence took a massive hit on April 30 when it was announced that the Fuhrer was dead. He had suicided in the bunkers of Berlin. The war was surely now over and the Germans must capitulate completely but it took a lot of persuading from his subordinate officers to make Haufhaus believe that, as their Fuhrer was no longer alive, his order of 'no surrender' was now null and void.

In England , HQ Southern Command had been earmarked to mount an invasion force to take back the Channel Islands and , armed with excellent intelligence as to the nature of the defence positions, had been in training in the south of England for some months.

On May 3, Supreme Headquarters of the Allied Expeditionary Force put HQ Southern Command on alert to open negotiations with Haufhaus and ascertain the nature of German intentions. Would they fight or would they surrender?

HQ Southern Command sent a wireless message to Haufhaus to the effect that they were authorised to accept his unconditional surrender. The Vice Admiral was annoyed by this and replied that he only took orders from his own government. Events in France overtook him, however, when the unconditional surrender of *all* German forces was signed in Rheims, France on May 7. All hostilities would cease at midnight on May 8 and so it was that, after a lot of ill-conceived hubris, he sent his deputy to sign the articles of unconditional surrender on a rum cask on the quarterdeck of a British warship four miles south of Guernsey near Les Hanois lighthouse.

The Liberation was complete and in the very early hours of 9 May 1945, five years of purgatory came to an end for the Channel Islands.

The morning before the official liberation was a morning of rumour and excited uncertainty. Bailiff Dechevaux put out a statement in a lunchtime Evening Post edition appealing for calm .That afternoon, a crowd of thousands poured into the Royal Square to listen to a broadcast on a hastily assembled public address system. Householders were standing in doorways, shopkeepers had Union Jacks in their display windows, there was bunting everywhere and at three o'clock in the afternoon the Prime Minister Winston Churchill made his historic speech to officially end the war. He made a passing reference to 'our dear Channel Islands also being freed' and the crowd erupted with unbridled joy.

When the speech was over, the crowd, emaciated from five years of constant hunger, attempted to sing 'God save the King'. The words, however, became strangled in their throats as emotions became unstoppable. Grown men and women simply broke down and cried. Months of conjecture and false dawns had led to this point and nobody could be prepared for the feelings that were unleashed when the end of the war became official.

Events moved fast from that moment. American and British prisoners held by the Germans were released. Church bells were ringing in every parish as the news travelled. The Electricity Company made sure the supply stayed on until midnight. There was no longer a curfew and people wandered the streets late into the evening simply because they could. Parishioners left their curtains open because there was no longer a 'blackout'. Young men were seen carrying their beds

out of the prison in Newgate Street. More importantly you could now openly discuss anything with your friends on street corners. All the restrictions of the last five years were gone. Once the Germans had signed the surrender, Operation Nestegg swung into action. Task Force 135 had been formed in July 1944 for the specific purpose of reoccupying the Channel Islands. Its personnel had been rejigged many times as many of their troops were needed to drive home the march to Berlin rather than defend Britain. TF135 was essentially an infantry brigade cobbled together from artillery regiments but nonetheless it had a big job to do. A Civil Affairs unit was allocated to help and liaise with Whitehall to collect urgent supplies for distribution to the islands. Using the extreme tides of the islands TF135 used landing craft to deliver these essentials right up to the sea wall in St Helier. Then there was the job of collecting over 25,000 German prisoners of war from all the islands and relocating them in prison camps all over mainland England. There were hand guns and rifles to collect and there were minefields and gun emplacements to be made safe. It was a huge task but the efficiency with which it was initiated spoke volumes of the British government's desire to make good the impression that they hadn't really cared too much about the plight of the islands over the last five years.
A small advance party arrived by boat on the afternoon of May 9 at St Helier Harbour and made its way through ecstatic crowds along the pier to the Kriegsmarine Headquarters at the Pomme D'Or hotel by the Weighbridge. The Officer Commanding the Forces in Jersey, Colonel Roberts , had arranged to meet Oberst Gruber, the Jersey Kommandant there at 4.30 p.m. to discuss the implementation of the terms of surrender. Colonel Roberts made a brief and historic speech from the first floor balcony of the hotel to the crowd below and then went back inside to keep his appointment. A few minutes later, the orders were given for the Germans to clear the quays and town by nightfall. Arms and ammunition were to be left in indicated places and Gruber was allowed a small percentage of

arms to be used by his own guards at those dumps. One of the British advance party commandeered a car and a German driver down at the harbour. The old Rolls Royce had itself been commandeered on the very same spot by the Germans in July 1940 where it had been abandoned by a fleeing English resident on his way back to Weymouth. There were no keys and the driver used a piece of copper wire to start the engine. The seats were leather and luxurious and Sergeant Major Barton thought it was brilliant. Under orders from Colonel Roberts , they hotfooted it to the Airport at St Peter where he was met by a Luftwaffe Oberleutnant who apologised for the state of the small number of aeroplanes that were left there and the lack of fuel. Still all alone, Barton was shepherded to the Officer's Mess where he was introduced as Acting Officer Barton and under British Mess rules he removed his webbing and weapon and hung them on a coat hook. The half dozen or so Luftwaffe officers then sat him down in front of a large brandy and turned up the volume on the wireless so they could all listen to Churchill's speech from London. At this point Barton glanced idly round at his prisoners and realised they still carried a veritable armoury of Lugers, Mausers and Berettas while he sat drinking their brandy......completely unarmed. He spotted a bottle marked 'Reserviet fur die Wehrmacht' and chuckled while they poured him another. Within an hour or two, a platoon of gunners arrived to seal the deal and the airport was back in Jersey hands. On the way back to St Helier, Barton ordered his driver to drive on the left hand side of the road. After five years of all and sundry driving on the right , German style, this produced a certain amount of chaos much to Barton's amusement. His argument was that they had to get used to it sometime and, to him , there was no time like the present. Within a week, the first of the Germans were transported to larger ships offshore by amphibious craft and then on to Southampton and beyond in Britain. Generally German prisoners of war were put to work in agricultural or reconstruction work and by 1946 were being repatriated. All prisoners were made to watch a film detailing the atrocities of the Nazi regime and practically all must have been appalled to find they had been fighting for such a rotten cause. The Luftwaffe band were shipped off, happily together, to a camp in Yorkshire where they spent a very cold few months before being allowed home. Others faced a dilemma inasmuch as their home towns were now on the wrong side of Berlin under Russian control. Saddest of all, many had no homes to go back to whatsoever.

The months following the liberation were a strange period of adjustment. The initial euphoria quickly drained away as the locals tried hard to get back to some sort of reality. Operation Nestegg was quickly put into operation. A wide range of foodstuffs was made available although still rationed under the old scheme. Medical supplies were abundant and at last those diabetics who had managed to survive the Occupation now had access to insulin. The islanders had been forced to use German marks as currency and these were to be exchanged, within three days, at the banks for pounds sterling at the rate of 9.36 to the pound. There was a mad rush and there were reports of one or two notorious black market traders turning up at the banks with wheelbarrows full of German cash. Rumours were rife and tempers flared. In more general terms, the islands were in a mess. The infrastructure which had generated the building of all the concrete and steel bunkers and defence positions left scars everywhere. Railway tracks criss crossed many major roads. These had to be dug up by the German prisoners but it was tedious hard work. Then there was the hardware of war. Field guns, large and small, were decommissioned and pushed over the cliffs into the sea. Explosives and ammunition were made safe. Rifles and side arms were stored before being shipped out. A lot of ordnance was also dumped in the Hurd Deep off the island of Alderney. All the hotels, guest houses and billets used by the Germans to house their troops had to be cleared and returned to their previous conditions. The German prisoners forced to do these tasks became fractious forcing

their British overseers to carry arms once again. Clearly everybody had had enough.
Klaus stayed on for three months of mine clearance on the south and east coasts. He had a good knowledge of all the maps which indicated where explosive devices were laid. He was taken each day to an HQ on Gorey Pier and worked on clearing the Common and golf course to the south and the many fields which were laden with anti tank and anti parachute structures. As he was still in Grouville parish, he took time out ,when allowed, to investigate the Glenn Miller mystery. He quizzed as many locals as he could but came up against a brick wall. Lots of people had been to the Christmas Fayre and enjoyed the Luftwaffe Band - but nobody knew anything about the Americans. Then one day in July he made a bit of a breakthrough. His work party stopped on the beach near the Grenadier Inn for lunch one day and Klaus asked his overseer Sergeant if they might all have a beer at the pub.
“Sounds like a good idea to me, Klaus. So long as you're paying. Lead the way!” said Sergeant Mainwaring in his broad Yorkshire accent.
Klaus was pleased his request had been fulfilled so easily and followed his instuctions. He pushed open the front door and made his way to the bar while the rest of the squad of six found a table near the window. Brian was delighted to see him and made a huge fuss.
“Feldwibblewobble Bucholz , you old bugger. We thought you must have left already! It's great to see you. What's going on?”
“Good to see you too, Brian. They put me in a mine clearing division. Only because I can ...er...read the maps. I will be leaving in a few days.....sadly.”
At that moment, Sergeant Mainwaring came up alongside them with the order for the drinks.
“Eee oop, Klaus. We'll have five pints of Mary Ann , please, in the far corner.”
Klaus, in his usual well mannered way, introduced Brian to his boss.

"Ah Sergeant, this is my good friend Brian who runs the island of Jersey. We sometimes shared some fish when we were all hungry. I was sometimes the ..er..guard...when they were out in his fishing boat."
Mainwaring smiled and shook Brian's hand.
"Sounds like you had a whale of a time while we were oop to our necks in desert sand fightin' off the likes of Rommel in North Africa!"
He was joking but the point had been made. Brian was aware of it too and guided the conversation back to calmer waters.
"Five pints, Sergeant? Have these on the house as a token of our gratitude at being finally liberated!"
Mainwaring beamed and made his way back to the table. When he was out of earshot Brian added quietly, "yeah ..finally liberated after being ignored for the best part of five years."
"What was that, Brian?" chimed in Klaus.
"Nothing, Klaus......nothing. Now , five pints of Mary Ann and what will you have?"

"Do you have a stein of ice cold German beer?" said Klaus, trying to wind Brian up.
Brian never even looked up. "We'll make that *six* pints of Mary Ann then, shall we?"
They smiled in unison, melded by the same thoughts.Brian pulled the pints slowly whilst filling Klaus in with all the latest news . Eventually the conversation swung back to the Christmas Fayre and the fun they had had that night.
"Now the war is over, Brian, you can tell me who the two Americans were ?"

"Okay, why not....... but I don't know a lot. You'd be better talking to Mac and Peter. The night before the Christmas Fayre it was really foggy and nearly dark when they heard a small aircraft overhead. The engine cut out and Mac said he heard a small explosion coming from the direction of the tower. He took Peter with him down towards low water and found two

Yanks wandering around in a state of shock. They were both officers but I can't tell you their names.....one was maybe a major. Peter and Mac hid them overnight and then moved them up to Mick's place, the night of the Fayre. Mac and Mick had the bright and stupid idea of bringing them up to the parish hall for a night out. Mick took them back to Sunny View later but by morning they had gone, vanished into thin air. We kept very quiet about the whole thing and held our breath, thinking they would soon be captured and possibly dob us all in under questioning. Then Christmas came and the Red Cross ship arrived and still absolutely nothing , which was best for everyone. My guess is they escaped and the mystery will be cleared up very soon when they tell their story. You should be talking to Mac and Peter as they were the ones who rescued them ....can you take these over to your mates?"

He poured the last of the drinks and Klaus delivered them before he returned to the bar to continue his chat with Brian.
"Mac and Peter should be in this evening if that's any good."
" No, I'll be back in the prison camp this evening anyway."
Klaus was beaming from ear to ear. " But it's good to know that at least the Americans existed, because you rescued them . How about that? Now I *know* it was Glenn Miller. I played with the Glenn Miller Luftwaffe Orchestra ! "
Brian burst out laughing. "Yes, that would look good on a job application. Good luck with that one!"
Klaus was pleased that a few facts had risen to the surface but he quickly returned to family matters.
Brian kept fiddling with the pumps while still talking.
"Peter is still loved up with Melody. Sophie starts big school in September but I haven't seen Christine for a couple of months. Mac has his ups and downs. You gotta love the man! My beloved wife should be here very soon. Her mother is old and frail so she's looking after her on the mainland. I'll be glad when she's back, she can run the pub while I go fishing! Anyway, what about you? When do you leave?"

Klaus took a large sip of his beer before replying.

“ I could leave any day now . The job is close to.....finish. I get the ship to Southampton and then I don't know....another prison camp somewhere. I shall miss this place and I shall miss you people. You have been good to me.”
In the corner Sergeant Mainwaring was stirring.
“Time to find some more mines, boys. Come on, look lively. Finish your drinks and fall in outside. Thank you, landlord!”
The squad shuffled off through the door. Brian came around to the other side of the bar and shook hands with Klaus.
“Good luck, my friend. Come back and see us one day. Promise me that.”
“Yes. Thank you, Brian. Please give all good luck to Mac and Peter and to Sophie and Christine. I shall miss you all.”
With a tear in his eye, Klaus turned and left to join the rest of the men. Two days later he was on a troop ship on his way to Southampton before boarding a train to Truro in Cornwall. His next job was on the land driving tractors on a farm. He loved the work and loved the farmer's daughter but he missed his family. He hadn't been home in three years. He was finally allowed home at Christmas 1946 and took his girlfriend Morwenna with him. She later became his wife and they had three sons, one of which became a keyboard player . He and Fritz met up ten years later to drink schnapps and talk of old times. He visited Jersey in the fifties and reconnected with the Marinelles, still convinced he had played piano for Glenn Miller.
Klaus Bucholz died in 2002 .

CHAPTER 72

Relief for Christine

Christine spent many anxious weeks waiting for her period to arrive. A potential pregnancy threw her into confusion. Some days she yearned for a memory of Hans but the rest of the time she spent with her head in her hands wondering how she would explain it all to Peter and Sophie and the rest of the world. The stigma attached to giving birth to a 'German baby' was overwhelming. There were girls in town who had been tarred and feathered for simply having a German boyfriend. The constant debate which raged in her mind was wearing her down. Despite a couple of bouts of sickness in the morning she certainly didn't feel pregnant. The poor diet of the years of occupation had taken its toll on the body clocks of the population and Christine was no exception. Her periods were not that regular and eventually, to her enormous relief, her menstrual cycle kicked reluctantly into gear and when it did, she mentally slapped herself to do better by her family. The cloud that had been sitting around her shoulders took off and dispersed. She had a good look around her and whilst things could have been better, she decided that life wasn't so bad. Hans had been a thrilling interlude but the price she paid with all the worry and deceit had weighed heavily on her. She looked forward to the end of this crappy war.

Mac however was sliding down to the other end of the spectrum. The sudden death of Hans had precipitated the confrontation with Christine and her subsequent confession of an affair. The weeks that followed left him angry and disappointed. When the Germans finally left, the structure they had all created to cope with life under the enemy suddenly fell away and they were left in a vacuum which would be hard to fill.

Peter was understandably preoccupied with his girlfriend and he was happy for him. He had seen the lad blossom through

loss, tragedy, puberty and more to become a handsome, honest young man who would do the right thing come what may. Melody was a nice girl and they were good for each other. He wished them well but he started to miss the excursions to low water with him and he spent more and more time alone with his dark thoughts. The nightmares became uncontrollable and he spiralled into depression.
One drizzly day in July he forced himself to follow the dropping tide just for something to do. The black and grey landscape matched his mood . He meandered between lobster lairs without success and skirted Seymour Tower as the sea fell away. He felt tired and sat on a comfortable outcrop of rock. He heard the scraping of boots on gravel and caught a whiff of the unmistakable smell of a French cigarette.
“Oh shit , the fucking Frenchman!” he said quietly.
Gaston Guilleaume crept into view, his shabby black coat contrasting against the grey sky. Mac didn't welcome him with open arms.
“Qu'est-ce-que vous avez dit ?” said the Frenchman. Mac was just not in the mood for the Gallic intruder and rounded aggressively on him.
“Why don't you fuck off back to France, you smelly bastard!” This seemed to deter Guillaume but he didn't back down. In his thick French accent, he was straight back at him.
“Eh bien! Why don't you fuck off back to Scotland and take that kraut loving whore Christine wiz you. She is only good for fucking German officers.”

There was a sharp intake of breath and even out there you could have heard a pin drop. Guilleaume's words flew through the air like machine gun bullets and the blood drained from Mac's face as his rage kicked in. His hands went immediately round the Frenchman's throat, pushing him over backwards . As he fell, his skull made a sickening thud as it struck the rocks, rendering him instantly unconscious with an ominous trickle of blood exuding from his ear.

Mac became unperturbed and remarkably calm. He spotted a puddle of sea water a few yards away and pulled the inert body towards it over the gravel and stones. He turned him over, pushed his face into the water and made sure his head was immersed.
"If he comes round, he comes round. If he doesn't, then he's gonna drown anyway. Useless fucker.

Mac then walked slowly away and left him there, feeling absolutely no remorse at all. He carried on exploring behind the Tower and returned to shore when the tide turned. The rain had set in and there was nobody else out there to bear witness to the Frenchman's demise. His body washed ashore behind Gorey Castle a couple of days later . There was a post mortem and the verdict was one of 'accidental death'. He had clearly struck his head on a rock and the coroner was not prepared to investigate further. Five people turned up at his funeral at St Patrick's Catholic Church in St Helier. Mac wasn't one of them.
A couple of evenings later, Mac was reading the Evening Post on the bar of the Grenadier. Brian was pulling a pint at the other end and casually remarked, his tongue firmly in his cheek,
"Now Mac, I have some bad news for you. It's your French mate. He's dead. The honorary police retrieved his body at low tide round the back of the Castle. Drowned by all accounts. Did you know ?"
Mac didn't even look up. "Yeah, useless fucker."
"You didn't go to the funeral then? Him being one of the brotherhood of low water men and all." said Brian, grinning as he gently wound him up. Mac wouldn't take the bait and simply repeated his first reply.
"Useless fucker. Glad he's dead."
After a couple of drinks he slouched off homeward with a big black dog at his heels.
Out came the Glenfiddich and he sat outside the back door to watch the light fade. The net curtain he had put up to keep

insects out suddenly floated up on the breeze and brushed his face. It was bloody Christine's hand again but tonight it was the final straw. He took his shirt off and let the curtain caress him once more before heading over the wall on to the beach. It was well after ten o'clock and there was still enough light to see the way directly to the sea to the east over shingle and sand. The tide was half way and it beckoned him as he quickened his pace. The line between reality and fantasy had become blurred by the alcohol and his depression. He suddenly perceived gunfire from the right, tracer bullets whizzed over his head and a shell exploded behind him. He was back in the trenches at the Somme and the fear clutched at him again. He started running but tripped over a body, sending him flying. A voice moaned from in front , 'help me help me'. A hand grabbed at the leg of his trousers .He undid his belt and wriggled free, leaving the garment in the grip of the dismembered arm. He rushed onward. He swerved round some more dead bodies and all the time there was the excruciatingly loud and violent noise of mortar bombs and hand grenades going off all round him. The figure of his old commanding officer, Major Moody, loomed out from the smoke in front. The Major yelled out,

"STAND STILL, MACKINTOSH!"

He gave Major Moody the finger and yelled back,

"Fuck off you sassenach prick! Stick yer bayonet up yer arrse!" and raced past him, heading for the sanctuary of the sea beyond.

He stood on the water's edge and took off the rest of his clothes. Sand dislodged by the explosions rained down all around him. Wading straight out he was quickly out of his depth and swimming strongly. The noise of gunfire ceased as quickly as it had begun. He stopped and turned to face the shore. Streetlights twinkled like stars along the shoreline and a fullish moon lit up the bay. There was not a breath of wind and the sea was like glass. His whole mind and body felt calm. The sea was his lover and he let her embrace him. He surrendered to the sensation. He took one last look around and let himself sink beneath the surface. He let the sea rush into his lungs and he started to see beautiful colours. It felt so easy and not at all unpleasant. The colours faded to black and Mac was free at last. No more noise, no more Krauts, no more unrequited love and no more black dog scraping at his heels.

They found his body the next morning on the high water mark close to his house. There were bits of clothing scattered along the shore and his death was a bit of a mystery until they read the letters he had left explaining the demons that were following him.

Christine cried like a baby when she read the letter addressed to her. She had never really gauged the depth of his affection for her. Given the age gap of fifteen or so years, she had never ever seen the pair of them as being together. She never disclosed what was in the letter, saying it was far too personal and something between her and Mac.

Peter was devastated. Mac was the one who took him through his teenage years. Always there but always not quite there, unobtrusive but attentive. The war had robbed him of his father, then his best friend and now his mentor. He had suffered the most of all of them and he wasn't even twenty years old. He was lucky he had the unconditional love of his mother, his sister and his girlfriend and he became very protective of all of them.

Sophie was sad also but too young to really understand that Uncle Mac was now gone forever.

His death also hit Brian very hard and he closed the pub for two days when he heard. He just sat in his upstairs lounge chair staring out across the road to the beach beyond, not quite believing that the old bastard had taken his own life. His funeral at St Peter La Rocque seemed to be the last chapter in their Occupation adventure. Brian pulled himself together just long enough to deliver the eulogy, outlining one or two stories of happy times spent together. He spoke of Mac's love of Scotland and scotch whisky, his love of La Rocque and its

landscapes and his love of low water fishing.
Brian managed to hold it together just long enough but when the lone Scottish piper squeezed the bagpipes for the opening skirl of Amazing Grace to lead the coffin party out to the graveside, he broke down altogether and had to be helped down from the lectern by the vicar.
The wake at the Grenadier Inn lasted two days and two nights. From those days on, when Brian called "time" in order to close the pub at 10.30pm, the last toast was always "Slainte Mhath" and he still hadn't a clue what it meant. He told anybody who enquired that it meant 'stupid bugger'.
The church of St Peter La Rocque seemed to be creaking under the weight of all the sad funerals that the war had offered up but the corner was turned when Peter and Melody were married there in September of 1945. It was a bit of a rushed affair. Sophie was one of the bridesmaids and Christine was ecstatic to hear she was to be a grandmother at the ripe old age of thirty nine. Mac had left Peter his house with the proviso that he lived in it himself .There was a huge turnout as the parish was well and truly looking forward to celebrating a happy event. There were flowers and happy tears . Sophie sang a song and Klaus was mentioned in conversations at the church and reception. Christine had recovered her health and had blossomed as her confidence returned. She made a new plan and set her sights on raising Sophie and lots of babysitting for her grandchildren in the future. She'd had her share of excitement but it was now all over. There would be no more mourning over lost loves and she built a new life.
The Germans were gone and now it was time to clear the islands of the memories of five years of hardship and uncertainty. It was time for regeneration. After a period of austerity and recriminations, the islands became the tourist hub it was before the invasion. The link to the mainland was quickly re-established and boat loads of trippers came to enjoy the beautiful beaches and nightlife. The government of Jersey cleverly maintained the income tax rate which was set during

the war and money flowed into the island's banks for the next fifty years.
Every Christmas and especially at the parish Christmas Fayre, there was discussion of the so called 'Glenn Miller 'concert but most of it revolved around Sophie and the musicians of the German band whose performances had been so outstanding that wet and windy night. As the years went by, Sophie's talent was recognised and she went on to study opera at the Royal College of Music in London. Her studies were paid for by the substantial amount of money that Mac had accumulated on the black market and left to Christine. The romance of the Miller story remained however and seemed to gain traction as the years passed but there was no solid evidence of his presence or involvement. Klaus and Fritz did return in the fifties to see old friends and places until eventually their own lives took over completely. Both remained convinced. Fritz had a light bulb moment in 1959 when he was reading an article about Miller's disappearance. The Noorduyn Norseman involved in the disappearance had a Prat and Whitney engine similar to the one Fritz had correctly identified near Seymour Tower the week before liberation. Fritz didn't need any proof, however, as he was one hundred per cent sure in his mind........but one small piece of evidence had been entirely overlooked.
When Peter moved into Mac's house, he did a monumental job of clearing out all the flotsam and jetsam that Mac had beachcombed during the war. Some of it held too many memories to throw away but there were certain pieces that had to be thrown out or given away. Out of a huge pile near the shed earmarked as junk, Peter offered it all first to neighbours and friends. Mrs Le Plongeon took a fancy to the leather satchel that Mac had grabbed at high tide a few days before Christmas, 1944. Hidden away in Mac's secret room, it had dried out naturally to reveal its original colour and quality. It contained a solid lump of papier maché, papers that had solidified into one mass after its soaking in the sea but the top sheet was clearly marked with musical notations. Edith threw

these out and used the satchel type brief case for her committee work. Twenty years of tireless work at the parish hall was suddenly terminated in 1960 when her heart gave out. She left the satchel for the next treasurer of the parish but he was a young ambitious accountant and preferred a new Samsonite briefcase funded by the parish. The satchel was put into a rubbish skip to be seen no more. Edith loved it because there was an inscription hand written on the inside of the flap in old fashioned black ink.
"It don't mean a thing if it ain't got that swing." She loved to quote that during boring moments in committee meetings. Also the initials embossed in faded gold on the outside were very apt for the work she was involved in.
A.G.M..
Clearly it stood for Annual General Meeting, an acronym used frequently in committee work and all the relevant papers and minutes were kept within it for many years.

It also stood for Alton Glenn Miller.

CHAPTER 73

March 2008

Peter Marinelle had felt a bit strange the last few days, as if he wasn't quite there. Now eighty one years old, he was winding down a long and happy life. After the Liberation, it had taken a few years to put things in order again. The owners of St Kitts never returned to the island and with the help of Mac's legacy , Christine had managed to buy it. Peter came to an arrangement with Brian to use his boat for fishing until eventually he bought the Crazy Doris and initially made a healthy living from it. Immediately he renamed Mac's house Slainte Mhath in honour of his good friend . No-one could pronounce it and he could imagine Mac chuckling as passers-by contemplated its meaning and pronunciation. When Melody gave birth to a fine baby boy in February 1946 they christened him Cameron which was Mac's middle name. Peter then set about extending the house and found he had a talent for building. He discovered that the construction industry had more to offer than commercial fishing and grew a very successful business extending the houses of the super rich who fetched up on the island trying to escape the UK tax system in the sixties and seventies. They had another child in 1949, this time a girl Crystal. Christine spent the rest of her life bringing up Sophie and doting on her grandchildren. Sophie became a famous international opera singer and Christine nearly burst with pride when she flew to London to watch her sing at Covent Garden in the late sixties. The jigsaw of Christine's life still had bits missing but she eventually reached a state of contentment before she died in 1989. Sophie enjoyed the the 'swinging sixties' and, after her initial success, achieved a certain notoriety as an eccentric diva. Her eccentricity, however, bordered on madness and on her rare visits back home to Jersey she was regarded with a certain amount of suspicion by the family. In her later years she turned to prescription drugs to ease her pain and died of an overdose in London in 1995 aged 55.

When his wife Melody died suddenly a year later, Peter sold the business and cursed the fact that he hadn't sold it years before. He was always so busy and should have spent more time at home with his family. Both Cameron and Crystal were good scholars and followed a path to university education. Both loved the island but, after moving to mainland universities, found returning home had become claustrophobic and they couldn't wait to move away permanently. As Peter grew older he became more isolated. He bought a smaller boat and it didn't take him long to rekindle his love affair with the seascape of La Rocque. He would be out in all weathers and when the tide was out, Old Pete could be seen down by Seymour Tower still plundering lobsters and crabs from crevices only he knew of.

The month of March had been milder and sunnier than usual . Peter packed some sandwiches and fishing tackle into an old backpack and walked from Slainte Mhath down the north slipway to where his bass boat Melody was moored. He had timed it to perfection and barely got his feet wet as he climbed awkwardly aboard. The rheumatism that had afflicted him for the last few years was getting worse. Within minutes the boat was afloat and the moorings were slipped. There was not a breath of wind and once again the visibility below water was stunning. He lowered his reliable outboard motor so that the propeller was in the water. It had an electric start button and it kicked quietly into life. He steered out along the side of the pier and a young boy, about ten years old, waved to him.

"That's strange. That looks a bit like Jimmy Le Cocq, haven't seen him for ....seventy years !" he thought to himself as he waved back. He laughed at the thought.

Despite the sun being out, the air was cool and Peter was glad he had put an extra jersey on. He pointed the bow towards the tower and glided slowly along, barely producing any wash at all. From all around, oystercatchers glared at him, Brent geese honked at him and generally everybody had a say as to Spring approaching. His heart seemed to miss a beat and he felt a bit dizzy but the feeling passed. He saw a figure waving from a rock a hundred yards away. As he got closer he saw that it was another young lad, this one a bit older.

"Over here, Pete, over here!"

The sun was shining from directly behind the rock and Peter could only see the boy's figure in silhouette. The temperature had risen quickly and it felt like a summer's day. As he got closer, the boy shouted,

"How are you doing, you old bugger? Can you give me a lift out to the tower?"

Peter squinted through old eyes, trying to identify the person and the voice. The voice was so familiar but it came from a long time ago. He thought hard until the voice clutched at him from the back of his mind.

"Johnnie? Johnnie boy?"

"Who the hell did you think it was, you old bugger. I've been looking out for you."

"What do you mean, Johnnie boy?" was all Peter could say.

"All your life, I've been looking out for you. Making sure you did the right thing. Boy, you had some fun with that French tart!"

Peter was dumbstruck but in that moment he knew that his time was up and he couldn't have been happier to see his old buddy again. He threw him a rope .

Johnnie stepped on board and they hugged each other.

"Good to see you, Johnnie. I really missed you when you went. I really did. It should have been me. I was so sorry. "

"I know, I know. It was just random but I got to keep my beautiful youth. Look at me. Not a wrinkle in sight and.... still no pubic hair!"

Peter observed Johnnie's youthful skin and gently reached forward to touch his face.

"Yes, Johnnie, you look ridiculous!"

They laughed together and Peter felt a pain in his chest.

"Come on," said John, "we're running late. Let's go !"

Peter cranked up the engine and they cruised further out. The boat guided itself onto the shingle at Seymour Tower where Mac stood waiting to give him a hug.
"Welcome, big man. Good to see you. We've been waiting for you."
They were both crying as they hugged but Mac was quick to tell him not to worry.
"It's okay, big fella. It's okay. You are not to be afraid. Come on now."
Johnnie beckoned him back into the boat.
"Hurry up, Pete. It's nearly time. Climb aboard."
Peter was feeling weak and dizzy but totally unafraid as they helped him over the side.
Johnnie pushed the wooden boat off the shingle and jumped aboard. Old Pete started the engine and they slid out over the crystal clear waters of La Rocque for the last time. He peered over the side and waved back at the bladder wrack at the bottom. John was fiddling around in Peter's backpack and pulled out a mackerel trace . He tied a piece of lead on the end and gingerly handed the feathered hooks to Peter.
"One last go. Go on, chuck 'em over! You always were a lucky bugger." said John.
Peter thought long and hard for a couple of minutes and then said,
"I was, wasn't I. I really was."
Peter lowered the tackle over the side and wound the line around the seat. He left his forefinger on the line and suddenly felt a bite on the end.
"Time to go, old buddy. See you on the other side." said John and he faded from view.
It grew colder once more and Peter slipped into unconsciousness easily and peacefully.
Two hours later the boat nudged gently back onto the beach. Peter was dead.

They are all still out there. In all weathers, the grey ghosts walk the tidal areas of La Rocque. They ebb and flow with the tides, watching over the seasons as they come and go. They stir the flocks of angry oyster catchers and they tell the swallows when they must leave to follow the sun. The egrets and herons, the kingfishers and gulls all see them and nod in acquiescence. On a calm day they will send dolphins to cheer your soul, but most of all they love a storm. Rain and wind will suck the colour from the terrain and the grey ghosts become as one, shuffling between sandbanks like mist on the move.

So, the next time you venture down with the kids to catch shrimps in the rock pools, just listen hard. That unexplained sound of footsteps on gravelly sand will be the low water men, just going about their business.

Printed in Poland
by Amazon Fulfillment
Poland Sp. z o.o., Wrocław

52157946R00265